THE
GOY

THE
GOY

by

MARK HARRIS

The Dial Press   New York 1970

ℓ·1

Acknowledgment

Lines from the Zutzky entry in
Westrum's Journal are from William Gibson,
A Mass for the Dead.

Library of Congress Catalog Card Number: 79–120467

Printed in the United States of America

Book design by Mel Brofman

First printing, 1970

Do you realize that you are also symbolically coming to terms with the Dark Man in your own depths? What you are doing outwardly is enacting a sort of inner drama in symbolic form. I dislike people who are averse to the dark races, not merely for humanitarian reasons, but because those who deny the dark are instinct suppressors and life deniers.

—letter to the author from Elizabeth Large, astrologer, Clennell, Harbottle, Morpeth, Northumberland, England

for AL HART

THE
GOY

This unique journal of self-exam-
ination reveals the inner attitudes
and reactions of W.A.S.P. historian.

1

In his rear-view mirror the bridge fell away, and behind the
bridge the city, where his mistress dwelled. From the high
windows of her home, or of his, or from the high windows of
the most frequent site of their rendezvous, the bridge was visible, and the Jersey side, and the highway beyond. "Your
brother has driven me into exile," he said to his wife on the
seat behind him, but it was Terence who replied, saying,
"You're driving yourself."

"Like Tusculum," said Westrum, for it was Tusculum
(though it might have been Marcus Livius Drusus) who had
taken himself into exile behind his own horses. He was cheered
that Terence should be so wise, so perceptive, and so frank.

Speak of Roman roads, they were nothing like these—a remark he had made in the merest passing in *A History of the
Past World*, and heard from this Benstock in a sour, stubborn
letter that Roman roads were superior to American roads. Benstock, having written a little sketch of Roman roads, apparently lay in wait for anyone daring to mention them. Soon
he'd see what this Benstock looked like. It had recently occurred to Westrum to reply to Benstock's letter, to rescue it
from his archives—his Journal in its gypsum vault—and aston-
ish Benstock by answering it, *I thank you for your letter of several years ago which the pressure of affairs has prevented my
answering until this moment*, but he had not done so.

Had Roman wagons air-conditioning? Westrum's wagon was
an Oldsmobile Custom Vista-Cruiser, warm gray and Brittany
blue, westward plowing with the power of three hundred
horses, whose passengers included, besides three human beings, a dog mostly Dalmatian, and a purebred alleycat black

1

and white like the dog, lying together entangled, entwined, black upon white and white upon black, cat upon dog and dog upon cat, making the best of a close place, and whose cargo included, besides cardboard boxes and expensive suitcases, Terence's motion-picture camera, motion-picture projector in a shockproof case, and enormous quantities of film given as a gift to the boy by the President of the United States.

Held fast by a Toter, a coppertone ten-speed bicycle rode the wagon's rear bumper, and beneath it, affixed to the bumper, the width of the wagon, a legend proclaimed TAXES TOO HIGH? DECLARE PEACE IN THE WORLD. But the bicycle was not the boy's: it was his father's.

On the radio, on the afternoon of their first day, they heard from New York that Beatrice's brother Tikvah had been struck —"grazed," said the announcer—by a brick hurled by someone outraged, and heard then Tikvah's own voice from the steps of University Hall, and heard him again that evening, but saw him as well on the television, with his handkerchief to his bald and bleeding head, one hand upraised, asking in the most reasonable manner for peace and tranquility. "I will not negotiate with anyone," said Tikvah through a cheerleader's megaphone, "with a brick in his hand. Friends, put down your bricks." The students chanted, "Amnesty, amnesty," and they wore black.

It was a grand and vulgar motel with a heated pool. While Westrum swam, Beatrice telephoned her brother to express their concern and to ask after his bleeding head. When Westrum returned, carrying his chronometer wrapped in a towel, she was treating with lotion the left side of her face, scorched by the sun through the dome of their wagon, and watching cowboys and Indians killing one another on television— "Watching your father killing Indians," she said, rebuking him for his past, not for the first time.

But his father had never killed Indians. "I swam a thousand yards in nineteen minutes," he said, recording that information upon a tablet he always carried with him and had carried for

2

thirty years to fit his pocket or the palm of his hand, writing also in his own private shorthand a brief record of other events occurring upon this day, which was the eighteen-thousand-three-hundred-and-fifty-third day of his life, Tuesday.

Then once again, on the second day, he drove westward into his imagined exile. "If it had hit him square," said Beatrice, "he'd have been killed," translating into her own distress the language of *The New York Times*, which would someday carry, Westrum trusted, an enormous obituary of his own dead self. If Tikvah died, how long would his obituary be? Imagining the death of Tikvah, his mind strayed from his driving, his three hundred horses strayed from their lane, and Terence glanced sharply sideways at his father to be sure that his father was aware of the drifting. Feeling Terence's eyes upon him, Westrum recovered himself and drifted back.

"How come Tikvah bugs you like he does?" Terence asked. His grammar was imperfect by intention, to dissociate himself from the perfect grammar of his father. The boy was not a boy of words. On his left wrist he wore his father's chronometer, with which by a calculation of his father's speed he reckoned mileage, or with which, by a calculation of mileage, he reckoned his father's speed. He could convert miles to kilometers or kilometers to miles without hesitation. With his binoculars he toured the horizon. On the whole he saw the world through the eye of his motion-picture camera, from five feet to infinity.

"It's our chemistry," said Westrum.

"I'll think it over," said Terence, who knew from old experience, young as he was, that things assumed his father's meaning with the passage of time.

In other years this route had been abundant with hitchhikers, but the Interstates discouraged them now. No pauses remained, no slowing, no crossings or intersections, no lights, no waiting places, and the cities and towns themselves were buried off the road. It seemed a shame to Westrum. He remembered in particular how once, somewhere between Brest and

3

Kansas City, he had stopped for a fine young lady, carried her through several states of the union, and she was grateful, and he reckoned now, by the device of his memory assisted by his Journal, that he belonged to that company of men more active than numerous who had had at least one lady, fine or otherwise, young or otherwise, in most of the states of the union (in more than half; in enough to win an election), and some ladies in more than one, and in some states more than one lady by far, and his wife and his mistress all over the place in a restless succession of imagined exiles.

And yet the same restlessness had compelled him once to tell Tikvah that he—Westrum—in his years of marriage had never so much as kissed any woman but his own wife. Tikvah, hearing this, sagged as if shot in the knees, staggered by the possibility. He believed, for he believed in Westrum. For weeks he gazed upon Westrum in a new way with a new respect, either for a man who told so bold a lie, or, more likely, lived so stern a life. Tikvah, possessing few of Westrum's advantages, had settled for his own, achieving contentment by necessity. He had often supposed, had he been Westrum—had he been Gentile not Jew, had he been tall not short, had he been graceful not awkward, had he been handsome, had his head been lush with hair, had his health shone upon his face as Westrum's did—that he might very well have run about, taken here or there a mistress, as he had always imagined Westrum did: for he imagined, given Westrum's charm and Westrum's fame, ladies everywhere eager to place themselves beneath him for the honor of it. The idea that Westrum forswore such opportunity elevated him in Tikvah's mind to a plane of moral sturdiness which accounted for everything else. Not Westrum's accidental blessing but Westrum's moral striving was the secret of his success. The doubts of years dissolved, and he saw Westrum anew as the man of labor, sobriety, industry, control, and rugged quietude.

It had been a coup, thought Westrum, who with a single fortunate sentence, delivered upon impulse, had dissolved in

Tikvah's mind the doubts between them. Tikvah said, "I suppose I should salute. All men are not created equal."

But if Westrum had expelled all mistrust of himself from the mind of Tikvah he had not yet expelled it from his own, for the fact remained that Tikvah's mistrust was earned, whether Tikvah knew it or not, and Westrum mistrusted himself to this very day. He had won Tikvah, but not himself, and he said to Terence, "Don't think yourself out of it, you may be more right than I."

"He might be jealous of you," said Terence, encouraged.

"That'd be part of the chemistry," his father replied.

"Or you might be jealous of him," said Beatrice from the back seat.

"For what?" said Westrum.

"He's his conscience," Beatrice said, but who was whose she did not make exactly clear. Her brother caused her husband much unhappiness, and her husband caused her brother the same, and she was disheartened by the struggle between them, for they were excellent men. Where was the world's hope if even excellent men were never at peace?

"He's your conscience," Terence said.

"No," said his father sharply.

The subject was raw. Why spoil the trip? Terence raised his binoculars to his eyes, touring the horizon, monitoring the interiors of other cars. He saw ladies with their dresses high. He saw flesh. Well, someday he would have his chance at flesh, for his father often said that everything happened to every man in time, that all the world and all the history of the world occurred within every man.

Then who was Tikvah to dislodge him from his place, to force him into exile behind his own horses? *I was here before Tikvah*, Westrum thought, *I have prior rights to the place.* But of course not. He knew better. The Chairman of the President's Inquiry on Population and Immigration knew better. He seldom permitted a thought so little generous to cross his mind, and certainly he never spoke of it when he did. *Hitler is*

5

alive and well and driving the Interstate, he thought. As well ask, "Am I not more entitled to this land than my wife?" As well ask, "Am I not more entitled to this land than my mistress?" Such thoughts being unthinkable, he attributed his thinking them to the very openness of his mind, the very action of his imagination, accepting the openness of his mind as the price of his talent, as an athlete accepts an enlarged muscle as the price of his specialized excellence.

Was he anti-Semitic? Did he hate foreigners? Did he yearn to kill Indians, as his grandfather before him? Was he the seed-bearer of fascism in America? But his wife and his mistress were Jews. On the surface he'd say No. Anyone who meant much to him was more likely than not to be a Jew, and his three sons were Jewish by half. "Well all right," said Westrum to Terence, "maybe he's my conscience."

"O.K.," said Terence, "that's what I said."

"It's the chemistry," said Westrum.

"Don't let it bug you," Terence said.

It had been their plan, on the third day of their journey, to stop at Brest before proceeding to the Center itself. At Brest lived Westrum's mother and father. There Westrum was born. There his father now lay dying, or so his mother said every week upon the telephone. Westrum did not believe her. Therefore a quarter-mile east of the off-ramp to Brest he changed his mind, saying, "You can't stop a car once it's moving."

This much of his Journal—these three days of travel and arrival—he composed on the night of the third day, upright in bed, two pillows behind his head, tablet in his palm, in his own private shorthand known but to him and to Miss Sanantone. His wife beside him lay still, across her eyes a sleep-mask, plugs in her ears, but whether she slept he could not tell, nor ever knew, for sleeping or waking she breathed shallow, always had, always would: any shallower and she'd be dead. *Then* what would he do?

He could not recall where they had eaten breakfast that

morning. Oh yes—a young couple from Punjab ate breakfast at the next table, and their baby in a high chair. They were students, they were traveling to Colorado, and if they liked it in America they would remain. Terence asked them that—"Do you intend to remain here permanent?"—the question arising in his mind from his conviction that anyone with any sense would naturally make every effort to settle in America. "Aren't you rather late for school?" Westrum asked. The Punjabi man replied, "Only three weeks." Would that dark Punjabi baby someday be Senator from Colorado? Westrum thought the very color of America would gradually deepen and darken, in a hundred years America would be markedly browner, the paleface exterminated at last, the land re-won, if not by red Indians at least by brown, and justice done if only indirectly. He mentioned at breakfast that he had been to Punjab—he'd been there on the Inquiry—but the Punjabi were unimpressed (they'd been there themselves), and at mid-morning it rained, and the dome leaked, as Terence predicted it would, and they arrived here up a long hill shaded by English maple still holding their leaves at half-past two on the afternoon of the eighteen-thousand-three-hundred-and-fifty-fifth day of his life, and opened the door with the key mailed to him by Benstock. This final solemn event was shot by Terence with his Super 8 manufactured in West Germany, whose father hated Germans East or West. Westrum, interrupting himself, wrote quickly to his brother-in-law:

My dear Tikvah,

Here we are, and just this note to tell you so. When Beatrice phoned you I was swimming, thinking of you under water, your bleeding bean, your megaphone, your cool voice, I swam a thousand yards in nineteen minutes as usual.

Forgive me for not being beside you deflecting bricks as they come—hurled through the air by lovers of freedom and amnesty—but I simply could not resist coming here

7

instead. You know I'm scouting only. If you'll ever have me back I'll go to you, of course, but *on my terms,* loving you as I do—on my terms. Beatrice is sleeping or would send her love too.

They were three here now in the twelve-room rented house, dog, cat, and every necessary luxury. Tikvah would twist his lips in scorn to see such power, who lived still within stained and fading walls in a small apartment in the north Bronx—air-conditioned, he joked, by the updraft from the garbage cans, through his open window, through his rooms, and through his open door, too, if the neighbors across the hall obliged by opening theirs. "With a little cooperation two families can make a breeze," said Tikvah. Become now First Vice-Chancellor, he lived as he had lived when he had been an assistant professor, altering his standards in no way, denying all rumors that he intended to go so far as to buy a hairpiece. He traveled by subway, carrying his lunch in a brown bag. He shined his own shoes, he blew his nose on toilet paper.

The rented house at the Center contained a darkroom for Terence, and the swimming pool was square. Those had been Westrum's demands. He'd not have come to a kidney-shaped pool, and he swam upon arrival today, as he had swum every day all summer, and every summer for years, a thousand yards in nineteen minutes, and returned to the house to dress, finding Beatrice dejected, far from anyone she knew. Often she wept upon arriving at a new place—perhaps she'd been weeping while he'd been swimming—but now she said only, "It's a hundred percent mechanical. The eternal light is in the bathroom." Indeed, the bathroom could never be darkened.

"Illuminated," said Westrum, "whether we like it or not."

He and Beatrice had chosen a bedroom for themselves, but now they could not find it again, and they went wandering through the house looking for their bedroom. Terence had found it—cries of discovery—entering it now (he'd never think to knock), foregathering at day's end, as they often did, which was also, for Westrum, the day's beginning, too, when he began to capture upon the tablet in his palm notes for his Journal. Westrum lived all life twice. Tikvah said that to live life twice was never to live it once. *So be it* he wrote, *we are overtaken, we shall speak from room to room on the intercom, we shall grind our garbage chemically, incinerate our trash in a flameless, smokeless, odorless pit at the bottom of a chute, we shall bake our meats instantaneously in an instantaneous oven, the house is an experiment by a scientist at the Center in solar* . . .

"It's a really neat place," said Terence, sitting heavily upon the bed.

"Your mother's asleep," said Westrum.

"No she's not," said Terence.

"I'm awake," Beatrice said.

Terence saw that his father's eyes were turned off. The day was beginning again. The Journal was turning, the film rerunning, but the boy had been meaning to say that the Agfa was supreme, it absolutely eliminated all jitter from the film.

"All right," his father said.

"Go to bed," his mother said, and her voice was filled with urgency and fear. The mood of the night alarmed her.

"Second point," said Terence, although he had no second point.

"You have no second point," said Westrum. "Please do go to bed." He heard in his own voice his own cold control, and he feared his voice, for it told him that so much claim to control was proof that he was near the end of it. It had not really been his decision to come here. Someone else had made this decision for him.

"The projector heats out bad," said Terence.

"That's nothing new," his father said.

Again his mother said, "Terence, go to bed," lifting her sleep-mask from her eyes, and her urgency was clear to the boy. He stood, releasing the bed from his weight, and he, too, felt the mood of the night as his mother felt it. It was the mood of the most terrible night of their lives, when they had fore-gathered, the three of them, like this, his father in exile or imagined exile, in cold control, or so it seemed, then heated, burst, went seemingly mad, and broke the boy's back with a blow of his hand.

2

In the morning he shopped for groceries with Beatrice. Does it amaze people that a renowned historian steers a rolling cart down the aisles of Meister's Ordinary Super Market? Yet it is true. How else can he eat? And what else had he to do? The work of his life was done. The author of *A History of the Past World* cared nothing for history now, or for the past, but cared only for the present and the future, his sons and the children of his sons. The *History* had swept everything, his effort was made, his fame was gained, and he could now spend the rest of his life shopping for groceries with his wife in supermarkets, accompanying his wife to galleries and concerts and theaters and the places of interest throughout the world, accompanying his son to events of his son's choosing, accompanying himself to pleasures of his own, meddling at public meetings, keeping up his health, examining his conscience, taking his pulse, reflecting upon his reflections, managing his investments, flying up and down with not much apparent purpose, killing time, playing games, keeping a scrupulous and infinite record of his own hours, flying through the air about the world, or flying through the air, as now, in his bathing trunks, into the pool behind his rented house, where he swam again today, as he had swum yesterday, one thousand yards in nineteen minutes.

In other weather he ran, or rode his bicycle. He ran two miles in thirteen minutes and thirty seconds every day in running weather, and he cycled eight miles in seventeen minutes and fifty seconds in cycling weather for the sake of his heart and the pulse of his body, to subdue the heat of his hatreds, and to ease or silence the dialogue between himself and imagined enemies. The more strenuous his exercise the less the vio-

11

lence of his antagonisms. In his heart lay murder. But his most favorite exercise was secret screwing recorded in his Journal, all names (but one), all private places, all dates, and amusing details bearing upon these meetings between himself and women and girls, old friends and passing strangers, ladies briefly encountered or mistresses known for years in all these states and cities beneath varieties of roofs in all weather in small hotels or grand apartments, of whom the most recent, best, and probably last was his excellent mistress, whose name, in that connection, he had never committed to his Journal. *Madame,* he called her, and so she signed herself.

Beatrice, at the poolside, when his distance was done, said that Benstock had telephoned: might a small delegation visit, to carry him to the Seating Committee?

"Of course," he said.

"I didn't know," she said. She never knew how he might feel about visitors. He was one day available to all the world, another day hiding, in spite of his claiming for himself absolute consistency.

Terence, coming to swim, shot his father with his Super 8 Agfa as he climbed from the pool. Westrum was six feet tall, slender, firm, and all his life so far afflicted with the gait, the stance, and every appearance of an athlete that he had been recruited as a boy for every sport in its season. He played with fair skill, stationed by coaches at those positions tall boys played. His body had been sufficiently in it. He was pleased to be often applauded, occasionally cheered, and to wear the letter upon his chest.

Of a man still so splendid at fifty, so trim, so even of teeth, so bright of eye, so outgoing of speech, so lithe, so smiling, so regular of habit, whose name was Westrum and who was born at Brest nearby, some men of another kind could believe only the worst. Such a man was Benstock, who soon appeared at Westrum's door, and with him Harvey Weinberg and Kenneth Silvers. "Gentlemen," said Westrum, smiling well, greeting this delegation of three small men, two with heavy spectacles, and the third with two teak canes. Terence, from the distance, shot them shaking hands in the doorway.

This was the very Benstock who had written Westrum years before on behalf of the superiority of Roman roads to American roads. From the instant now of the first meeting of their eyes it was clear that Benstock lacked confidence in Westrum. He did not smile. Something preoccupied him.

His chairmanship of the Seating Committee was a grave responsibility. It was a most awful weight upon him, whose shoulders were rounded and his chest sunken. His hair was long and black, but thin, so that his skull shone bare amidst its plenty. His hair curled at his temples, fell about his ears, and flowed between his collar and his coat. "Before I forget," he said, "I'm supposed to ask you and Mrs. Westrum to dinner tonight."

"You make it sound like a duty," said Harvey Weinberg.

"We'll come," said Westrum.

"It's a duty *and* a pleasure," Benstock said, but no pleasure showed upon his face.

Westrum placed Benstock by his accents upon the sidewalks of New York. "I go to every dinner party," he said. It was not true—he lied sparingly, always with clear purpose—but he'd go to all the dinner parties here, at least to begin with. It was where the women were. He hoped, moreover, that by his free mingling here he might stir up a new life for himself, force a future by inviting complications, begin himself again, start himself over, restore for himself that urgency he had formerly felt about men and affairs. Urgency had once inspired him.

Beatrice brought coffee. Benstock, when he saw her, rested his eyes upon her face a moment, and then upon Westrum's, and then upon hers again, and his own face was filled with that old question Westrum would answer in his own time at a right moment: was she Jewish? Benstock's face was filled with hope, for if Westrum were married to a Jew he must therefore be in some degree better than he appeared to be. She served Kenneth Silvers his coffee where he sat—he had not risen to be introduced—and Harvey Weinberg with shaking hands carried cream and sugar to Silvers, a wordless deference to affliction which warmed Westrum, touched him, affected him, filling him with shame at his own complaints, whereupon he vowed to himself the vow he never kept—to dismiss every complaint, to love, to solicit love and to evoke love. At this moment, had Tikvah himself entered the room, Westrum would have leaped to embrace him and ask his forgiveness for having complicated his life and made it sometimes miserable. *But on the other hand*, he thought, *forgiveness for what? If not for him I wouldn't be here in exile.* Toward these three men and toward his wife he now felt for several minutes the strongest and most unbearable connections of love and commonality. He was exalted by the idea—civilized men on a sunshining morning sitting in perfect harmony, *Benstock, Weinberg, Silvers*, he thought, committing their names to his mind for his Journal, *Beatrice brought coffee, Benstock's face lit up a little bit at her Jewish mug, Terence shot a long shot, Silvers a cripple, Weinberg a shaking wreck.* Now they were in. Entering this house, they walked through the doorway into the history his Journal was, and may have been shyly pleased, as some men were, to have become figures upon an eternal page, or may have been, as other men were—as Tikvah was—dismayed by any vision of themselves not their own: little cheer, he supposed, to Kenneth Silvers, to be signaled to history as the companion of two canes, who had had, before his calamity, the plan of becoming famous as attorney to the poor.

"Did your girl get here?" Benstock asked.

"Not yet," said Westrum. "We've been wondering about that."

"We couldn't supply you a girl," said Benstock.

"I'd think not," said Westrum. Upon that point he was definite.

"He's got to have just the right girl," Kenneth Silvers said.

"Nobody knows my shorthand but her," said Westrum.

"We have plenty of girls," said Harvey.

"We have more girls than work," said Benstock.

"It's against the rules of the Center to fire any," said Harvey Weinberg, whose face was familiar to Westrum from somewhere out of the past. When the Journal came he'd look him up. Harvey's face was round and pink and sparkled with sweat. His left eye drained and wept. When the weeping became copious he wore dark glasses, and the eye dried. He was an ornithologist, distinguishd for having devised a shelter enabling African equatorial birds to survive in North America. Westrum's mind bent to the effort of restoring to Harvey the face of his youth or young manhood. *Interested in birds,* he thought. Well, he'd place it some sleepless night, or, as often happened, in the moment of his head's falling upon the pillow —"at Michigan," someone was saying, the eyes of the men upon Westrum, quite as if he'd been listening.

They were perplexed, of course, about his having come to the Center at all, and they could not imagine that he would remain. Humble men imagine limitless freedom. He would need an answer, and he tried one now. "I was born down the road," he said, "at Brest." It was true enough, although it was not why he had come: the reason he had come was to fetch better terms from Tikvah back home. But his having offered a sentimental reason awakened his sentiment, and he drank off his coffee swiftly to free his hands, and addressed his new friends with animation. "It's really a big thing with me to come back so close to home, to bring myself within range of so many old memories." To this he added an invention. "My father's bought me a plot in the graveyard there," he said.

"We play Brest at football," Benstock said, whose son was a star at Center High.

"I don't suppose they've much of a team any more," said Westrum.

"I believe it's a shrinking town," said Benstock.

"Rotting," Westrum said, introducing Terence arriving dripping, naming the men without hesitation, he'd sorted them alliterately—Benstock's hair black and Weinberg's eye weeping and Silvers a-sitting.

Terence toured the room shaking hands. He observed the canes lying crossed at Silvers's feet. For a time Terence had used a cane to ease the fatigue of his back, but then in a seizure of resolution he had thrown it away. His back was weary this morning, he'd swum too hard, but there was something in this scene he wanted. "Can I shoot you?" he asked, but he was already shooting their faces and their coffee cups and at last in the most casual way the canes crossed at Silvers's feet, though it had been all along the canes he was after, and he retreated up the stairs now, his father's eye following his disappearance, head gone, body gone, feet gone, Terence gone, recalling to Westrum's mind his own Uncle Nelson, his father's brother, in the garden of the house at Brest forty years ago and more, telling a small boy who could only have been Westrum himself that he—his Uncle Nelson—could perform the magic trick of making his own head disappear. Oh yes indeed, sailing near home *did* carry the mind within range of old memory. Alarmed, fascinated, the boy pleaded with his uncle to do so, who then walked across the garden calling, "Watch now, watch my head disappear," while the boy in direst apprehension watched for his uncle's head to fly from his shoulders. In fact, his uncle, who was then or afterward or had already been Representative to Congress from New Hamburg, merely hid behind a rosebush, calling again to the boy, "Do you see my head? You don't, you don't. Then I have made it disappear, haven't I?" Uncle Nelson's head, even in death, never entirely disappeared, remaining more or less in prominence on the frieze of the New Hamburg County Courthouse, and in a portrait on the wall of the dining room of the Willard Hotel in Washington, where Westrum sometimes entertained his mistress. But of the inside of his uncle's head Westrum knew nothing. His uncle had left no record of his thought—no letters, no memoranda, no Journal—and Westrum's only clue was the faint but encouraging memory of his uncle and his father in constant dispute, which must have meant, since his father was virtually a fascist, that his uncle was probably possessed of intimations of decency. He read Uncle Nelson's obituary in *The New York Times* on the train from Paris to Le Havre, discovering now that he was rising, that the delegation was rising, that Silvers was groping for his canes—"one car's enough," someone was saying. Apparently Westrum had offered his own, since that was the car they took.

The Center boasted of itself (or Harvey Weinberg on the Center's behalf) that it was the fifth largest building in America in total square footage. Harvey pressed the argument that he meant *single* building, and that in the present case the single building must be permitted to include its Wings— Computing Wing, Medical Wing, Environment Wing, and Residence Wing. The Wings were connected to one another, and to the History Wing, by tunnels, by walkways through the air, and by lateral belts at several levels, although it was also possible for a man or a woman of imagination to cross from one Wing to another upon his or her own feet on Nature's grass.

Large as it was, the Center was destined yet to be larger, expanding in time Wing beyond Wing to the river's edge, confronting there, across the water, the city of New Hamburg. Once upon a time New Hamburg, too, had been a center of things, but its soul and essential existence and balance of mind had been destroyed, sucked dry by the Center which, intending no harm, had nevertheless usurped, absorbed, and taken to itself all the opportunities for a higher life than commercial labor. The Center was devoted to inquiry. Its work was its play. New Hamburg was devoted to the granaries, and its profit was a pall hiding all the outer world. Unable to see beyond its own city limits, enclosed in gray smoke, New Hamburg imagined that this was how life must be. Its streets, for some reason, had never been well-kept: from boyhood Westrum had always associated it with litter flying loose, sew-

17

ers backed up. Had the river not lain between, New Hamburg might have shared with the Center forms of play promoting imagination, but all traffic passed between the two places upon an old bridge, narrow and discouraging, nor had anyone on either side of the river the inspiration to build another. Here at the Center, Mukden translated *Life at the Poles* in eighteen months, leaving the grounds but once (for a day, to carry his squash racquets for repair in Paree), here Topkin completed *Sephardic Studies* without drawing a single breath of fresh air, and here three scholars-in-exile from Cuba had revolutionized mathematical biology on the sundeck of the History Wing, descending to their rooms at night by walkways, thereby avoiding, for the better part of their Three-Year Seat, all contact with earth.

"My mother was born in New Hamburg," Westrum said, driving underground through a winding tunnel at whose end a versatile machine issued him a ticket permitting his Oldsmobile Custom Vista-Cruiser, whose license plate it had photographed, to park for an hour or a month or a year at designated rates, and urged him in a courteous male voice to park between white lines only facing forward, to remember to turn off his motor and extinguish his lights, lock his car, and follow green flashing arrows to the elevator. In deference to Kenneth Silvers struggling upon his canes, Westrum and the delegation walked slowly from his car to the elevator, rising swiftly then twelve floors and walking slowly down the long corridor carpeted in red, past a group of foreigners amusingly debating in broken English, to the suite reserved for him. The building hummed of systems flowing behind walls.

Outside the door to Westrum's suite four men stood waiting whose names he was unable to receive, so speedy was his introduction, nor would he ever learn their names, nor meet the men again. They were members of the Seating Committee, which seldom met, which had not met in months and was unlikely to resume, convening now to receive and welcome West-

rum in a salute to his distinction and in obedience to the Code
and Constitution of the Center requiring that the Seating Committee convene, if only to report its having done so.

Westrum and the committee stood in the corridor awaiting
Benstock's secretary—his *girl* he called her—who might or
might not oblige them by appearing. It was she, apparently,
who held the keys to Westrum's suite, and she was famous
among the men of the committee for neglect, forgetfulness,
and impudence, although she very well might be, said Benstock, simply deaf. Had he believed her willful he would have
passed her along to someone else, he said, someone he disliked,
someone who didn't need a secretary anyhow, but he sym-
pathetically suspected that her seeming willfulness was partial
deafness, and thus he endured her, as he endured all doubtful
cases, all hacks, dunces, pretenders, eloquent frauds, special
pleaders, freeloaders, learned charlatans, deluded amateurs,
and professional fakes.

"What are you planning?" a committeeman asked.

"We mustn't ask," said Harvey Weinberg.

"He's planning to open his door," said Benstock, "if my girl
brings the key."

"I didn't mean to pry," the committeeman said. "You needn't
tell us anything, you know."

"I'd tell you," said Westrum, "if I knew myself." He was
amused by his own sentence. But he might, in fact, here, he
thought, a stranger in a new place, come to know himself,
make acquaintance with himself, reveal himself to himself. It
had happened before. In isolation he had met himself. What
had *A History of the Past World* been, really, but self-
instruction? He had discovered to his chagrin when the work
was done that he had written less a history of the world than
an account of his own mind, carved from his Journal. For many
months he had resisted the idea of sending it anywhere except
back to his vault. Surely anyone would see how poor a print it
was of the face of the world, how bad a likeness of its supposed

19

subject. He capitulated at last to the persuasion of friends, especially Tikvah, and only when the deed was done was he satisfied that he could not have done otherwise.

The principal value of the work had been its freeing him into a knowledge of himself as he had been. With the fame of the book (whose title, as time passed, the publisher subtly changed from *A* to *The*) Westrum became new beyond the Westrum he had been, oddly celebrated, whose reward was his release from anonymity or material care into freedom and a vast confidence to proceed knowingly and consciously now upon lines established by accident. It was the confidence of immunity. Having revealed so much of the world in the disguise of historian, he believed he could now reveal even more as Westrum himself, throwing off all disguise, with a craft greater and deeper now because more conscious, tell the world not the history of a safe past but the perilous history of the present world, and that by telling the history of a white Protestant man born at Brest, heir to an older time, farther removed from Europe than the scholars of the present, and almost alone in his willingness to divulge it, prepared by training and by inclination to display for the mind of history his own true mind and passion heretofore concealed, the worst or most violent or secret parts of himself, along with the noblest. He would prepare his Journal for the eye of the public world, if not in his own generation then afterward. Thereby he would perform the single service within his power. "I'm only thinking," Westrum continued, to the committeeman, "of keeping up my Journal."

"We once seated a man," said Benstock—seating himself now, lowering himself to the floor because he was suddenly faint—"who came with the same idea."

"Hiram Browning," said Harvey Weinberg.

"His name makes me ill," said Benstock. "He promised us the journal of his life." Harvey sat, too, beside Benstock, but Kenneth Silvers could not sit, and Westrum therefore remained standing. "He was an old man by then," said Benstock, "with

20

nice gray hair, I should have grabbed him by it and thrown him off the roof."

"We never expected he'd live out the Seat to begin with," said Harvey.

"He lived out two," said Benstock. "He lived halfway into a third. Two Five-Year Seats and then some."

"Twelve years," said Harvey.

"At twelve thousand a year," said Benstock. "He ate corn flakes and saved eleven. Finally he died, the son of a bitch, he died and was buried and everything was legal, and I went downstairs. We have wonderful vaults downstairs, you lock them up, you set the combination for seven o'clock in the morning twenty years from today, and it opens on time, so they tell me. His particular vault could only be opened after three witnesses affirmed his death. I was one. I saw him dead. The coroner had to be the other, and a judge had to be the third. A judge came over from New Hamburg. He had a hundred packages of journal in the vault, they were all tied up in neat bundles, me, the coroner, the judge, and all the chairmen of all the committees in all the Wings, lawyers, members of the family, we were certified, we were witnesses, we began opening these little neat bundles. It was my honor to open the first one. I paid a hundred and fifty thousand dollars for the privilege. Do you know what it was?"

"Blank paper," said Westrum.

"Blank," said Benstock.

"All blank," said Harvey.

"The other ninety-nine were also blank," said Benstock. "We paid a hundred and fifty thousand dollars for a hundred dollars' worth of paper."

"My Journal's not blank," said Westrum swiftly.

"No no, of course not," Benstock said. Yet he must have thought of his story as a parable of his own misgivings, for his pale cheeks reddened.

"I've got fifty thousand pages," said Westrum, "and they're all written on."

"You've got half a dozen more histories there," a committee-man said.

"Yes," said Westrum, "but it's not what I want to do. I could carve books. The *History* was carved that way, but it'd been better never carved."

"Carving is art," the committeeman said, but his conviction was shallow, and when Rosalie approached he dispersed with the others, assuring Westrum it would all work out, all shaking hands, all wandering down the corridors to work, golf, tennis, lunch, and here was Rosalie. She was hardly more than a child, neither deaf nor willful, Westrum guessed, but only bored. "I'm sorry if I was late," she said, passing the keys to Benstock, and bringing to Westrum's mind the daughter of his mistress, of whom he unaccountably dreamed, his dream of her the more mysterious to him in view of his so seldom dreaming of his mistress herself except in the most impersonal way: in dreams his mistress appeared to him always as the officer of a vehicle, in a peaked cap—taxicab driver, elevator operator. At moments of passion he exacted from his mistress the promise of her daughter as a gift, but when passion was spent the promise was forgotten, withdrawn, between passion and passion never mentioned. He desired his mistress's daughter as a plaything, he'd not damage her innocence, he promised, although how he might play with her in the way he had in mind without damaging her innocence he had never explained to himself.

"It's a wonder she brought the right one," said Benstock, turning the key in the lock. "Isn't she something?" he asked, passing the key to Westrum, who took from his pocket a Winding Reel coiled in a chrome base—tangle-free, Terence's gift—upon which he carried the keys to his life, his house here, his apartment in New York, keys to car and bicycle, and the key to his vault where he kept the second copy of his Journal in a room in the apartment twenty stories high where he and his mistress met.

"Oh, say, splendid," Westrum said, entering the suite with Benstock.

"It's our best," said Benstock.

Westrum could imagine working well here. Space was broad. The walls consumed echo, and a colorful Finnish rug absorbed footfalls. The principal room (though not the second room) was illuminated by the same constant light of which Beatrice complained. "My wife likes the dark," said Westrum. *Watch now*, he thought, *he'll probe*.

"Your wife is a beautiful woman," Benstock said, seating himself at the second desk. He had yet to smile.

"Miss Sanantone will work there," said Westrum.

"I've got a machine ordered for her," said Benstock.

"She'll probably bring her own," said Westrum. "What she'll need is ashtrays. She smokes like a furnace."

"Ashtrays," said Benstock, committing them to his mind. "No problem."

Long Formica shelves would hold the Journal. Westrum ran one hand along a shelf to feel its sheen.

"It's dust-free," said Benstock. "That's what they tell me. If you see any dust you mustn't believe it. Those shelves cost three dollars a foot, I'm told."

"The windows don't open," Westrum said.

"I never saw one open," Benstock said. "They're not even glass, they're something else, some stainless miracle, better than glass. The real thing's never good enough for us here."

"Well, the real thing's often *not* much good," said Westrum. Across the valley of the river New Hamburg lay beneath the pall of its own making, arousing in Westrum pity for its victims, and yet a certain contempt for their resignation to their own pollution. "They consent to live in that," he said.

"*That* I can't do anything about," said Benstock. "I have no jurisdiction outside the Wing."

"That's the steeple of the courthouse," Westrum said. "It's all you can see. In the old days you could see the whole city from this side. The air was clear. The first research I ever did I did in the courthouse. I looked up my parents' births. It turned out they'd been lying to me. They told me my mother was eleven months younger than my father. Turned out she was really a month older. They live in Brest now."

"I've driven through Brest," said Benstock. "I don't think I like it."

"Oh, it's a nice little fascist town," said Westrum.

The second room of the suite was less elegant, furnished with a daybed, two chairs at a small coffee table, bare bookshelves, and, beyond the room, a bathroom with a shower in a stall of frosted glass.

"How fascist?" Benstock asked.

"Like you'd expect," said Westrum. "White Protestant, no Jews, Catholics, Negroes, poor, liquor, speeding, smoke, dirt, unions, third parties, hardly even any children any more because the old folks won't bear the school tax. One thing I might carve out of my Journal is a nice bitter little book about Brest."

"I think people would be interested in a book from you about Washington," Benstock said.

"Or maybe I'll make no book at all," said Westrum.

"A book about the Population Inquiry maybe," Benstock said. "It would be nice if I knew what you plan to do."

"One of the gentlemen in the hall said I needn't tell you."

"That's fine too," said Benstock. "You know best."

"Why don't you get the Center to buy my Journal?" Westrum said.

"Could we see it," Benstock asked.

"Could you buy it blind?" Westrum asked kindly. "See it when I'm dead. Once somebody sees it it's not a Journal any more. The seal is broken." They strolled back from the second room.

"Your girl sees it," Benstock said.

"She types it," said Westrum.

"Not reads it?"

"That's hard to tell. I've never known. I have very little idea what's in her mind."

"Maybe nothing," said Benstock. "How long have you had her?"

24

"A couple of weeks ago," said Westrum, "we celebrated our tenth anniversary. I said, 'Miss Sanantone, do you realize you've been with me ten years today?' She took her cigarette out of her mouth and put it back again."

"Have a cigarette," said Benstock. "You don't smoke?"

"No," said Westrum, "I just never seem to have got started on it." Yet in fact he smoked from time to time, big cigars when he was at particular peace with the world, and cigarettes when he drank, and at sporting events (especially outdoors), and with his mistress. "Suppose you took it on faith," he said. "Suppose you paid me a certain sum. Suppose you gave me a Seven-Year Seat at a certain sum a year. Suppose you paid me thirty thousand dollars a year for seven years. The Journal is yours for that, all that's been done and all that will be done."

"We never gave anybody seven years," said Benstock. Westrum's directness made him most uneasy, and he began to walk slowly between the rooms, puffing quickly and deeply upon his cigarette. "We never paid anybody anything like thirty thousand, either," he said, sitting in exhaustion upon the daybed upon which, he had supposed (although now, for some reason, he was not so certain), Westrum's girl from time to time would lie.

"Is it so much?" Westrum asked. "You pay three dollars a foot for shelves."

"Not *ordinary* shelves," said Benstock. He wished he had not sat upon the daybed, for Westrum had strolled after him to the second room, and loomed above him a thousand feet tall, and he was trapped in an old familiar way, in the shadow of a big threatening boy who might or might not intend harm, and a goy at that of the sort whom he had often disarmed with a bit of a joke learned from his father and told in his father's weary tones. "I'll tell you the difference between capital and labor," he said. "The money the other fellow has is capital. Getting it away from him is labor."

Westrum, unhappy to be at such a height, sat at the coffee table, winding his long legs like rubber about the legs of the chair. He cared nothing, really, for arrangements or talk of arrangements, for Seat or money, but only for Benstock, whose faith he coveted, whose timidity moved him. "Do you exercise? " he asked.

"I know I don't look well," said Benstock. "It's this job. If I could get out from under I'd be better off. Today I got a letter telling me what a liar I am, I'm accused of breaking a promise I never made. People apply for a Seat, and they think their application is the same as acceptance. They pack their bags. They break all their connections. They announce their Seat to the local paper, they send me clippings showing the wonderful publicity the Center is getting in Chapel Hill. I'm supposed to be grateful for that."

"People think their dreams are true because they dreamed them," Westrum said.

"I dream nightmares," Benstock said. "I don't know the territories. How do I know the value of anything? Everybody thinks his own work is valuable, everybody has a prejudice in his own favor. Maybe your Journal is the great work of the century. I'm always afraid of turning down something wonderful, I'll be the laughingstock of history, Bonehead Benstock, he turned down the invention of the wheel, he said it was too round. How do I really know you've got anything there?"

"You don't," said Westrum.

"Maybe it's fifty thousand pages of old sheet music," Benstock said. "I understand why you can't show us the Journal. For the benefit of the committee, let's say you're writing a specific book about a specific subject, Washington, Brest, the Inquiry. The committee feels better if you name it."

"You're the committee," Westrum said. It was a fact and he knew it.

"No, no," said Benstock, "I present it to the committee."

"I think you present it to yourself," said Westrum gently.

It was a fact, and Benstock knew it, too. He *was* the committee. Deny it as he might, he ruled the Wing. All decision was his. Poet turned historian, if Benstock was neither poet nor historian any longer he nevertheless retained the poet's instinct for fire in the ashes, and the historian's exactitude. He was right for the job. The poet was swift to suspect the worst of men, but the historian too far respected the facts of any case to condemn or reject any man without hard evidence. His reigning fear was his fear of denying a Seat to a worthy or needy candidate, and in the process of striving for justice he was consuming himself with exhaustion.

How could he finally be the judge of men or their hopes? How could he know which man's work was done, and which man's work was about to begin? Men worked in ways beyond his imagination, in fields he had never heard of, couldn't pronounce, and hadn't the time to read in. He didn't know the territory, he often said, and he therefore judged the *man*—the man's credentials, the man's letters of reference, the face, the eyes, the brows of the eyes, chance impressions, his wife's impression, rumors, dreams—ending by knowing as much as he'd have known by the toss of a coin.

"I can't name it if I'm not doing it," Westrum said.

"I wouldn't want you to lie," said Benstock.

"All right," said Westrum, "it happens I'm writing a little book."

"Tell me a title," Benstock said. "Make up a title if you don't have one."

"It's called *Potentialities for Fascism in America*," said Westrum, who from time to time had contemplated such a book. But the title was not his. It belonged to his brother-in-law, Tikvah, who twenty-five years before had written a small pamphlet of that name.

"Don't tell me how it comes out," said Benstock. "No, tell me. The question of my own skin is always timely. Shall I pack my bags?" His wife, Sally, had been rescued as a child from the Nazis in the hour of her execution. She bore upon her arm a tattooed number. He walked quickly to the bathroom to douse his cigarette. "I'll remember the ashtrays," he said. "I'll tell my girl, although I can't guarantee she'll hear me. She doesn't answer me. She won't say Yes, No, Maybe, Tomorrow, or Ho-hum. Her mind is far away. Maybe sometimes I don't actually ask her. My mind is also far away."

Westrum wrote upon his tablet *ashtrays for Miss Sanantone* and tore away the page. Benstock took the page. "Years ago I gave up writing things down," said Benstock.

"You're as well off," said Westrum. "A Journal's a prison."

"Good," said Benstock, walking to the door with sudden energy. "Very good. I'll do everything I can with the committee. Prospects for fascism in America," he said, writing it down upon the page Westrum had given him.

"Potentialities," said Westrum.

"Correct," said Benstock, "I've got it," and he smiled at last, if only fleetingly, for Westrum appeared new to him, and he recalled, yes, the *History* (given a small lapse on the subject of Roman roads) was a labor not only as perfect as one man could make it but anti-fascist to the tail of the final comma, and Westrum was known for having fought those good fights, he'd churned up the right waters in Washington, he'd been the one good strong voice on the team of the Inquiry. Benstock was confident of Westrum, and he said, "Potentialities for fascism in America, or, the secret of your goyim heart. That's what we really want to know."

"That might be what my Journal might tell," said Westrum.

Westrum accompanied Benstock down the corridor—formerly guest, suddenly he was host—parting from him at an intersection of corridors where signs and arrows of several colors pointed the ways to distant Wings, to ramps and walkways, to banks of elevators controlled by sequence timers, Westrum descending to his car. *Don't establish inconvenient virtues,* he thought. Now he could never, in Benstock's presence, smoke. *Good,* he thought, *overwhelm him with moral accomplishment,* he'd play the part of austerity here, he'd be old settler, old upright self-denying American, cling to old virtues for the eyes of new Jews, who'd give him all the Seat he wanted out of their own scrupulous love of justice. Benstock would give him every benefit of every doubt, as Tikvah always had, soon speeding to his house, and up the long gravel driveway.

Benstock had forgotten to return for his car. It was a robin's-egg blue Ford Falcon still coated with the summer's dust, all hubcaps gone but one, a football banner flying from its radio aerial, and a bumper sticker urging caution—SCHOOL'S OPEN, DRIVE CAREFULLY. In the house Terence awaited his father.

But Terence's father could never instantly depart for anywhere. He must always, between one errand and the next, write his thoughts upon one or another of his tablets already accumulating here in the new house upon tables and the arms of chairs, upon the piano, the television set, windowsills and mantelpiece, standing scribbling quickly now in his private shorthand *to the supermarket, thousand yards in nineteen minutes getting too cold for swimming, Beatrice brought coffee, Benstock thin black hair, Weinberg weeping eye, Silvers sitting, Terence shot all, "a duty AND a pleasure," presented myself as one returning home, thought of Uncle Nelson's head, ritual meeting of Seating Committee, Benstock is bugged by the fraud of the blank Journal (Horace Browning?), suspicious and mistrustful toward me, dropped dead when I asked 30G but softened when he remembered my reputation for antifascism, forgot his car,* and upon another page of his tablet swiftly began a letter to Miss Sanantone, not in the shorthand she well enough knew but in the plainest schoolboy script, the simplest sentences in the simplest and most direct order, without humor or irony or any form or sort of indirection likely to confuse her mind.

We have arrived here in good health after a good trip with no car trouble or other trouble of any kind. Today everything was arranged in all final details for you to come. The right people have approved it. Come as quick as you can.

29

> I have been expecting that you would be here by now, but possibly you have not been able to pack the pages as fast as we thought. Do not hurry. It is better to do it right than fast.
>
> I have seen your quarters where you will stay. They are in the Residence Wing, as it is called. Everything there is very clean and modern. Above all, everything there is very air-conditioned, so none of your allergies will be able to get at you and give you a hard time.

It was a natural question Benstock raised. Could she really see it, type it, without reading it? Westrum had asked himself the question so long ago, and so long ago settled it for himself, that he was unprepared to hear it again. It seemed impossible indeed that Miss Sanantone could be at once so efficient and so little observant, so merely neutral moral agent, through whom everything passed and upon whom everything was lost. She spelled everything but knew nothing. How could she on one hand so intelligently find her way through the forest of his shorthand, the interlinear of his drafts, without on the other hand absorbing his meaning? Undoubtedly such people existed. He continued:

> Remember to lock all doors and windows and bring all the extra keys with you. Ask Hermie the doorman to clear away from the front door all papers or other material which pile up there. Stop the milk man and the bread man from delivering. Give Hermie five dollars for those services and, of course, keep track of all money you pay out for me to repay you.
>
> Now, about the matter of carrying the footlockers down to the street. If your friend helps you you may settle up with him in any way you see fit. If Hermie the doorman helps you, pay him ten dollars *more*.
>
> The name of the airplane medicine is Dramamine. You can buy it at a drugstore. Follow the directions on the bot-

tle. My wife believes that it is sold in both liquid form and tablets. Enjoy your traveling and do not fear it. St. Christopher is the patron saint of traveling and has never failed anybody.

The main thing you must do is be happy about leaving New York. It is not as if you are going to some foreign country. We will undoubtedly go back soon. If by any chance you need advice, please telephone me at the number below.

He would enter the telephone number later, for Terence was waiting, driving off with Terence to meet the principal, who had sounded, on the telephone, tough, defensive, as if Westrum's desire to visit the school implied criticism sight unseen. The principal was wife to Harvey Weinberg, and Westrum supposed, judging from Harvey, that she'd be plain, since Harvey was awkward, unconfident, unlikely to have imagined himself winning beauty in a wife.

The school was glass, long, low, and new, and well-provided in the way of a school whose children were the children of parents whose own business, too, was education. The football practice-field adjoined the school, and the boys were assembling now, some in short suits, some in full armor. It was Friday, and practice would be light. Years ago, for Brest—before the coming of the Center, and before the new stadium had been built—Westrum had played on this practice field. He could not recall where the old schoolhouse had been, but it hadn't been here, nor did the principal know, but the coach would, they'd ask the coach, she said, who was coming down the corridor now, and who, as he approached, feasted his eyes upon Terence. Terence was tall and well-made, and a coach might imagine in Terence an agile boy with able hands, whose American face—so much the coach's own—suggested less the city than the country, less an indoors boy addicted to books than one who, in a phrase of the coach, "takes care of himself like a man."

How lovely the principal was! How dark she was! How West-rum did love dark, dark-eyed women, his wife and his mistress were dark with dark eyes, and he said to Coach Wilson, "I played for Brest once upon a time," to which the coach replied that he himself had played for New Hamburg, and named the years, and mentioned, by the way, now that he thought of it, the honor he'd had of being selected two consecutive years All-State. His voice was hoarse, as it always was during foot-ball season. About his neck he wore a whistle on a white shoe-string. But his eyes drifted to Terence in spite of every effort to keep them upon Westrum, and he said, "You're a new student."

"I'm a student," Terence said.

"Some of our best students," said the coach, "are on the foot-ball team."

"Is that true?" asked Terence, not of the coach but of Har-riet Weinberg, as if one stood the chance of hearing truth from a principal if not from a coach.

"A boy wants to learn to take care of himself," said Coach Wilson.

"I'm a student," Terence said. "I might have been an athlete." He might have been an athlete, or he might not have been an athlete. How could it be known? One of his brothers had been an athlete, and one of his brothers had not, but for Terence the question had been foreclosed forever by a blow of his father's hand in awful wrath. "But I'm not," he said.

"You'd never regret it," said the coach.

"Don't look at me," said Terence, "because I'm not," whose words turned the coach's eyes to Westrum. Coach Wilson ex-pected Westrum to assist him, for Westrum had a sensible, trust-worthy face. Upon such men as Westrum the coach depended, home folk with a face and a voice he knew, someone he'd fol-low if the time came to follow, someone he'd vote for, someone he could count upon as he could not count upon these shaggy scholars. He winked at Westrum.

Terence's firmness charmed Harriet. Her contempt for the

coach was a source of much conflict in the school, in the Center, and through the community. She hoped to put an end someday to football at Center High. Every Saturday, with a picket sign, she marched against it.

"Football coaches," said Westrum, when the coach had passed beyond their hearing, "are sophomores at heart." Coach Wilson's condescending wink of the eye irritated him.

She was delighted. By the sound of Westrum's voice on the telephone, and by the sight of him, she had anticipated no ally: he could have been the coach's father beside him there in the corridor. The twang of his accent she mistrusted. "Don't underestimate our sophomores," she said.

"Football is fascist," said Westrum, to whom the idea occurred now for the first time.

"That's rather strong," she said.

"My father feels everything strong," Terence said.

"Some people feel so little," she said, walking with the delightful boy and his father down the corridor of a school she'd never meant to be principal of. She had had her heart set on schools in slums and ghettoes whose children were dark and deprived. For a decade she had taught Indian children where the need was most, Cherokee and Tuscarora in the Carolinas, Utes in Utah, Ojibway in Minnesota. "Then I followed the birds here," she said, for Harvey had exhausted the birds where the Indians were, and he was offered a Seat at the Center and irresistible resources, and they came, though it was always a question in playful minds whether the Center hadn't really offered the Seat to Harvey to nail his wife as principal.

"All right," said Westrum, "look upon it as an intellectual ghetto."

"You don't have to be an Indian to be hung up," said Terence.

"All rather homogeneous I suppose," said Westrum.

Terence paused to survey a bulletin board, and Westrum and the principal paused behind him, and the down of her cheek tempted Westrum's touch. Had Terence not been there

33

he'd have touched her. More than once, in a career of capitulating to his own temptations, he had touched lovely women upon the cheek, upon the neck, and been rewarded for his good sense by ladies who, like Harriet Weinberg, he guessed, were prepared in their imaginations to receive him.

"It's all white," she said, "except for the janitor's daughter."

The bulletin board featured entries in last year's Father Contest, won by a boy named Jerome Weiss, whose father thereby was acknowledged for his general excellence and his superiority as a father, the boy himself winning the prize of a free trip to a far place.

"Where did he go?" asked Terence.

"I think Los Angeles," Harriet said.

Jerome Weiss had extolled his father in eighty prize-winning heroic couplets, not themselves faultless, but anyhow different from the orthodox prose of competitors, winning more by novelty than merit.

> *I sing of him, my father, you'll say he's nice,*
> *I give you now the chemist, Samuel C. Weiss.*

The boy then enumerated in rhyme the data of his father's life, his birth (in Germany), his flight to "these free shores," the names and locations of the public schools, colleges, and universities he attended, degrees and honors, positions held, the titles of his professional papers, and excerpts from statements solicited by the boy in behalf of his father's character and achievement from other chemists likewise endowed, and telling, too, of his father's noblest moment, who had once saved the life of a child not his own by swiftly carrying the child to a hospital: the child, while roller-skating, had been struck by a vehicle driven by a person crazed with drugs.

> *The name of him who struck I shall not mention.*
> *The case, in fact, is still in litigation.*
>
> *Down rushed my father to the stricken child,*
> *So cool of head amidst the scene so wild.*

Terence read. His mind raced with exalted thoughts, afire with visions of triumph. He'd enter such a contest, he'd contend, he'd win, he'd be carried down this hallway upon the shoulders of his proud friends. In the eye of his mind he viewed a film of himself borne high in victory, asking neither who shot the film if not he, nor who the friends might be, for he hadn't any here.

He'd not go to Los Angeles, though. He'd be original, he'd go some obscure place nobody thought of going, he'd go to Little Rock or Racine, he'd not be obvious nor do the obvious: all geniuses were slightly peculiar. He'd heard it said his father was peculiar, too, his work was unorthodox, his politics quixotic. But Terence would reply to all that in the prize-winning essay he would write. If only he could write! The trouble was, he couldn't write. He hadn't his father's talent for writing, and hardly even Jerome Weiss's talent for writing, either, whose epic ended:

> *I've told you now of Weiss the chemist wise.*
> *Don't you agree his son should win the prize?*

"No," cried Terence. But even if he could write he hadn't much of a subject to work with. Terence's father, unfortunately, or so it seemed to Terence, for all his reputed achievement, was light on the spectacular, hadn't saved any children, hadn't fought in the war. He followed his father and the principal down the hallway. They walked in step. How dramatize his father? Where was his father's passion? Ice Water Westrum indeed—so they called him in Washington. Her hips rolled. *My father takes a deep interest in school affairs,* thought Terence, it was a virtue, it was a point, put enough virtues and points together and he'd write a prize-winning essay, if only he could write. *Gather notes,* he thought, *start a collection, jot down virtues and points as they come to mind.* He overtook them. Something his father had said had caused the principal to smile with pleasure. *My father is kind to ladies,* Terence thought.

"Why is he so hoarse?" his father was asking.

"He swears at the boys," Harriet said.

On the wall of her office were several photographs of Indians in tribal dress and business suits on a railroad platform somewhere, and she and Harvey in their midst. In the photographs she wore her hair in a single braid falling to her left shoulder. "You've given up the braid?" Westrum asked.

"Indians liked it," she said.

"I'm a white man," said Westrum. "I like it."

"Then I might braid it again," she said. She was confident, she said to Terence, that he'd catch up his schoolwork in spite of a late start, and he said he was confident, too, he'd been late before. She gave him papers to complete, and she walked with them to the doorway of the schoolhouse, where she and Westrum shook hands, and her flesh was cool, and Westrum followed Terence to the car, observing as he settled behind the wheel that although she had withdrawn into the darkness of the corridor she remained to watch them go; unseen, she thought; or perhaps she meant to be seen; and Terence shot her from the car, and shot the sunlight dancing down the rows of glass windows as they drove from the parking lot, and shot the football squad running behind Coach Wilson on the practice field.

"How is football fascist?" Terence asked.

"They do what they're told," his father said. "It's only to win, no matter how."

"I'll think it over," Terence said. "Was that a good poem on the wall?"

"Not very," Westrum said. "I didn't read the whole thing."

"It was good enough to win," said Terence.

"Well, it was *different*," his father said.

He'd do something *different*, then, thought Terence. He'd win. The winning was all. He'd make his father and his mother proud, first by his winning and next by the message he'd win with, he'd show his father's goodness off, shooting the receding school, shooting the neighborhood, shooting up the long hill

36

between the rows of English maple, shooting his Dalmatian waiting, shooting his mother swimming, and behind her the comic sign hung upon the pumphouse, WE DON'T SWIM IN YOUR TOILET, PLEASE DON'T PEE IN OUR POOL. His father objected to the sign—low humor bored him—and his mother's bathing cap was new, borrowed, found in the house, bright green, ill-fitting. She appeared hairless and earless beneath the cap, and it wasn't her face at all, unless, seen another way, thought Terence, it *was* her face, her natural face, her unadorned, unpainted, undisguised face. "You look very Jewish in that cap," he said.

Without haste, but nevertheless without hesitation, Beatrice removed her cap, and she floated upon her back, her hair spread upon the water. Yes, thought Westrum, in a canvas chair at his tablet, deeper than anything else she was Jewish, it was where she lived, and wrote the telephone number on the letter to Miss Sanantone, and upon his tablet wrote *to the school with Terence, he put the football coach down, one Wilson whom I might have become.* If Terence had said, "You look very ugly in that cap," or even if he had said, "You look very old in that cap," she'd not have removed it, she'd have said, "Terence, go soak your head," and wrote upon his tablet *hard to match up the principal with her husband, dark Jewish women rescued me from a life of dull sin, I might have been the football coach.*

"I don't care what I look like," Beatrice said, poor woman, twice trapped for eternity by her son's film and by her husband's Journal. She seldom watched herself upon film nor ever read her husband's Journal except once when she came upon two pages fluttering loose from a cardboard carton on the shoulder of a truckman moving them in (or was it out?) the house in Leipzig, and read a half a dozen lines before she realized it was her husband's Journal she was reading, and read the pages through because she was powerless to resist, but never knew and surely never asked when they had been written, or when the event had occurred, or whether the lady was

37

herself or some other, or whether it was all a young man's theoretical plan or a seasoned man's experience of love's excitement. He had sometimes urged her to read his Journal, not in the present but in the far past, to take it up a day at a time twenty or thirty years ago, thousands of days ago, reading slowly forward, remaining always long behind events and therefore far from pain, but she preferred to hear nothing, as someone, hearing her name beyond a door, instinctively pauses before moving quickly, sensibly on, not to hear, and thus by denying him, in fact, that single listener he most desired, goaded him endlessly on.

there because I'd never really get to go down on her, which was my ambition of the hour, until I could help her to ripen herself by admitting me of her own will into her own imagination in such a way as to think me possible. I appeared to her ghetto eye so different from herself, and I knew that she wasn't seeing me at all but only seeing an image of me her whole lifetime had produced. I was not a man but a type, and an alien type, creature out of a western jungle, animal with the wrong nose and the wrong sound to his howling. Besides, she thought herself beneath me (so to say) as well as above me, or anyhow certainly apart from me, so that until she saw clearly that I truly wanted *her* (in spite of my wanting several others, too, all dark Jewish girls and ladies) she couldn't begin to think in practical terms how she might give herself to me.

Educator, educate. I'll teach her that I want her, that it's not my idea to go and catch an American beauty, though they're fine, too, with their golden hair—teach her not by teaching her who I am but who she is or might be, by giving her a greater idea of herself, by extending her sense of herself, by boosting her up so she'll transcend herself, help hoist her out of her mind, which now recognizes only the one issue, the Jews and the plight of the Jews.

They thought I was some sort of spy from the Gentile world. I wandered through the house, and a fellow named Yasef politely said, "Why are you wandering through the house?" Everybody was wandering through the house for reasons of his own. "Studying the bookshelves," I said, and he nodded, remembering, *Oh, that's right, the beast can read.*

I'll be giving her every opportunity to eavesdrop on me, so that she may arrive by degrees at her own decisions and conclusions, and one thing may lead to another, agreement upon agreement leading to understanding, understanding leading to affection, affection leading finally to the fucking bed, and all this she must gather for herself, not by my persuading her but by her own apprehending.

I am more radical than she. She thinks she's more radical than I. But as her curiosity becomes aroused her thinking will begin to pursue mine, now and again she will call upon me for a bit of advice, assistance, support, and in these conversations she will see that my radicalism extends beyond the mere acts of marching with her on her various picket lines, although of course I'll do that, too, and march my very soles and heels into oblivion and hope at the moment of the harvest of my ambition that I shall be able to say to my shoes, as I drop them to the floor, "Well done, you led me here," for if all goes well she'll go down with me at last with confidence and conviction because I am on her side and she will have found it out for herself, and she'll believe in me, and she'll know that I am of her, and she will marvel at her own having first mistook me for a dirty thing from way out west where the KKK rides. Educator, you will have taught her (of all things the most difficult) to discriminate between appearance and reality.

Yet as I write this I am aware minute by minute that at the end of everything the bed stands, all roads lead to the bedroom, and I question myself and leap to the question of history besides: if all my life's learning is directed to no end but hers (and taking myself as a representative man), is it not very probable that much of history can only be understood in terms of men's acting out events to verify their own theories? Whole towns have been bombarded, I suspect, to give the generals a chance to try out their guns,

From the water she called, "Benstock phoned."

"What did he want?" Westrum asked, beginning a new letter upon a fresh page of his tablet: *Madame, I have just discovered in the little groin pocket of my bathing trunks a piece of paper I put there two weeks ago at the University pool. It shows a phone number where you were.*

"He was looking for his car," she said. "He knew he'd left it somewhere."

Benstock would never remember Miss Sanantone's ashtrays, either, Westrum thought, and wrote *ashtrays* upon his tablet and drew a ring around it, and he tore to small pieces the paper he had taken from the pocket of his bathing trunks.

My father is very athletic, thought Terence, whose father flew through the air, diving shallow and swimming to Beatrice's side, *but not exciting,* Terence thought, he'd saved nobody's child from the madness of a drug addict with quick thinking or fast driving through red lights to the hospital. "Did you ever save anybody's life?" he asked his father.

"Only my own," said Westrum, treading water beside his wife.

"Did you ever produce anything useful for mankind?" asked Terence, pursuing his father into the water.

"Nothing useful like a chemist produces," Westrum said. "I'm working on the abolition of war."

It occurred to Terence to *invent* brave deeds for his father to have performed, or invent useful products for his father to have produced, he'd lie a little, everybody lied to some extent.

40

"What was your most exciting moment?" he asked his father. "What do you consider your most notable achievement?"

"I'm the only father on the block," said Westrum, "whose Journal is fifty thousand pages long."

The statistics were inspiring to Terence, who felt that he was getting somewhere now. He'd reckon how high the pages would reach in a single climbing pile, or, better still, more impressive, how far they'd reach laid end to end, a simple calculation, *my father's Journal end to end would reach from the steps of Center High to—*then, too, a few selected excerpts might be telling. "What's the chances of glancing it over?" he asked.

"You might not enjoy what you glance at," his father said. "You might read things you'd prefer not to know." But that was too little to say, and not at all what he meant, and Westrum submerged to think, swimming under water to the shallow end of the pool and wading out. "You're at liberty to read any part of my Journal any time at your own risk," he said, a sentence delivered earlier upon two occasions to each of Terence's brothers, neither of whom had yet taken the liberty or the risk. He lifted from its hooks the sign reading WE DON'T SWIM IN YOUR TOILET, PLEASE DON'T PEE IN OUR POOL, and opened the pumphouse door and tossed it in.

"What happens to his Journal when he dies?" Terence asked his mother.

"It stops," she said.

"Who gets it?" Terence asked.

"You do," she said. "You boys."

"Not you?" he asked.

"I've not put in for it," she said.

"I accept human nature," Terence said.

Westrum intended his Journal to pass to his sons. It would be, perhaps, their fortune, and at best a gift of wisdom and reconciliation, put them at ease with themselves who might otherwise imagine, knowing their own worst natures or foulest fantasies, that they were but bad, weak sons of a powerful father,

41

poor tainted copies of a sublime model. He hoped his sons might know him as he truly was.

If this way of speaking to his sons was monstrously elaborate it was nevertheless the only way he knew to proceed, for whom not speech but the page was the coin of the country. In the beginning he had learned all he knew of the world from printed pages. He knew no other way of talking back or telling out. From his own detestable father he had learned very little, and that all wrong, where coldness and silence were the code of the house. Thus, when the time came, and he fell among the Jews, he rejoiced, he admired them to extravagance, he envied them their talk, their frankness, their uncensored passion, the unfenced limits of their debate, partaking without repaying in kind, sitting silent and seeming cold, not because he chose that way but because he was incapable of passion except upon paper.

And he married into them as soon as he could, and there they were, a Jew and a half floating upon the water, and West-rum discreetly behind the hangings of the clothesline, removing his seeping trunks and exchanging them for a dry pair, draping the wet trunks upon the line and emerging to discover wife and son smiling from the water at the head and ankles of the bodiless man, and sitting in the sunshine continuing his letter to his mistress. *It's Tikvah who made me come here. He could keep me there if he wanted to. He sent me into exile. He plotted and planned it this way,* which his reason told him was untrue, and he drew a line through it. Yet accusation drifted toward truth in the moment of utterance. *I might be right,* he thought, he'd expand it a little and see if any truth were there. *Put the pressure on Tikvah. Figure out how. Enlist an ally whose name I won't mention, have him bring to bear upon Tikvah every gun and cannon and poison dart and camouflage and trickery in his vast armory and arsenal until the enemy surrenders,* ceasing there at the ringing of the telephone.

Often history was best understood less by the logic of decisive men than by the logistics of men and their mistresses. So he had written in the *History* and brought down upon himself the criticism of men who were either quite right, or who had no experience of mistresses (or who took this way of denying it). It was Benstock on the telephone again, who now believed, he said, that he'd not only left his car there, but the keys in the ignition, too. "I'll check," said Westrum, affecting a voice deeper than his normal voice, having been told on the telephone by Tikvah twenty-five years ago, "On the telephone you sound like a cowboy moved to town," for which he had never forgiven Tikvah, which Tikvah himself had forgotten instantly, and walked to the car and saw the keys there. "There they are," he said to Benstock.

Would Westrum bring them? Just stick them in his pocket?

"Certainly," said Westrum, "stick the car in my pocket, too, if you like." He'd take the car. He'd not smoke. He'd not drink. He'd be kind to everyone and know the joy of new beginnings after old lacerations.

"I'll appease their fears," he said to Beatrice, who was dressing now in a fine and simple dress from Pauline Trigère, pewter gray she'd shopped for with Winnie Tikvah the day before they'd left New York. For Beatrice, dressing was a discreet act. His mistress, on the other hand, dressed parading, flinging herself about, talking to her mirror, praising her own flesh, speaking things she never spoke but to him.

"Yes," said Beatrice, "appease them. Taxes are too high, declare peace."

"Life is conflict," he said.

"Appease them," she said. "They're nervous, don't quibble, you're the well-known pacifist."

"Conflict is how people work," he said.

"We didn't come to fight," she said.

"Thought is dispute," he said. "Dialogue is thought. Fighting is a way of thinking."

"I'm ready if you are," she said, turning off the lights as she

43

went, old economy, old habit, old love of the dark, passing behind him through the house, hesitant among unfamiliar turnings, downstairs past Terence at the television.

"Have a good time," said Terence, "write if you get work," not turning his head. He had discovered an American flag in the basement. It lay upon his lap.

"We always do," his father said, he'd appease them, he'd stress the anti-fascism of his pacifism, he'd deal right and put them at their ease. He'd help them to trust him, for they must make their acquaintance anew with every Gentile, and he took Tikvah into his mind as the means of knowing Benstock's heart.

"Go to bed at a decent hour," Beatrice said.

"I'll go when I'm tired," Terence said. He had not yet chosen a bedroom for himself. He'd not sleep tonight where he slept last night.

"Don't talk like that to your mother," Westrum said. "No swimming."

"I'll do as you say, Mother dear," said the boy. *My father is a very social man,* he thought, *he goes to many dinner parties.* But was that a prize-winning virtue? And how could he write when he could not write? He heard them depart in two cars, his father in Benstock's corny blue Falcon, gone at last, hurrah, he'd prowl the house, he'd reconnoiter, he'd turn the TV up as loud as he cared to, he'd swim naked in the night.

Lost for the moment, Westrum leading, Beatrice following, they drove up and down the hills looking for Benstock's street, and back and forth on Benstock's street looking for his house. Its lights were lit from porch to attic. Two bicycles lay upon the lawn. Rain had begun.

A girl, nine years old, answered Westrum's knock. She was Gretchen, and she said, "How nice of you to come," whose mother behind her instantly said the same thing in an accent faintly foreign. She was a frail woman with a melancholy face, whose smile for Westrum, like her husband's invitation of the

morning, was rather duty than enthusiasm—how nice of them
to come, she said, how weary they must be from traveling—
and who, after this first greeting, never again that evening, nor
for weeks afterward, permitted herself to look into Westrum's
face. Her eyes avoided his as if he were death itself. Upon her
forearm tattooed numbers told that she had once been a cap-
tive of the Nazis.

Benstock named their liquor. He had begun to drink in advance of his guests, and he had been unable to dispel a
depression which had enveloped him all day. Quietly, in order
not to be overheard, Westrum declined to drink, he'd take, he
said, a glass of iced water if it weren't too much trouble, meeting then, in the living room, two men of the Center, and their
wives, though which woman was which man's wife he never
clearly established, and Philip Benstock, with golden hairs
upon his chin.

Taller by a head than his father, Philip nevertheless gave the
impression of breadth, not height, for he was a wide boy, pow-
erfully solid and sound. The newspaper called him "Little Gibraltar." It was he who brought the iced water to Westrum.
His hand could crush the glass it held. From his shirt pocket a
toothbrush protruded, bristles up. "You're right ready to brush
on a moment's notice," Westrum said.

"I was in a hurry," Philip explained, smiling with all good
humor. Indeed, his teeth were brilliant. Neither he nor his sister appeared to have inherited melancholy. "You're the gent
who played for Brest," he said.

"I'm the gent," said Westrum.

And there was Harvey Weinberg at the door, whom no one
heard, knocking with his umbrella, whom Westrum himself admitted to the house, and with him Harriet. The rain had
begun, and their faces were wet, for Harvey had forgotten to
open his umbrella between the car and the house. He had forgotten, also, to complete the buckling of his belt, whose
dangling end swung from his waist. He handed his umbrella
with trembling hands to Gretchen, who said to him, "How nice

45

of you to come," and with the drying of the rain upon his face he began to sweat, and his weeping eye drained and ran, and he reddened ferociously as he entered the living room, his neck swelling in the prison of his collar, and the reason he was late, he said—but only Westrum was listening—was that he had misplaced his medicine. "It's my weight medicine," he said, grateful to Westrum for listening, and turning to him fully. "It's made of the urine of pregnant horses. I can't tell you much more than that."

"You've been quite specific," Westrum said.

"Harriet read about it in a ladies' magazine," said Harvey. "I'll bring the article in. I'll drop it in your box. It's either a miracle or a fraud." With difficulty, with his trembling hands, he carried his drink to his lips. He was flattered that Westrum should speak to him, Westrum was "distinguished," Harvey said.

Harvey Weinberg's own existence embarrassed him. Somewhere out of the past Westrum had known someone embarrassed by his own existence, years and years ago it was, he'd written it down, he'd find it when the Journal came. Perhaps he was closer to it now than he had been this morning. It seemed so. His mind tended to grind upon things, to keep shuffling through memories. *Damn,* he thought, feeling the letter to Miss Sanantone in his pocket, he'd forgotten to mail it on the way over, *all Jews here but me,* he thought.

"We'll be playing Brest next week," Philip said.

"Will you beat them?" Westrum asked.

Philip, like a sensible athlete, was wary of prediction. "We beat them by a lot last year," he said.

"He's great," said Harvey.

"You don't drink," said Benstock, who stood with them now.

"He's drinking," Harvey said.

"I have no prejudice against drinking," Westrum said.

"Aren't you drinking?" Harvey asked.

"It makes me ill," said Westrum.

"Then anyhow you tried it once," said Benstock.

"Once," said Westrum.

"You didn't give it a fair test," Benstock said.

"What position does Philip play?" asked Westrum.

"In what sport? He plays everything. In football he's a line-backer. His mother hates it. I hate it, too. Philip loves it. It's what he's good at. All his friends are on the honor roll, he's on the football team."

"I was never on either," said Harvey.

"He's the only Jew on the team," said Benstock, who had vowed to himself beforehand not to say so to Westrum, nor to ask Westrum if Beatrice were Jewish, nor to probe, nor to guess. But he was exhausted, and when he was exhausted his vows broke down. "But you do eat," he said to Westrum, "my wife is sending us messages," and they drifted to the dining room, ten souls in a small place, Westrum beside Sally Benstock on his right, and upon his left the nameless wife of a nameless man in "gust alleviation" (unless it was "dust alleviation"), and he fixed in his mind the plan of their sitting, and he retained in his mind as well as he could the order of the topics they discussed, beginning first with the question of luxury and whether to despise it in a world so hungry, and asking whether in their hearts' depths all white people did not in fact wish the death of all colored people, and whether the Governor of the State was or was not cripplingly neurotic, as he seemed to be— if so, what *could* be done?

Harvey Weinberg as often as possible ate with his fingers, whose trembling hands caused his silverware to clatter upon his plate. It was a triumph for him to raise his cup to his lips, but having done so he always drank even the hottest scalding liquid, in order not to waste his triumph. With Harriet and their son, Reuben, he had recently been to Africa—"birding," he said—and he was eager to tell of his journey, but although he several times began, "Recently, in Africa . . ." he was always interrupted by someone with something more important to say. He appeared not to mind. He listened attentively to everyone else. "You *can't* see our house," someone was saying,

47

"it's covered with plastic toys," and Westrum held it in his mind for his Journal, with the urine of pregnant horses, gust alleviation, and the supposition that Benstock was heavily tranquilized, that between the drug and the liquor he might yet arrive by the end of the evening almost at the verge of a smile.

"Austrian," said Sally Benstock, "I am Austrian. I was Austrian." But she never turned her eyes toward him. Her mind, he supposed, was mainly on the roast, which the company praised, but whose success, she modestly said, was due to the supremacy of her new stove. Someone asked the price, and she told it. Prices were high these days, someone said, the Governor was neurotic, traffic was thickening, the races were warring, violence was alarming, the poor grew poorer, and everyone Westrum knew grew guiltier among luxuries. The size of his own fortune dismayed him, and he sometimes dreamed of scattering it to good use. But upon the whole body of the world it would spread thin indeed, and he said softly and privately to Gretchen Benstock at his elbow, "I *heard* that you were pretty, and now I believe it," which pleased her, and she served him sherbet, and cookies glistening with crystals, and her smile was as white as her brother's. The lady upon his left said *assept* for *accept*. He placed her therefore somewhere southeast, basing his guess upon a memory of his grandmother's speech, with whom he had traveled once, forty years ago, on the train from Brest to Northern Florida, where she had been born and to which she frequently returned for final farewells. Would the little girl remember forty years hence that Westrum had told her, in exchange for sherbet and cookies, that she was pretty? A good compliment earnestly said might last a lifetime. Would she come upon herself someday in Westrum's Journal? The library at the Center, someone was saying, was not keeping up as it should, real estate had doubled in ten years, and Harvey was speaking of Africa, having recently been there: wouldn't somebody please kindly notice, he seemed to be saying, his having recently been there?

To a historian of experience not much was news. Governors

were neurotic, every age was dangerous, and Westrum was adrift in disengagement when he heard Harriet say with good cheer, "Oh yes, I'm in trouble now."

"How is she in trouble?" he asked Sally Benstock.

"I did not hear," said Sally, for to explain it she would have been forced in courtesy to turn her head to Westrum.

The question was, Could the principal legally picket her own school? "Ken Silvers says I can," said Harriet. She wore a long Indian braid which persistently presented itself to Westrum as his own braided beard, for it would surely be the form his play would take, her braid was the logical thing, he'd tie himself to her by the braid of her head, he'd strangle her if she wished by her own braid, he'd lead her about, it would serve as gag or blindfold or any old thing for him or her, it was all in fun, it was all in play. *I'd stay here,* he thought, *for her,* but he found difficulty associating Harriet and Harvey in his mind. It was a marriage of grace and awkwardness, of the well and the afflicted, of beauty and grossness, of skill and bumbling, of repose and trembling.

"Not the school," Benstock corrected. "The football games."

"On what grounds?" Westrum asked. It was the first time he had addressed the company as a whole. In deference to a new voice the table immediately grew quiet.

"On the stadium grounds," said Benstock, vexed and irritated by the dispute. "On the grounds that the school puts too much emphasis on football. It's an old issue and it makes me sleepy."

"The world demands its games," said Westrum.

"Right," said Benstock eagerly.

"But we needn't like the idea," said Westrum.

"Listen," said Benstock, "a few Saturday afternoons a year I go to the stupid game. It doesn't destroy my mind. I like to watch the girls jump up and down."

"Philip is on the team," said Sally. "That's why we go."

"Eleven boys are on the team," said Harriet, "eleven hundred are watching."

49

"You were an athlete," said Sally Benstock, addressing Westrum roundabout. "Philip is distinguished in the football game. You must know how it is to be a boy."

"The trouble with football," said Westrum sharply and decisively, "is that it's fascist."

His remark astonished Beatrice. She lowered her eyes as if she had lied. They went frequently to football games with the Tikvahs.

But Westrum himself was less astonished, for he had said as much to Harriet Weinberg this afternoon, and a venture grew easier with repetition. He'd picket with Harriet if he thought much more about it, though he hated picketing. Yes, he'd picket, he'd touch the back of her neck with the tips of his fingers on the picket line, he'd stand shoulder to shoulder and hip to hip with Harriet.

"Off the football field," said Benstock, "Philip can't spell *cat* on the first try."

"How can it be fascist?" said Sally. "The word is very big."

"Kill a little now," said Westrum. "Kill more later. Get in practice now for killing."

"But they don't *kill*," said Sally.

"Go down some afternoon," said Westrum, "and watch them practice. Listen to the coaches. Kill him, kill him, kill him, get him, kill him, that's what they say. Believe me, I remember very well how it is to be a boy."

"The coach would not say that," said Sally. But she suspected that he would. "We have so many controversies," she said.

"Yes he would," Benstock confessed.

"But he would not mean it," Sally said.

"He doesn't know what he means," said Benstock.

"He swears at the boys," said Harriet.

"He's a nice big, blond, dull, stupid, insensitive . . ."

"Yes," said Westrum to Benstock, "I met him this afternoon," who himself was big, blond.

"Philip adores him," Sally said.

"Coaches are boys at heart," said Westrum, "and boys love to play at killing. If that weren't so, the military service wouldn't be as attractive as it is, and we wouldn't be able to have wars."

"You were not in the military," Sally said.

"Something in my imagination," said Westrum, "told me to refuse."

"You *refused?*" she asked.

"Bravo," cried Harvey Weinberg.

But if he had not been in the military, Sally knew, he had not fought fascism. From what point of view had he not been in the military? She must know. She must find out. Philip was eager for the military. Coach Wilson was acquainted with one of the coaches at one of the service academies, and he would help. Already Philip was practicing throwing his cap in the air. He mystified her. American boyhood mystified her (she had never had her own childhood), but she possessed a most favorable feeling toward the American military, for it had been an American soldier who had carried her off from captivity to a new life. He drove a quartermaster truck, and he lifted her up to the seat beside him and carried her away, and he kissed her upon the cheek and said to her in poor Yiddish, "Big girls don't cry."

Sally Benstock had been born, she believed, at Eisenstadt, or nearby. Her father was licensed to sell tobacco in Eisenstadt, as her father's father had been licensed before him. The line of the family was ancient.

Even so, the worst happened. It appeared to her at first, when the soldiers wickedly sheared her grandfather's beard, that the beard itself was the cause of all trouble. So her father said, too. "Yes, yes," he said, "it is only because of grandfather's beard." Yet the mystery was deeper than the beard, and they were warned by neighbors to flee, to whom her father replied that their license and their line were ancient, the little girl adding, "It is only because of his beard," as she believed.

Of course she remembered best one neighbor in particular,

first in Eisenstadt, and afterward in the countryside, who disputed with her father ceaselessly, insisting that things would be worse before they were better, the danger was great. It was he who drove them into the countryside in a van filled with everything they owned. She remembered kitchen chairs in the van. He took them to a house with a roof of green tiles, and she felt that the tiles protected her from an atmosphere ominous in ways she could not name. Her father said yes, it was true, the green tiles protected them. The neighbor who had driven the van was a tall, blond man, and he lived in the countryside, too. She must have known his name—she must have called him *something* at the time—but she lost his name afterward. For a time she lost her own as well.

Once at bedtime, between sleeping and waking, she was carried from her house to a stone church. The night was filled with confusion, someone rapping terribly upon the door, not with a human hand but too loud and hard for a human hand, knocking with a hard object, no doubt, although she never knew the object, for she fell asleep. It was the last night's easy sleep she ever knew: afterward, she fought sleep every night of her life, unable to endure the moment between waking and sleeping. She awoke upon the following day among children in the stone church, and received from them the impression that she, and each of them, would soon be carried home again, for ransom, as in a story.

Nor was this true, either, but a false hope like the roof of green tile. Not deliverance was here but death. Here German doctors performed experiments upon children, and here she waited her turn with other children, vaguely fearful. One day a number was burned into her arm. She held forth her arm, as she was instructed. When the doctor asked her her name she could not remember it. Yet soon she remembered it again, but withheld it from everyone nevertheless, as the single thing still hers after all else had been taken.

One day, as she stood among children, playing near the

52

chancel, after long discomfort, unwell, sleepless, humiliated, after the ransom failed, her name forgotten and then secretly remembered, she was seized where she stood by the tall, blond man, her neighbor once, who ordered her in the fiercest and most urgent voice to follow him. She refused. It was he with whom her father ceaselessly argued, he who had driven them to the false safety of the house with the roof of green tile, and he who now gripped her shoulder savagely, forcing her to run before the pain, out of the stone church, through the grave-yard, through the fields, and to the roadway. From there he carried her to his own house not far from the house with the green roof, where she had once lived and to which she expected to return.

He kept her prisoner, refusing to permit her to return to her house. When she pleaded to be allowed to go home he was stern, and he said, "You don't dare, or you will die."

Sometimes, at night, upon her promise to hold his hand and to be as silent as the stars, they walked together down the road and back; now and then, if the night was black, he permitted her to accompany him to the well, where they drew water. When he called her by name she denied that the name was hers. She resented him, associating him with dispute, pain, and the stone church, as if he were her oppressor, when in fact he was her savior, and she saw him for the last time when he took her by day, actually, the night having ended at last, to Eisen-stadt, and handed her up to an American soldier in a quarter-master truck.

"But was it possible to simply refuse?" Sally Benstock asked the company at large.

"Recently, in Africa," said Harvey Weinberg, waiting to be interrupted.

"What about Africa?" Westrum asked. He'd give Harvey his moment at last. "When were you there?"

"Recently," said Harvey, wiping his spoon with the napkin tucked like a bib beneath his collar and telling Westrum how

Africa was, the cities and countries he'd been to and the birds he'd seen on the deserts they'd crossed, and the cost of things. "You'll come and see the movies we took," he said.

"Must we?" said Benstock.

"I'd be delighted," Westrum said. "I'm a fan of home movies."

"I'd be honored," Harvey said, but he doubted, he said, that Westrum could spare the time for *him*, a famous historian was too busy, his time was too valuable (they'd be more comfortable in the living room, Sally said), taking Westrum's arm, Harvey's napkin still beneath his chin, his belt still flapping, and the zipper of his trousers crawling downward beneath the weight of his dinner. "You mean to steal the napkin do you?" Westrum asked, but Harvey Weinberg hardly heard. He seldom any longer felt awkward. Embarrassed by his own existence, yes, but that was the way of his life, and sugar crystals sparkled in the creases of the flesh about his lips. "Air rates to Africa are favorable for groups," he said—there are several time zones in Africa, he said, he'd met the chiefs of several kingdoms, they'd palavered with him in palaver huts. He was grateful for the opportunity to have gone, and grateful for Westrum's listening, for Westrum was a busy and distinguished man, his time was much taken up, no doubt.

"Not really," Westrum said, "I'm really rather idle."

"The busiest people have the most time," said Harvey. "The most productive man I know has seven hobbies," and he named the man and the hobbies, and the sweat coursed down his face, and his weeping eye drained, and Westrum now thought he could almost see in Harvey Weinberg's face that face out of the past evoked this morning when they first met, but who it was he could not yet say—easy does it, he thought, let the mind grind it—*somebody from Brest*, he thought. It would rise to his mind; somebody whose forehead glistened with sweat as Harvey's did, not in beads but in a single sheet, lowering itself like a glacial mass, whereupon Westrum, taking the napkin from Harvey's hand, mopped Harvey's forehead, who barely noticed this kindness, but said, "Lord, I do sweat," continuing his tour of Africa.

"He reminds me of somebody," Westrum said, driving at midnight over the hills as they had come.

"Everybody reminds you of somebody," Beatrice said. Now he'd go tracking his memory for a name to put to a face, and he'd forget when he found it why he had wanted it. "You were well-behaved," she said.

"What does Benstock think of me?" he asked.

"He didn't say," she said.

"His wife never looked at me once," he said.

"He's honored to think you want a Seat," she said, but Benstock hadn't said that at all. He'd said nothing. "He's too smart to judge fast," she said. What did her husband expect of Benstock all upon a single day? She herself had begun in mistrust, for Westrum, when she first knew him, was everything she had never known before. He might have been a captain of marines, or an airlines pilot, sitting among them in the old days, all Jews but him, adoring them all beyond anything they merited, sitting silent among them as he'd mainly sat tonight except that in the old days he'd been captivated by their irreverence—how they dismissed God and the State. In recent years, however, his silence was only cordial at best. He'd gone beyond irreverence, caught up to the Jews and passed them by; not that the world was well, or that he approved of it, only that he refused to jerk with old reflexes. Thus it must appear to Benstock that Westrum was content, as complacent in mind as he was in appearance, old settler, champion of old standard virtues, dry county in a wet country, long and blond and free of horror because he had never known horror. He must have appeared to the eye of Benstock this morning as he had appeared to her own upon their first meeting.

For a moment they were uncertain of the house. Harsh lights blazed up from fixtures planted in the lawn, focused upon the flag upon the staff. The flag hung limp, drenched by

55

the evening rain, and they walked through the light beneath the flag, and Terence from the window shot them with his Super 8.

He claimed he had not been swimming. "Would I swim in the rain?" he asked, who, after swimming, had dried his body with the flag to test the omniscience of God or the F.B.I. or the C.I.A. or his grandfather or whoever it was who was in charge of apprehending dangerous skeptics, and dragged the flag across the floor, and stomped upon it, and tied it to himself like a jockstrap, and raised it on the staff upon the lawn like many another man or boy, to hide from his neighbors the doubts within his heart, and drank a quart of milk before the television, and wrote two letters to his brothers seeking data for his essay upon their father, and attempted, in the same cause, but without success, to decipher his father's shorthand on the tablets scattered everywhere. "I really like this joint," he said. "I hope they give you a Seat." The place was new, the rules were down.

"Isn't there some sort of law against flying the flag at night?" his father asked.

"Consider 'The Star-Spangled Banner,'" Terence said. "It flew through the night."

"There was a battle on," his father said.

"I'll take it down," Terence said.

"Don't take it down for *me*," his father said.

"There was a sweet boy there tonight," said Beatrice.

"The Weinbergs are big on home movies," Westrum said. "He has a Bolex."

"No kidding," Terence said.

"But he can't work it," Westrum said.

"You can shoot pictures," said Beatrice, "of your father picketing the football team."

"I shoot anything that moves," said Terence.

Madame, thought Westrum. He'd continue his letter to her, assembling his tablets, which appeared to be elsewhere than

56

he had left them—in a new house things jumped about on their own; Beatrice calling down, she'd lost the bedroom again —and carrying the tablets to a leather chair beside the picture window facing east. He'd know the time by the light of the sky, he'd write until dawn, but not to her, no, he'd write Journal, loosening his shoes, beginning his day again, living his life twice to understand it once, swiftly scribbling upon his tablets all the loose, stray fragments of speech and sight brought home like souvenirs, as some people carry home from dinner parties napkin rings or place cards or recipes, *Gretchen was nine, her mother's tattoo, her father tranquilized, Little Gibraltar, pregnant horses, is football fascist?, sweat in a glacier, home to the flag,* from which point he might begin to work backward and forward upon this day which was the eighteen-thousand-three-hundred-and-fifty-sixth day of his life in a private shorthand all his own, to be raised then by Miss Sanantone to black and white in the communal English of the world, made multiple by her and separately reposited, upon pages now numbered in five figures and one day six, God willing: it was a long-lived family.

Terence, passing, said he'd found the bedroom for his mother, and taken in the flag. "Anything else?" he asked.

"Yes, tell me what kind of bird it is that sings at this hour," said Westrum, for outside his window a bird sang in a tree.

"The bird's problem," said Terence after a short study of the problem, "is that he doesn't know the hour. He thinks it's day on account of your lamp."

Indeed, when Westrum in the spirit of experiment turned off the lamp the bird ceased its singing, and when Westrum turned on the lamp again the bird resumed, and he said to Terence, "Very smart of you," and Beatrice called, "Terence, get to bed, leave your father alone," and Terence called back to her, "Keep your powder dry," and his father said, "Don't talk like that to your mother." But Westrum's support was routine only. His eyes had turned off. He had entered his Journal. But

57

suddenly, instead, he resumed his letter to his mistress, translating his shorthand to longhand with minor revisions, and continuing:

Madame, this afternoon I discovered in the little groin pocket of my bathing trunks a piece of paper I put there two weeks ago at the University pool. It showed a number where you were, some shop, some beauty parlor, but when I called you there you'd flown. Think of the fortune in dimes I've dropped for you. Suppose I'd dropped it instead into the palms of beggars around the world.

We had a good trip, and now that I am here the temptation to remain is almost irresistible. The Center has offered me a "Seat" for seven years. It has also offered to purchase my Journal for a sum in six figures, each and every figure to the left of the decimal. Why are we always valued in proportion to our distance from home? I invent an expression: "The prophet is without honor in his own land."

It's Tikvah who made me come here. He could have kept me there if he wanted to. I feel quite exiled, and put upon, too, as if he planned it this way. It will finally be up to you to put the pressure on him to recall me. Enlist an ally whose name I won't mention, have him bring to bear upon Tikvah every possible weight and pressure. Cause to be implanted in Tikvah's most honest mind the idea that his resistance to me must certainly be some buried prejudice of his own. We may depend upon his scrupulous conscience to consider the question seriously. He'll be forced by introspection to ask himself, "My God, how's this? Everybody is bidding for my old friend Westrum, and here I am resisting his modest desire. I must examine my hidden prejudices." He will puzzle it over, and end by blaming himself, as the purest people do. He'll say, "Indeed, I guess the truth is that I really am *jealous* of Westrum, I envy Westrum his moral purity, I'm a goy-hater after all, Dr. Freud would make much of it all: how'd you like your sister to marry one?" His did. Four exclamation points. It just occurred to me.

Be ingenious. Be devious. It's down your line, it's up your alley, nobody lies better than you.

Thinking, Madame, of Tikvah's bald bean, I wonder if I've ever told you of the wittiest remark I ever heard. I intend to think of it on my deathbed, and float away to God with a smile. It was just after the war. It was in the war that his hair was blown off. We were sitting in a meeting room at the University, young instructors, maybe our first or second year on the job (I could look it up), waiting for things to begin. Into the room walked another young instructor, a fellow with an Italian name I can't recall—Lastrucci, Lavoli, Maroni, Bastandi—an art historian who has become famous for a book on the Florentines. I was sitting beside Tikvah. Italian Name walked down the aisle searching for a seat. He saw one behind Tikvah. He went to it. As he sat down he passed his hand across Tikvah's head and said, "Do you know, your head feels like my wife's ass," whereupon Tikvah, passing his own hand thoughtfully over his own bald head, replied, "Say, it does, doesn't it?"

Today I met the principal of Terence's school. I have befriended her, and I think she may be generous with me as well. The way to a woman's heart may be through her politics. Or the way to a woman's heart may be through her husband. Once, when I was a schoolboy, I did a very wicked thing. Therefore my father caused the principal to be fired. Clearly my father then had an underdeveloped sense of justice, nor has it developed with the years. One day soon I must pay him a visit, though I don't look forward to it, His Honor the Mayor of Mayhem, Injustice of the Peace, Chief of the Volunteer Arson

Department. He'll scold me once more for my Jewish wife and for not having donated my mortal body to the war effort, although he himself hadn't been much for the war, either: he thought F. D. Roosevelt was fighting the war to save the Jews, and my father saw no purpose in *that*. And he'd scold me too for my Jewish mistress if he knew. I won't mention her.

Brest lies down the road not far, but it's the mental preparation that takes the time to get there. When I go there my soul sinks to think of the man I might have become.

Very well, write me, phone me at the Center, tell me how things go, give me news of my friends, tell me which gentlemen try to make love to you, and which don't. I dream of you, you are an elevator operator carrying us to our sunken pool on floor twenty. Outside my window a bird sings. Au revoir, Madame.

When he extinguished his lamp the bird ceased its singing. To think, to rest his eyes, to begin upon his Journal now, Westrum sat back, his head against cool leather, and at that moment he saw clearly the face of the principal at Brest whom his father had driven from the school and from the town, and he saw the face of a schoolmate, too. It was a boy. And he saw the circumstances, too, himself, his father, the principal, the boy, clear faces in a distant clouded circumstance, and he knew in this instant who Harvey Weinberg was.

3

But it was five days before the name of the boy drifted to the surface of his mind, cruising Old Road past Brest to the airport, having run this morning two miles in fourteen minutes and thirty seconds upon the eighteen-thousand-three-hundred-and-sixty-first morning of his life—it was Wednesday —having given up swimming and eased into his running, autumn was here, he'd run, he'd cycle, he'd run it in fourteen-flat tomorrow and settle at thirteen-thirty Friday, singing as he drove, *Choose now one fair maid from all the rest, And we'll hail her as our queen of May.* It must have been a song of spring, thus *May* (not for nothing was he acclaimed historian), and he remembered that they sang it with the windows of the schoolroom open, hearing it now forty years after the day, cruising past Brest, and the voices of little girls inexpressibly sweet, and the wondrous sight of their teacher whose bosom enraptured his eye, she'd be seventy now and her bosom down, or dead, and the little girls gone, for Brest had declined among the cornfields. He could have driven the Interstate to the airport, but he knew Old Road better, and he remembered once, in the company of children, they'd gone to the airport when the airport was new, to see the rare sight of an airplane landing, whereupon the name drifted upward to his mind and exposed itself, *Turtleman,* yes, yes, there it was, there he was, Turtleman, with a round pink face sparkling with sweat who never quite buttoned all his buttons. He was always late. He always arrived after the door was closed, and when he opened it everyone laughed, and he stood in the doorway red-faced from running, and stumbled upon the threshold. His family owned the smoke shop, and among themselves they talked

61

Yiddish, and formed a congregation of the Jews of Brest, who numbered, once, ten families or more, and one by one removed to New Hamburg for some reason or other, *driven out, no doubt, by my father*, thought Westrum, or who, if he hadn't driven them out, certainly hadn't urged them to stay.

Imagine thinking of Turtleman, whose name or face had scarcely crossed his mind five times in thirty-five years, but whose face had hung before him now for five straight days like a painted moon. He saw him once in uniform, off to war. They talked at the railroad depot, and their talk had been unpleasant. The mood had been mistrust, cruelty. The details were now hidden from Westrum. Someone had been hurt, someone forgiven, someone aided, someone betrayed, not bones broken but only principles, which had mystified Westrum at the time: if no one was hurt, did it matter? A boy saw no connection between objects unalike, as between bones and principles, or between the sweet voices of little girls and the full bosom of their teacher singing, sweeping into the airport now, following signs telling which way Departures, which way Arrivals, and he supposed it was Arrivals he was after. He parked his car.

For ten cents, on the pavilion, he could watch the airplanes arrive and depart. Cheap at the price, he thought, dropping his dime into the slot, turning the turnstile, and sitting on the sky-watching bench. Before watching the sky, however, he thought to commit a few words to his tablet, *up, ran two miles in fourteen-thirty, drove Old Road to airport, thought of school-room singing, thought of name Turtleman*, and upon a fresh page he wrote *My dear Tikvah*, and read again the letter from Tikvah.

> Dear Brother Wes,
> My bleeding bean has stopped bleeding. It wasn't much. The "lovers of freedom and amnesty" have ceased for the moment, but we expect more bricks to fly before it's over. The wound to my scalp made me go on thinking of my head as a whole. Another bald fellow told me he has defeated the common cold with something called a head

warmer he wears at night, and I might buy one myself. The man at the head warmer store wants to sell me a wig, too, but I've been so long bald I don't plan to grow hair from a store.

As for having you back *on your terms,* love I can give you, but all the money you want I don't have. I'm bald of money. Such special funds as we do have we've turned over to various projects involving Negroes (say *blacks,* I am instructed), whom the University has discovered at last, guilty over neglect, and therefore gone overboard. You and I discovered Negroes years and years ago or more. So be it. That much is good. Let the world catch up with us at last.

You may be interested to know that I have just had a telephone call from Justice Lerman. He is taking up your "case," as he calls it, putting pressure on me with his own influential bricks. If I do not meet your terms I will be embarrassed (he will embarrass me) not only in the eyes of the world but worse—at the meeting of the Trustees. He is preparing a "long brief." Posterity will laugh at me, history will sneer at me, and the Trustees will rebuke me. I find his aggressiveness mysterious, since he understands well enough that one of the real sources of our trouble has been absentee professors. When students come here from far places seeking you it is painful to tell them that you have been gone for some years and appear to wish to be gone for some years more. They properly ask, why then do we keep your name in the catalogue. Why indeed? Sadly I must tell you, as I have just told Justice Lerman, that if you do not indicate soon your intention to return we must announce your place vacated.

I'll write you more soon. Please do kiss Beatrice and Terence for me, and accept my love to you, as ever.

Westrum replied to his brother-in-law Tikvah.

My dear Tikvah,

Here I am at the airport watching airplanes come and go. Your letter is here. Speaking of hair or its absence, do you remember the name of the fellow—an Italian name; he became an authority on the Florentines—the one who rubbed your head that time and said it was like his wife's ass? To that you made a most splendid reply, a choice moment in the history of the wit of the world, but I cannot recall his name.

Certainly I am flattered to hear that Judge Lerman or anyone else has taken up my case with long briefs or brief briefs. Nobody who fights on my behalf can be all bad. I had no idea he was so far persuaded of my value as to trouble himself for me, but apparently he goes sleepless thinking up ways for me to be of use to mankind. He made the President make me chairman of the Population Inquiry, and after the Inquiry was done he got me the good situation in Washington.

I'd not be intimidated, if I were you, by the prospect of future generations sneering at you. On the other hand, I do often wonder why it is you resist me. Why don't you want me there, when strangers so much want me elsewhere? Arrangements are under way here for my Journal's being preserved for history under conditions agreeable both to students in the future and myself in the present, in deep fireproof cellars immune from civil disturbance and international warfare, which I hope will not occur: who will read my Journal if everyone's dead?

I've persuaded the appropriate people here to beg you to come, too, and take a Seat, and finish the *Potentialities*. But the airplane comes. I send you and Winnie all my love. Beatrice is perfectly well. We have a very good house. Terence sleeps in a different room every night.

For one more dime he searched the sky through binoculars fixed to an iron stanchion for the airplane he had announced to

Tikvah. *Not so much a lie,* he thought, *as a premature truth,* and there it was anyhow, a speck in the sky with his Journal in the hold telling the names of the schoolroom songs and the little girls who sang them, the true history of faint forgotten moments sometimes retrieved, he suspected, only to test the Index to the Text. He'd learn the name of the chap who passed his hand across Tikvah's head, and he'd extract Turtleman, too, and down from the sky they came, and down she came, too.

She was the first to debark. She had sat at the back of the airplane where, she supposed, the danger was least, and she tested the steps now beneath her feet, as if they, too, because of their association with the airplane, were likewise unworthy of her confidence, carrying her portable typewriter and her black, patent-leather handbag shining to match her patent-leather black pumps gapping and stretching for the relief of her swollen ankles. She wore the only coat he had ever seen her wear, green plaid for every season, and her face was as white as new paper, but here and there stabbed with red as if stung by bees. With her teeth she gripped a long, unlighted cigarette. By the time Westrum reached her at the level below the pavilion she had smoked the cigarette half through, puffing deeply and continuously with pleasure and gratitude, compensating for time lost from smoking, stunned, stupefied, nauseous, searching about for savage rapacious Indians, unable to believe that she was here when she had, after all, almost always been *there,* and taking his arm for a moment's support. "Never again," she said.

"You were sick," he said.

"Was I *sick,*" she said.

Had she ever touched him before? He could not remember that she had ever taken his arm. Did it occur to her that they had never touched before? He had no idea of her mind. "The medicine didn't help?" he asked.

"It will pass," she said. Her swollen ankles distorted her legs. Her legs, at better moments, pleased Westrum's sight. She released his arm and walked ahead of him through the terminal on swollen ankles, abandoning him, to show him that she was angry with him, but at the baggage claim he joined her again, and she said to him in sudden irritation, in a voice she had never used for him before, "Why did you bring me here? What are you thinking about?" But when she saw by the amazement of his face the wild error of her accusation she relented, explaining, "I'm sick, but I'll be better." Indeed, her face had begun to regain its color, and the points of her rash had begun to fade.

Her suitcase, which Westrum hoisted from the moving belt, was smart but borrowed, marked with initials not her own. She had brought also a straw trunk, an old family possession, hasps and hinges hanging loose, but her own name recently affixed in half-a-dozen places with Dymo tape, which amused Westrum, who could not imagine its being falsely claimed by either error or design.

As for the two footlockers which were his, obviously she had placed the highest value on their safety, for they were not only locked, but tied with stout rope, and the rope in turn drawn tight by spurs devised of wire twisted and knotted by someone with the keenest eye to security, and the strongest hands, and Westrum asked in the way of compliment, in that simple, direct, humorless language he had found most useful with Miss Sanantone, "Who tied it up that way? Did Hermie tie it up for you?"

"It was sure to get here the way he did it," she said.

"The way Hermie did it?" he asked.

"I paid him five dollars," she said.

"You should have paid him more than that," said Westrum. "Did you get my letter?"

"Only if he carried them down," she said. "He didn't carry them down."

"Did somebody else carry them down?" asked Westrum.

"Yes," she said.

"Then somebody else tied them, too," said Westrum.

"Yes," she said, someone else had locked the locks and tied

the rope and drawn the rope tight with wire, and said to her when that was done, "I wish the son of a bitch himself was in them," for he was persuaded—her friend Hawkes was persuaded—or anyhow pretended to believe that Dr. Westrum was carrying Miss Sanantone west for immoral purposes, even as he believed, or pretended to believe when he found it convenient to do so, that Miss Sanantone went every day to Dr. Westrum's house for the same immoral purposes, or anyhow partly so, that Dr. Westrum paid her money for the service of her body and for her skill at typing up something said to be a Journal of his life, as if any man really wrote down his life all day, or even if he did he took a little time for pleasure, too. Nor had Miss Sanantone, in fact, ever denied that maybe now and then when Dr. Westrum's life was all caught up she put off typing for the moment and took up fucking. Did Hawkes own her? Like hell he did. Would Hawkes marry her? Like hell he would. "I have the keys," she said.

But Hawkes did own her, and Miss Sanantone owned Hawkes, too. They drifted apart and they always returned, one to the other, he whom she called her friend.

"Then who tied them?" Westrum asked.

"My friend," she said, hailing a Negro skycap who viewed the load and said he would return. "He won't," she said. "They never do. They don't want to work," although the skycap shortly did return with a handcart and wheeled the footlockers, trunk, suitcase, and typewriter to Westrum's wagon. Westrum and the skycap loaded the wagon.

Beside him in the car she smoked. "I'd have been worse off without the medicine," she said. "I guess it helped." But had she given Hermie five dollars? She knew she couldn't be sure. She'd given five dollars to Hawkes for Hermie, which might have been a gift, therefore, to Hawkes himself. Hawkes wasn't particular. Besides, Hawkes deserved it, he'd tied and wired them and carried them on his shoulders from the Westrums' apartment to the airport, insisting upon every assurance from the airport people that the footlockers would travel on the same plane with her and arrive as safely as she, "and no monkey business and no excuses," said Hawkes to the airport people. He told them. Nobody stepped on Hawkes. He knew how to get things done, and he never really failed her when she needed him. He was her friend, and he was more. She believed that he did love her, too, friend and lover both. Why else did they always return to one another after parting—why she to him if not for love? Men were easy got, but only Hawkes was Hawkes, and Miss Sanantone believed that she loved Hawkes and Hawkes loved her, and there it was.

Nevertheless, he insisted that she go. Of course he'd miss her, he'd be out of his mind with loneliness. Nevertheless, go, he said, and he'd bring her back as quick as he could.

"Get me back," she said.

"I'll get you back good and quick," he said at the airport, kissing her again and again. "Find me out who his mistress is."

"He never writes her name," she said.

"He writes her letters," said Hawkes.

"But not her name," she said. "He writes her box number."

"He writes her envelopes," said Hawkes.

"But I don't see them," she said.

"See them then," he ordered. "Send her box number to my box number."

Still, he might have given the five dollars to Hermie the doorman, for he had just come off a case and he was flush, and Hawkes flush was the most generous man in the world. He'd not have kept five dollars he didn't need, though when she asked him, "Did you give the five dollars to Hermie?" he didn't say yes and he didn't say no, but kissed her again and again as he often kissed her when he was flush and couldn't wait to be rid of her.

"Tell me everything you spent," said Westrum. "Charge me for the medicine, too. Are you feeling better now? Are you hungry?" Ahead lay the Clover Leaf Motel, which had a decent restaurant.

"I can't eat yet," she said. "It's all so flat." She had never been among cornfields. She had never been west of Riverside Drive. She had been with the Westrums in Washington, but she had never been south of Washington and never been north of the Bronx. At the junction with Old Road, Westrum pointed out to her the way to Brest. "Brest?" she asked.

"It's my old home town," he said. Had she never heard of Brest? Did it mean nothing to her? Impossible. He had named Brest a thousand or ten thousand times in his Journal, she typed out the name of Brest a thousand or ten thousand times in the text and at least half again as often in the Index to the Text, so she must have retained its name somewhere in her mind, if not out of her own interest at least beneath the weight of its frequency.

"When will we go back?" she asked. She could not believe she had consented to come. Yet here she was: she must have consented. "Nobody forced you to go," said Hawkes, and he was right, she'd come of her own will, but when she said to Hawkes, "Stop me, make me stay here," he'd made no effort in that direction, saying bitterly, grimly, like one who was powerless against injustice, "Don't think I don't know why he's bringing you there. I know what he's thinking about," dumping the blame upon her. Briefly, in the airplane, she thought he might be right, perhaps she was a party to something both Hawkes and Dr. Westrum understood, but when she landed she saw in Dr. Westrum's face that it wasn't so, it couldn't be so. She had never imagined herself his mistress, she wasn't eligible, he'd had a number of ladies over the years but never a stenographer among them. Well, Hawkes had done that before, too, misunderstanding, dumping the blame on her, confusing in her mind the order of events, accepting choice while disclaiming all responsibility for the choice she finally made. "How many women does a man need?" said Hawkes. "You're driving me out of my mind," he said. Sometimes he accused her of driving him into the arms of other women. Sometimes she drove him back to his wife. But he returned to Miss Sanantone.

"Maybe soon," said Westrum. "Maybe in a few months,

69

maybe in a year. We'll see how things turn out. You'll like it here. You'll see."

"You never know how things will turn out," she said.

"Do light me a cigarette," he said. "Don't tell anybody here I'm smoking."

"Don't you worry," she said. "Is my apartment air-conditioned?"

"Everything is air-conditioned," Westrum said. "The whole place is really fantastic."

"How far from the movies?" she asked.

"I haven't noticed," he said. "They must have movies somewhere. They have dancing, bridge, television, swimming, concerts, bars, restaurants, a theater. A lot of people never leave the building at all."

"That's something," she said. "And everything is paid for."

"Everything is paid for and everything is air-conditioned," he said. "You'll be untouched by fresh air. It's like some sort of great hotel, a luxury ship."

"I'll be saving money," she said.

"For any particular purpose?" he asked.

"For when we go back," she said, and down they went to the end of her journey, into the winding tunnel beneath the Center where for a moment she fell ill again, her nausea returned, and she became pale. But at the loading platform, where Westrum stopped his wagon, and where her bag and trunk and typewriter were taken by a young country fellow with red hair— who, lifting her straw trunk to his shoulder, smiled at her—she imagined the possibility of recovery. She'd not be here long. She'd find a way back. They'd go back. She'd figure out how, and Hawkes would help too.

He'd need a wire-cutter, surely, to unstrangle his Journal, which Miss Sanantone's gentleman friend had so beautifully and effectively made safe for its journey, for Westrum never doubted it was he, her gentleman friend. For some reason of her own she was reluctant to name him. His name was in the

Journal somewhere, once or twice, here or there, the brief name of an animal or bird of the class rather of arrogant beasts than meek—ferret, eagle, wolverine, though none of those either.

He removed one footlocker from his wagon and locked the wagon and carried the footlocker on his shoulder to his suite, and locked his suite and returned for the second footlocker. In his suite now he telephoned Benstock's office to ask if someone might be sent to him with a wire-cutter. Benstock's girl Rosalie asked, "With what?" With a wire-cutter, Westrum said. Rosalie asked, "For what?" To cut wire with, Westrum patiently said, who could not remember Rosalie's name, either, it was a pretty name, it tinkled like a bell. He thought it proper to mention to history the names of everyone however obscure, Benstock's girl, or Miss Sanantone's gentleman friend whose humble role it had been to lock and tie and wire the Journal for its safety during its passage upon a certain day from New York to the Center, just so that history might have all those haunting details Westrum himself was pleased to have: he loved, from history, the names of stablemen who saddled heroes' horses, maids, scribes, children who died in infancy. Now his own history waited upon a wire-cutter. He waited thirty minutes.

When he began to suspect that Benstock's girl would never put his message through he left his suite, locking the door by latch and by key. The value of the suite had suddenly soared. So he hoped. So he imagined. In any case, if he didn't believe in himself nobody else could be expected to. If the work were not the work he thought it was it was nothing at all, he'd been spending these years upon nothing, with plans to spend all future years in the same way, setting off down the corridor through the vast Wing still unfamiliar to him, past the offices and suites of other men and women persuaded, too, of the worth of their own work, the topologist, the mathematical biologist, past the sound of a typewriter, past the sound of chalk upon a blackboard, past silent rooms either empty or filled with silent thinking, past names upon the doors, algebraist, oceanographer, geneticist, enzymologist, Egyptologist, Copticologist, some of which contained neither thought nor emptiness but the bodies of men only resting, sleeping, gazing out of stainproof windows, several of whom, over the years, so Benstock told him, had discovered not the worth but the impossibility of their work, and in these rooms took up despair, solitaire, drinking, drugs, and three suicide, by the nameplates on their doors at least half Jews—ah, *Westrum* by the nameplate, who'd made a wrong turn and come back to himself, starting out a new way now. Not only Jews, of course, but Jews on the whole had always made him think his work made sense. They believed in the perilous world and therefore in every effort, whether history or introspection, to find it out, explain it, clarify it, and maybe even partly solve it. They feared the outside danger. They thought that books, art, history, science, inquiry mattered, and the private man's own history, too, and so it had always been mainly Jews consenting to his waywardness, his experiment with history as one man's tale told daily to the length of his life. No other way had necessarily succeeded, give *that* way a try, give it a fling, and they valued him, they hired him, they conferred fees and degrees upon him, they passed him along from opportunity to opportunity, place to place, as Tikvah did and Judge Lerman did and as Benstock was probably prepared to do, down the corridor to Benstock's office for a wire-cutter to get at his life which lay in two footlockers. "My girl's arrived," he said to Benstock.

"In footlockers?" Benstock asked, whose girl had delivered Westrum's message after all, the wire-cutter was on the way.

It was brought to them by the young red-haired man who had carried Miss Sanantone's luggage to the Residence Wing. He wore suntan overalls jangling with small tools of every sort suspended through loops, a New Hamburg County farm boy who had already this day harvested corn before coming to work. He maintained a discreet distance behind Westrum and Benstock, back up the corridor to Westrum's suite, where he crouched beside the footlockers and proceeded to untwist the wires, for he thought not to destroy them by cutting them, he'd save the wire for another use. "Just cut them, just cut them," said Benstock impatiently to the country boy in his own country.

"You'll want your wire," said the red-haired boy.

"I don't want it," Benstock said.

"*He* wants it," Westrum said.

"Yes sir," the boy said, "I want it." He was grateful to Westrum for having translated his meaning to the foreign-looking man with long black hair covering up his ears, and he worked slowly, untwisting the wire he had chosen not to cut, accepting Westrum as authority to proceed in any way he saw fit, although he must have known that Benstock was chairman of the Wing and Westrum but a recent arrival. But Westrum was the face of all the authority the boy had ever known, and much the larger man besides, someone he had always known and trusted and could trust now because he had always known him, no foreigner like the other, and slowly and with care he untwisted the wire and thereby released the clutch of the rope upon the first of the two footlockers. The boy, to release the hasps, knelt upon the footlocker, and when the hasps were free the boy rose, and the lid of the footlocker sprang like a living thing, and he opened the locker to light and air, revealing the upper layer of Journal. "That's what it was," the boy said, and he asked, "That's paper clear through?" He'd harvest a continent of corn before he'd read his eyes out on paper. He pitied these people their worship of paper—all the suites and rooms were filled with paper—if it was up to him he'd take and turn the building over and dump it clean.

"There's a girl underneath," said Benstock, and the boy smiled. He knew a joke when he heard one.

Yes, true, there were girls in there, and the girls turned to women as time went by, many girls at first, and a few women afterward, and his wife and his mistress finally. "Paper clear through," said Westrum.

73

Benstock said, looking down into the footlocker, "You're an industrious man."

"Or anyhow a compulsive man," said Westrum.

"Then you won't want the wire," the young man said.

"What would I want with the wire?" said Benstock. "Dispose of it."

"I'll dispose of it," said the young man, who would not dispose of it, who would keep it for himself, who knew *useful* things when he saw them, and opened the second footlocker, too, as he had opened the first, and again the lid sprang as if it lived, calling to Benstock's mind carcasses upon hooks in his father's shop, swinging like living things when touched by some commotion of the air, and the young man carried away with him the wires intact, and the rope, too.

"Industry and compulsion may be something alike," said Benstock.

"Or the paper clear through might all be blank," said Westrum, whose joke went far awry, and who was amazed to hear now from Benstock, not for the second time but for the third time, which he had heard first upon the morning of their first meeting, and again that night at Benstock's dinner party, the account of one Hiram Browning, historian-turned-fraud whom Benstock had seated, who had promised the Center the Journal of his life, who received twelve thousand dollars a year for twelve idle years and more, who died, who was buried, whose pages were then with all propriety opened and found to be blank. It was Benstock's grand disaster in a life otherwise of small, sound, solid, responsible achievement—he'd seated Duerden, he'd seated Millender, he'd seated S. Cohen, Kidd, Georgeoff, Tod Solomon and M. B. Flaherty in History alone and he'd likely seat Westrum—but no pleasure of achievement, no small triumph or sound gratification would ever lie upon his memory with the weight of the trick played upon him by Hiram Browning. "Imagine when we opened the first ream of paper," said Benstock. "It was my honor to open it. I thought it was some mistake, maybe some package of new paper was

74

packed in there by mistake. Even after the second package, maybe two blank reams of paper got mixed in with the rest. It was possible. But after I opened the third it wasn't possible." He lay then for weeks in the Infirmary in a state of exhaustion otherwise unnamed and undiagnosed, collapse and bereavement, shame, chagrin, nightmare and self-recrimination. "If only the committee could see *something*," he said.

"You don't really need to," Westrum said.

"It's in the rules," said Benstock.

"It's not in the rules at all," said Westrum.

"Who said not?" asked Benstock, and he sat upon the daybed, although he had hoped to avoid it—it placed him too low, and Westrum too high above him. "It's the rules of the committee."

"Harvey Weinberg said not," said Westrum.

"Oh, Harvey."

"Harvey's the committee, too," said Westrum.

"I'm the committee," said Benstock.

"Good," said Westrum. "That's clear then."

"That not how I meant it," Benstock said.

"We say what we mean," said Westrum, but he said it kindly.

"I can't buy anything I can't see," said Benstock. "No more."

"Nobody has ever seen my Journal," Westrum said.

"Your girl sees it," Benstock said.

"She types it," Westrum said.

"So she sees it," Benstock said.

"I've never known if it registers," Westrum said.

"Of course it registers," Benstock said. "She's a human being, so it registers."

"I have no idea of her mind," said Westrum. Ten years before, on the day of their first encounter, he told her that he wished her to be a sieve through which all things cleanly passed and nothing clung, and she had obliged him ever since with mindlessness and obliviousness, by seeing nothing, by reacting to nothing, by recording all things promptly and forgetting all things instantly. She was an attachment to a typewriter. She could raise shorthand to typescript, and tangled typescript to clean, she numbered the pages of his Journal, and she kept current his Index to the Text, but none of it, as far as Westrum could tell, had ever touched her mind. Her interest never appeared to quicken nor her pace to break or alter, though all his life passed through her fingertips. She said but the single word, "Well," with a slight exclamation so that it might have been "Well!" when he presented her with a copy of *A History of the Past World,* for whose "patient, silent assistance" he had expressed grateful acknowledgment upon a printed page. She carried the book home with her that day, but never mentioned it afterward, and as far as he knew she had never opened it nor ever knew that her own name was in it, nor would have cared if she knew, since as far as Westrum knew she never read any book at all. He had come to assume that she was what she seemed to be, serving him with a faith not even flattering because she would have served anyone at all who supplied her with her wage.

Upon that account he disliked her. She appeared to him to be a neutral moral agent and therefore, all paradox aside, both contemptible to his own moral sight, and unbelievable to his imagination. She would as willingly have served any wicked purpose as well as she served his own, and he had often envisioned her typing long lists upon German machines of persons marched or to be marched to chambers of death, and very neat lists they would be, too, and perfectly alphabetized and unerringly categorized, here men, here women, here boys, here girls, servant of any master and compliant to any purpose.

"Impossible," said Benstock. But he knew how possible it was.

"Oh no," said Westrum. "Possible. You know it's possible."

"She must be in there herself," said Benstock.

"I omit nobody," said Westrum. "I do my best."

"Now I'm in there, I suppose," said Benstock.

"Years ago you were."

"How so?"

"You wrote me a letter," said Westrum.

"I was hoping you'd forgotten," Benstock said.

"On Roman roads," said Westrum.

"I apologize. I felt an awful need to say something. I wanted to bring you down a little. You know, your damn book made a lot of people stop in their tracks."

"I had a lot of letters," Westrum said.

"What about herself?" Benstock asked. "How about when she sees her own name? A person can be a neutral moral agent, but when he sees his own name he takes a little notice."

"A thousand times," said Westrum. "More. Three hundred days a year . . . three thousand times now. But just a note—'Miss Sanantone came today.' That's all."

"Someday somebody's going to ask, 'Who was Miss Sanantone? What was she to Westrum?'"

"He won't have much to go on," Westrum said. "I went to her father's funeral. I think that's the only continuous passage she was ever in."

"If I were a historian someday," said Benstock, "I'd wonder, though, here's a woman, she came every working day and everything the man did or said or knew passed through her mind."

"I'll show you her father's funeral," Westrum said.

"No no no, for God's sake, don't show me anything," said Benstock, "I believe you, the committee believes you, forgive me for my skepticism," but Westrum's own curiosity had been aroused, and the name of her gentleman friend would be there, too, for he'd met him at the funeral. It was in the rain, he now recalled, the rain ran down off her gentleman friend's umbrella, it was a short name, the name of a fierce beast such as a wolverine, but not *wolverine*, not so long as *wolverine*, rather the length of *tiger*, but not *tiger*, either, and he found her name in the Index to the Text, and the pages where the Index said they'd be. "We could do it with computers," said Benstock, "in twice the time."

"Yes, Miss Sanantone out-computes computers," Westrum said, and sat to read beside Benstock on the daybed.

On Monday, the sixteen-thousand-four-hundred-and-thirty-fifth day of my life Miss Sanantone telephoned by nine o'clock to say that her father died (Friday night) and to extend to me a "cordial invitation" to attend his funeral, whereupon I dressed as black as possible, partly in selfish mourning for the loss of half-a-day's work. I seldom thought of her as having a father at all. I knew he was a policeman, and that was all. But then, she never mentions anyone to me, we keep our distance between, our little lives apart, our souls segregated, separate but equal. She also neglected to mention the funeral parlor I was to go to. I rang her back quickly, but her line was busy, and several times more with the same result, and when it finally did ring nobody answered. Beatrice suggested that I call the Police Department, which I did, and was told that normally a funeral "detail" gathered in the department's own chapel, but not today, nothing was "on tap" there. "Are you sure of your party's name?" the policeman asked. I said I was. I said I was certain that Mr. Sanantone, a policeman, was to be buried today, for his daughter had told me so. "She wouldn't have told you if it wasn't so," he said, speaking for his own benefit, really, or perhaps to someone aside, for when he came back at me again it was in a loud, direct voice, "Hold the wire," he said, "I'm finding something out," setting down the open phone. He was gone long, but he assumed that I was waiting, for when he returned he did not ask if I were still there; rather, he shouted into the phone, "Here's the picture."

The picture was this: because of some sort of confusion in the records of Officer Sanantone his status was unclear. All that was certain was that he was dead—"you're right about that"—but whether he was entitled to an officer's full and official burial was undetermined, or whether he was entitled to begin his final journey from the department's own chapel, or whether police vehicles were to be lent to him, or whether department musicians and official mourners were to be given to him at the last—all that was unclarified, a poor picture not well-developed. Shriven in the eyes of his Church and God he may have been, but the regulations of the Police Department are more exacting. He had been guilty at some time or other, whether long ago or recently, of some sort of falsification of department records. I was to hear more of this as the day progressed.

Miss Sanantone had decided, in spite of friendly advice to the contrary, to proceed as if her father were entitled to nothing, that is to say to bury him in decent time rather than await the decision of department lawyers. She ordered therefore a funeral at her own expense, engaging one Tucci & Sons, Morticians of Manhattan. In this, of course, Tucci and his sons encouraged her, although several members of the department, including officials of the policemen's fraternal order, warned her that her hiring a private funeral director and doing all these things on her own will jeopardize her subsequent rights and claims by deepening the case against her: that is to say, having waived her right to the chapel, her right to the vehicles, her right to the Funeral Band, and her right to official mourners (who are apparently paid regular wages to attend and mourn in principle) she will appear to any Board of Review of the future to have admitted and conceded at the time of her father's death that she was aware that her father was not then entitled to funeral benefits.

Aspects of this delicate controversy were revealed to me as I rode in the rain in one of the funeral cars, in argument or debate among three policemen who had never personally known Officer Sanantone, but attended him to his grave upon the strength of fraternal conviction, as a kind of labor-union matter. They abused the driver of the car

79

(one of the Tucci sons himself) upon the grounds that the firm had been too anxious to snap up the job.

The day was right for a funeral. Let it be gloomy, let it rain, so that we may feel that the poor departed friend is missing out upon little. The rain poured down. The little plot so kindly provided by the Tuccis was a mudhole just off Gowanus Parkway about 53rd Street, Brooklyn. The service was conducted by a clergyman whose name I may be forgiven for not having determined, who himself had not the conscientiousness to determine the name of the deceased person, either, and so referred to him with alternating evasions as "our friend" and "our fellow-worker," groping meanwhile among his skirts for a slip of paper he knew he had, showing the name of the stiff, which he pronounced, when he found it, "Santoney," dropping a syllable, adding a sound: for what is a syllable more or less on a wet morning to a slipshod priest in a hurry?

Miss Sanantone's face was erupted in a rash, all blotched with red spots the size of a nickel, all scaling and peeling, no very pretty sight at all, which she dabbed with a handkerchief from moment to moment while, in the most controlled manner, she supervised the conduct of the ceremony—welcoming friends to the funeral home; thanking them for coming with that old political all-purpose lie we heard so much in Washington, "It's good to see you again," most of whom she had never seen before, and some of whom had never known her father, either, but had come in the name of solidarity. Above the head of the coffin was mounted a large wreath in the shape of a policeman's badge bearing his number.

At the cemetery one person stood slightly apart, one Hawkes, her gentleman friend, a detective of some sort, who told me something of her father. Poor fellow (Hawkes), his teeth were bad with big black holes. Calling cards stood in his hatband. He frequently begins sentences with the irrelevance, "I'm a poor man." He viewed me with suspicion. He declined to stand with me beneath my umbrella. The rain ran down his hat, pouring off the brim like a waterfall.

His thoughts (he said) were all for Miss Sanantone, and for the rights and benefits and privileges she had so regrettably waived. "Poor people bleed," he said, "rich people own all the knives." He associated me with the rich. His face is indented, nose aimed down, chin aimed up: extend their directions and they'll meet two inches in front of his mouth. "She's the sweetest kid in the world," he said, and then, as if he had not shown sufficient force, he added, "I love her deeply," but that dissatisfied him, too, and on his third effort he gave forth sufficient feeling to please him and to persuade him that he persuaded me, saying, "She deserves better than this. She deserves the best. They're making her sweat to get back at her father."

Miss Sanantone's father had had, said Hawkes, "a sharp head." The implication of the tense was unclear: had the mind failed in life or in death? Failed in life, Hawkes meant, under the following circumstance: Officer Sanantone, not for his own gain but to assist a distressed or impoverished friend, had falsified certain records of the Police Department, been discovered in his dereliction, and suffered as a penalty certain losses of rank, pay, and privileges. Hawkes's objection to the quality of mind of Miss Sanantone's father is less objection to his having tampered with records or even to his having been stupidly caught at it, but, beyond all that, to his having stubbornly and vaingloriously refused to reveal his partners in falsification. Thus all the penalties fell upon him, whereas *had his mind been good and not failed* he would have named the others, permitted them to share the penalties with him, and thereby lightened the burden upon himself.

81

"Good for him," I said, "there's your fraternal principle at its best," but Hawkes objected: "Every man for himself," he said, and offered with rapidity a series of supporting platitudes, looking for the right one, "Every rabbit knows his own hole. It's a dog-eat-dog world. . . God helps him that helps himself," but none of these served him, and he turned upon me instead. "It's easy for the rich to say," he said, "maybe you can afford fraternal principle but I can't. What do you do with her all day long, that's what I want to know. How many women does a man need?"

"We have lost the thread of the conversation," I said.

"If you don't see it I can't explain it to you," he said, pointing to the grave site for an emphasis to supply, I suppose, some connection I should have made. "But it all comes down to the same end," he said.

"Then she saw this," Benstock said. "Was it ever settled?"

"Was what?" asked Westrum.

"The funeral benefits," Benstock said.

"I have no idea," said Westrum. "I knew it was the name of a bird. I'm bad on names." But now that he had Hawkes's name he had no use for it. He carried the pages from the daybed to the desk Miss Sanantone would use, and placed them among new pages of Journal still in shorthand and a memorandum *Pull Turtleman*, and he thought he'd search himself for the Italian name of the man who had passed his hand across Tikvah's head: Tikvah's entries were numerous, hundreds and hundreds of hours with Tikvah, especially years ago before they drifted apart. Turtleman, Tikvah, Benstock, Harvey Weinberg, they were upon his mind for reasons known to the mind if not to Westrum. "I could have sworn he had his own umbrella," he said.

"I won't hold you to it," Benstock said.

"The rain was coming off his hat, not off his umbrella," he said, but whether history could care he did not know, it seemed a small point, and perhaps the whole thing, the whole fifty thousand pages, would hardly prove more relevant to any-thing than the question of who stood beneath whose umbrella. For a moment, casting himself in Benstock's place, he saw the risk in disbursing so much money for secrets which would never reveal—whatever they *would* reveal—the cure for the common cold or the way to make rain in dry seasons or new sources of fuel, food, energy. "Anyhow," he said, "there are no blank pages here. So be easy."

"I'm easy," Benstock said, for whom the little he had read was enough. His former mistrust embarrassed him, he'd not been fair to Westrum. He saw that the Journal might be, by seeing one man so close in infinite detail, a portrait of many men themselves revealed by symbol, clarified, renewed, re-freshed, made well, relieved to discover themselves not uni-quely troubled but eternally natural children of creation. And here he was! *Shithouse lawyer*, he thought. Here he was, shit-house lawyer standing here quibbling in the presence of a work perhaps great, mistrusting, doubting, bargaining, asking for impossible proofs, infected by his own narrow stinking sus-picion, history's joke who'd measured the Journal of Westrum against the budget of his little domain, his Wing, his petty pre-serve. Brace up, he thought, be big, be worthy, discriminate, distinguish, notice true eminence under your nose, when Miss Sanantone appeared with her handbag and typewriter, carry-ing her mismatched cotton fleece slippers, who could only re-side, thought Benstock, this side true eminence.

Her face was in a rash still. But Benstock had had the im-pression that her father's death was long ago, months or years. This then was a new rash in a new crisis, a new minting of nickels upon a face remembered by Benstock as the map, the mug, the puss of that one alien, that one *schicksa* flung down like an oddity or a sample and exemplum of unclean life among the Jews in every neighborhood he had ever lived. Her face was stupid, dumb, blank, ignorant, the face of all tawdry side-walk life, the first girl on the street in the morning, still running the streets after dark, whose cry he heard from his bed, the girl with bruised legs, whore of the alleys, shoes without socks, the mouth of the gutter, Jew-hater, cop's daughter, the first girl he had ever kissed, and the last *schicksa*, to whom he now said most cordially, "I see that you found your way."

"I was sick on the plane," she said.

"I mean," said Benstock, "you found your way here from your room."

"I followed the signs," she said, strolling through the suite. "It's very very nice," she said. "A bed," she said, returning to the desk she saw would be hers, and pouring from her handbag packages of cigarettes and ball-point pens. Soon her hands and her forearms would be streaked by the pens. Sometimes, confusing pens with cigarettes, she took them to her mouth and streaked her lips, her chin. Her cigarettes, it seemed to Westrum, were the principal pleasure of her little life. She smoked the day through. Nor would she surrender her cigarettes no matter how many people told her (as Westrum sometimes did) how bad they were for her health, for she loved her cigarettes more than she loved her health, and her lips soon would be hung with shreds of white paper and strings of brown leaf. Her fingers were stained to the second joints, her eyes were always squinting against the smoke, and a stranger from another world might ask, "Is she smoking while tending the man's Journal, or is she tending the man's Journal while smoking?" But she had never burned a hole in a page. She forgot nothing. She neglected nothing. She never paused in the rhythm of her work. In the wintertime she seldom ate during working hours, whose lunch was fresh air taken in a turn around the block, and in summertime took neither food nor air, for the air was deathly pollinated. She was allergic also to airplanes, elevators, and reports of death, whether of someone she knew or someone she felt she knew, such as a star of screen or television, a President, or someone prominent over the years in Dr. Westrum's Journal.

"Do your quarters suit you?" Benstock asked. She stirred an old excitement within him.

84

"You really can't call it an apartment," she said, "it's only a room. I thought it'd be an apartment," but it was air-conditioned, she said, and the young man with red hair had helped her settle in a bit (she did not say). On the way to Dr. Westrum's suite she had passed a glass room filled with computers, lights flashing, wheels spinning, attended by young men with their sleeves rolled, one of whom, as she passed by, flattened his nose and his lips against the glass in a clever charade signifying a prisoner famished, and her sneezing had stopped and her eyes had dried, so it might not be bad. "It'll be all right," she said to Benstock. *A Jew*, she thought, *another*, having come, actually, even to a kind of taste for these mad scientists and dreary scholars with their hair curled down their necks. She had met a good many Jews in and out paying calls upon Dr. Westrum, and she had read a good deal about them, too, in Dr. Westrum's Journal, which was all the reading she ever did, all her education, and the best excitement of her life, quite in a class with movies and the New York *Daily News*, and met them down in Washington, too, and they were polite, though Hawkes said they were tricky and cheated on their wives. "We'll need ashtrays," she said—"I'll need ashtrays," she amended—folding pieces of paper into ashtrays.

"No problem," said Benstock. "I'll tell my girl."

But he'd forget to tell his girl, thought Westrum, and blame it upon her willfulness. "I'll bring ashtrays," Westrum said.

She removed her shoes and stepped into her slippers, and she blew upon the dustless shelves awaiting Dr. Westrum's Journal. "It'll be like home," she said. Her slippers were leather with cotton fleece and mismatched pompons. All day her shoes stood in the well of her desk, and all night her slippers. Today one slipper was bright red and the other bright yellow, and the colors were always bright but changing, now green and red, now yellow and blue, and Dr. Westrum thought she went out of her way to find them, but that was not true. Let him think so. On her way back to the Residence Wing she'd pass the glass room again, and she'd know Benstock soon, too. Perhaps he cheated on his wife, perhaps he didn't, she'd know more about him than he'd like her to know, he'd be popping up in Dr. Westrum's Journal: everybody popped up, and she especially enjoyed reading of people she'd actually met, coming upon them in their proper order and finding out about them. She never came to anybody before his time, she never read ahead—it spoiled the story. "I'm over a week behind," she said, "I didn't get out of New York as quick as I wanted to," spying at the end of a dustless shelf a brown paper sack filled, she knew, with quarters and dimes he called his mistress with when they were parted. He was regular and faithful. They were good for each other, whoever she was and whatever her name, whom Dr. Westrum solemnly promised never to name but who had otherwise no objection, so long as she remained nameless, to entering history known to the world as a healthy, robust, humorous, comical, passionate, superstitious, intellectual naked lady lying for years and years and pages and pages with Dr. Westrum, but never up and dressed, as far as the world would know, until such time, at least, as someone with a bright eye would name her in a simple early footnote; for she also appeared frequently elsewhere in the Journal beneath her proper name, who was in private life—that is to say, in public life—a woman of influence. Miss Sanantone had clues and divinations. She was either the wife of an eminent man, or the wife of a man sounding eminent to Miss Sanantone, wife of a scholar or entertainer or psychiatrist or candidate for high office (surely not the wife of a makework detective), or notable in her own right, lovely singer, brilliant lady scientist, lady lawyer, lady stockbroker, lady historian met at a conference, or both married to an eminent man and notable in her own right as well, for such women appeared in Dr. Westrum's Journal, and never a stenographer among them.

Whoever the lady was, and whatever her name, Miss Sanantone admired her for having made herself so indispensable to Dr. Westrum, and for her very interesting style of writing, too, whose letters Miss Sanantone read with the most powerful sensations of pleasure, wishing only that she knew someone to write to in that way, and had the talent to do it with, who'd have written Hawkes in that way if she could—she'd put together snips and patches of Madame's dirty letters: *Darling* she would write *so splendid to hear you say* . . . but she was too shy to copy it out.

With Dr. Westrum she'd have gone gladly nameless into history herself, for the pleasure of it. The man himself she admired in spite of his peculiarity. Did you ever hear of a man who spent half his life writing down the other half? And yet the University paid him for it, or the Government paid him for it, or even for a while the President of the United States paid him for it, and now the Center was paying him for it, and sometimes one party was still paying for it before the other had even stopped, so it must have some sort of value for them, too, as well as for her, all the more incredible in view of their not having even read it, as she had, and Hawkes had, too, in search of Dr. Westrum's mistress's name.

"What was it kept you?" Westrum asked.

"Getting it packed and tied," she said.

"They were tied to stay," said Westrum. "Did your friend Hawkes tie them?"

She was displeased to hear Hawkes's name. "No, not him," she said. "He was out of my life long ago."

"I'm sorry," said Westrum.

"Don't be sorry," she said. "Be glad."

"I'm only sorry I mentioned him," said Westrum. Very well, then, not Hawkes, or anyhow she'd not say so, nor say who tied it up if not Hawkes. It might have been another gentleman friend, or a boy, a brother, a cousin, a policeman, a janitor, an expressman, or someone from the airlines.

"*I'm* sorry," she said. "It was a friend, let's say."

"Say no more," said Westrum.

"A *personal* friend," she said, pleased to say no more of Hawkes who had packed Dr. Westrum's Journal and Index to the Text, and tied and wired the footlockers, and carried them

87

down upon his shoulders past Hermie to the airport, and
through the airport on his shoulders again and made very
damn sure they'd travel out on the same plane as she, though
not before reading the Journal himself, here swiftly, turning
whole handfuls of pages, but elsewhere with utmost care and
absorption.

Thus it would never be Benstock or the Seating Committee
or any chairman or committee anywhere before or after Westrum's death, nor Beatrice reading thirty years late, nor Westrum's sons, but Hawkes, a makework detective, squatting
upon his heels for two days and a night in Westrum's apartment, who would be—who already was—the first man in all
history to read Westrum's Journal. His wire and his rope lay
beside him on the floor as if at any moment he would turn from
his reading to the job he came to do. But these years had been
Hawkes's years, too, and he leaped and skipped about among
the years, jumping philosophy, meditation, rumination, heading
for hot spots as you'd do with any regular bound book—he'd
read a million sitting waiting for something to happen, someone to appear, in his parked car across the highway from a
hundred motels.

His being in the apartment at all rather disturbed Miss Sanantone. She should have given the work in the first place to
Hermie the doorman. "I'm only running my eye over a page or
two," Hawkes said, but he was an hour, and then he was all
day, and then he was all night and the next day, too, for he was
very fond of descriptions of flowers, trees, children, and sporting events, too, not only women, and he loved dirty jokes, analyses of dreams, the details of business arrangements, the private lives of political persons, the inside dope on big decisions,
and accounts of foreign places, especially when accompanied
by photographs, observations upon races and religions, memories of scenes of boyhood, and above all scenes of dispute between Dr. Westrum and his family, for Hawkes was at war
with his wife and his children and had been so for years, and
slammed them about when they needed it. He was gratified to

come upon the account of Dr. Westrum's breaking Terence's back, but he felt himself superior to Dr. Westrum, whose remorse appeared to Hawkes both prolonged and tedious: Hawkes himself had busted a bone or two when somebody needed it, and never thought a thing about it.

Imagine his surprise at coming upon himself, in the rain, in the graveyard, five years ago. "A detective of some sort," he said. "What in hell does he mean by that?" Nor was he pleased to read of his bad teeth or his indented face, he knew the trouble with his teeth—he'd always had bad teeth—and his face was his face, he was born with it. If he'd had a different face he might have been another man. "What business is it of his?" he asked, and smashed the page between his hands.

"You can't do that," said Miss Sanantone, and retrieved the page and returned it to its place in the order of things, and upon further thought took it to her typewriter and copied it new. He had a short temper. He wasn't to blame. He was by trade a makework detective, he lived by his wits, he was only a man. Now and then he took a lady instead of her fee. He had a way with women, bad teeth and bad face and all, he'd not been entirely faithful to anyone, if you must know, nor even entirely faithful to Miss Sanantone, either, though she'd been best and lasted longest and was his now. When all was said and done, calculated and counted, it was Miss Sanantone who was different from all the women he knew or had known, and he loved her. Or now and then he took a lady and her fee, too, helplessly seduced by the very subject he'd been hired to peach upon, victim of dire circumstance, in which case he sometimes even reported the lady's bad liability to promiscuity, neglecting to mention that it had been himself she was promiscuous with (it was relevant anyhow?), and in the end no harm came of it all, for in every case at law somebody had to win, somebody had to lose, and Hawkes did, on the whole when conditions permitted, if it was no strenuous inconvenience, the fair thing, as often as not.

"I can do what I please," said Hawkes. "You prefer his face

89

to mine." He had read through the night, and in the morning he was ill-tempered, as if he had been drinking, and he pretended to believe, as if no evidence were before him, that Dr. Westrum kept no Journal but only pretended to do so, to lure Miss Sanantone day by day, as he was luring her now to distant parts upon the same pretext, tying and wiring the footlockers and wishing, as he said, it was the son of a bitch himself who was in them, and carrying them off upon his shoulders with the bitterness of a poor man harassed and outclassed by the very rich. "How many women does a man need?" he asked. It proved ideas he firmly held of the inequality of men, whereby some men lived above the law, while others, like himself, were compelled to live legal lives. His face, his teeth, had been his misfortune. He knew it. The Journal had named his most tender and unmentionable parts, once more the poor man was bled by the rich, once more he was humiliated by a better face.

"He only has the two," she said.

"And you makes three," he said.

"You don't even believe that," she said.

"I know why he's bringing you there," said Hawkes. "I know what he's thinking about."

"Say one single word," she said, "and I won't go."

"Find out who his lady is," said Hawkes. "That's how we'll do it."

"You don't care if I go," she said. "You've got fish to fry." To the last moment, to the calling of the airplane, she'd have stayed if Hawkes had given her a word.

"It's too late now," he said. "The footlockers are all shipped through," and he was flush, he'd just come off a good case, he was overflowing with affection—not quite for her: for someone else he'd soon tire of, and ring Miss Sanantone when he was ready. He had that tendency. He needed to run about a bit before coming again to her whom he loved. He chose the moments, springing to view suddenly when his mood was right. She'd not stay long. She'd fly to him this very moment if she could, and meanwhile be busy, reading along, keeping up, not falling behind. She said to Westrum, "I'll have it on the shelves in no time."

"I know you will," said Westrum, taking his brown paper sack from the shelf, and departing with Benstock. "That's my girl," said Westrum. "You seemed curious."

"She gives me the impression—I don't know what," Benstock said. *"Resourceful."*

"That's one of the things she is," said Westrum. "Yes, right, resourceful."

"You're lucky," Benstock said, whose own girls—two, three, four a year—were often sweet, tidy, pleasant, attractive, but never resourceful. "When I have them I can't keep them. If I keep them I can't trust them."

"Loyal and resourceful," Westrum said. "She's made a career of tending my Journal."

"She worries about it," Benstock said, "because she worries about you. Of course she's very fond of you. It's in her eyes. She still has a rash on her face."

"Still?" asked Westrum, walking with Benstock past the glass room of computers.

"From the funeral," Benstock said.

"Oh my God no," said Westrum. "That was years ago. She's had ten rashes since. This one's an airplane rash."

"When her skin is clear she must be attractive," Benstock said.

"I believe she is," said Westrum.

"Does your Journal shock her?" Benstock asked.

"There's nothing shocking in it," Westrum said.

"But you put everything in," said Benstock.

"Everything, yes, of course, everything, it wouldn't be a Journal otherwise."

"Regardless of every adventure?" Benstock asked, but even as he asked his question an answer came to him: Miss Sanantone was everything Benstock thought she was, street girl beyond shock, whore of the alleys grown up and gone to business

91

school, and beyond that, as he had feared and suspected, West-rum's mistress besides, so that he'd not only brought Westrum here, but his mistress, too. By God, then, he'd give Westrum no Seat at all, not Five or even Three but only One and up and out for him. He'd give a Seat to someone silent, unheralded, un-wanted, someone modest and alone, some small contributor to the life of mankind, some small discoverer of a small relief for a small pain, not some star of arrogance keeping in fifty thou-sand pages a Journal of a single life in the best suite in the Wing in the best house in town, and his mistress along for the ride besides.

"Well, so far," said Westrum, "no, nothing seems to have shocked her. Nothing seems to have made an awful lot of im-pression, either. She just lights up another cigarette."

"I'll remember ashtrays," Benstock said. But why should he remember ashtrays for Westrum's mistress? What was this? What had things come to? Was the chairman of the Wing a bellboy with a tray? What next? Whiskey? Ice? True, Westrum did not drink.

"Anyhow," said Westrum, "I've no adventures of the kind I'm sure you mean." His blood stirred, rising and pumping, his pulse leaped, it was ninety at least, and a lie was in his throat likely to be the right lie. It was the lie he had lied to Tikvah and kept him at bay forever by proving everything that Tikvah had feared: by proving that Westrum's success at life, his ca-pacity for work, for organization, his perseverance, his fame, his fortune, all these so far exceeding Tikvah's—even his body, his face, the hair of his head—were the divine rewards of moral supremacy. He would have preferred to have been praised by Tikvah for *A History of the Past World*, but that praise had never come, and so he had rocked and shaken Tikvah with the most astounding lie he had ever dared, and lived with the hope that he'd never need to dare it again—it was a strain upon him—however amusing posterity might find it in the narrative of his Journal. Casually he tossed his paper sack from hand to hand, coins packed tight, they'd bring the voice of his mistress to his ear.

"Adventures are in the mind, too," said Benstock.

"But you don't mean in the mind," said Westrum.

"To be truthful," said Benstock, "no, in the flesh I meant." Beside the elevator his finger searched the wall. He could not find the button. He could not remove his eyes from Westrum, to whom once more he owed apologies for unjust thoughts, for doubting, for a quibbling pride. If Westrum took his girl for mistress, good for him, nice catch. Wouldn't Benstock himself have taken Rosalie if he could?

"I thought so," Westrum said.

"You're not exactly an ordinary man," said Benstock, his finger finding the button at last, whereupon it lit up.

"I keep at the work," said Westrum. "The rest is ordinary."

"You're famous," said Benstock. "You're known."

"That's not what I admire about myself," said Westrum.

"A famous man," said Benstock, "a man who is known, he's not Tom, Dick, and Irving, he's somebody, he's bigger than ordinary, women pursue him, I'm sure." It was a venture, a probing, it was a question—really, wasn't it true, if the reward of work was fame, wasn't the reward of fame lovely ladies coming running, lovely ladies happily thinking, I who am ordinary exceed myself by getting fucked by fame? Wasn't that how fame was, Benstock was saying, don't fail, be human, don't let him think that the difference between Westrum and himself was a tremendous moral difference beyond apprehension. "I'm always wondering if I'd be exactly myself if I'd made it big," he said. By God, if Westrum told him *that* he'd have a Seat for Three or Five, and every other hospitality, for Westrum would then have carried the good news to Benstock that the difference between them was luck, and luck alone, when the elevator came, and they entered. But Benstock, in his distraction, waiting for a reply, neglected to indicate their destination, whereupon the elevator, so perfectly was it made, began to hum with impatience, its humming gradually gaining force, then breaking, then beginning again, awaiting the will of its passengers.

"I have no adventures," Westrum said. "Only in the mind. What floor are we going to?"

"None," said Benstock. He was astonished.

"You imagine I have mistresses and all that," said Westrum.

"Not mistresses," said Benstock.

"One mistress?"

"A man might have one mistress," said Benstock, pushing the button. "It's natural. When he accused you of it you didn't deny it."

"Who accused me? Of what?"

"At the funeral," said Benstock. "He indicated your girl was your mistress."

"It was beneath denial," Westrum said, and the doors of the elevator closed, and they were alone.

"Please," said Benstock, "I'm sorry it all came up." Indeed he was. He blamed his own indolence. Indolent, he had sometimes been accused by men less indolent than he of a failure to appreciate the true nature of hard or steady labor. He had once gained a small start upon both poetry and history—a few poems, a small monograph of Roman roads—then paused forever, failed, slid, drifted, too much savored continuous society or empty-handed meditation, sank from the business of work to the business of administering the work of others. He could manage a Wing of men at work, but he could conclude nothing of his own. With as much grace as he could command he praised and supported the men and women he sheltered, but he allowed himself to feel that behind their closed doors they were as indolent as he. In moments more honest he confessed to himself that he was too indolent even to try to understand the things they were doing: he could describe in two concise sentences the work any gifted man was up to, and prepare an annual report. He knew finally, as he knew now, or thought he knew, in this moment, in the elevator, that his innocence of

work defined the poverty of his moral character. He had ma-
ligned Westrum, harboring unjust thoughts against him, for
Benstock was innocent not only of work but of the emotions or
consequences of fame. Jealousy, envy, and suspicion were the
signs of his decay, Westrum was industrious, Westrum was
great, Westrum was fine, pure, and Benstock said senselessly,
lunging for the final proof beyond all necessary proof, "Beatrice is Jewish, I take it."

"Something I might say," said Westrum, in the privacy of
the elevator, "to clarify—to you—something I've never said before, though my Journal knows, for some reason or other it's
how I am, it's my constitution, I take no credit for it: the first
woman I slept with was my wife on the night of our marriage.
I've never so much as kissed another woman since."

4

With Beatrice and Terence, and their dog and their cat (left sleeping in the car), Westrum drove to the Infirmary to visit Benstock, who had fallen ill. His illness had been marked by chills and a rocketing fever, delirium, and a probable complication of ulcers, a mystery even to physicians so fortunate as to be able to draw upon the resources of the Center.

But where knowledge was so far advanced, so also were doubt, skepticism, imagination, and obscene articulation: Benstock was a bad patient. For a week he had refused to allow anything dramatic to be done to him, resisting every medicine but the mildest old pills and tonics remembered from his mother's cabinet and therefore trustworthy, and refusing with fevered oaths any capsule or needle, especially if it was accompanied by anyone's assertion that "we are just going to try this . . . we are just going to see what this will do." Knowing how little he knew of his own territory, suspecting how little anybody knew of any other, he was warned above all by his poet's imagination against experiments upon human beings. Such talk had too much the sound of the advanced stage of medicine said to have been in progress in Nazi Germany.

He was obsessed at one hundred and five degrees by the resemblance between the white chamber in which he lay and the photographs he had seen, tales he had heard, of the German dungeons scrubbed pure to assure death of the right thing. During the first three days of his hospitalization, when his fever was high, he accused the young doctors of crimes of which they had never heard, calling, "What have you done to the Jewish doctors?" He was obsessed, too, by the moral neutrality of the young doctors, who in any case were scarcely offended by his peculiar accusations. Their memories were shorter than his. They had been children at play when he was at war. For them, Hitler's name was one of several out of a fixed, standing past, a figure painted flat in history, neither nearer nor farther in time than Bonaparte, the Kaiser, Alexander, or the Emperor of Japan. When he accused the young doctors of moral neutrality they ignored him—they hadn't known it was anything bad—and when in moments of recovery he apologized to them for his disgraceful behavior they thought his apology but a farther part of his first delirium.

The doctors, unable to name a cause for the rising and the falling of his fever, or for the erratic pattern of his chilling, unable to fix any sort of name to his affliction, baffled here, pressed elsewhere, lost interest altogether in his body when his chart stabilized. Now, for two full days, he had felt quite all right, "Sick of sickness," he said, expressing to the Westrums his gratitude for their having come.

"He doesn't really look sick at all," said Philip, arriving shortly with his mother and his sister.

"You really don't," said Westrum.

"Something came and went," said Benstock.

Indeed, Philip Benstock looked more the patient than his father, for his face had been bruised at football. His left cheek was patched with tape below a blackened eye, and his upper lip was split—a small thing, he said, considering what they'd done to *them*. They'd beaten Paree Catholic by forty points yesterday, as they'd beaten Brest the week before. With his broken lip he kissed his father upon the mouth.

"Did you feel bad," Gretchen asked Westrum, "when Philip beat Brest?"

"I took it philosophically," Westrum said.

His answer was important to her. She hoped for Philip's winning, but not for Westrum's disappointment. One recent night he had told her not only that she was pretty but that he had heard rumors of her beauty beforehand, and she was fond of him for having been the bearer of such good news. She jumped from her chair to sit beside him, and she asked, "You aren't angry at Philip for beating Brest?"

"No no," said Westrum, "it's what he set out to do."

Terence avoided the eye of his father. He had not kissed his father in years, and he was distressed to see Philip and Benstock kissing now. He had supposed it wasn't done. Beyond a certain age father and son no longer kissed, and yet there they were, Philip and Benstock, kissing warm and hard with evident affection, and upon the mouth besides. Perhaps they did not know the rules of life. Yet Dr. Benstock was a worldly man, the very chairman of the Wing. Terence thought Philip Benstock in any case not intelligent, or if intelligent somehow reluctant to appear so. His teeth were too white—their brilliant whiteness definitely irritated Terence, who in this moment unaccountably and guiltily enjoyed a secret, shameful pleasure in the broken lip subduing the whiteness of Philip's smile.

His enjoyment confused him. The emotion was new. He had swiftly become a loyal citizen of Center High, and he therefore wished its football team well. But he felt himself wishing it well with the strange qualification that it succeed without the heroism of Philip Benstock. Twice now, upon two Saturdays, Philip was everybody's hero. At some moments Terence's thoughts drifted so sullenly that he wished no football games occurred at all, although he could not go so far as to condemn football altogether, as his father did. Yesterday he'd shot his father picketing football, carrying a sign, FOOTBALL = FASCISM, but Terence couldn't possibly go so far as to say that football was fascism, and he wondered whether his father believed it, either. This morning, in the early hours, in his new darkroom in his new house, developing, editing, playing his new film upon the wall, Terence observed with deep interest that his father's face beneath the picket sign was amused, not indignant, that his father was rather detached than involved, rather spectator than participant, even as he was at this very moment, talking with Gretchen Benstock.

True, Benstock really didn't look sick at all. He had slept a good deal, consequently smoked less, drunk nothing spirituous at all, and tormented himself by imagining himself living up to resolutions he knew he'd never keep—to go on, when he was once more abroad, neither smoking nor drinking nor keeping late hours, just as he had always resolved in the past when he was stricken by this mysterious failure which the doctors called, as they called it now, exhaustion. "But why should I be exhausted?" he asked Westrum. "I don't work very hard. I'm not entitled to exhaustion. I'll tell you who's entitled to exhaustion: *my* father. *My* father worked fourteen, sixteen, eighteen hours a day, and overtime on Friday. On Friday he worked from dawn to sundown. Friday night he slept until Sunday morning and went back to work."

Benstock's father had been a butcher, and Benstock had been thinking of his father here upon his back, speculating, as a matter of fact, about his father's—what name had he and Westrum given it?—*adventures*, as they called it. Where, he had wondered, would his father have found an hour for an adventure? He never left the shop. He walked in blood, in daily fear of the knives of his trade, forbidding his sons to touch a knife, although each son at some time of his own life had offered to relieve the infinity of his father's labor, forbidding, finally, each son in turn, to enter the shop at all, lest he enter it forever. No, he could not have had a free hour, and therefore no adventure, either. Beautiful things were for his sons, not for him, who defined his own life in two sentences often announced. "I should have been born the next time," he often said, and again, "A knife don't think."

"He never saw Saturday," said Sally Benstock. She meant Westrum to hear her, for she thought Westrum ought to know how difficult the past had been, and she tried to raise her eyes to his. But she could lift her eyes only to his hands upon his lap holding Gretchen's white gloves, as Gretchen had asked him to.

"But I'm sure this is uninteresting to you," said Benstock to Westrum who had come and gone with the butcher through

Benstock's mind, and Miss Sanantone in his fever, too, who might have gone to the back of the shop with his father in his bloody apron for the swiftest adventure in exchange for kosher meat for a week for a *goyim* family. Benstock had also resolved, ascending from his exhaustion, to begin a Journal of his own, whose most recent affliction had been precipitated, he felt, by Westrum's coming to the Center, or if not then then certainly in Westrum's suite above the mass of the Journal kicking itself free of confinement, or if not then then certainly in the elevator afterward.

"Of *course* it's interesting," Westrum said.

"He's taking every word in," said Beatrice.

"My father's nuts about other people's family history," Terence said.

"I see," said Benstock. "I forgot. I keep forgetting I'm a character in your father's Journal."

"And now *your* father's a character, too," Terence replied.

"The stink of that shop," said Philip, "was the most awful stink I ever smelled."

"Rest your lips," his mother said.

"The bleeding's stopped for good," said Philip, tenderly touching his wound, linebacker extraordinary, Little Gibraltar, at the center of every play, driven by loyalty to his school and to himself to risk himself by acts of unremitting valor. Who'd not give up a bit of blood to be named in Monday's newspaper Player of the Week? Nor for the first time. Triumph inspired triumph. He lived for autumn Saturdays, days of his distinction, whose penalty was always a little pain on Sunday, recuperation on Monday, light action on Tuesday, and glory again on Saturday, grandson of the butcher who in all his life never saw a football game because he never saw Saturday. "What's all this picketing jazz?" he asked Westrum.

"You can't be speaking so rudely to Dr. Westrum," his mother said.

"Do you read his Journal?" Benstock asked Beatrice.

"Never," said Beatrice.

101

"That's all right," said Westrum. "He's not rude," but when he turned his eyes to Sally Benstock she looked away.

"*You* played football," Philip said. "You *know* it's worthwhile."

"Be nice," his mother said. "Speak nicely."

"How many people picketed?" Benstock asked.

"Not as many as saw the game," said Philip, laughing.

"That's why I picketed," Westrum said, "to balance it out," who had also picketed, on the whole, because Harriet Weinberg hoped he would.

"I bet you wouldn't picket if Terence was on the team," said Philip.

"It's an interesting question," Westrum said.

"I think you would," said Benstock.

"I don't really know," said Westrum.

"You would," said Benstock firmly, who, in this happy moment at least, emerging from exhaustion on the most splendid Sunday of autumn, had arrived at simple reconciliation: some men were better men than others, Westrum was a better man than he, and it was the duty of lesser men to believe in better men. Westrum, in his passage these few days through Benstock's agitated mind, appeared to Benstock not less virtuous than Benstock's own father. Both were sober, principled monogamous men, whose adventure was their labor. If one had existed, why should he doubt the other?

"It's good of you to think so," Westrum said.

"A principal's got no right to picket," Philip said. "She should be loyal to her school. They'll make her be."

"A principal should be loyal to her principles," his father said.

"She's a bitch," said Philip.

"Who'll make her be?" asked Westrum.

"You *played* football," said Philip. "That's what kills me— you played. That's why you should *know*."

"Who'll make her be?" asked Westrum again.

"The Board will," said Philip.

"Make her be what?" asked Westrum.

"The coach says the Board will," said Philip.

"Make her be what?" asked Westrum again.

"Make her be loyal," said Philip.

"Your lip will bleed," said Sally Benstock to her son, "so rest your lip, don't talk, be nice."

"Football is fascist," said Westrum.

"It is very warm in here," said Sally, hastening to the window. But the windows of the Infirmary, like the windows of all the Wings, had never been made for opening.

"My mother hates arguing," Gretchen said.

"She panics easy," Philip said.

"Take your feet off the bed," said Sally to Philip.

Westrum smiled inwardly. Once, somewhere, his mistress walked on a bed in high-heeled shoes because her mother hated anybody's feet on a bed. Sometimes she sent her husband to the hospital, too, a silly little pleasure all her own, to get him out of the way for five days for his health and her better freedom, though he hadn't in any case the least suspicion of her. He was never really in the way, no match for her endless invention: she could create from the most minute fragment of a suggestion accidents, crises, and obstacles sufficiently formidable to account for a delay of two hours between any two points on the island of Manhattan, or a delay of two days between any two points on the globe. She could describe to her husband in her charming way a hundred details of a traffic jam which never happened, caused by a parade which never occurred in celebration of a holiday which never existed in honor of a hero never born, airplanes with motor troubles, airports fogged in, business entanglements, subcommittee meetings, the unexpected arrival of an invaluable visitor, all for the real end of serving her pleasure and Westrum's in committee in their own rooms. And yet, when imagination created emergency it created reality, too. Westrum's eye, falling here or there upon certain passages or pages of *A History of the Past World*, was often reminded that a point might have been

103

better made or a cluster of data more strategically formed had he not, upon a certain evening, been rather with his mistress than at his desk.

On the other hand, his mistress was his equilibrium. All other gain would have been loss without her, for she cost him only here or there, now and again, some part of one day in the cycle of his days for the release and disburdening of wild private passions. All history, after all, was complete with appointments not kept, meetings abbreviated, decisions hastened, orders detained because generals or couriers fell to mistresses. It was true. Westrum had facts. Moreover, he had before him his own example: it appeared to him now that he would remain here or go home depending upon nothing so much as his good or bad fortune in going down upon Harriet Weinberg, whom he was daily more eager, you may believe, to go down upon, to see how he liked it, and how she liked it, and whether it would last beyond first curiosity.

"Your mind goes away on frequent trips," said Benstock from his bed.

"Comes right back again," said Westrum.

"Sooner or later," said Beatrice.

"He's thinking," Terence said. "Give him a chance." *My father is a thinker*, Terence thought, *my father takes precious time to visit people in hospitals.* These good things he would emphasize in his essay, if only he could write. But he could not write. He never knew where to begin an essay. He could *outline* an essay very well, but he could never put the meat on.

"I was right here all the time," said Westrum to Benstock, turning to Philip. "I *did* play," he said to Philip, "and that's why I know, because I played it, and I played it right here, too, and I think I know what the boys are like in these parts, and what they're susceptible to, and the terrible things these damn sports breed in you."

"They teach you to hate," said Terence. Although he had not picketed he knew his father's argument. But he had never heard his father state it with quite such force before.

104

"You need hate to build fight," said Philip, his hand to his lip, examining his hand then to be sure his epigram had not reopened his wound.

"Why do you need fight?" his mother asked.

"You need fight to *win*," said Philip, looking with pity upon his mother's ignorance.

"Why not lose?" asked Beatrice.

"You want to learn to take care of yourself like a man," said Philip.

"It's a long leap from football to fascism," Benstock said.

"Maybe so," said Westrum. "Maybe not. Tikvah wrote a little book. You should bring Tikvah here."

"To do what?" Benstock asked.

"To finish his book. To do it new. I know I mentioned it to you—on the potentialities for fascism in America."

"He wrote it or you wrote it?" Benstock asked.

"He did."

"I thought you said you," said Benstock.

"No, no," said Westrum. "He."

"Then I misunderstood," said Benstock.

"You never read it?" Westrum asked, choosing to be astonished, tripped upon his own forgetful lie. "Tikvah has the most extraordinary mind I know," he continued, astonishing Beatrice now, who had never heard her husband speak with such enthusiasm of her brother's mind. Moreover, it was no book, it was scarcely a pamphlet, fifteen pages at most (she hadn't seen a copy in twenty years), begun by her brother in an hour of inspiration, with the idea of producing a comprehensive work. Tikvah had begun many comprehensive works, none ever resumed after the hour of inspiration. His talent for abandoning comprehensive works in the hour of their inspiration was equaled by her husband's talent for inspired lies leading to comprehensive truth. He'd claim tonight that he had *always* believed Tikvah's mind extraordinary, that he'd never said a word against it. He cultivated obsessions—somehow they served him—and as far as Beatrice knew no harm had ever

105

come of them, and sometimes good. Sometimes he whimsically declared his faith in someone, as in Tikvah now, as a means of turning faith to fact.

Consider Beatrice herself! He had raised her up in her own eyes. He had brought her to his idea of her, given her, out of his imagination of her, his creation of her, invention of her, a sense of herself much different from herself as she had been, so that in fact she became herself as she was now, learning from him to believe beyond her own vision to his. He had been alien. He was Gentile. He belonged to all that country out there in the wild west beyond the Hudson, beyond the Jersey shore, alien, Gentile, smelling of horses and guns and the Jew-hating Ku Klux Klan and mute straight-nosed even-featured stupid bookless men named Jackson and Johnson and Smith and Jones and Black and Westrum, whose course—Westrum's course—in modern history she almost spurned *precisely* because of the name in the catalogue. At the last moment she signed for it, however, when her brother said, "Try it, I'm told that he's unusual," though even then she'd not have taken someone named Westrum had she found a better name at the same hour. She preferred a safe-sounding name more or less guaranteeing someone who'd see modern history as she preferred it to be seen, life was too dangerous and too crucial to leave it open to speculation, good guys were good guys, and bad guys were bad guys, and this Westrum—what was he? bad or good?—neither looked nor sounded like anyone she had ever known, and he followed her down the street one day, and took her arm, and turned her out of her way into another.

They pleased one another. Sometimes she thought of the oddness of the possibility of marrying him, and she wrote upon an end-page of the strange text he had chosen—old Charles Homer Haskins's *The Renaissance of the Twelfth Century*—her imagined name, *Beatrice Westrum*, so stark beside other possibilities, *Beatrice Feinberg, Beatrice Katz, Beatrice Rosenberg*, and kept the book forever, with her name inside an anachronism, a puzzle to the painstaking historian who would natu-

106

rally conclude that she had written her name not before but afterward.

She'd be marrying into the country then, into all that territory heretofore so alien to her. In his presence, in those first days, she was never herself, she was someone else, she was outside herself and disloyal to herself, and she could not have lived long with herself that way had he not shared with her the same sense of flight from old past to new being. Together they remained who they had been even as they became who they now were. If she had married out of the north Bronx into everything alien he, too, had come far from Brest to Manhattan, twelve hundred miles upright overnight in a railroad coach, his pockets filled with dollar bills and nickels. The bills were his worldly fortune. His father allowed him nothing. "Beg from the Jews," his father said. "They have it all." The nickels were for telephone calls.

"All right, I'll write an invitation to Tikvah," Benstock said.

"Is he nice?" Sally Benstock asked Beatrice. For Sally, niceness was all, the Center needed nice people, everyone saw a great deal of everyone else. In all life only harmony mattered to her, for she had seen too much of the depths of hatred.

"Some of the most productive people aren't the least bit nice," her husband said.

"Let them be productive of niceness," Sally said.

"I'm supposed to write somebody named Jim O'Brien," Benstock said, writing Tikvah's name below O'Brien's. "History of the rise of the Serbs and Poles. I often find it hard to square the name and the work. O'Brien's no Serb and Pole."

"What you should do," Terence suggested, "is put the name of the applicant on the *back* of the application."

"I'd peek," said Benstock. A weakness had come over him, but whether it would turn to chills or fever he did not know. He hoped it would pass. He lowered himself in his bed and lay flat.

"Everybody has prejudices," Philip said. "It's natural. Nothing can be done about them."

107

"It's too big a subject for today," his father said, beginning to perspire, but whether it was the cold sweat of a chill or the hot sweat of a fever he was no more certain than before. Whichever it was, though—this he knew—he'd take below with him the question of whether to honor his promise to Westrum, for he was wary of friends attracting friends (and would have been wary, too, had he known the facts, of brother-in-law attracting brother-in-law); and carry below, too, disappointment with himself for not having defended Philip: what possible harm could there be in football? If Westrum had had his pleasure at it once upon a time why shouldn't Philip have his pleasure, too? He shouldn't have been so quick to disagree with Philip— Philip was right. Perhaps, maybe so, perhaps if Terence played football Westrum would see it in another light. It was all so trivial; unless, of course, football *was* fascist, in which case it was no longer trivial, and it would be well for the world to hear from Tikvah or from anyone else on the potentialities for fascism in America. He called to Philip, as from a distance, weakly, "Play football."

"We've stayed too long," said Beatrice.

"He's all right," said Philip. He was beside his father now.

"I might not be as well as I thought I was," Benstock said, kissing his son again, as before, with heat and the gift of guilt-lessness, no doubt because he had never mauled his own son, thought Westrum, never assaulted him, never broken his back. "How beautiful your wife is," Benstock said. "My father never drank," he said. *It's possible*, he thought, possible that Westrum never drank, possible that Westrum never kissed another woman, and he saw from his bed, in the lowering of Beatrice's eyes, a little Jewish girl praised before company, and if she was Jewish then Westrum must be as good and as true as he seemed to be, and if Westrum was as good and as true as he seemed to be then Benstock would give him everything he wanted.

Westrum saw Sally then. Plainly Benstock had told her, and plainly she was doubtful. She was troubled by Westrum because her husband was troubled. Westrum would exhaust him. These crises exhausted him. The doctors said her husband must relax, let down, be loose, stop taking everything so seriously. Philip was right, everyone was prejudiced, and so was she, she could not help herself, she had mistrusted Westrum upon the first instant of their meeting, she mistrusted him now, she'd mistrust him forever, no matter what, though her husband might give him a Three or a Five. Let him do so. Let him choose always to give every man the benefit of doubt, and take upon himself the breakdowns which always followed. She was beside her husband now, Sally and Philip and Benstock all kissing, all embracing. It was how the Jews were, thought Westrum, they wept and kissed and told one another how beautiful they were, and how soon they would be well: it was for this he had married into the Jews as quick as he could, to share the warmth of it, who would himself have flung himself upon Benstock and kissed him, embraced him, kissed Sally and Philip, too, if only he could have brought himself to do so—they had all stayed too long, the nurse said, arriving with a young doctor.

Gretchen was frightened. In the confusion she had been forgotten, and she stood alone, seeking some instruction—shall she sit, shall she stand, shall she remain, shall she go. "Is something happening?" she said, whose mother once, when she was a child, in a moment of utter mortal danger had been taken by the hand by a tall Gentile whom she afterward associated in her heart, in spite of the knowledge of her mind, with death and captivity, as Westrum took Gretchen by the hand now, and said, "We're too many in here. I've got your gloves," and walked with her to the physicians' consulting room, where they waited for her mother and her brother.

From the Infirmary to the History Wing was a perfect distance. The day, too, was perfect, cool upon the flesh of his legs. Beside his car he climbed from his trousers, removed his shirt, tied up his running shoes, taped the key of his suite to his

109

sweatband, and wound and set his chronometer. "They're off," called Terence, but only Westrum was off.

By the time the wagon passed him he had already settled into a wise pace, bearing in mind two grades ahead to conquer. Beatrice waved. Terence, cross-legged in the wagon, shot Westrum through the rear window, the dog barked, and Westrum, by an involuntary action exceedingly interesting to himself— crazy, quixotic, stupid—suddenly spurted, sprinting as if to overtake the car, arms flung before him. In this foolish way he continued not more than twenty feet, brought himself into control, and resumed his sensible pace.

But his shoes were cracking leather at the instep, or else his socks were bunching, *see to shoes, see to socks,* and Philip was right, hatred helped, Westrum hated the road and conquered it by hating it, hated the running, hated the swimming, hated the cycling. He knew better, however, than to take water or road by force, he'd taken them always by wisdom, by the right stroke and the right pace, *never fight it, easy does it, play it cool, show no temper, see to shoes,* and it was always then, cheering himself forward, telling wise things to himself, that his body won, his lungs filled and floated him, and he could run forever, passing down a street of old houses now quite like the street where he had grown, with swings upon the porches, hammocks slung between ancient shade trees, boiling attics and cool cellars, hearing as he ran a rake among the leaves, and passing fifty paces farther the eyes of a child: so Westrum was sailing through somebody's childhood who might remember forever this briefest vision of a tall blond man with a big silver watch upon his wrist and a band around his head, and having run indoors to say a man was running down the street in his underwear—nonsense, child, you never saw any such thing, though the child would refuse for a while to mistrust his senses until he finally learned, for fear of ridicule, to see only those things everybody saw and not to see anything everybody else didn't see. Just so Westrum had been told in his own childhood. The world was as it was, he was always told, and a fine place, too, and all was well, count your blessings, the poor we will always have, the Indians were savages, the Jews are greedy, the blacks are lazy, the railroad is here to stay. His father fought to save the trees. That was to say, Westrum later understood, his father fought to prevent anyone from altering the landscape as he had known it. To whom, after all, did the country belong if not to the Westrums? Who was here first if not the Westrums?

He conquered the first grade with no greater loss than he had anticipated, and thus he took the first mile in six minutes and fifty seconds upon the eighteen-thousand-three-hundred-and-seventy-second day of his life, and began the second mile, and took the second grade in good style soon after. He was running as well this year as last, and he expected to continue. No reason existed why, in any department of life, he should do less well this year than last, for every year had always been better than the year before. He was a blessed man and he knew it, and he could not understand why, in this moment, breathing so well, running so precisely, exalted in every cell, whose wife was so beautiful, whose sons were so successful and devoted, for whom life was so agreeable, whose options were always so numerous, whose stock was always so on the rise, who felt himself balanced so well between labor and ease, between solitude and society—why then was he so determined to make Tikvah unhappy? He was ashamed that he had introduced the matter of Tikvah. He should never have done so. No good could come of it. Even if Benstock remembered to write Tikvah a letter of invitation Tikvah couldn't accept, and even if he ever accepted he would never complete the work: *Potentialities for Fascism in America* was a pamphlet without a future.

Only mischief had been in Westrum's mind, his tongue had spoken without permission, something within him wished unhappiness and complication upon Tikvah (and upon Benstock, too, for that was what it would come to), for some reason not clear to Westrum, some resentment there, some hatred or antagonism he had never been able to explain, nothing so clear as a crease in his shoe.

Ahead, where the hedge began beside the walkway to the Wing, he sighted the line of his finish, broke stride and sprinted—once more the winner!—stopping his chronometer and slowing, his momentum carrying him almost to the door of the Wing, so that he was forced to veer, rounding the hedge, feeling a grace in his swooping and a deep pleasure in his body's anticipation of his mind. If he ran that route again he'd end his sprint ten strides sooner, consulting his time now, removing his shoe, and discovering a weakened seam. He was always discovering exactly what he expected to discover. His time was exactly thirteen-thirty for two miles.

In this moment, exalted from running, he was unable to believe that an hour before he had so perversely raised Tikvah's name. The running had cleansed his body, as heavy exertion always cleansed him; drawn out, somehow, the poisons of his heart, pumped his blood clean, lightened his brain of some weight upon it. Yet his joy was cautious. He knew the true nature of the moment, surcease only between one perversity and the next. In another twenty-four hours his bile would flow again. Well then, he'd run again through the leaves of autumn and the snow to follow, cool his lungs, open his heart, lift off the top of his brain to the sunshine.

He entered the Wing, walking these corridors unerringly now, independent of signs and arrows, knowing his way. Most suites were locked and silent. Even here, insulated from all natural light or air, things had the feel of Sunday. Sound had its day on Sunday—currents of air racing through the walls to cool the computers for Monday; light flowing; water flowing; and Westrum, striding quickly still to keep from cooling, heard Miss Sanantone's typewriter, distinguishable to his ears from any other. He removed his sweatband from his head, and his key from his sweatband. For an instant, as he entered, she was diverted, but in the next instant she resumed, her eyes rising not even as high as his face, whom she'd know anyhow by the

112

smell of him. "Two miles in thirteen-thirty," he said, entering the fact upon a chart upon the wall beside his desk.

"Very good," she said.

"I wish you wouldn't feel compelled to work on Sunday," he said.

"Every day is like the rest around here," she said.

Yet her spirits appeared to Westrum to have lifted. She was typing with energy. She had emptied the footlockers, put up all the years upon the shelves, caught up the Index to the Text, and raised recent shorthand to Journal, following with absorption the journey of the Westrums west, driving with them, swimming with them, eavesdropping, in on everything, meeting the committee, knowing Benstock, Weinberg, Harriet, Coach Wilson, handsome Philip, lovely little Gretchen. Would Harriet fall in love with Dr. Westrum? Why did Dr. Westrum tell such an awful lie to Dr. Benstock in the elevator? Even she was there among it all—"Miss Sanantone arrived by air from New York this morning"—not for long, to be sure, not nearly the attention he gave to the footlockers: not that she minded, for she herself took pride in the Journal. It was in some sense a creation of her own hands as well as his. Not long ago, when they reached the fifty-thousandth page, she had thought the event worth mentioning, and he'd been giddy about it, too, gay and boyish, not at all like himself. "I bet I'm the only man on the block," he said, "whose Journal reached fifty thousand today. Keep going, let's try for six figures, we're a long-lived family." He declared the day therefore a holiday, though she couldn't see how, he'd gone right back to work as always, writing, reading, talking on the telephone, she supposed you'd *call* it work, though it wasn't the work men ordinarily did, peculiar work it was, and a wonder how a man lived at it, stopping his life every few hours to write up his Journal.

"It's the Jews," Hawkes explained to her. "They pay him to do it, don't they?" He knew the angles, Hawkes did. Oh well, some of it passed down the line to her, and some she passed along to Hawkes, too, when his luck was low, though Dr. Westrum said it wasn't stopping his life, it *was* his life, it was a thing he made, as he'd made a whole book once and given it to her, which she cherished, valued, guarded with her life, just a little something, he said, for the world to remember him by.

"It might not be so bad," she said, "if I got an apartment in town."

"We'll manage it," he said.

"It will cost money," she said.

"We'll manage that, too," he said. "Don't be unhappy."

"It's too much like a hotel," she said. "The days are the same and the nights are too long."

"There seems to be so much going on," he said. "Concerts and plays and movies."

"It's all families," she said. "I don't like concerts and plays, and the movies are all foreign."

"All right," he said, "we'll see about an apartment in town."

"I mean New Hamburg," she said."

"Yes," he said. "I assumed so."

"I don't have a car," she said.

"We'll get you a car, too," he said.

"I don't drive," she said.

"You can learn to drive," he said.

"So many people do," she said.

"Benstock will teach you," he said, laughing inwardly with some bitterness at his own instinct for cruelty: having imposed everything else upon Benstock, he thought now to make him driving teacher to Miss Sanantone.

"When will we go back?" she asked.

"Everything will work out," he said, hearing in his phrase his mother's voice, who might have been right after all, everything had worked out, dropping his running shoes into the wastebasket. They were done. Lately he bought running shoes more frequently, ran them less, and threw them away: it wasn't the old days when he ran them a second life or a third—ran them into the ground, so to speak, taping and stitching old shoes. His life had passed the point of need or narrow care, he hadn't

114

been to a shoemaker in years. On the Population Inquiry he'd
met people who fed a family for a month on the cost of a pair
of his running shoes, and he told the President so, and the President said, to hide his own embarrassment, "Buy cheaper running shoes," and Lerman said afterward to Westrum, "You
shouldn't have told him that, never tell him sad news," passing
to the inner room of the suite and to the bathroom beyond.
The hot water was endless—for him if not for them—the
power plant of the whole Center serving up Westrum's shower
on a Sunday afternoon, laughing beneath the water to think of
Benstock teaching Miss Sanantone to drive, who probably
would if Westrum asked him to, who might even ask to *see* if
he would, who might present it to Benstock as a *moral obligation,* laughing at himself in the shower.

It was surely a comment upon his own bad character, he
thought, that when he needed someone, as he needed Miss
Sanantone, he preserved her from all pain, nor ever played his
whimsy upon her, as he played it upon others, expecially those
whom he should have loved best—rather a bad sort, this Westrum—trying experiments upon human beings, producing little
shocks to see how people jumped, asssembling it all in the com-
pletest Journal of any man who ever lived, passing it to history
in an act, he often felt, of religious devotion, the secular hereaf-
ter, a gift to posterity at immense cost to himself, who'd draw
for history a portrait of a mind not uncommon to his time or
place except insofar as it knew itself wholly and described itself willingly, offering itself generously, entirely, and com-
pletely for study not less valuable than the study of the liver or
the lungs, withholding from his Journal no significant sensation, dressing in clean clothes and passing through the suite
again, smelling of toothpaste and soap: except, of course, any
significant sensation he might ever have experienced regarding
Miss Sanantone.

As he had never touched her flesh, so had he kept her at a
distance in his work. Between him and her no conflict must
arise. He feared to divert her, or cause her to falter. With every

115

human being he sought engagement, but not with her, denying her as much as possible to his mind, as he denied her to the pages of his Journal. Benstock said that history would search her out—poor Benstock, he couldn't keep his eyes off the girl. All right, let history run her down if it could. He'd fool history there, let a legend thrive. "I had a splendid shower," he said.

"Very good," she said.

He carried the empty footlockers from the outer room of his suite to the inner room, where he stood them upon end. They'd been around. Heavy in appearance, they were light in fact, manufactured of fireproof gypsum, like the vault he kept in the apartment he shared with his mistress. He had been told by the man he bought the footlockers from that they had been used by a popular evangelist to carry his money about, whose faith in God exceeded his faith in banks.

Upon his desk lay a memorandum from Miss Sanantone— duplicate of a memoradum to herself—*Turtleman pulled pp. 161-166*—joined beneath a paper clip to the designated pages; and a letter from his mistress, too, upon orange paper recommended by her astrologer, whose name Miss Sanantone had never known but hoped to know soon; to whom Miss Sanantone occasionally alluded, when the necessity arose, as "your friend," whose undated letters Miss Sanantone dated according to the day of their receipt, and "numbered in," as they said between themselves, and assigned to the Index to the Text—for want of a more regular name—beneath the entry *Madame*.

Now Hawkes knew who Madame was. He had seen her. Then why didn't he tell her when he knew she was dying to know? He had not written to her since her coming west, running around having a good time all by himself with someone else. When he kissed her at the airport he was really thinking about somebody else, standing there faking grieving. He could make tears come to his eyes, and when the tears came she'd do anything he wanted her to, and she'd sent him the box number now, but never a word back from him through his crocodile tears, louse, rat, scum of the earth, bum, bastard, snake in the grass, he was indispensable to her happiness. It was better to have Hawkes part of the time than none at all. If he hadn't written to her it was only because he thought it bad policy to put anything to paper, the less he was known the better things went, no names, no photographs. He had promised her a photograph for years, but he had never delivered. *Pull Hawkes,* she thought, *pull Hawkes too, pull him out of there forever.* He hadn't liked the look of himself on the page, his bad teeth and battered face. *A detective of some sort!* He hadn't liked that at all. He *was* a detective. Watch him track Madame down now and see if he's a detective or not. He'd smashed the page in his hand, and would have destroyed it altogether if she hadn't made him stop. He'd been a sidewalk photographer once himself. Of course he'd been a lot of things. He'd been a taxicab driver under another name. His wallet was full of photographs of people he was on the lookout for: now and then he'd nab one and win the bounty and go about for a week feeling good.

When Dr. Westrum read a letter from his mistress he swiveled away, turning his face from her. It was a habit he had. If the letter was particularly dirty the backs of his ears would redden, and she wished she could write such letters as his mistress wrote, she'd give Hawkes a jolt. She had once struck off a few lines of Madame's writing, and she carried them in her purse. One day she'd send them off to Hawkes as her own, he'd sit up and take notice, he'd hurry up and bring her home. Now Dr. Westrum swiveled away, turning his face from her, reading again the letter from his mistress. It had arrived yesterday special-delivery.

> Dear Friend,
> I do not know how urgent I should feel, nor whether to trouble you with it. But I know that you would rather share it with me than leave me to suffer alone. Even so, I put off writing you, waiting to see if things improved. Instead, things worsened, in the form of a telephone call telling me I must bring you back alive. "Bring Westrum back alive."

117

Last week, after your call, I went for your letter at the
post office. As I took it from the box a voice behind me
said, "So you are Madame." Like an idiot I turned
around. A man stood in my path. "Madame," he said,
"bring him back alive," the message I received on the
phone today, in the same voice, I am sure, amended only
by his using your name today, as he had not done at the
post office. I had no time to say anything to him. He hung
up. At the post office I said, "Excuse me, you're standing
in my way," and he politely stepped aside.

Should I have told you this? Does it matter? He was a
friendly man, but his tone was definitely ominous, and I
am above all frightened to think that he possesses a bit
of information we always thought nobody on earth possessed but us. To hear your name delivered by a stranger
is a shock to my system. Does he want money? Then why
doesn't he ask for it like a gentleman? If it's only malice,
in the hope of destroying one of the main pleasures of
my life, he has almost succeeded, but not quite, for one
of the pleasures of my life is to write you answers to your
letters, perhaps in the hope my letters to you will affect
you as yours affect me. I took your letter to the bath with
me in the hope it would inspire me to masturbate, with
positive and beneficial results to my soul.

Tikvah didn't send you into exile. You sent yourself. Of
course I am putting every pressure upon Tikvah all the
same, and our mutual friend has begun to do everything
within his power. I cannot bear the thought that the
Center will give you a "Seat" for seven years. I am sure
they do not know the trouble you will cause as soon as
you begin to sit, for you will go on and on cultivating obsessions, hoping people will therefore mistake you for a
Jew. Dear man, there's not a chance in the world of that
happening. It's not that Tikvah is jealous of you, or en-
vies your moral purity, or is a goy-hater, or resents your
having married his sister. It is only that you are so far

118

away. I have asked Winifred several times to invite us to dinner together so that I might meet you. They speak frequently of you—you are their most famous friend. "Yes," she says, "but Wes is always away. The last time we invited him he called at the last minute to beg out, though we had gathered a crowd, and the time before that he didn't even call at all. We don't know if we'll ever invite him again."

You are foolish to make life so hard for old friends who love you so much, and would love you more if only you gave them the chance. If you were to express to Tikvah only a few words of love he would melt, but you keep silent while adding distance besides, and when you keep going away from people they cannot help but see a meaning in it. They want you. It is their achievement that they had you once.

My husband is home from his tour and has brought with him a staff of Spaniards for home and office. They laugh at my Spanish, but I understand it well enough to eavesdrop on their romantic secrets. One of them boasts behind kitchen doors that he will seduce me. He is Pisces with Sagittarius rising. My husband knows a few words of Spanish and imagines he's conversing in it.

Do not befriend high-school principals. They are notorious germ-carriers.

I see by the papers that the Willard Hotel is "closing its doors." It was "a favorite spot for many Presidents up to recent years." It lost its "competitive position." Who can forget the Willard Hotel with its 450 rooms? If we did not patronize all 450 rooms it was nevertheless none of our fault that the hotel lost its competitive position. We could not do it all. I think of all the distinguished Senators from their great states, and I often wonder—without the deep curiosity to find out—if their screwing is as platitudinous as their speeches from the Floor or the thoughts of their heads. Can a United States Senator, al-

119

ways prepared to advocate bloody war, always by instinct defender of private avarice, finally actually share himself with someone? The food was very good, and you always checked to make sure your uncle hadn't been taken down from the wall—all those Presidents and members of Congress watching us from the walls as we dined, all goys there but me.

"Number it in," said Westrum to Miss Sanantone, swiveling to his desk. She took the letter from him and dated it and numbered its pages and entered it beneath *Madame* in the Index to the Text, all in five puffs of her cigarette, shaking her slippers from her feet and preparing to leave.

Quickly, in his shorthand, in absorption, his mind spilling, Westrum wrote of his visit to Benstock at the Infirmary, Benstock's allusions to experiments upon human beings, Philip arriving with his bruised face, how Philip kissed his father, how Westrum had felt Terence's eyes upon him, connecting the kiss with himself and his own father, as he felt Miss Sanantone's eyes upon him now, for whom the days were indistinguishable and the nights too long: therefore she worked on Sunday.

Where was the urgency? He knew less than he had known yesterday, when the letter arrived, his perplexity increased, and with the expansion of possibility he saw the letter as a lie —she lied, she was lying, her foremost talent, after all, was her skill at fabrication: their very confidence in one another rested upon their mutual confidence in their mutual capacity for clever and dexterous invention.

She had made it up. The man at the post office was fiction. Invented once, he was easily reinvented: the man at the post office took to the telephone. Bring him back alive. Who wanted him back? It was *she*, after all, who wanted him back, *she* who lamented his distance, *she* who valued his fame, *she* who'd melt for a few words of love, *she* who kept seeing a meaning to his going, *she* who invented a hot imported Latin and threw him in, too, with all the rest of the fiction. Why now news of the Willard Hotel, word of whose closing he'd seen in the papers months ago? How many months to carry the news these days from D.C. to New York?

"Good night," said Miss Sanantone, "I'll see you tomorrow."

"Many thanks," said Westrum. "You really mustn't work on Sunday any more."

"When will I move to New Hamburg?" she asked.

"We'll take care of it all when Benstock is well," he said.

"When will Dr. Benstock be well?" she asked.

"Never, really," said Westrum.

"Thank you," she said. "Good night. I'll see you tomorrow," closing the door behind her upon Dr. Westrum back at his shorthand now—how Sally scolded Philip for his feet upon the bed (for his supposed rudeness to Westrum, actually), and Benstock's account of his father, the butcher. Yes, these Jewish boys and girls, they were raised in the backs of shops, Benstock in a butcher's shop, Sally in a tobacconist's shop, gathering there to talk up their innermost minds. Their capitalist fathers gave them the backs of shops to talk up socialism in. Their very church gave them rooms to talk up atheism in. He envied them, even as Terence envied Philip. *I had none of their advantages, growing alone, isolated, reading smuggled books in my father's attic.* He'd been himself (smiling at the language of it) a deprived child owning nothing but the perfect credentials of face, name, skin, church, heritage. Who among the sons of shopkeepers had an uncle in Congress? He should have flung himself upon Benstock and by a single kiss eased his pain, kissed everyone, touched everyone, kissed Terence and been kissed by Terence. Instead, he waited with Gretchen for Sally and Philip, and he went then in the most methodical manner to his running (entering here, for all history to know, as he'd already entered it for quick reference upon the chart upon the wall, today's running time), recalling now how, when Terence shot him from the window of the wagon, when Beatrice waved, he'd not acknowledged them with his mind but with his body which suddenly, senselessly, purposelessly spurted, sprinted—foolishly broke his calculated pace—as if to overtake them and throw himself aboard and kiss them and embrace them and lavish them with the heat of his body; but restrained himself and ran well instead, conquering the upgrades, showered and shaved and brushed his teeth, never felt better, never more reconciled to the bloody world, no man more fortunate, footlockers empty, Journal on shelves, all passions idling, this much of this day re-created, brought up to this hour in his shorthand.

Shifting his position slightly, he reached for the Turtleman pages Miss Sanantone had pulled, removing with his thumbnail the paper clip joining Miss Sanantone's memorandum to the pages he had some days ago required, but he could not now remember why he required them, although if he'd more or less read along a little in them, he supposed, he might remember, suffering himself to read his tender style: his striving for elegance had produced only pomposity. The very young man, in those old days, had begun to see life with his own eyes, but his language was still the language of the commonplace press, for he knew no other, nor any society beyond Brest, only the solitude of his father's attic, pen, paper, ink, where he perfected a bastard shorthand mixed of two approved methods and a third which was his own, as the speedy means to write up everything that happened, and thereby view himself "in the mirror of life."

> Experience is truly amazing. Trite. In the afternoon I had another experience at seeing myself in the mirror of life, this time through the good offices of Turtleman, a fellow I haven't mentioned before, having no occasion to. We were once the central figures in a schoolyard brawl. It's a haunting experience to find out how you look to someone else, especially someone you never thought about, and whom you never suspected thought about you. It was more than a little shocking to hear his opinion of me, to wit that I have Nazi sympathies, and I defended myself ably and

vigorously in true pacifistic style. I may have changed his mind about some of the things he said.

This time it was at the depot. I walked from the house to the depot, Mr. Otterbein having called to say the box arrived, which I must now go back for tomorrow, because the distraction of my conversation with Turtleman caused me to forget what I had gone for—not what I had gone for, but to forget that I had gone for anything at all. I am becoming like the proverbial "absentminded professor."

The depot was so crowded you could hardly move. I saw various families or individual members of families there, some fellows in uniform, some just going, and I received the usual hostile stares with equanimity. The up train was late. The two of them finally arrived at the same time. Among the various families I noted there, all or in part, were the Shueys, the Fultzes, the Kerkhoffs, the Mussers, the Pedigos, the Norfleets, the Shoafs, the Kittles, and others, everyone coming or going, somewhere, or just gaping and milling. Delbert Enyart is missing and presumed dead.

I noted a soldier sitting on a bench reading a book, and I sidled close to him, more to see the book he was reading than anything else. It was *Berlin Diary* by William Shirer. Of more importance, the reader was Turtleman, as I discovered when he looked up at me. I recognized him instantly in spite of not having seen him in more than a year, and he certainly recognized me, too, in no uncertain terms, and with a vitriolic venom which caught me off balance and chilled my blood, staring at me for several seconds with blazing hatred, and then returning to his book and reading, or pretending to read, without answering my cordial greeting to him. I greeted him a second time, and he looked up at me again and said in a trembling voice, "Westrum, I don't have any business with you."

He looked wild and frightened, leaning sideways and looking up at me, as you do when you're sitting and some-

123

one stops to talk with you. Rather than hover over him I sat down on the bench. He was sweating. His whole forehead was a sheet of sweat, really just absolutely shining with sweat, and several times he took off his cap to get at his forehead, taking off his cap with one hand and his eyeglasses with the other hand and wiping his face with his coat sleeve, and then he'd sort of sit his cap back on his head and his eyeglasses back on his nose, and then he'd adjust the cap, which was too tight because he needed a haircut. He wasn't the natty soldier of song and story. His coat was all bunched up on his chest, and various things were sticking out of his pockets. He continued to sweat in an uncontrollable manner.

"I am at a loss to understand your statement," I exclaimed. "You wouldn't," he replied. He picked up his duffel bag and began to walk down the platform toward Mulberry Street, and I pursued him, insisting upon some sort of explanation of his inexplicable behavior. He turned to me sharply. "Get the hell away from me, you—" No doubt he had some oath in mind, but he did not go through with it. "Some serious misunderstanding exists," I asserted. "Let's bring it to a head."

"No business with you," was his response, over and over, "I have no business with you. It's over. It's past. I'm going away."

"You'll be back," I reminded him.

"Never."

"Don't say that."

"I'll say what I f——— please. If I ever get out of this f——— war alive this town is the last place I'll ever come back to anyhow."

"I am going away myself," I offered in agreement.

"You drove me out," he charged.

"I WHAT?"

"You drove me out," he repeated.

"You had better explain that statement," I requested.

"Your father drove us out," he clarified.

"I am not my father."

"He drove all the Jews out one way or another."

"I am still not my father," I reiterated.

"You're a f——— Nazi, you f——— Nazi bastard."

At these harsh words I could not conceal my consternation. I can't get down on paper how I felt. I cannot exactly remember what I even said in reply, but of one thing I am certain. That is, that my pacifistic demeanor, the nonresistant tone of my voice, my relaxed, composed posture, and my ever-present effort to smile produced upon Turtleman's being a sudden and dramatic effect, for with his final harsh oath all his hatred toward me was suddenly spent. He now recognized that he had been in error, since, if I WERE the things he accused me of being I would have retaliated with oaths or shouts of anger of my own; whereas, not having responded in that way, I was therefore not the man he thought I was; I was therefore someone else. This forced him to a reexamination of his position.

"I do not believe that anyone hates Nazism more than I," I stated.

"You ARE Westrum?" he meekly inquired. "Your father is who I think he is?"

"Yes, but I—''

"But you are not your father. I understand. I apologize for the things I said." He was truly mortified at having sworn those oaths at me, but what the tongue issues nought can recall, and I believe he learned a lesson he will never forget. The sins of the fathers shall not be visited upon the sons.

"No apology is necessary. I am glad we met, and I am glad we were able to bring this matter to a head after all. I hope you have good luck in the war, although I'm sorry to see that you have chosen resort to arms."

"We must defeat Hitler," he indicated.

125

I began to offer him my short course in philosophy, which was going to have to be very short since the trains were announced. "Hitler is not a cause of the sickness of society," I argued, "but a symptom. The more we rely upon resort to arms the more will we come to depend upon arms. Our enemy is not Hitler but war."

"Oh, sure," he countered. "But we must defeat Hitler before we can attack the symptoms. Either you're against him or you're for him."

"That is a two-valued orientation," I pointed out.

"I am a Jew," he proudly informed me.

"I am a pacifist," I replied with equal pride.

"If only we had time to discuss this fully—" he began.

"Above all we are human beings and brothers," I declared.

"I can't afford to be a pacifist," he argued.

"You can't afford not to be," I countered.

We could hardly hear ourselves talk above the roar of the incoming trains. The up train was late and the two of them pulled in at the same time. Turtleman consulted his watch, and he looked all around him, as if he were looking for a way to escape the trains, escape returning to the inferno of war. "I wish I could stay and talk with you," he said above the din, thrusting out his hand. We firmly shook. Then he took me by the shoulders and embraced me, which was rather embarrassing, speaking in the loudest possible voice up into my ear. "Listen, it's the most awful thing. The things I said to you were awful and you must forget them. But what's more awful is these awful thoughts I've had of you for more than a year, because of your father. All this time we could have been very good friends if only I didn't have these terrible ideas of you. You should have identified yourself to me. All these years we lived in the same lousy town and never identified ourselves. I will write you a letter," he concluded, starting to board the train.

126

"Keep a Journal of your experiences," I advised him. "I've begun a Journal. I've got over a hundred pages."

"Terrific," he called . . .

stepping into the railroad car, departing from Westrum's sight then and forever. Whether he survived the war Westrum never heard, and he wondered now how to find out. What happened to Turtleman, was he living or dead, last seen boarding the train at the depot at Brest with a duffel bag and a copy of *Berlin Diary* on the seven-thousand-nine-hundred-and-forty-first day of Westrum's life—more than ten thousand days ago, more than half Westrum's lifetime ago—soon dead perhaps, or alive and well, or somewhere between in one of those military hospitals concealed from view to spare the public morbid sights? Perhaps Turtleman was the American soldier in the quartermaster truck who took Sally Benstock from the hand of the tall blond man on the street in Eisenstadt and lifted her to the seat beside him, and kissed her and said to her in poor Yiddish, "Big girls don't cry," although she was at the point of tears when he saw her last this afternoon in the physicians' consulting room, Philip bruised, Gretchen frightened, and her husband flattened by exhaustion. Benstock was a type, thought Westrum, he'd seen them topple, these chunky fellows with their passion for justice.

Then I must identify myself to them, he wrote, *go to them as I went to Beatrice. Cross over. Become. Cease to withhold. Give, give.* As he went to his mistress, he thought. *Subtlety's no match for fear*, he wrote, *give good friends the chance to love you, thaw out Ice Water Westrum*, but upon paper, rather to see what it looked like than to act upon it.

Telephone Benstock. Tell him that since you saw him this afternoon you have been praying for his recovery, not that you wrote up your visit for your Journal, not that you ran two miles in thirteen-thirty (though it is true you did), not that your girl complains of long nights and dull days or requires driving lessons. Don't parade your wonderful health to him. On the contrary, let him see your suffering, too; it may ease his; it may perk him up right away. Shoot him full of the serum of love, nothing's more bracing. Oh, how you sat with such good posture looking healthy and moral, arguing against Philip's pleasure at football as if *you* knew any more than anybody else where the roots of fascism lie. You were too cool. You were too distracted. You were thinking of your mistress walking on a bed, you were imagining yourself going down on Harriet, you were thinking of outsmarting the two uphill grades between there and here. You plainly showed you were there out of duty only, and you introduced the question of Tikvah because of course it wasn't enough to have one Jew flat on his back, you needed two. You delivered neat analyses of hatred, but it wasn't the time for it: not a maxim, but love, dissolves hatred, you're driving him to exhaustion, nothing's so restful as love, you drove Tikvah to exhaustion, too, with tricks and distractions, testing at every turn his devotion to justice—that is to say, his devotion to *you*—and you're doing it still by mail.

He would telephone Benstock. He rose to do so. But thinking of Benstock and Tikvah produced a thought he believed he should write before he lost it, and he wrote in his shorthand: *But I thought that the appearance of perfect moral posture was all I had. It was what I had instead of Jewishness. It was my price of admission. I didn't know I had other virtues, and when I found out it was too late to break my habits.* The Jews needed all the decent friends they could get in a world which, despising itself for its crimes against itself, despised the Jews as an alternative to self-contempt, with results very clear and recent, having blown the hair from Tikvah's head in the war against fascism, and burned the numbers in Gretchen's arm (*Sally's* arm, he meant to think). Therefore this very instant he would telephone Benstock at the Infirmary. But as he touched the telephone it rang itself, and Beatrice said, "Are you ready?"

"Ah, my prompt Jewish wife," said Westrum. "I was never readier."

Some misunderstanding had occurred. The Westrums arrived at the Weinbergs under the impression they were arriving for dinner, and afterward film, only to discover that dinner had never been intended, just cake and coffee, and that later.

Of course, with Harvey, it was wise to count upon misunderstanding. The telephone was not his medium, it induced mumbling and forgetfulness. Sometimes, even as he dialed, he forgot whom he was calling. Thus, although he had intended to invite the Westrums, he hadn't meant to invite Bill and Betty Brown at all, who were doomed now to see his film of Africa for the second time. He had muffed the message to Kenneth Silvers, who would therefore be late, but done quite well with an old gentleman named Weiner, notable for his work in chemical equilibria. Harvey came to the door for the Westrums, rushing back then to the living room where he was mildly humiliated at the failure of his Bolex 18-5 Super. His eye was draining badly this evening, and he wore dark glasses. "I can't thread it," he said. "It won't thread." However, when Terence pressed a switch the machine brilliantly threaded itself, and Bill and Betty Brown applauded. Brown's work was in infrared energy, by means of which, with computers and satellites, he was upon the point of offering the world an accurate means of measuring crop production. He said that he and Westrum had met once at an Inquiry meeting in London—he didn't expect Westrum to remember. Westrum did not remember, but he said he did, and Brown appeared pleased.

Terence sat for comfort upon the windowseat. From time to time he moaned low in his throat, a sound familiar to Beatrice and Westrum who, when they first heard it years ago, thought Terence was imitating the cat. It indicated hunger, or pain (as when his back was broken), or, as in the present moment, acute mental distress, misery of the mind induced by Harvey's film.

129

Of course the work was bad. The film jittered, fluttered. The sequences were perfectly chronological, lacking all organization, all transition, leaping senselessly from badly focused objects to others ill-lit, a saga beginning at the Weinbergs' front door on the morning of their departure for Africa (one saw their cabdriver stowing their bags in the trunk of his car), showing the wing of their airplane as they took flight, certain portions of the anatomy of an unidentified fellow-traveler, Harriet emerging from the lavatory, and suddenly a lion. Film was not his medium, either.

"We'd been rather planning on dinner," said Westrum frankly to Harriet in a low voice in the low light.

"Yes, I'm sorry about that," she said. "He didn't communicate."

"We'll picket him," said Westrum, but perhaps she did not hear. Certainly she did not smile. Perhaps jokes about picketing weren't funny. He could feel her intense awareness of his being near. To any motion of his she responded with a motion of her own. When he crossed his legs she touched her chin, and when he uncrossed his legs she stiffened and sat ever more erect, her gaze forward upon the screen, but her thought essentially upon him. At his slightest motion she leaned toward him, as if in expectation of a message. She wore her hair in a single braid falling to her left shoulder, once more for him, as she had worn it to dinner at the Benstocks', and he knew the message she expected, and the reply she was prepared to give. In love she'd be enormously serious, it all mattered very much, everything was critical. So had his mistress begun, too. He'd be, therefore, as serious or as casual as the lady liked, they'd work it out. But he observed with optimism her close attentiveness to the sight of her own body upon the screen (at a campsite somewhere in Africa), she was pleasing to herself, nor too shy. The spirit of reform he had so strongly felt while writing in his Journal had vanished in an hour. He blamed it upon the bitterness of hunger. "Octar the Hun betrayed his army at the smell of broiling pig," he said.

"Try to hold out," she said. "It won't be long."

There she was in Africa, and here she was beside him, viewing this film for the tenth time, and even so with pleasure at the sight of herself. How had it served her to marry Harvey? They had one child, a son, Reuben. He joined the company now, filling the room with a moment's light from the kitchen, carrying his sterling-silver flute and saying, as he came, "I always show up for my favorite scene." He was a slight boy not likely to grow—a light-boned boy with small hands, small feet, with wide eyes and sailing ears, brisk in his movements and extremely fond of Terence. Their birthdays occurred upon the same day, they rode everywhere together in white helmets upon Reuben's Honda 300, and they shared an earnest distaste for Philip Benstock. He sat beside Terence on the windowseat, and he sympathized with Terence's mental distress, the disembodied pain of the craftsman.

"It's not supposed to be *good*," Reuben said.

"It's a nice projector," Terence said.

"Don't look if you don't want to," Reuben said.

"I'm fascinated," said Terence, still sarcastic.

Westrum was fascinated, too, by the peculiar narration of Harvey Weinberg, whose fate it was to be most amusing when he least intended it, and least amusing when he most thought he was. When he became irretrievably entangled in irrelevance he was brought back to the company by Reuben's toots upon the flute, sufficiently varied to be newly amusing each time. Nothing happened to Harvey in Africa that didn't happen to him every day at home, his belt flapped, his shirttails flew, his good humor prevailed. "This is exotic Khartoum," he announced, and so it must have been if Harvey said so, but his film showed only a city street which might almost have been New Hamburg. "Notice the women bearing burdens upon their heads," he said, noticing the inescapable, zooming in upon the obvious. It was nothing anyone could possibly have missed unless, like Westrum, one had closed one's eyes for a moment to arrange his thoughts. He had never touched

Harriet, except to shake her hand. Here in the dark, if he liked, he could touch the back of her neck. "Notice the bare-breasted women," said Harvey, whereupon Westrum slightly opened his eyes to bare-breasted women washing clothes at a stream. Had Turtleman ever written the letter he promised? No, for it would have been entered in the Journal. Every letter was entered. Benstock's letter on Roman roads was entered. No, that was the end of him, off on the up train to oblivion. Surely he could learn where the family had gone, they'd owned the smoke shop on the Square before the Jews were driven from Brest, someone must know where old smoke-shop families go. "By the way, is your son living or dead? He's owed me a letter for thirty years." In those days it was difficult if not impossible to argue the merits of the war with Jews no matter how much history they knew or you knew, no matter how deeply your instincts told you the implications of the war as they would be seen by history. It was very personal. *All Jews here but me and the Bill Browns,* thought Westrum, *and half of Terence.* His stomach growled with hunger. "Did you say something?" Harriet asked in a whisper in the dark.

"I could eat a lion," he said.

"I'll get you something," she said, but he restrained her, holding her by the hand. "I'm so angry at myself for disappointing you," she said.

"I'll eat a lady finger," he said, drawing her hand to his mouth and kissing her finger. With her whole body she gave him her finger. He'd nibble her fingers, he thought, and the back of her neck and her swinging braid, she'd tell him of her experiences among the Indians, they'd picket the football games carrying their signs side by side and hip to hip. Would she judge Terence's essay winner of the Father Contest? Would she give him the prize? Would she dare? Would she dare not? Luckily, since Terence's excellence lay elsewhere than in his writing, the issue of collusion was remote, and yet suppose—just suppose—a boy's receiving a public prize from his father's mistress, rather a tangle, that, and rather mournful, too, for the boy to read years hence in his father's Journal that he'd won by collusion the prize he'd always thought he'd won by skill.

"Now watch this," cried Reuben Weinberg, "my favorite scene."

The film had suddenly become steady. Apparently the camera was now held not by Harvey Weinberg with his fluttering hands but by Reuben, whose hands were steady. Harvey and Harriet stood beside a stream. Harvey had captured a small bird he had long sought, and he was speaking softly to the bird to ease its fright when the earth gave way, and Harriet stepped to safety, and the bird flew off, and Harvey slid down the bank, falling and tumbling to the water, and Reuben ran, camera still shooting, to help his father. Seeing, however, that his father required no help the boy wisely continued to shoot instead, and Harvey climbed dripping up the bank of the stream, his face absent of any expression either of alarm or chagrin, a man who had fallen into the water more than once before, under whose feet the earth was bound to crumble wherever he was. It was only an insult of accidental nature and therefore acceptable, unavoidable, inevitable, as fixed as fear in a bird. The face of Harvey Weinberg placed no blame upon any man, smiling into the camera and into Westrum's eyes, too, as the boy Turtleman had smiled into Westrum's eyes, too, once upon the schoolyard, having fallen like that, or perhaps having been struck to the ground, not for offense but by the accidental nature which was the nature of boys who knew no better, and someone called, "Attaboy, Wes, give it to the Jew." It was nothing extraordinary. Yet if it were nothing extraordinary why had a certain controversy ensued? It had, yes, yes, everyone was in upon it, the teacher came running, the principal came running, and in the hours which followed Westrum's father came running from the house and Turtleman's father came running from the smoke shop. Westrum was commanded to apologize. If only he would apologize all would be forgiven, apologize once to Turtleman for the blow itself and once to the class itself for having

set a bad example—a boy so tall as Westrum was expected to
set a moral example as tall as himself—but he refused upon
every count to apologize to anyone for a crime he refused to
admit.

A meeting was called, of men, not boys, and his father
praised him, not for his refusal to confess but for his having
struck Turtleman to begin with, old Indian fighters struck
without apology, and anyhow (his father said) a knuckle in
the eye was good enough for a Jew, and an oath against a Jew
nothing improper, and Westrum stood before the table of men
unable to make them see how his view was different from his
father's, not that he wouldn't apologize but that he hadn't done
it in the first place, and in the end, to settle the matter, the
principal was dismissed, for Westrum's father thought it well,
as he often said, to keep principals upon their toes.

"Do it again," said Bill Brown.

"Harvey," called Westrum, to nobody's surprise more than
Harvey's own, "those are the most wonderful pictures I've ever
seen."

Terence moaned, pushing off angrily from the window seat,
taking up a can of his own film, shaking it open, threading the
film swiftly, and throwing upon the screen the title *The Westrums Come West in Seven Minutes by Wagon and Water*, in
which his mother and his father flew into swimming pools at
motels between New York and the Center, and finally into the
swimming pool behind the house they presently occupied,
where his mother, without haste, as if to say "We have
arrived," removed her bright-green bathing cap, and the Westrums' Dalmatian was reading the sign posted upon the pumphouse WE DON'T SWIM IN YOUR TOILET, PLEASE DON'T PEE IN
OUR POOL—laughter in the living room and a snicker from Reuben upon his flute. Now Terence's mother and father advanced
through the night beneath the flag hanging drenched and limp
upon the staff, and now, too, but by day, not by night, the delegation of three men approached by the same path, Benstock,
Harvey, and Kenneth Silvers upon two teak canes. In the door-

way they shook hands with Westrum. "That's no good," said Terence in apology, "it's lousy when you get one tall man in a picture," and the men were seated now, and the canes were crossed at Kenneth Silvers's feet. And there stood the Center in the distance, and soon, in particular, the History Wing. The eye of the camera wound underground, photographing the machine photographing his father's license plate, and caught with their lids up two footlockers filled with his father's Journal.

"Tell me when it's over," Beatrice said to Terence. She never watched herself upon film, never willingly posed for a photograph, never willingly spoke into a tape recorder, kept no Journal nor read her husband's, wrote no letters, closing her eyes, bowing her head.

"Thanks a whole hell of a lot for your interest," Terence said, whose art was his vision of detail, his genius for preserving essences—not so much the dog and the cat but their blackness and their whiteness, Miss Sanantone's legs upon a walkway of the Center, her slippers beneath her desk, Reuben Weinberg's lips upon his flute. He'd shoot a hundred feet of film for fifteen telling seconds—Philip Benstock's toothbrush upright in his pocket, and Philip's mother who, at the sight of the camera, concealed her tattooed forearm, Coach Wilson stalking the sidelines, cursing, swearing, enraged, spitting with disappointment although the scoreboard showed triumph.

Harriet sighed now to see herself in the schoolhouse doorway. "I didn't realize you could see me," she said, and sighed again to see herself upon the picket line. Terence had shot her from the roof of the grandstand, first picket line, then ball field, now Harriet with set face, now Philip with set face, now Harriet's passionate will in her face, now Philip's passionate will in his own. They were short studies, one might say, in conflicting determination, except that they were more in likeness than in difference when seen against Westrum's face, who appeared not even to be participant, but only observer, holding a sign, FOOTBALL = FASCISM, but who might have been holding it only as a favor to someone expected shortly who would come and take it from him and carry it high with a passion equal to Harriet's or Philip's, or who might have been a mercenary picket, one of those men professionally on strike every working day. He appeared amused, detached, aloof, disengaged—and then he vanished, replaced by Terence himself walking also with detachment, aloof, into the eye of his own free-standing camera behind the floating title *Now I Shall Turn on the Lights*, which he did, to the applause of everyone but his father who, alarmed by the absence of conviction his face had revealed, appeared for a moment stunned by the sudden light.

"Actually," said Terence, "it smelled."

"Not at all," his father said. "It was superb."

"You forgot to clap," said Terence.

"Let's have dessert," said Westrum. "Then we'll go somewhere for dinner."

"But *his*," said Terence, standing apart with his father, "really *stank*."

"I was only trying to be polite," said Westrum.

"You overdid it," Terence said. His hatred for Harvey's bad work was relentless. "You have to go to *do* it to shoot the wrong speed in the wrong light. He's a goddam moron."

"No," said Westrum, "his hands tremble. Watch out, your own hands might tremble someday."

"One of those monkeys in a tree could have done better," said Terence, "it's a crime against the equipment," capping the can, drifting away from his father now to make room for the principal. He wished he'd not be invited places where the principal was. He'd not kiss up to anybody. Why hadn't his father applauded? He had no objection to dessert before dinner—he ate cake with both hands. His mother hadn't even watched. She wasn't eating cake, either. She had not moved from her chair, and he sat beside his mother to complain of his father's not applauding, not reacting to the film.

"Maybe he was too moved," his mother said.

"There was nothing moving in it," Terence said.

"It was a moving picture," Beatrice said.

"He was only trying to be polite to Mr. Weinberg," Terence said, "that's all it was," taking a cheerful view of it suddenly: *my father is a polite man*, he thought, it was a point he'd make in his essay, the whole goddam educational establishment was nuts for politeness.

"I know that's all it was," his mother said.

But it was not Harvey Weinberg whom Westrum hailed with praise out of the darkness. It was Turtleman. Owing Turtleman, he repaid Harvey. Turtleman gone, here was Harvey now. Westrum the boy gone, here was Westrum the man now. Had they made their peace in that last moment beneath the thunder of the trains, or did Turtleman carry with him down the years the memory of Westrum as the son of his father, who drove the smoke shop out? Perhaps he had died in the war. Then if he had died in the war who lifted Sally Benstock to the seat of the truck? No, if Turtleman were dead the memory nevertheless remained, and Westrum existed in other minds as the ultimate Gentile. Every Jew had his Gentile, and Westrum existed therefore in other minds, if not beneath his own name then as surrogate Gentile guilty of crimes and offenses committed by persons who merely looked like him. Every Jew retained one outstanding memory of nature's insult, and Westrum was, God knows, in Terence's film or any other, Gentile incarnate, his face his doom, his name his doom, his twang his doom, standing eating strawberry shortcake beside Harriet Weinberg, he was famished, inquiring of Beatrice across the room, by holding up his cup, whether she wished coffee. She declined. She was comforting Terence, and Harvey was telling Terence, too, how superior his film was—and ah! poor Terence, there he was, forced to the civilized moment, telling Harvey that Harvey's film, too, was fine.

"Say when," said Westrum to Harriet, pouring cream into her coffee.

But she was speechless. *Whenever you say*, she thought. Her cup clattered upon her saucer. But her trembling was not her condition, it was the moment only, this man was most admira-

137

ble to have sung out his praise for Harvey, as he was most admirable to have joined her at the picketing. He had courage, he had sympathies, he was stalwart, he was whole, he was handsome, his hands were steady, the world needed Westrums. "You have a good way with Terence," she said.

"He's angry at me at the moment," Westrum said. "I didn't praise his film sufficiently."

"We must praise all children all the time," she said.

"Praise everyone all the time," said Westrum.

"There should never be winners and losers," she said.

"I understand," he said.

"Yes," she said. "You do."

"I thank you," he said.

"I seem to be trembling," she said.

"I understand that, too," he said. "Put down your cup until you stop," and with pleasure she did as he suggested, and he fed a strawberry into her mouth, *putting a little something of mine in you*, he thought, *all Jews here but me and half of Terence*, for he saw Bill and Betty Brown letting themselves out the front door, and the door closed, and there followed then the sound of loud rapping upon the door, not of a human hand but too loud and hard for a human hand, and therefore the sound, no doubt, of a hand holding a hard object, a terrible rapping, really, a terrible knocking in the night, *the police* (he ate another strawberry) *coming to collect the Jews*, for everyone had been betrayed by Bill and Betty Brown. Had he assaulted Turtleman upon the schoolyard? Had he called Terence *Jew* when he broke his back? Whom could he trust if not himself? In Terence's movie Westrum looked for conviction upon his face but had not found it. The line had been straight down the years from the schoolyard at Brest to Harvey's living room, some cruelty had been born in him, or early trained, he was his father's son. He knew of no time in his life when he had been free of his own cruelty, and he'd fought it down, perhaps confining its general spreading by focusing it always upon

138

a single person, first Turtleman, always Tikvah, now Benstock, once even Terence for a moment.

Fascism came not in a moment with a knock upon the door, but hour by hour by hour by hour in the gestures of daily life. So he had said in *A History of the Past World*, and been roasted by historians who said, "But that's not history." Fascism was no system of government. The thing that was fascism was the playing out of one's pleasure at another man's expense, and the closing of the mind to the act. Whose pleasure had it been to burn the numbers in Sally's arm? "I'll get the door," he said to Harriet, briskly, swiftly, urgently crossing the room, past Harvey who saw with surprise that Westrum had undertaken to get the door, past the old man Weiner who was about to get it himself and who saw upon Westrum's face the most violent conviction—these young men so determined about *everything*. "Pigs," said Westrum's lips, "you must collect me, too, with the Jews," flinging open the door, revealing Kenneth Silvers there bent upon one teak cane, the other cane upraised to rap again, perplexed by the ferocity of Westrum's face, and puzzled by the sight of so much strawberry shortcake so soon, for he had come to dinner.

5

Madame, he wrote, replying at last to his mistress's letter, *you're suspiciously late with news of the closing of the good old Willard Hotel,* borrowing one cigarette from Miss Sanantone to smoke before Benstock dropped by.

Miss Sanantone had already smoked fifteen cigarettes this morning. She had also, in the cleverest manner, for the first time in her years with Dr. Westrum, altered pages of his Journal. Had he known her crime he would have discharged her.

Therefore she applied all craft. Upon paper of the same grade as the surrounding matter, her typewriter ribbon worn to the same degree of faintness, and margins widened imperceptibly to preserve the appearance of body even against the excision of seven paragraphs, she deleted from the sixteen-thousand-four-hundred-and-thirty-fifth day of Dr. Westrum's life all reference to her gentleman friend, Hawkes. The old pages, the former pages (themselves copied new after Hawkes had smashed the original pages between his hands, sitting upon his heels in the Westrums' apartment), she now tore to several pieces and collected beneath a paper clip and dropped into her handbag.

She removed, too, from the Index to the Text, the white card alluding to Hawkes—*friend of Miss Sanantone, at her father's funeral, pp. 44,375-6*—and the card, too, she tore to pieces and placed beneath the paper clip, those paragraphs gone, deleted, ruined, Hawkes dead, disappeared, vanished and erased forever. How could he ever be missed? History would never find Hawkes.

It was as Hawkes wished it. Hawkes knew best, and she'd

141

tell him that she had done it, and he would pinch her cheek and say, "That's the trick." She would write him a letter.

But she had written Hawkes twice in three weeks, once to send him the number of Madame's box, once to tell him of Madame's alarm, and received no reply although she had told Hawkes too how unhappy she was, and how far from everything, how dreary the days and the nights were. He could have sent her at least a postcard. "No time," he'd say, "I'm run ragged making ends meet," but he was run ragged running around, and forgetting his promise to bring her home as he said he would, though she'd kept her end of the bargain, and at a risk, too.

Lately she had it in her mind to write Hawkes a fetching, stimulating letter put together of bits and pieces of letters from Madame to Dr. Westrum, but each time she began she lost her nerve. *Darling,* she would write, *so splendid to hear you say "I'm in your cunt, I'm in you, you," calling my name while coming,* but she had been too shy to copy it out, she'd been brought up too well.

In the very beginning, in her first months of service to Dr. Westrum, she had sometimes been almost unable to transcribe bold passages, frank ruminations, dirty talk, oaths he swore against sacred things, jokes he made at the expense of God or country or any number of revered objects. She was upon the verge of quitting. "Hang in there," said Hawkes, "ride with the times," and she persevered beyond shame and through the heat of her flushing face for the sake of her job. As time went by she discovered herself working less against shame and heat, descending more easily as time went by into excursions into various violations of her former self, out of shock into amazement that Dr. Westrum was actually, on the other hand, a man so proper, so widely respected, and so decently rewarded.

Hadn't she sent him the number of Madame's box? Now she had taken him out of the Journal, too. She'd been prompt with him. When Hawkes asked, she gave. Let him deny it. He knew she was dying to know who Madame was, but he was holding out on her, it seemed. Perhaps he'd like to be put *back* in the Journal. She could do that, too, you know. There was still the carbon copy in New York, you know. She could make a little fuss and ruckus herself one of these days, this little thing or that little thing the police or someone or other would be delighted to hear about, for Hawkes had not always been perfectly businesslike. Why didn't he bring her home, even a postcard would ease her—Dr. Westrum was smoking a cigarette and writing a letter to his mistress. "You know that Dr. Benstock is coming," she said.

"I know," he said. "I thank you." It was his cigarette she had in mind, he'd clear away the evidence before Benstock came, resuming his letter to his mistress.

Madame, you're suspiciously late with news of the closing of the good old Willard Hotel, which makes me question, too, not the urgency but the truth of the friendly but definitely ominous man sneaking up behind you in the post office, shouting my name on the telephone wires. I know you want me back. That's the theme of your little fiction, isn't it? Don't worry, I'll be back, I'll be in your box.

I have heard from Tikvah, too, who tells me that Justice Lerman has taken up my case. I have been wondering whether it is the best possible argument to threaten Tikvah with history. The Judge should try another sort of thing, for Tikvah's conscience lives in the present, not in the future: he'd rather be right than immortal.

Let us consider our past lives. Between Tikvah and me lie thirty years of tension and rivalry, distance and intimacy and swordplay, the advantage being all mine since my arms are longer, my footwork defter, my endurance greater, I am in much better all-around physical athletic condition than he. He tires. Instead of fighting, he picks his teeth with his sword, putting my chivalry to the test, knowing how difficult it is for a knight like me to run him through, since it violates the regulations of the Interstate

143

Knighthood Commission to run a man through when he's picking his teeth. Besides, I love him. Besides that, I am a pacifist and don't even own a late-model sword.

Why then does he keep me here in exile? In a way you are right, it's because I am "so far away," and because he wants me to "express . . . only a few words of love," he would "melt," and so forth. But it's not "love" he wants expressed, it's statement, commitment, an absolutely clear and unambiguous and unartistic positive and categorical assertion and description of my politics.

You see, I am still to many eyes the latent American fascist. I notice that among some associates here. In the particular matter of Tikvah, his mistrust of me goes back to our very beginnings. On the first day we ever met he blurted, "What's in your heart?" Not *my* heart he meant, the Gentile heart. He was sleepless from a night-long bout with *Potentialities for Fascism in America*, which my coming upon the scene stopped forever. Its thesis is that every goy is a Jew-hater somewhere just below the surface, but as long as I appeared to be the exception to his theory he couldn't go on, he had no theory, his theory went bust. He has been waiting for thirty years for me to slip and provide him the evidence to free him at last from his final doubt. If he can manage, after thirty years of taunting and tempting me, to extract one little vile word from me to prove his theory, he will be ratified. The world will prove to be as he says it is. I shall give him no such comfort, nor is it within me to do so even if I had the will. At any rate, there's a line of argument for the Justice to consider. Whisper it into his learned ear.

I am in haste because my friend Benstock is knocking upon my door, who objects, as Tikvah does, to the idea of my holding two jobs at once, occupying two places. I think he is prepared, however, to offer me a situation here to last five lifetimes.

Two jobs are better than one. Don't they pay twice as

much? Isn't twice better than once, if you're up to it? Ask anyone. Wouldn't you rather have two elephants than one? God gave us two arms, two legs, two eyes, two ears, and two of everything else without exception except noses and navels, for we would certainly look very foolish with two navels. Everyone has two names. God made two sexes. Ask any bird if two wings aren't better than one, that's why the bird created himself in the image of the airplane. Did God mean every man to have two mistresses, one at home and one away, as He meant a baseball player to have two uniforms, one for home, one away? My principal needs me and depends upon me. Yet the long search for talent ended with you, nobody frees me from my body but you, so bring me home—but there, my friend raps upon the door, wherefore I remain, as always.

In fact, however, Benstock had not yet arrived, leaving time for Westrum to dispose of the evidence of his cigarette. Nor was Benstock alone when he came. Harvey Weinberg was with him, to keep an eye on things, to advise, rightful member of the Seating Committee, heretofore silent, now newly determined to have a hand in things, after all.

Harvey had none of Benstock's doubts about Westrum. He thought Westrum super—an opinion applauded by his wife. He had never met such an honest man, nor such a gentleman, such a fine father, such an admirable husband (married to a Jewish girl, by the way), their sons were intimate friends riding everywhere upon Reuben's Honda 300: in their white helmets they were almost twins. Westrum's presence at the Center cheered and uplifted Harvey, inspired positive thoughts and fresh confidence, rejuvenated him, dried up his weeping eye. New energy flowed to his body: as soon as feasible he intended to begin running with Westrum several miles a day or more, and he'd swim with him, too, when summer came.

Even this moment he was planning to return to work, to several projects neglected for years, not only to African equatorial

birds but to a theory of molting likely to have shattering reper-
cussions to students of birding the entire length of the Missis-
sippi Valley. In the past he had puttered only. He was prepared to admit that now. But here in Westrum's presence,
among these shelves of relentless industry, he could imagine
life's taking a new turn for himself, he'd reform, he'd finish
things begun, he had power, he had muscle.

Between Harvey and Benstock the question of Westrum had
become a point of dispute. "You're beginning to disgust me,"
Harvey said to Benstock in private arguments extremely de-
pressing to both men, for they had never argued with one another before. "You're not reasonable. Buy his Journal if he
wants. Give him all the Seat he wants, make him king if he
wants because it's a noble work and has a unique viewpoint."

"We all have unique viewpoints," Benstock said.

How did Harvey know the work was noble or unique? In
such matters Harvey depended to some extent upon his wife's
eloquence and insight. It was a noble work, he said, avoiding
as much as possible her exact language, because Westrum had
played a role of significance both in the composition of history
and in the affairs of men. It was the Journal of a man who had
acted upon the public scene without sacrifice of his private vision. Westrum was a rare man, therefore, last of an old breed,
Puritan, Gentile, gentleman, the end of that succession which
had once owned America and seen it slip away, and yet without bitterness, greeting history as it came. "It's *unique*,"
Harvey argued, almost in his wife's very words, "because we
very seldom get a record of the class deposed."

But if Harvey was renewed Benstock was not. He was recov-
ering poorly from his recent exhaustion. He had regained most
of his lost weight, but artificially, too fast, and much of it had
simply formed a dewlap. This morning his mood was good, but
that was the work of a tranquilizing drug. Without the drug his
mood darkened, his mind ran ahead of things, his suspicions as-
sailed him, the poet within him implored him to battle. He ar-

gued with Harvey that something was "fishy," that somehow
the Westrum seen by the Weinbergs wasn't at all the Westrum
seen by the Benstocks. "We mustn't be his leverage here for
something he wants somewhere else," Benstock said, feeling
himself betrayed by the Weinbergs, too, whose sentiments
were entangled in the football controversy, in Reuben, in home
movies and God knew what else, who loved Westrum for the
very reason the lamb loved Mary.

> *"Why does the lamb love Mary so?"*
> *The eager children cry.*
> *"Mary loves the lamb, you know,"*
> *The teacher did reply.*

But he had no evidence, his ulcer rebelled, and he began to
fear that his blackness and suspicion were their own sources,
feeding upon themselves and upon fantasies of his own creation, or upon mistaken identity: he had for a moment mistaken
Westrum's Journal for the blank, white Journal of an old fraud-
ulent man named Hiram Browning, and Sally had mistaken
Westrum for a tall blond Austrian whom Westrum couldn't be.

For the lightening of Benstock's mood a physician at the
Infirmary recommended modest outdoor exercise, and Benstock had begun a program of walking. One day he walked a
mile, and the next day half a mile before discontinuing his program. To gain the benefit of the outdoors, however, he sat
every afternoon in blanket and shawl in the grandstand at the
practice field, watching Philip practice football and watching
Westrum, upon occasion, so regular, with such grace, such for-
titude, and such ease run two miles about the cinder track,
who, by that discipline, said Coach Wilson, would undoubtedly live forever or longer. The coach's admiration for Westrum was boundless.

The coach advised Benstock, too, to take up running as the
means to long life and certain happiness, for the coach could
see, he said, that Benstock lived too much indoors among

paper and books, worried too much, brooded too much, imagined too much, drank and smoked too much. "It's never too late," said Coach Wilson, "to get yourself in shape."

"Long life," replied Benstock, "may not even be desirable," which the coach thought a good joke, for Coach Wilson's will was a boy's will, everything one desired was desirable, winning was all, who pursued the scrimmage up and down the sidelines, crying, "Hit low, hit hard," crying, "Don't listen for the whistle, I tell you, never stop," crying, "Charge, men, charge, kill him, he's not your mother," and crying most often an indistinct message which Benstock at last interpreted as "Don't protect," for the boys—as Coach Wilson explained—had the bad habit of protecting themselves, of fearing injury. The boys often forgot that the best protection was indifference to protection, that the boy most likely to be hurt was the boy who most feared being hurt, some of his men worried too much, thought too much, brooded too much. "My men want to learn to take care of themselves and be men," he said.

In moments of guilty fantasy Benstock in the grandstand had visions of Westrum falling dead upon the cinder track, studying now upon the wall of Westrum's suite Westrum's daily record of his running time. "By now," he said, "I suppose there's a lot of Center in your Journal."

"Well, wherever I am," said Westrum, "that's the life I see."

"Birds nest with close makings," Harvey said.

"That's concisely said," said Westrum, who'd put it in his Journal.

"I've said it before," Harvey confessed.

"Many times," Benstock irritably said.

"It was appropriate, I thought," said Harvey.

"Tell posterity," said Benstock to Westrum, "that the Center is a site of pure industry."

Miss Sanantone brought coffee in paper cups. Her perfection as a waitress was marred, Benstock thought, by the cigarette hanging from her mouth, and he irresistibly formed an image, such was the pleasure of his drug, of Miss Sanantone abed

148

smoking and waiting for him, she'd be casual, who could pour coffee with her cigarette in her mouth and could probably therefore screw with her cigarette in her mouth, too, and poured a fourth cup, too, still without removing her cigarette from her mouth, and carried the cup back to her desk where she began to type up, such was Benstock's illusion, a storm of smoke and steam.

"It may not be a site of pure industry," said Harvey, "but I for one am beginning a new life." His hands shook. He could not manage his cup. He'd let it cool before he tried again.

"A new life," said Westrum, "that's how I feel. This being back close to home starts me up again."

"It's because you were born down the road," said Harvey. He recalled, too, Westrum's saying he'd lie in his family grave. "You *see*," said Harvey to Benstock, for these were points he had raised to quiet Benstock's doubts. "Now you'll be here forever," he said, excited by the prospect of the long future. He foresaw years and years of friendship, Westrum and he running and swimming and working, Terence and Reuben, Beatrice and Harriet.

"You turn him on," said Benstock.

"Isn't that what friends are for?" Westrum asked.

"I imagine I'm a fool," said Benstock.

"Yes, you're a fool," Harvey said.

"Gentlemen," said Westrum.

"I should have faith," said Benstock.

"It's only what I said," said Harvey. "Have faith, we must show faith, we must proceed on faith and trust, that's the whole thing. Didn't I say so?"

"I'm sure you did if you say you did," Benstock said.

"Who's for a ride to New Hamburg?" Westrum asked.

"You're not saying I didn't say so," Harvey said. "I hope not."

"You say so many things," Benstock said, "it's hard to keep track."

"Slow," said Westrum, in a voice he'd use to Terence. "I as-

149

sume it's me you're talking about. I appreciate your faith. I also appreciate the committee's reluctance."

"I'm also the committee now," said Harvey. "I always was, but now I really am."

"Harvey's emerging," said Benstock.

"I'm an emerging nation of Africa," Harvey said.

"Don't emerge too fast," Benstock said, "you'll break a leg."

"I'm too impulsive," Harvey said.

"Frankly," said Benstock, "I wonder about your being in two places. It's a question I ask. If my committee doesn't ask it I must ask it myself."

"You tell me what you want me to do," Westrum said. "If you want me here like Five or Seven or whatever, say so. If you don't want me here, say so. You mustn't fight over me. You mustn't ruin your health over me."

"That's a noble position," Harvey said, raising his cup to his lips, and vaguely conscious, in his excitement, of hot coffee spilling to his knees.

"Or you could share me," Westrum said, who saw the beauty of being shared, of coming and going between the Center and New York, between one society and another, between the great city and the landscape of his beginnings. "The more I'm shared," he said, "the freer I am." Ideas of Harriet sang in his mind, his letter to his mistress reposed in his pocket, and Miss Sanantone came to them with fresh paper cups, and steaming coffee, and a towel to serve as a napkin across Harvey's knees.

"No more for me," said Harvey, "it's back to work for me," who, rising to his feet, collided with the table, as Turtleman years and years ago, in Brest just down the road, collided with any object too witless to avoid him, and whose face, like Harvey's now, transcended embarrassment, so accustomed was he to collisions and falling and the laughter of children which became afterward the courteous blindness of adults. Westrum remembered Turtleman as being often down upon hands and knees searching for lost objects in the cloakroom, and arriving late to school—yes, always late, his face scarlet from running,

150

opening the door to laughter with his fluttering hands, whose clothes were freshly stained from the meal just eaten, who existed as that model of ineptitude furnishing proof to everyone else of one's own grace, diverting attention from one's own awkward lapses; whom Westrum, too, from time to time taunted or derided, yes, yes, that was true, he'd admit it, he had been an imperfect boy like most of the others. But he'd never called him *Jew*, not even in games, though it was thought to be helpful in games to set one's mind against the other fellow, rattle him in his most sensitive part. Was it a wall? Was it a tree? Was it the bank of a stream? No, the bank of the stream was Harvey himself in Africa, and this was a fall in the schoolyard at Brest, and Westrum had rescued him, or gone to rescue him, or only invented the rescue afterward, and Turtleman fell not because Westrum had taunted or rattled or failed him but because of the magnitude of his surprise at being assisted by anyone at all, staring at Westrum in amazement, disbelieving that it was either help which Westrum had come with or Westrum who had come with help, amazed, astonished, speechless indeed, so that when, by a sign of his hands in lieu of speech, Turtleman attempted to express gratitude, he fell. But he fell without injury to himself, thus he must have fallen only a short way to a soft landing, perhaps to gymnasium mats, in which case it might have been the climbing ropes he'd fallen from, and indoors, not upon the schoolyard, in any case dewinded but unhurt, and someone called, "Attaboy, Wes, give it to the Jew," and teachers and principal and fathers came running, and Westrum refused upon every count to apologize for a crime he had not committed, and his father fired the principal, if that was how it was, or even how it might have been.

"Half a cup," said Benstock to Miss Sanantone, "it's not back to work for me."

"Take a ride to New Hamburg with us," Westrum said.

"All right, I think I will," said Benstock, and to Miss Sanantone he said, "I'm sorry you don't like it on this side." But she did not appear to know she had been addressed, and he spoke to her again, addressing her by name.

"It wasn't that I don't like it," she said, but she did not explain herself.

"Just give me a minute to change," Westrum said, withdrawing to the inner room of his suite.

Miss Sanantone cleared away the cups, pulled the plug of the coffeemaker, stepped from her mismatched slippers into her shoes, and locked her desk with jingling keys. It amused Benstock that she locked her desk but that the Journal lay upon open shelves, who had himself his own magic jingling keys admitting him, Chairman of the Wing, to any desk or drawer or closet through the door of any room or suite, whose sense of honor and trust and responsibility had prevented his ever using his keys improperly. Yet it had sometimes occurred to him that his exhaustion would have now and then been less had he abandoned honor more. A little reading among forbidden pages might have helped him to distinguish between true laborers and frauds. A little reading of Westrum's Journal at three o'clock some morning might assist his body and his health to lighten his suspicion. "You must find the Journal enormously interesting," he said.

"It wasn't that I don't like it," she said, "but it's so far from everything. The nights are too long. I'd really rather go back to New York."

"The nights are just as long in New Hamburg," said Benstock.

"It's near the movies," she said. "I don't drive. He said you'd teach me to drive. Will we be staying here or going back?"

"He said I'd teach you to drive?" Benstock asked. Again she amused him.

"You're the committee," she said. "It's up to you if we're staying or going."

"Does he say I'm the committee?" Benstock asked. "No," he said, "don't tell me," holding up his hands. "Don't tell me any-

152

thing. I'm no detective, and I'm no driving teacher either. I can hardly drive myself."

"He doesn't say so," she said, "but he thinks so."

"We don't know what anyone thinks," Benstock said.

"There's nothing wrong with a detective," said Miss Sanantone a little defensively. "I have a good friend who's a detective."

"Yes, a detective may be very fine," said Benstock.

"My father was a detective," she said. "He's in love with me. We may be married."

"He's a lucky fellow," Benstock said. "Then you'll be going back anyhow."

"I wonder," she said. Hawkes would never marry her, it was a lie she told so stark and so vivid as to make her see that she was much more likely to be here forever than to return to New York, and she became very angry with Hawkes now, she hated him, she wished him dead, she knew what he was thinking: he was thinking he'd never marry her, keep her as mistress only and have her when he wanted her, and cast her away between times, men deceived their mistresses, Dr. Westrum had one mistress there and another he'd like to have here, and she said, still defensively, even a little angrily, "We know what someone thinks. I am his mistress. I know what he thinks. I know him as well as anyone, don't you think?"

"As well as who thinks?" asked Benstock, "I've lost it," amused for the third time now. Not her father's mistress, surely, he thought, although on the whole he was prepared to believe the weirdest things of her or anyone. But her father was dead, that much he had read in Westrum's Journal—not her own dead father's mistress surely, for that was weird beyond belief. Her detective's mistress? It was what she meant, no doubt, asking then in sudden alarm, in terrible weakness of mind and body, "Whose mistress do you mean?" In his exhaustion he sat at her desk. She was Westrum's aide, assistant, secretary, amanuensis, his confidante, keeper of his

153

Journal, keeper of his Index to his Text, but not his mistress, too. True, in the beginning he had thought so. But in the beginning he had even feared the pages were blank, and then he had routed all suspicion, not without shock and exhaustion, and his mind struggled in this moment to regain Westrum at Westrum's best: in Harvey's view, for example, who saw Westrum as ideal Christian to whom any grateful Jew ought to award as many Seats or years or sums or prices the good man needed or only asked.

"I mean his," she said. "Everybody knows."

"No more," said Benstock. "Be silent."

"Dr. Westrum's mistress," she said.

"I didn't hear you," said Benstock, holding his hands to his ears and rocking from side to side in pain.

"I'm changed," said Westrum, emerging from the inner room of his suite into the silence lying here between Benstock and Miss Sanantone. Obviously something had gone wrong between them, she was red and Benstock was white, some intrigue here between woman and man, perhaps a proposal. *Splendid,* he thought, *it's all in fun, no harm can come of it, the twentieth century is upon us,* and he thought, *Benstock, my dear fellow, why so ashen?*

"You changed?" Benstock asked in a low, dry throat.

"So to speak," said Westrum.

"He means he changed underneath," Miss Sanantone explained to Benstock—mad scientist, she thought, with his long black hair curling down the back of his neck, she'd give it a little trim if she were Sally. *Another Jew,* she thought. Hawkes said they were tricky and cheated on their wives. Yes, he had his eye on her. She could tell. Very well, two could play at that game, too, she had her way of keeping her eye on him, too, following him everywhere in Dr. Westrum's Journal, from the first morning when he forgot his car, to his dinner party—the very liquor and food and wine he served and who was all there and what they talked about—and visiting him in the Infirmary, and talking right here in the suite, opening the footlockers and

154

reading about her father's funeral. She knew Sally. She knew Philip. She knew Gretchen without ever having met any of them, and the grand lie Dr. Westrum told Dr. Benstock in the elevator, though what could be the point of it she'd never know (he'd told the same to Dr. Tikvah once). Her work was her pleasure, her education, her excitement, it was better than a book, for often the very characters walked in and out right under your nose, accompanying Dr. Westrum and Dr. Benstock down the corridor and into the elevator. She was allergic to elevators, and she sneezed.

Westrum recalled the last occasion of his having been in this elevator with Benstock, who may or may not have recalled it himself. Miss Sanantone said to Westrum, "Don't forget to mail your letter," and on the walkway between the History Wing and the Residence Wing Westrum dropped his letter to his mistress into a mailbox, and all three went up again by elevator to Miss Sanantone's room for her smart suitcase and her old straw trunk.

They swung up out of the underground garage into a light rain, and they crossed the bridge to New Hamburg, where his mother had been born, he said, whose birth had occurred not eleven months after his father's, as he had first been told, but, in fact, thirty days earlier. It was necessary to talk, for Benstock beside him was sullenly silent. It was right there, he said, up ahead, in the New Hamburg County Courthouse that he'd gone for the truth of the matter, when he was twelve years old or thereabouts, very young historian then, first learning there in the courthouse to satisfy his historical curiosity, looking himself up, too, to be sure that he'd been born, pursuing himself backward to his grandparents, uncles, aunts, and the plats of the houses they'd built or lived in or bought or sold, discovering here for the first time that things had never occurred precisely as his father said they had, nor precisely for the reasons his father gave.

Lies could not be imposed forever upon a young historian so

inquisitive as he. His mother's ancestral house, for example, had not been "stolen," as his father said, by Jews and eastern bankers, but sold to New Hamburg Gentiles, who knocked it down for a granary, so that Westrum had begun to suspect as a boy that if his father lied in one matter he lied in others, pausing now before the courthouse to point out to Benstock and to Miss Sanantone his Uncle Nelson's head among others upon the frieze. "Or alleged head anyhow," said Westrum, "because I never thought it looked much like him," whose head was also on a wall of the Willard Hotel in Washington, D.C., soon to be knocked down, too, he supposed, and someday the courthouse, too, and Uncle Nelson's head forever, never to reappear from behind a rosebush, driving on and asking Miss Sanantone, "Which way?"

"To my apartment," she said, as if Westrum knew where her apartment was—as if he had been there before—lighting a cigarette from the cigarette she was smoking, and opening her window to throw the old cigarette out, and taking from her handbag, too, while it was on her mind and the window open anyway, those pages of Westrum's Journal from which she had deleted seven paragraphs (and surrounding matter to preserve the pagination) and torn to pieces, and the card, too, from the Index to the Text, which she had also torn to pieces, removing the paper clip which held the pieces together and permitting the pieces themselves to flutter from her hand, sucked by the draft, out and away. "Keep going straight," she said, and dropped the paper clip back into her handbag.

"Say when," said Westrum, beyond the courthouse, past the post office, and beyond the square itself.

She had found an apartment not actually "on the square," as the advertisement claimed, but near enough to everything that mattered. Three movie houses were situated within five blocks of her apartment, and the bus to the Center stopped at her corner, carrying, in the main, Negro women serving scholars' wives.

It was a characteristic New Hamburg street, a neighborhood

156

of workingmen's small houses, reassuring to her because of its resemblance to the places of her childhood in Brooklyn. If much had changed in New Hamburg since Westrum's last tour of these streets it had not changed for the better. The city was poorly kept. The granaries were prosperous, but the men who owned them lived beyond the Interstate, or in Brest or Paree or Center, entrusting the care of the city to modest local men whose service to the granaries could not have been more slavish had it been deliberate. It was not that New Hamburg admired its own pollution—mist, fog, smoke, haze, steam—but that its citizens could imagine no alternative. The granaries were the source of all life. Beneath those smokestacks all men worked, and there the men would work who now were boys. All roads led to the granaries, and all men's memories back to boyhood—the passion of the city was games, its only heroes were stars of sport. New Hamburg's sacred places were the high-school stadium and the high-school gymnasium, each in its season, and its high priest was its football coach, whose salary was nine thousand dollars a year in addition to a sum thrice that size taken up by private subscription.

"Turn," said Miss Sanantone.

"Left?" asked Westrum. "Right?"

"Right," she said. "Correct. Where the statue is." Her apartment was in a brick building three stories high. Adjacent buildings, now rooming houses, had once been private homes, but hers had been built for its present purpose, ludicrously narrow —a shoebox upended—compressed between two houses whose residents had already been close enough for easy greeting from window to window. Its brick was chipped and scarred, bearing every sign of neglect and defacement. Hundreds of families had abused it.

In its courtyard, beside a small pool of pebbles and floating trash, stood a stone maiden once sculpted in explicit detail but so weathered now that her nakedness appeared most modest. In one outstretched hand she held several cigarette butts and the cork of a wine bottle.

Westrum carried Miss Sanantone's trunk and suitcase above. Almost instantly he returned to his car, trousers and shirt upon his arm, chronometer upon his wrist, sweatband about his head. He sat beside Benstock, who was behind the wheel and who had not recovered from his sullen silence; who, having spent half a day last week scouring up budget for an apartment for Westrum's secretary, and having inadvertently discovered that she was not only Westrum's secretary but mistress, now found himself chauffeur to both besides. He stared forward. Of course he should have known. He should have relied upon his intuition. Westrum, for all his industry, was merely human, and the girl was all flesh, the Journal was full of intimate secrets, and intimacy led to intimacy naturally enough. Very well, then, he knew more now than he had known an hour ago, and he trusted that he would remember it forever, nor ever again abandon intuition.

"These are new shoes," said Westrum, tying up his new running shoes.

"How do I work the windshield wipers?" Benstock asked.

Westrum showed Benstock the switch to the wipers, and Miss Sanantone came hastening through the courtyard, tossing her cigarette into the pool and seating herself behind the gentlemen again among discarded boxes and cans from the supply of film given to Terence by the President of the United States, and Dr. Westrum's shirt and trousers and shoes, lighting a cigarette.

Benstock drove to the bridge, where Westrum alighted. He had not yet run these shoes in rain, but they gripped the cement well, and he ran slowly across the bridge to warm before running, setting his chronometer at zero. Had his wagon passed? No, there went his wagon, they'd stopped for Miss Sanantone to move up front, and they were disappearing now ahead, at the western edge of the bridge, sinking with the downgrade. *Benstock sullen and silent today,* he thought, but he'd recover if he didn't drop dead first. He *did* worry too much, brood too much, imagine too much, the coach was right

—*go, man, go,* and he was off now and into a right pace instantly, himself not likely to drop dead, whose father was dying at eighty and his mother thirty days older, a secret they'd not been able to keep from an eminent twelve-year-old historian.

But he feared that he had spoken to Benstock unfairly of his father. If it was true that his father lied in one matter or another, nevertheless compare green little Brest with the pollution of New Hamburg. Lying was a form of resistance. His father had refused to relinquish himself or his past or his grounds or the boards of his house to commerce and pollution, the Mayor of Mayhem had led Brest against encroachment, invasion, that leveling called improvement, that plunder called development, restraining himself upon the downgrade, *don't over-pace, don't let gravity deceive you,* taking his first mile in six minutes and forty seconds, a gift to himself of ten seconds he'd lose on the bluff to the Center, he'd have done no better on a dry day, good shoes these were, he floated, he was serene, his body was lighter than air, any moment he'd float away like a feather. They'd smoke their way from New Hamburg. What would they talk about, who had nothing between them but Westrum? He trusted Benstock's absolute discretion, which he felt he knew by having known Tikvah's: Tikvah, wrapped in smoke in an automobile with Miss Sanantone, would have refrained in the most deliberate exercise of friendship and faith and confidence and honor from inviting any knowledge or privileged information he ought not to have. He would indeed have warned her to be silent if she appeared to approach a secret; or who would, if anything escaped her, erase it from his mind like a perfect juryman under instructions of the judge, which was more than Westrum could say for himself, who sometimes solved little riddles and puzzles and mysteries by pumping other people's secretaries, wives, children, mistresses, friends, enemies, associates, colleagues, and maids in the kitchen. But then, of course, Westrum told only his Journal, all secrets remained secret, he'd never yet let a secret out, and

when he did they'd all be let out at once at the discretion of his
heirs yet unborn, by which time moldering lovers and mistresses alike would hardly care.

Unfortunately, one hundred yards from the beginning of the
hedgerow approaching the History Wing Westrum's right heel
turned upon a pebble. It was a wrench whose cause he deplored even before he felt its pain. He'd been stupidly running
overconfident and inattentive. *Stupid bastard,* he thought.
Good, he thought, listening to his own first involuntary protest,
he'd blamed himself and not the pebble, not the rain nor the
pavement nor Beatrice nor the Jews, he was a bigger man than
his father, who might have argued that Jews and eastern bankers had scattered his path with pebbles. It would be his ankle.
He knew it would be his ankle which would suffer, for he had
turned his heel in that way before, he knew the extent of his
injury and the probable progress of its mending, regaining his
stride and sprinting, completing his run where the hedgerow
began in a burst of ninety yards and stopping his chronometer
at thirteen-thirty.

When he slowed, the ankle tightened. A slight throbbing
began, and the ankle resisted the pressure of his weight, filling
with rushing blood, and the throbbing eased a little then, as his
heart slowed. He walked swiftly down the ramp to the underground garage, stepping for amusement upon the treadle of
the computer which, believing that Westrum was an automobile, issued him a ticket permitting him to park himself, photographed him, and urged him in a courteous male voice to park
himself between white lines only facing forward, to turn off his
motor and his lights and lock himself up. His key was in the
switch. Benstock had adjusted the driver's seat to suit shorter
legs than Westrum's, and Westrum readjusted the seat to suit
himself, and he started the motor. Then he turned off the
motor and removed his running shoes, and turned on his motor
again, and backed out, and drove away in his socks. They'd
been here. The car was full of their smoke still clinging, but
she'd have told him only the sort of thing she had told students

or journalists from time to time, who found the things she told more useful than the things Westrum told, she was clear and direct, not roundabout and full of qualifications, as Westrum was—how he sometimes sang or talked to himself, she told them, argued with himself, wasted simply tons of paper, broke typewriters by pounding too hard upon them, spent a hundred dollars a year for pencils and tablets alone, sent her upon the strangest errands to find out the color of somebody's car, the name of a child (he was very fond of children), the name of a certain dish served at a certain dinner party, pull this, pull that, put it back, number it in (that's how they talked between them), spent twenty-five dollars a year for Index cards alone, he'd always been extremely nice to her, he never docked her sick days, he paid her a pension plan, he wrote down all the most amazing scraps of things and nothing was too personal, which people put up with at the universities but got very upset over in Washington, D.C., which was why they didn't stay in Washington, D.C., though he got three full years of Journal there (about six thousand pages if you wanted to count it in pages), it hadn't been exactly what the President had in mind, he had a regular cross-section on a person, a whole portrait or picture, he kept a daily record of his running or his swimming or his bicycling (you can see the chart there on the wall if you like), he cracked his head once on the side of a swimming pool, so he won't go anywhere there's a kidney-shaped pool but only a square pool, he gets calluses on his hands from bicycling, or sometimes he turns his ankle running—entering his house now in his socks, in the light rain, favoring his ankle, carrying upon his arm his shirt and his trousers, and in his hands his running shoes and his street shoes.

Beatrice was dressed for going. "Unless," she said, half hoping, "you've changed your mind."

"No," he said, "we'll go."

Terence, too, was dressed for going, in a white shirt with a dark tie, and his hair was damp with a grease he'd seen adver-

161

tised as guaranteed to give him irresistible sex appeal. Mr.
Weinberg's Bauer C2B, on loan, was strapped to his hand. It
wasn't any better, Terence said, than the C2A. He had begun
to observe that all cameras were much the same, the difference
was in the shooter, and he was appalled by advertising claims
that anybody could make good movies simply by turning a
switch. Terence had spoken of these things frankly enough to
Mr. Weinberg, offering a blunt evaluation of Mr. Weinberg's
film of Africa, which Mr. Weinberg accepted in the best spirit,
forcing upon Terence the C2B nonetheless. All Weinbergs had
become exceedingly fond of all Westrums.

Westrum, after showering, wrapped his ankle tight in an
elastic bandage, and he wore his right shoe loose. He was hungry, but he ate no lunch, and Beatrice drove.

"I hope your old man doesn't die while we're on the prem-
ises," Terence said.

"It would be a bother," Westrum said.

"How will you feel when he dies?" Terence asked.

"Same as you'll feel when *your* old man dies," Westrum said.

"I'll say 'There goes the old meal ticket,' " Terence said.

"How do you know what a meal ticket is?" Beatrice asked.

"Haven't the faintest idea," Terence said, shooting cornfields
through the open window. "I get the idea, though. The coach
calls Philip Benstock his meal ticket."

It was Old Road here, a two-lane highway as straight as the
line of sight north from the Interstate to Brest. For the first
quarter-mile the cornfields lay broken by bulldozers, where the
road was to have been widened for the encouragement of commerce, but the town of Brest resisted, the road was halted, the
invaders turned back, Jews and eastern bankers repulsed,
driven off like the Indians before them, commerce gone to New
Hamburg, Brest preserved. "When he dies," said Westrum,
"they'll resume the road."

"There he'll be," said Terence, shooting the cemetery as Beatrice drove past, shooting the iron fence with its spikes to the

sky protecting the stones of the dead. In the rain the stones gleamed.

"You wouldn't care," said Westrum, "to stop and see the graves of a whole bunch of dead Westrums."

"Not particularly," said Beatrice.

"I would," said Terence. Like his father, he stalked his own past.

"Another time," said Beatrice.

"I'll come out one day with you," said Westrum to Terence. "We needn't impose it on your mother."

"It's enough to go see live Westrums," Beatrice said.

"When your old meal ticket expires," said Westrum to Terence, "bury me there, but do me a favor and put me in a cheap box. Don't let the undertaker talk you into anything. A very cheap stone will do. Save the difference, take a cruise to the moon."

"The fuzz," said Terence, for ahead of them, at the limits of Brest, a policeman of the town sat in a black Comet station wagon. Its wagon was screened, less for prisoners than for dogs, for policemen here were dog-catchers, too, sitting in wait for stray dogs or stray men. The visor of the policeman's cap concealed his eyes. The cap lay forward upon his head. His hair was blond, and he was very young, whose orders were to resist all alien men or dogs.

Brest. Historic Homes
Local Option

The policeman lifted his hand to the Westrums as they passed, whose car was fine, whose skin was white, and who were therefore admissible upon whatever business they might have: they came, perhaps, to see in the Indian Museum arrowheads, implements, headdresses, and peace pipes, and to read explanatory legends assuring any critical visitor that these relics had always been obtained from the Indians by legal and peaceful means, that the conquest of the Indians had been as hu-

manitarian as it was thorough, that the settlers at Old Fort
Brest had never tortured or lynched Indians in spite of reports
to the contrary, nor taken Indian women prisoners, as certain
historians asserted. Or they came to stroll through old houses
existing as fine examples of early Victorian style adapted to
frontier conditions, rifle-rests beside bedroom windows, bar-
rel-thrusts through knotholes in the walls, some houses still
occupied (as Westrum's father's was) by descendants of the
families who had built them, who, in some cases (not Westrum's father, however), conducted short tours for visitors
whose interests were serious. Or Westrum and Beatrice and
Terence might have been behind a family disguise promoters
and developers from New Hamburg or Paree, surveying Brest
with the idea of resuming abandoned plans—to clean out the
cornfields, seize the land, widen the road, and advance commerce by buying out the last resistance of old families too fee-
ble for further struggle.

Or they might have been, as Westrum was, blood visiting,
kin come home. Westrum had been home ten times in thirty
years, sometimes with Beatrice, sometimes with his sons,
sometimes alone. In the past such visits were crises of his life,
but today his sensations were subdued, lying low. His principal
feeling throbbed mainly in his ankle. *My father loves his old
home town,* thought Terence, shooting the Lutheran steeple,
and Beatrice drove, at Westrum's direction, to the railroad
depot. There she paused. There Westrum and Turtleman, on a
Sunday afternoon thirty years ago, argued the question of the
war. "In those days," said Westrum, "if you hung around the
depot for a couple of hours you saw half the people you'd ever
known," but now the platform was barren except for an old
snub-nosed Chevrolet pickup truck, tailgate down and dripping, its door ajar, but its driver nowhere evident, its bed
empty, waiting to bear away into Brest whatever the freight
might bring, but expecting nothing from the train, to which it
had nothing to deliver, either. Nothing was manufactured

here. "I came down to pick up a box that day," said Westrum, "but I forget what was in it."

"Keep the hot bulletins coming," Terence said.

"There were eighteen trains a day," Westrum said, "nine up, nine down."

There was the bench where Turtleman sat reading *Berlin Diary*, and they'd walked *that* way toward Mulberry Street (he pointed), "and he called me a fucking Nazi bastard," Westrum said, and he boarded the train and glided off to war to rescue Sally Benstock in a quartermaster truck on the street in Eisenstadt, one abused child rescuing another. True, Turtleman might have glided off on the train to his death, too, who might have been lying these thirty years in one of the graveyards of Europe. Westrum had employed a single photograph of the American military cemetery at Draguignan to illustrate a bloody chapter of *A History of the Past World*—perhaps the most memorable chapter of the book, famous now, in which, in the coldest objective prose, he had hardly done more than to name the names of five hundred wars, reviewed the issues said to have precipitated them, and counted the numbers slain. For a moment the face of Turtleman appeared clearly to his imagination, and might have remained longer had not Terence interrupted to offer a practical suggestion. "I realize it's too simple," Terence said, "but it's loony to keep thinking about it. Couldn't you look it up somewhere? Couldn't you write a letter to the Pentagon? I noticed the postal system went right into Washington, D.C."

"I could," said Westrum. "I guess that's not how I'm interested in it."

"All right," said Terence, "Do it your way."

"He will," said Beatrice. "Shall we go?"

"Apparently," said Westrum, "I'm more interested in speculating about what might have happened to him than I am in knowing."

"Apparently," said Terence.

"It's what *happened*, it's not *him*, if you know what I mean."

"I get it," said Terence, who'd get it, he was sure, if he cared to think about it, who would have shot a train if a train had come, or shot the truck if the truck had moved, but who would never shoot anything stationary when he himself was stationary. Something had to be moving. When Beatrice started the car he shot the old chalkboard flowing past, PASSENGER SCHEDULE BREST AND FORT BREST, but nothing was posted, for the passenger trains had been discontinued, and the only motion was their own.

But Westrum's father was clearly not dying or thinking of dying. The clasp of his hand was never firmer, the hand never steadier, his spirit never more suspicious, shaking Terence's hand, too, with his eye upon Beatrice.

She remained her distance, evading his hand or any touch of him, whom she never forgave for the brutality of his tongue, old fascist he was, old rotter, old lecher, old viper—she didn't like him. Sometimes she wondered if she would have married Wes had she met his father beforehand. She bowed slightly with respect for anyone who had lived so long so mean, so narrow, so wicked, so fond of blood and guns, and she lightly kissed Westrum's mother, who had been to Beatrice kinder, however distant, who frequently said, "Pay no attention to him, it's not him you married, he doesn't mean half he says."

But half was more than twice enough, Beatrice had always thought, declining to remove her coat in the cool house, and because, too, if she did, the old man's eyes would play upon her body. He had said once, in her hearing, many years ago, "She'll grow fat," for he believed that all Jewish women grew quickly fat, objecting to his daughter-in-law not because she was Jewish but because she'd grow fat. His language was always enveloped in a system of euphemism clear to everyone, responsible to nothing—eastern money, eastern bankers, fat women, "brains," professors, scientists, liquor interests, tobacco interests, motion-picture producers, advocates of peace, friends

of the Indians, newspaper columnists, Quakers, Unitarians, and
television reporters, all, all were Jews or names for Jews. "We
can't stay long," she said. "We just dropped by. Wes had the
afternoon free."

"Free from what?" the old man asked. "What are you doing
over there at that joint? I thought you were determined you'd
never come back to these parts. I said you would, didn't I? You
can't stay back east. They ripped you up, didn't they, tore you
up?" He turned to Terence. "What you got there?"

"A movie camera," Terence said.

"Lights, camera, action," the old man said, dancing sidesteps
to his chair between fireplace and television set, and sitting,
whereupon his black cat leaped to his lap. The name of the cat
was Nigger. "How do *you* like it over there at that joint," he
asked Terence, "in there with all those brains?"

"It's pretty good," said Terence, who thought he'd shot a
most unusual shot there of the old man dancing, the cat springing, the old man coming to rest in his chair at the same split-
second the cat came to rest on the old man's lap, the two sitting as one, and Terence shot the flickering fire, too, and he
said to his grandfather, "You shouldn't call a cat that."

"He's my cat," the old man said.

"It isn't right," said Terence.

"We won't dispute," said Terence's grandmother.

"The cat's black, isn't he?" the old man asked.

"Yes," said Terence.

"And a nigger's black," the old man said.

"That's not the point," Terence said.

"Then tell me what the point is," his grandfather said,
turning the television high. In the garden his Doberman
Pinscher howled. The dog was fierce, dangerous, and objected
to visitors. His howling was ceaseless. But the old man appeared to hear neither the machine nor the animal.

"Do you mean to say," Westrum asked, "that we've no more
passenger trains?"

"They've passed," his mother said.

167

"We've no more a lot of things," the old man said, "and a lot of things you've got elsewhere we can do without."

"Brest has stayed quiet," Westrum's mother said.

"I'll say," said Terence.

"We've no riots in the streets," his grandfather said. "I saw your brother bleeding all over the place," he said to Beatrice, pointing to the television. "Hit in the head by a student's brick. Do you approve of that?"

"They don't know who threw the brick," Terence said.

"I know who threw it," his grandfather said. "But I don't see you on television any more," he said to Westrum. "They drove you out of Washington, too, did they, and now out of New York as well. The knives are out for the likes of you, you know. They'll rip you up, those professors will."

"New Hamburg is livelier," said Westrum's mother, "but we don't go there any more. He's not well."

"He looks well," said Westrum.

"I'm perfectly well," his father said.

"He's not well," Westrum's mother insisted.

"I am quite well. Your mother likes to think I'm not."

"I hurt my ankle," Westrum said, elevating it to the chair facing his own.

"I haven't an ache or a pain," his father said. "I don't wear eyeglasses or batteries in my ears."

"I wrenched it running," Westrum said.

"I don't run," the old man said. "I never ran. This is malarkey, all this keeping fit. You run after girls, that's what you run for." He knew where all this free-thinking led, and he smiled at Beatrice.

Terence smiled, too, to think of his father running after girls. Would that he did, it was only human, but his father had never revealed to Terence tendencies along those lines, never whistled between his teeth at the sight of shapely girls, as the fathers of other boys did. "When will the dog stop barking?" he asked, lowering the volume of the television.

168

"What dog?" his grandfather asked.

"He hasn't been out of the house since July," said Westrum's mother.

"I gave the oration," her husband said.

"What oration?" Terence asked.

"Oh no," his grandfather said, "you'd never hear of it in the schools you go to. They wouldn't teach it over there where the brains are, would they? It's all one world to them, though I suppose they teach you all about Yugoslavia and your yellow brothers across the sea."

"May I ask," said Terence, "what was the subject of your oration?"

"Work," his grandfather said.

"How many people were there?" Terence asked.

"Everybody was there," said his grandfather.

"You've orated on that subject before," Westrum said.

"I repeat myself," his father said. "If you tell me something new to say I'll take the greatest pleasure in saying it. You know nothing new beneath the sun. Learn to work. Stay at some one thing all day long and every day and you'll arrive someplace yet. That's why they drove you out, you know. They *abhor* the idea of work."

"We saw you running," said Westrum's mother—on the television, she meant, Ice Water Westrum running two miles in thirteen minutes and thirty seconds down the streets of Washington. "He ran all over town," she said to Beatrice. "He ran around the square, he ran around the schoolyard, he ran around the fort, he ran through the park, he ran behind the snowplow."

"Six and a half times around the square," said Westrum, "was two miles."

"Still is," his father said. "Stop running after the girls. You're too old to run after the girls."

"He's running *away* from them," Terence said, and smiled again, and laid aside his camera, and removed the firescreen

169

and poked the fire, and laid a fresh log upon it. He stood with his back to the warmth of the fire, for the day was damp, and his back was stiff.

"They'll drive you out of that joint, too," the old man said to Westrum.

"Who's *they?*" asked Terence.

"The brains," said his grandfather. "They'll run him through, they'll rip him up, way down deep they really hate his kind, you know." He did not address Terence, but Westrum. To Terence he said, "Old men stand like that. Don't stand like that, you're not an old man."

"He has a little difficulty with his back," said Beatrice. It was how she spoke of it always to strangers—a little difficulty, a bit of trouble, a slight matter hardly worth mentioning. The thing was done, and there had never been any blame-placing or any recrimination, and she and Westrum and Terence had lived with it among themselves only, never mentioning the unmentionable, never speaking of the unspeakable.

"It's his imagination," the old man said. "He's too young for that."

"But he has," said Beatrice.

"You imagine it," the old man said, and when she did not reply he added, "You imagine too much," and when, even to that, she did not reply, he added further not to her but to everyone generally, his eyes upon the screen of his television set, "You all imagine too much. You all imagine sicknesses and thoughts that don't exist, and aches and pains and cures that don't exist. You all study yourselves too much."

"All who?" asked Terence.

"You *all*," said the old man with vigor—Terence, his father, his mother, everyone but the cat, whom he tenderly stroked.

"I have studied myself," said Terence, "and I imagine that I'm hungry." He thought he understood. Yet it was difficult for him to believe that his grandfather, so kind to the cat, could possibly be, as Westrum and Beatrice said he was, vestige and seed-bearer of everything worst and most sinister in America,

170

His Honor the Mayor of Mayhem, Injustice of the Peace, Chief of the Volunteer Arson Department. Terence remembered, upon occasions of these visits in the past, having been delighted by the vehemence of his grandfather's prejudices. Today, however, he heard the substance behind the vehemence. He remembered, from visits in the past, having been delighted by his grandfather's accounts of how he killed Indians. Today, however, Terence was depressed by the memory of those accounts, for in fact his grandfather had never killed Indians at all, but only wished he had, or would if he could, or might find someone else to kill instead, and so feel worthy and manly and duly entitled to all these pleasures he had never even worked for, either, much less killed Indians for. "When I was little," said Terence, "I took everything at face value. Nowadays I'd rather study myself too much than too little."

"On the whole," said his grandmother, "I'd rather clothe than feed it," and she went to the kitchen.

"I don't study myself *ever*," the old man said, his eyes upon Beatrice now. The rising fire having heated the room, she slipped from her coat. She laid it upon her lap.

"No," said Westrum. "You never have."

"I do only what's right," his father said. "Things that were right for me are right for you. That's all they do over there, they study themselves."

"Over where?" asked Westrum.

"Over there at that joint," his father said. "In among the brains."

"We won't dispute," said Westrum's mother, returning from the kitchen with a bowl of fruit.

The sight of the bowl was chilling to Westrum. His eyes met Beatrice's. But the bowl apparently bore no meaning for Terence—it bore fruit only—who took from it an orange and two bananas.

The bowl was of a set of chinaware called Ancient Malacca Distinctive, translucent, agreeable to the hand, a wedding gift

171

—dinner plates, soup stands, creamers, oval platters, cups, saucers, sauce boats, and two ashtrays the old man dropped in the garbage as he took them from the box, for he forbade smoking in his house. The bed of the bowl would reveal, once the fruit was taken, a lavender lady shading a lavender house with a lavender parasol, perspective so badly seen that Westrum from childhood had gazed upon it with tireless fascination. Just such a bowl Terence had dropped and broken on that most terrible night of their lives, when Westrum in seeming madness broke the boy's back with a blow of his hand.

"Be careful of the bowl," said Beatrice to Terence.

"He *came* to dispute," the old man said, "and he's got Terence in the habit now too." His thin white hair was combed forward: at eighty he'd still admit to no man that he was on toward baldness.

"You have a similar bowl," said Westrum's mother to Beatrice.

"You gave us one," said Beatrice, as if to say it still existed, last seen, in fact, broken to pieces beside Terence's body upon the floor, and the boy lay moaning low in his throat, accusing his father, "You didn't have to do it, it was only an old bowl, it wasn't all that much of a crime," as indeed, of course, it was not, had not been, as Westrum instantly confessed upon his knees beside his boy, third son, baby, in the sight of his own violence. Who swept up the pieces of the bowl? She did not know. She did not remember. She disliked looking back. Perhaps she had swept up the pieces herself, it seemed likely, nor could she remember afterward whether her husband had called Terence *Jew* or *little Jew* or *you little Jew,* or whether anybody had called anybody anything. He had asked her that almost in the moment of the blow, sitting and awaiting the doctor, and asked her again from time to time down the years, but she remembered only the sight of the boy struck to the floor, violated by a rage her husband pursued to this day, still in the hope of knowing its source.

"I don't see what's wrong with brains," Terence said.

"They make you study every little item," his grandfather said. "They make you imagine too much. They don't let you be natural and do what you like." His rage was rising. "They make people argumentative. That's the kind of people they are. Look at you, you come here and you argue with me, and you heat up my house. If you need all that heat at sixteen what'll you need at sixty?"

I wrote a letter to my mistress, Westrum thought, fixing in his mind the order of the day as the means to its center, *Benstock and Harvey came, "birds nest with close makings," Benstock's mood was high and clear and good then turning silent and sullen in the car to New Hamburg and ran back and sprained right ankle, Beatrice drove to Brest and we looked at the depot, Terence eats two bananas in four bites from the Ancient Malacca bowl.* Yes, his father was right, he'd come to dispute, so that Terence might hear his grandfather's mouth with his own ears for himself through his own consciousness, and so hear his own history from its own source. He hoped that Terence might arrive at conviction by conviction, not by hearsay, choosing, selecting, listening.

"You don't have an airport," Terence said.

"I wouldn't have one of those," his grandfather said. "Do I want airplanes falling down on my house?"

"They're so noisy," Terence's grandmother said.

"No train, no airport," said Terence. "How do you get in and out?"

"There's a bus," his grandmother said. "You mustn't worry about us."

"What will happen to the house?" Terence asked.

The question had occurred to Westrum, too. He could imagine himself returning to this house. Ten years ago the prospect would have sickened him—five years, even, last year perhaps —but he was immune now from its contamination, free of every fear of the influence of place, his ideas and convictions too dearly won and held to be threatened by mere rooms. Once he had exiled himself, but he could return home now, he'd build a

173

workplace in the attic and he would enter into his Journal *Today I am writing once more back in the attic having stepped outdoors for thirty years.*

"When I'm dead?" the old man asked.

"I meant, for example, in case you move," said Terence, whose question had escaped his tact.

"We hadn't planned on moving," his grandfather said. "I was born in this house and it suits us. I know my way around in it. What do I care what happens to this house or anything else once I'm dead?"

"We have a responsibility to the future," Terence said.

"That's for your father and the brains over there. Let them think about the future. That's what they're paid for." He gave some consideration to what he had said, and he added, "God damn the future."

"He doesn't mean it," said Westrum's mother. "He doesn't mean half the things he says."

"Don't ask me any more questions," the old man said. "If you don't know I won't tell you." He stared at Beatrice. His eyes upon her routed her, and she rose and carried her coat to the closet. He had not thought the marriage would last, but it had lasted twenty-five years, and that was well, for the sake of the children. She had not grown fat. She had borne three sons, but how could sons named Westrum be half Jews, two of whom had married Jews producing Westrums now three-quarters Jews? The name was become a Jew-name, and Terence, too, was beyond recall, his mouth was filled with fruit and questions, and the old man cried fiercely to the boy, "Why do you come here and eat up my fruit?"

"We asked them to come," his wife said.

"They only came because they thought I was on my death-bed."

"We knew you weren't," Terence said, who knew it wasn't the fruit at stake and began upon an orange.

"You know everything," his grandfather said.

"I wish I did," said Terence.

174

"Do you remember a family named Turtleman?" Westrum asked.

"I remember everybody," his father said.

"They owned the smoke shop," Westrum said.

"No," said his father, "they didn't own the smoke shop, they owned the liquor shop. It was another one owned the smoke shop. You're getting your Hebrews mixed up in your mind."

"They were Jewish folks," said Westrum's mother kindly, as if the fact would be pleasing to Beatrice, "and quite nice, as I recall."

"They had a son," Westrum said.

"Indeed they did," his father said.

"Do you recall what happened to the son?" Westrum asked.

"I have not been informed," his father said.

"He went to war," Westrum said.

"It was more than you did," his father said.

"But you don't know if he lived or died," Westrum said.

"They came and they went," his father said.

"More or less driven out, as I recall," Westrum said.

"You recall wrong," his father said. "Nobody was ever driven out. We voted option. If you own a liquor store where the citizens vote option you better load up your pack on your back."

"But you voted option as a means of driving him out," Westrum said.

"Your mind is mixed up," his father said.

"I'm trying to unmix it," Westrum said. "Once there was an incident in the school. He fell from the climbing ropes, and I was blamed for making him fall, and somebody ordered me to apologize."

"The principal ordered you to apologize," his father said.

"It wasn't from the ropes," said Westrum's mother, "it was from the principal's window."

"Whoever ordered," said Westrum, "or whatever it was he fell from, I wouldn't apologize."

"It wasn't your fault," his mother said.

"But he was a boy we always taunted," Westrum said.

175

"All that may be," his father said.

"So you fired the principal," Westrum said.

"We keep principals on their toes," his father said.

"You fired the principal," Westrum said, "and you drove the liquor store out."

"That was over the course of years," his father said. "It was none of it connected."

"It was all connected," Westrum said. "There are no Jews in Brest."

"People come and go," his father said.

"You exile people," Westrum said.

"*You* come and go," his father said. "You're coming and going over there, aren't you? Mind your manners and speak the right things or they'll drive you out of there, too, like we drove the liquor store out. It's in nature. I know what I am and I know what they are."

"What who are?" Terence asked.

"The brains over there. It's natural, and I am a natural man. It's in my nature to close myself off from the people I'm not, and I respect them more when they close themselves off from me, too. I don't go where I'm not wanted. This cat's no dog. He'll spit at a dog. He'll rip at a dog and tear him up. If you bring my dog in here this cat'll hump his back and spit and rip, he's a natural cat. A cat's a cat and a dog's a dog."

"America is a democracy," said Terence.

"Cats and dogs together," his grandfather said, "but apart, not all of a heap."

"Our cat and dog live together very peacefully," Terence said.

"I'm certain they do," his grandfather said.

"Then your argument is baseless," Terence said.

"It would be baseless," said his grandfather, "if it was cats and dogs we're talking about," and he said to Westrum then, "Keep guard of your back and flanks, keep your eyes all around your head, they'll come at you more ways than one. They don't like your looks. They'll drive you back and forth like they

176

drove you out of there," he said, pointing at the television—
Washington, he meant.

"Who will?" Terence asked.

"They will," his grandfather said, softly, weakly, almost in-
audibly, weary of the varieties of avoidance—fat, eastern
money-loving scholars and scientists drinking liquor and
smoking cigarettes and selling off America to the international
colored races of the world. That was who. His country had
been seized, his nation taken by the enemy. His son had sur-
rendered, his grandsons were half-Jews and his great-
grandsons three-quarters. "They'll use you," he said, "and
they'll throw you away." His cat, feeling the old man about to
rise, leaped from his lap to the hearth.

"I'm sorry if I asked too many questions," Terence said at
the door.

"It can't be helped," said his grandfather, "it's too late."

"I'm sorry we can't stay longer," said Westrum to his mother.

"They're all sorry for something," the old man said. "You
could have stayed longer if you wanted to. You came too late
for lunch and too soon for dinner."

"You can't fool him," said Westrum's mother, crossing the
porch with Westrum, her arms folded against the dampness of
the day, her husband having already closed the door behind
them, at his television already whose screen had revealed to
him in recent years even the face of his own son so cheerfully,
all facts in mind, all eloquence ready, clarifying the situation of
the world—the poor were poor but need not be always, peace
was possible, color was only skin-deep, the world was one,
minds must meet, hands must join, guns must go, for whose
song of democratic love he was paid a tidy price by the Jews
no doubt, who'd give it all back to the Indians by and by. The
Doberman in the garden was silent at last, his teeth were fear-
fully bared, and he was eager to devour them. Westrum was
pleased to reach the gate. He kissed his mother. "But I believe
you were right about the Turtlemans," she said.

"I'm sure I am," said Westrum.

"It's a long story," she said.

"With a short meaning," Westrum said.

"That's something you'd understand," his mother said. "I don't meddle. We won't dispute." She said to Beatrice, "Drive carefully," and Beatrice promised that she would, Westrum in the back seat with his ankle elevated, and Terence shooting his grandmother as she swung the gate closed and stood to watch them go, who would telephone again within a week to say that her husband was dying.

"It's not her fear," said Westrum, "it's her wish."

"He's a fascist," said Terence, as a matter of fact.

"You wouldn't want your daughter to marry him," said Beatrice, driving at Westrum's direction to the schoolhouse, and Terence rolled his window down and shot his father's school. *My father loves his old home town and school,* he thought, but such sentences lacked flair, he thought, won no prizes at essays, and he had begun to despair. He could not write. Reuben Weinberg could write well and play the flute besides, Philip Benstock was an athlete, but Terence lacked all skill, he was nothing, he was nobody, walking beside his father in his father's old schoolyard, in the dusk, in the rain.

Here and there in the schoolhouse the lights were on. The light in the principal's office hung from the ceiling at the end of a chain whose links were threaded with an electric wire. Westrum felt that he could see the wire itself, even at this distance, and the slight swaying of the light, too, but in fact the only motion discernible at this distance was the motion of the pendulum of the clock upon the principal's wall. By daylight the pendulum flashed once every second if the sun was right. The boys in the schoolyard often sent a small boy up a large boy's back, to seize the ledge, hold fast, consult the time, and report to his mates below.

"They probably still do," Terence said. He shot the pendulum.

Any agile boy could then easily drop to the ground. But Turtleman had been no agile boy, and he feared the fall, nor could he climb upward to the ledge, either, and when Westrum went to assist him Turtleman fell of astonishment. "Therefore my father fired the principal," said Westrum to Terence, walking with his son beside the schoolhouse now, too close any longer to see the clock.

"That was nice and logical of him," Terence said.

"But that wasn't enough," Westrum said. "He drove the whole Turtleman family out, too, and all the Jews besides. He was a terror."

"He doesn't *terrify* me," said Terence, "but I don't think we agree on any issues at all."

"He terrified anybody he cared to terrify," Westrum said. "He'd pick and choose. He liked his victims weak. Something in us makes us happy to see other people suffer. He was always at work on somebody, grinding somebody down, making life miserable for somebody, this principal if not that one, this teacher if not that one. He always had a target. He'd terrify one dog but not another."

"He seems to love his cat," said Terence. "I *know* I got some good shots of him there with the cat." But nothing was moving here except his father's mind putting pieces together, and you couldn't shoot that.

The red light lazily revolved on the roof of the policeman's Comet at the limits of Brest. Perhaps the policeman was the blond young man, as before, but it was too dark to know, and they were gone from Brest, down the straight road through the broken cornfields to the Interstate, intending to dine at the Clover Leaf Motel, where Westrum had come the day before yesterday with Harriet Weinberg. It was an event he had omitted to mention to Beatrice at the time, and felt no necessity to mention now, his heart lunging at the thought of Harriet, and his ankle throbbing as a souvenir of this day which was the eighteen-thousand-three-hundred-and-eighty-third of his life. She'd be his mistress if he wanted her. That he knew: every sign was there, and he an old hand at knowing the signs.

179

MARK HARRIS

He'd sat with her on these high stools in the darkened bar, passing his hand now across the smooth, cool, Naugahyde seat of the stool. "Listen," he said to Beatrice, "let's have a good stiff drink before we eat."

Terence protested. Saloons bored him, and he was starving to death, he said. He went ahead alone to the buffet, his mother and father remaining in the saloon, at the bar, up upon the stools, Westrum once more passing his hand across the seat of the stool where Harriet had sat, whereupon an old lost name came to him—*Gagliano*. Then who was Gagliano? And now that Westrum had it, what was the use of it? Yes, yes, his field was Florentine art—*Gagliano, Gagliano*—and it was he who had passed his hand across Tikvah's bald head at a meeting of young faculty twenty-five years ago and said, "Your head feels like my wife's ass," to which Tikvah speedily replied, passing his hand across his own head, "Say, it does, doesn't it?" and filled the meeting room with laughter, and sent the laughter down a quarter of a century, too, reviving a smile upon Westrum's face a quarter of a century afterward twelve hundred miles to the west, which the bartender at the Clover Leaf Motel accepted as a smile of recognition for himself, and said, "Happy to have you back."

"I'll have a whiskey double on ice," said Westrum.

"I'll have the same," said Beatrice.

"What kind of whiskey?" the bartender asked.

"Any kind," said Westrum, "as long as it's advertised."

"Have you been here?" Beatrice asked Westrum.

"Not in years," said Westrum.

"He said *back*," she said.

"If he meant it," said Westrum, "he shouldn't have said it."

Yet the bartender perfectly well knew that he'd seen Westrum here not long ago, and not with this woman, either, and not with that big boy, either, and not in the evening, either, but in the middle of the afternoon, because they glanced toward the door whenever it opened to daylight to see who might be entering with no more business here than they in the

180

middle of the afternoon; and as for her (although of course he'd never eavesdrop), she was in the middle of some trouble or crisis she was revealing to him, and she drank Ballerina vodka in the belief that it was odorless, and her tongue quickened and her confidence grew; and as for the tall man, however, he'd been no sale, he drank iced water, sipping it like wine and taking her trouble or her crisis in and writing on a tablet, too, as she talked, as if he were a lawyer and she a client. Whatever they were, they were neither man and wife, nor cool detached friends, nor brother and sister, nor uncle and niece, oh no, not by his way now and again of touching her neck to comfort her, who, when his hand was upon her neck, sat stiff, erect, neither inviting his hand nor wishing it away but beginning, as their hour passed, to bathe in the pleasure of his hand.

Yet now he ordered whiskey doubled and drank it instantly and ordered the same again, whereupon the bartender began to wonder whether, indeed, it was the man he remembered, or thought he remembered, since the lady now drinking with him was his wife, no doubt, and the boy passing beyond to the buffet their son without doubt, and it was the bartender's observation, based upon extensive experience, that a man never took his family where he took his mistresses or mistresses-potential, unless, of course, the man was some sort of daredevil. The bartender stood with his shoulder blades to the mirror behind him, his towel upon his arm, and his eyes upon the ceiling.

"The trouble with my fascist father," said Westrum, "is that he never let himself go," writing upon his tablet *Gagliano*.

"Don't let yourself go," said Beatrice. "You need two weeks' notice to yourself to let yourself go." His trouble was, when he let himself go, he came back too soon, he moaned at the neglect of his Journal, his work, engagements missed, his running unrun or his swimming unswum. "It'll all pass tomorrow," she said, "when your father and the whiskey wear off."

"Let's go to New York and have dinner with Tikvah and Winnie," he said.

181

"No," she said, "let's go somewhere we haven't been. Let's go to the airport and take the first plane out."

"It might not be going anywhere good," he said.

"Wherever it goes they've got bottles and beds," she said.

"He accuses me of running after women," said Westrum, kissing her, his fingertips upon her cheek, here where Harriet Weinberg sat. The day before yesterday he had engaged a room for their nuptials, marriage, and life together, but he'd sat here with Harriet instead, writing out the Rider and Recommendation on his tablet because it appeared to him that she needed him more in that way than in another, and he dropped the key into a mailbox afterward, and ran two miles in thirteen-thirty as a stay against his passion.

"Terence was amused," Beatrice said.

Even so he might have taken Harriet, too, but for the feeling he had that his face was absent of conviction, as it had been in Terence's film, that all this love he had always had for Jewish women was but the outward part of his brutal center. Was he anti-Semitic? Did he hate foreigners? Did he yearn to kill Indians like his grandfather before him? Was he the seed-bearer of fascism in America? But his wife and his mistress were Jews. On the surface he'd say No. Anyone who meant much to him was more likely than not to be a Jew, and his three sons were Jewish by half. "Knowing my father," he said to Beatrice, "how do you know I'm not an undercover man for the Ku Klux Klan?"

"Then let's go somewhere and get under covers," she said, "while the whiskey's still hot."

"Benstock's got a hard-on for Miss Sanantone," he said.

"You saw it?" she asked.

"I can tell by the way he looks at her," said Westrum. "I came on them by surprise this morning and they were looking guilty."

"Then he'll want all the more to keep you here," she said.

"The bartender is eavesdropping on our obscene conversation," he softly said, and he kissed her again, and Terence came shooting.

"Do you have any idea what *time* it is?" he asked.

"I object to being photographed in a bar with a drunken woman," Westrum said, seizing Terence by the buckle of his belt and pulling him to him, encircling the boy's waist, to the boy's most awful pleasure and embarrassment, who feared, even, that his father might kiss him, as Philip Benstock's father kissed Philip, and his father said, "What would your fascist grandfather say of your drunken Jewish mother?"

"I'm not supposed to be in the bar," Terence said. "Let me go, I'm a minor."

"Then why aren't you mining?" his father asked, but he would not release the boy.

"You're crushing my camera," Terence said.

"I'll buy you another," his father said.

"Aren't you going to eat?" Terence asked.

"There isn't time," Westrum said.

"You had no lunch, either," Beatrice said. "Now you'll be irritable. You'll sober up and be irritable and depressed."

"Who'll drive?" Terence asked, delighted at his parents' drunkenness, proud of them and pleased with his father especially, who so seldom let himself go. He'd got a rare shot of them embracing, though whether the film would develop out of such darkness he could not be sure—he hoped so—"I'll drive," he said.

He drove, they were drunk, his mother between his father and himself, and the whiskey in Terence's nose.

"Put on your lights," his father said.

"They're on," said Terence.

"Never shoot while driving movies," his father said.

"It's a lucky thing somebody's sober here," said Terence.

"Keep to the right," his mother said.

"Unless we're in England," his father said.

"I am, I am," said Terence, seldom so happy. *My father is*

183

the life of the party, he thought, *my father likes a good time.* Last year Jerome Weiss had won the prize with heroic couplets, and Terence had recently been thinking of limericks.

> My father's a good man from Brest,
> Definitely best by test . . .

But none of his limericks ever advanced beyond the second line. He was no poet, either, as he was no writer, and the shortness of time had begun to depress him.

"Your mother and I are going on a trip," said Westrum, "as soon as I give myself notice."

"We're taking the first plane out wherever it goes," said Beatrice.

"Never happen," Terence said. "You're always going on a trip after a couple drinks," driving home with perfect skill.

Westrum, behind the wheel now, sober, glum, and hungry—sober, irritable, and depressed, as Beatrice knew he'd be—parked his Oldsmobile Custom Vista-Cruiser before the high school in the space reserved for the principal, who said she'd save her space for him, he could park in her space any time, she said, *putting a little something of mine in you,* he'd thought, popping a strawberry into her mouth. He'd give a good sum for a quart of strawberries now, and a second good sum for a bucket of ice to plunge his throbbing ankle in. He should have eaten at the Clover Leaf Motel, not drunk, his father would be scornful of Westrum's stupidity. Half a day without food reduced a man to the temper of an animal.

On the other hand, half of this gathering crowd had eaten dinner as usual without losing its appetite for the principal. It would devour her if it could. In the past, before the coming of Harriet Weinberg, the school had run itself without the aid of parents, and they resented her intrusion upon their evening. This was not the first time she had routed them from their homes, their newspapers, their card games, the warm glow of their television. Why was the auditorium dark? Who had the

keys to the lights to the auditorium? Surely the President of
the Board had the keys, but where was he—where was the
Board? But the crowd was leaderless.

Nor had Benstock eaten, either, standing for support with
his back to the wall of the corridor, gazing into a distance suddenly foreshortened by the very head of Westrum, of whom he
had been thinking this moment and continuously since this
morning, nor kindly thoughts, either, but the bitterest thoughts,
for he felt himself most cruelly betrayed.

"I'm starving," Westrum said. "Is there a candy machine
anywhere?"

At one point of the day Benstock had sworn to himself that
he would grant no Seat to Westrum, not a Five or a Three or
even a One, and risk the wrath of Harvey Weinberg if he must,
and be the fool and laughingstock of history, too. *You're killing
me,* he'd say, *you're ruining my health,* or if by chance he actually granted Westrum a Seat he'd say, *Take it, but we must
never speak.* As far as possible he would never again speak to
Westrum. He had been betrayed. He had been lied to. The girl
was Westrum's mistress, and Benstock the fool of both, lied to,
deceived, betrayed, stepped upon.

However, in all his life he had never so far broken with any
man as to end speech between them, and he had no idea how
far into action he could pursue such a devastating intention.
Then, too, in the case of Westrum the matter was far from
clear. Perhaps it was the girl who lied. Perhaps Benstock had
been too far influenced by Sally's prejudice. "I wouldn't know,"
said Benstock, as coolly as he could.

"There must be," said Westrum. "You can't have a school
without a candy machine. I'd sell my soul for a bag of Planter's
salted peanuts," and he smiled a good smile and he said,
"Cheer me up, I've just been to see my father."

So see, he's got troubles too, thought Benstock, who for all
his sullen mood this day had carried with him, too, a last vision
of Westrum seen upon the bridge through his own rear-view
mirror, in running suit and sweatband, with straining face. The

185

sight had touched Benstock in spite of himself, and he said suddenly now, breaking all vows of eternal estrangement, "Come to the toilet"—old north Bronx schoolhouse word for the Boys' Room, share a cigarette, exchange a secret, plot an action—emerging with Westrum from the heat of the crowd, extricated, disentangled, alone with Westrum now, apart from these others. And when Benstock considered those others he knew that whatever Westrum was or was not he was, at any rate, above all other objections, finally and fundamentally indispensable, civilized, sophisticated, in the largest sense a friend however difficult. They paused a moment to greet Coach Wilson.

"Who are all those strange people?" Westrum asked.

"Friends of football," Benstock said.

"From the Center?" Westrum asked.

"A few," said Benstock, "maybe from the Computing Wing, but they're mainly business people from New Hamburg. They only sleep here. You never see them in the daytime."

"Factory managers," Westrum said, "plant superintendents, vice-presidents, heirs to granaries."

"Legionnaires," said Benstock. "You see them at the football lunches. Rotarians, deacons of the churches, bookkeepers, and accountants."

Here in this corridor Westrum had walked with Harriet when first they met. Jerome Weiss's eighty heroic couplets still hung upon the bulletin board. "Anti-Semites and fascists," Westrum said.

"How would I know?"

"Take my word for it," Westrum said.

"Maybe you know the territory," Benstock said.

"It's worse than you think," said Westrum.

In the Boys' Room Benstock drank from a plastic flask borrowed or stolen from his son, property of the Center High football team, whose ordinary use was to squirt water into the parched and gaping mouths of the players, but which was employed by Benstock now to squirt whiskey. The flask fit neatly

186

the breast pocket of his coat among the week's accumulation of applications for Seats, often accompanied by the most desperate appeal for that single year of blessed leisure the applicant was certain would free him to advance or complete or perhaps only to begin that work his whole life had prepared him to do. Benstock drank one short quick mouthful of whiskey and offered the flask to Westrum, saying, "Have a swallow to cheer you up," and who said then, when Westrum gently declined, "Then I'll swallow a swallow for you, too," and drank a second drink, longer this time and not so quick—not one squirt but two—and screwed the top of the flask again, and he said, "What do I get myself into these things for? I'm no friend of football, I'm only a friend of Philip. I could be home drinking milk."

"If Terence played I might be on the other side," said Westrum. "There was a Lombard king who suddenly became a pacifist when his son reached military age."

"Bless his soul," said Benstock, "I'm glad to hear you say so." The whiskey scorched his ulcer, and he thought to leave the flask behind, but as he was about to drop it into the wastebin he decided, instead, to drink once more, offering Westrum a drink again, who again declined.

Now Benstock had the strangest sensation. He thought that he smelled liquor upon Westrum's breath. But he disbelieved his own nose, for Westrum never drank: undoubtedly the odor was the odor of his own flask, or the odor of himself, and he drained the flask by wrenching the cork from the bunghole itself and tipping it upside down for the last good drop of his own stolen whiskey smuggled from his own house beneath the eyes of his wife and children. "My physician would disown me," he said. But nobody liked fighting at public meetings and everyone tanked up against it, except a few, perhaps, who were very strong, as Westrum was, Ice Water Westrum looming above him here in the Boys' Room. "In my opinion," Benstock agreeably said, "Harriet Weinberg's a pain in the ass."

"Oh no, I *like* her," Westrum said. "I like them both."

"They're both a pain in the ass," Benstock said, even more agreeably than before. "I like them, too."

"Maybe we'll be the first school in the county to abolish football," Westrum said.

"What have I got against football?" Benstock asked.

"She's very beautiful," Westrum said. "Football is fascist."

"You don't believe that."

"Then why did I say it?" Westrum asked.

"Listen," said Benstock, "I'd give a lot to play a game of football myself, running around like that at the top of my health. Do you really think she's beautiful?"

"Oh certainly," said Westrum. "Don't you?"

"Your girl is beautiful," Benstock said. "We had a good little talk in the car. Tell me the truth now—did you really tell her I'd teach her to drive?"

Westrum smiled. "I said something like that," he said. "I was satirizing something unreasonable she said. She's got a very literal mind."

"Does she tell lies?" Benstock asked.

"Maybe little small lies," Westrum said. "I never think of her as beautiful, not even attractive, I'd say. She's not the sort of girl I went for when I was a young man."

"You went for Jewish girls," Benstock said.

"That's how it turned out," said Westrum.

"Harriet got you into this," Benstock said. "I wish I had more whiskey. You're a sucker for Jewish girls, I'm a sucker for Philip, let's get ourselves out of it. You're hungry, let's go somewhere and eat. You eat, I'll drink."

"Afterward," said Westrum.

"Never mind afterward, I'll be sober afterward. There's a little place across the river, they broil steaks, the bar is noisy, a little girl sings, a big girl strips, she'll wave her titties in your face. I'm sorry to report they're not Jewish, however."

Westrum laughed and took Benstock affectionately by the arm. "Not that," he said, and held the swinging door, and they passed into the corridor, which was silent and echoless now, the crowd having entered the auditorium leaving Westrum and Benstock alone and behind, two bad boys late for class, who might have turned accident to opportunity as bad boys often did, and fled, disappeared, flown out across the river to broiled steaks. *Why not why not?* thought Westrum, for he loved noisy little bars and big girls and little girls singing and stripping. From the auditorium a single voice could be heard. It was Harriet's, deep and low. But why not go instead with Benstock, who needed him now more than Harriet did, why not relieve Benstock this night of the burden of Westrum, come clean with Benstock, do a kindness, show Benstock that he, too, Westrum, was only a man like any other, nothing superior about him at all, hungry for a broiled steak, nor above a whiskey, either? Such moments as these he had had with Tikvah, too, but never been able to abandon the person he had become, always one sort of man in the presence of other men and a second sort of man in the presence of women, now one, now the other, here one, there one, without reason except that life had gone best for him that way, instinct had hardened to policy, his very voice in this moment carrying policy forward in spite of his will to break with himself, saying, "Afterward, maybe after the meeting, maybe another time," which was clearly to say to Benstock *Never, little fellow,* turning the corner of the corridor with Benstock and holding the door of the auditorium to permit Benstock to enter first, who was the weaker, the smaller, the less sober, the frailer, the more helpless, the poorer, the more in pain, the sufferer, the less famous, the more ill and trampled.

Benstock was also at this moment upon the wrong side of the public question, joined for Philip's sake with his natural enemies—the boosters and Legionnaires hidden from themselves, themselves denied, incapable of imagining lives more gracious. They loved football, and everyone they knew loved football, and people who did not love football were people they did not know with long hair and foreign names and accents, and mainly of the History Wing of the Center, where they lived in idleness.

Heads turned when Westrum and Benstock entered the auditorium, to see if this was friend or enemy, who proved to be not one man but two and probably one friend and one enemy, depending upon anyone's point of view. The small man with the long flowing hair would be the enemy of football, and the other the friend. They sat together.

The crowd, whose mass, whose heat, and whose single muttering voice had so ominously oppressed Westrum in the corridor, here in the auditorium had surrendered its unity to space. It was scattered, broken, as leaderless as before without even the reassurance of the compactness of bodies. Moreover, the principal, Harriet Weinberg, violated the easy expectations with which the crowd had come. Her reasonable tone disarmed it. Rumor and report had given her the wild features of a revolutionary leading children down base paths upon a picket line, but this evening she spoke in the kindest way, in the gentlest manner, apologizing for the confusion regarding the lights, expressing her appreciation for their interest and attendance, and hoping to clarify for everyone present—for herself as well as for them, she said—this intricate matter of the budget. Her braid fell to her shoulder, her turquoise clip twinkled, and her eyes, which had followed Westrum down the aisle to his seat, remained with him now.

How could Benstock question her beauty? Except, of course, Benstock questioned Westrum at every turn, he couldn't help himself, as Tikvah couldn't help himself, either. He had parked in her space. Had he turned off his lights? He'd been a little drunk, and he might have left his lights on, drinking made him forgetful. But no, his keys were in his pocket, and therefore he had probably remembered, too, to turn off his lights, hoisting his right ankle now to his left thigh. The throbbing and the pain distracted him, and she said something amusing which he missed—everyone laughed but Benstock—and the whiteness of her teeth soothed Westrum's eye, he'd popped a strawberry between her teeth, putting something of his in her. She'd been a grateful mistress. Gratitude, beauty, humor, and conviction made a perfect mistress. *Madame,* he wrote in his mind to his mistress, *with the most painful regret I must inform you that I shall now return to my home, having been thirty years away,* he'd close out their fine apartment on the twentieth floor with sunken pool, and he'd transport his gypsum vault from exile in New York to his attic in Brest, and he'd love Harriet Weinberg long hours while Harvey went birding. "Where's Harvey?" Westrum asked Benstock.

"He's not here," Benstock said. "He's somewhere being industrious."

"Ah yes," said Westrum, "turning over a new leaf," and he asked, "Where's his whistle?"—Coach Wilson's whistle, he meant, for Coach Wilson stood before the meeting now in a blue suit, offering the impression, Westrum thought, of a man pleading his own case at the gallows. The coach's collar choked him. Apparently he had earlier loosened collar and tie for relief with the intention of restoring both when he should rise to speak, but he had remembered his collar only, forgetting to pull his necktie snug. His voice was hoarse, as it would be until the end of the season, which had thus far been, he said, successful in every way and promised to be successful to the end: he expected that Center High might "win the County," he said, and not for the first time, either, he said, and he named the years he had won it before and mentioned, by the way, now that he thought of it, the honor he'd had of being twice selected All-State Coach of the Year.

"May we proceed," said Kenneth Silvers, presiding officer of the Board. His two teak canes were crossed at his feet. But his chest, arms, and shoulders above his table suggested the stoutness and strength of an athlete, too. Someone initiated applause with a single clap of two hands, but the applause was not for Kenneth Silvers but for Coach Wilson who, with this encouragement, unfurled a scroll and proceeded to read, item

191

by item, a monologue of irrelevance which was the football budget—for sweat socks, he read, so much and so much, for practice pants so much and so much, for award sweaters so much and so much, for insurance and film and inner soles and gasoline mileage for transportation and Ananase tablets and physician's services so much and so much, for ointments and mouthwash and laces and cleats and helmets and girdle hip pads (as opposed to rib pads) and practice balls and game balls so much and so much—which had never, item by item, been placed in question, nobody ever having doubted the budget but only its disproportion where other things were needed, and finally the idea of so much stress upon football, which tended, said the Rider and Recommendation to the Budget, composed by Westrum and Harriet at the bar of the Clover Leaf Motel, to emphasize winning at the expense of play, to cultivate brute strength at the expense of subtlety, to focus upon single heroes at the expense of general participation, to favor mob noise above reflective silence, to divert attention from the essential purposes of a school to contests for public notice, wherefore it was the will of the Board to resist expansion of the program in football, not unmindful of the danger or the prospect whereby the failure to expand the program in football might lead in the course of years to its extinction altogether.

"You may be seated," said Kenneth Silvers to the coach, as to a child who had recited sums. "What is your wish?" he asked of the crowd, but it was Coach Wilson who replied. "I wish we'd accept the Budget but not the Rider and Recommendation," he said.

"A motion is in order," Kenneth Silvers said. "You are out of order."

"I wish to make a motion," said the coach, "that the Budget be accepted without the Rider and Recommendation."

"You may do so," Kenneth Silvers said.

"I make a motion," said the coach, "that the Budget be accepted without the Rider and Recommendation."

"The motion is out of order," said Kenneth Silvers. "The Budget cannot be accepted without the Rider and Recommendation. They are of a piece and inseparable."

"I make a motion that the principal be refrained from picketing the football games," said Coach Wilson.

"The motion is out of order," said Kenneth Silvers. "This is a meeting of the Budget. We may discuss only the Budget."

"May we hear the Rider and Recommendation?" called Benstock from the floor.

"We have heard it," Kenneth Silvers replied. "I believe you had not yet arrived."

"We were caucusing in the toilet," Westrum said.

"Did you write it?" Benstock asked.

"Did someone say I wrote it?" Westrum asked.

"She said you wrote it," Benstock said, who had heard it in fact from Harvey, not from Harriet, but Harvey got everything a little wrong, of course, and might have got this a little wrong with everything else or else Westrum was lying. God knows why. Who cared? Who cared if Westrum wrote it? Who cared if Westrum took a drink? "I don't care one way or the other," Benstock said.

"May I hear a motion?" Kenneth Silvers asked. "The Budget with Rider and Recommendation is before us. We really have no alternative to accepting or rejecting it all of a piece and inseparable."

"Mr. Chairman," said Westrum, "I feel that I am about to make a motion," rising so that he might be seen as well as heard, his body seen and the twang of his voice heard, to win this moment for Harriet by reassuring all friends of football, all factory managers, all heirs to granaries that they, too, in the company of aliens if need be, should support the Budget with Rider and Recommendation too, and go home then to the warm glow of the late movie on television.

"May the assembly know the name of the speaker?" Kenneth Silvers asked.

"I'm Westrum," said Westrum, "I'm a resident of Brest, born

193

and raised there, my father lives there still, and my mother, too, though to tell you the truth about my mother she was born in New Hamburg," meeting Harriet's smile with his own during the brief moment of pleasant general laughter, whom he would take now, but not tonight upon this throbbing ankle. Furthermore, he thought, if they went back to the Clover Leaf Motel tonight they'd terribly confuse the bartender. "I have studied the Budget very carefully," he said, "and the Rider and Recommendation, too, and I feel that what the principal and the Board have in mind is really in the very best interests of all of us. Therefore I move that the Budget be accepted."

"It has been moved and seconded," said Kenneth Silvers, "that the Budget be accepted."

"Second me," said Westrum to Benstock beside him.

"Do I hear a second to the motion?" Kenneth Silvers asked.

"Second yourself," said Benstock sadly, sinking into his seat, slouching upon his backbone, hiding, concealed, who would in this moment have seconded Westrum upon no imaginable issue, who might have seconded him five minutes ago or an hour ago or yesterday, and might second him again someday, but not soon. For the moment, for now and for the immediate future he would second nothing Westrum stood for, and oppose his Seat, too, at whatever consequence to himself because tonight his wounds were fresh and painful, his body bled with Westrum's lies. Perhaps they were not lies. But tonight they felt like lies and his body felt therefore wounded and bleeding —not even wounds inflicted in passion but worse, not lies told in passion but lies deliberate and therefore not even wounds so much as incisions in the spirit of experiment, the spirit of play, an experiment by one human being upon another no less calculated than the experiments of the young physicians of the Infirmary—lies, lies, lies, the Gentile torturing the Jew. Did Westrum truly believe that football was incipient fascism? Did Westrum drink? A smell was a smell, Benstock knew liquor when he smelled it, unless it was himself he was smelling: could a man's nose be smelling his own mouth? The lines of the

194

battle were drawn. Harriet had spoken, Coach Wilson had spoken, Kenneth Silvers had spoken, Westrum had spoken. According to the rules something must happen. But whatever happened would exhaust him, encourage the insurrection of his ulcer and the acceleration of his heart, dissipate one whole evening of his life in a battle he never invited, whose outcome would change nothing anyhow. His body clamored for an end to all suspense. He hadn't the strength to go on contending further, it would kill him, the doctor said so.

"Yes," said Westrum, "wouldn't it be lovely if we were allowed to second ourselves?"

"I second the motion," Coach Wilson called, for Westrum's voice and face he trusted, and Benstock was Philip's father, they had entered together, they sat together, he'd seen them go deep in discussion down the corridor to the Boys' Room together, and he knew that they must know what they were doing.

"Does he know what he's done?" Westrum asked.

"Don't talk to me," said Benstock, "you're killing me."

"*He'll* kill you," Westrum said. "Anything to win. It's only to win, no matter how."

"Philip admires him extravagantly," said Benstock.

"Philip's a boy," said Westrum. "The coach is my father's son."

True, Benstock thought, Philip was a boy. It was no secret. Yet where would Philip shine if he had no football field to shine upon? He shone at feats of bodily strength. He was built for such things. They exhilarated him. They gave him a sense of his own worth, his own value. Again he smelled liquor. Did Westrum drink? Who wrote *Potentialities for Fascism in America*? Did Westrum write it or did his brother-in-law Tikvah write it? Was it a book or was it a pamphlet? Who wrote the Rider and Recommendation? Harvey said Westrum wrote it, Westrum denied it. The fantastic thought crossed Benstock's mind that something in the nature of a secret lay between Westrum and Harriet. Then was Miss Sanantone his mistress?

Did she tell big lies or small? What was all this pretense this morning, turn left, turn right, straight ahead, to the statue, if she were his mistress he knew where the apartment was, and if she were not his mistress she was a very great poisonous liar. Westrum thought her a small liar only. So he said. And he said once, too . . . in the elevator . . . "Mr. Chairman," Benstock called, but in the cry of the vote his voice was lost. "Mr Chairman," he called, "may I speak, may I speak?"

"Speak to me," Westrum said.

"Never," said Benstock, "never again."

"Let's go for that steak," said Westrum.

"Never," said Benstock, fleeing from Westrum, down the row, cracking his shins upon empty seats, and up the aisle into the night.

6

For the relief of his ankle he had taken to his bicycle, spinning now eight miles in nineteen minutes on the cinder track of the football stadium early on the eighteen-thousand-three-hundred-and-ninety-second day of his life, after a poor sleep. He had been awakened at three o'clock in the morning by the sound of Reuben Weinberg playing his flute in the kitchen, finding there Terence fully dressed, sitting upright and asleep, and upon the kitchen table his tape recorder playing. The tape recorder smelled of its own heat. "You'll set the house on fire," Westrum said.

"It's insured," said Terence, coming quickly awake.

"Get some sleep," his father said. "Get to bed."

"I can't sleep," said Terence. "There's no use trying."

"Then keep it very low," his father said.

Nor could Westrum sleep, either. He lay for an hour with his hands clasped behind his head, staring at the dark ceiling which began, at length, to lighten, hearing below Reuben Weinberg's flute playing not songs but short quotations. He was on the point of rising, upon the theory that one hard hour of sleep at dawn was worse than none at all, when sleep came at last, and he dreamed that his mistress, wearing a policeman's cap, was driving a busload of football players from the Willard Hotel in Washington, D.C., to Nazi Party headquarters in Eisenstadt, and awoke from that ride to find Terence below at the kitchen table at seven o'clock exactly as he'd been at three, and the flute still playing. Terence held in his hands, for some reason or other, the fireplace bellows.

The boy was too far in fatigue to explain the bellows. He was at the end of long labor. He had devoted a week of sleep-

197

less nights to the preparation of a most precise and painstaking documentation of his father's excellence, with the goal of winning for himself a free trip to a North American city of his choice. He would draw distinction to himself, elevate and uplift himself in the eyes of his fellows, and charm, excite, fascinate all girls. His own distinction lay in question, his mind troubled by its own secret suspicion that if he were offered the range of all distinctions he'd choose above the winning of the Father Contest the chance to run ninety yards with the football for the winning touchdown against New Hamburg, and be borne from the field on the shoulders of his mates, and escort the Queen to the Victory Screamer, limping, bleeding, aching, bandaged. His eyes were glazed and swollen. "Go ride your bicycle," he said to his father.

Eight miles in nineteen minutes was extremely cautious time for Westrum, even on cinder, but he mistrusted his ankle, and his mistrust affected his rhythm. He had misjudged the progress of his ankle's mending—unless it were the wheels that needed greasing. This afternoon he'd greased the wheels. He hadn't greased them since New York. He'd grease the wheels and tape his ankle fresh, and he would nap, too. Calluses stung his palms. He'd go buy a pair of golf gloves. One way or another all pleasure was hazardous, all hazards tempting, and certain discomforts a kind of pleasure, too. His cyclometer stood at something over a thousand miles, or the distance between himself and his mistress, whose face he was lately confusing with Harriet's.

In his dreams he had taken Harriet as mistress, but in his waking day he'd not progressed so far, ending by feeling that he was betraying her by not taking her whose cause he had supported with her body in mind. Convinced of the cause now, he abandoned for the moment the dream of her body, and found himself condemning himself as severely as if, having won her body, he had abandoned her cause.

Such a turn of affairs had the quality of a dream all ironic— Terence fully-dressed at dawn in the kitchen asleep with the

198

fireplace bellows, Reuben Weinberg's flute in the night, whose mother Westrum would take as new mistress (depending upon Benstock, Chairman of the Seating Committee, father of the linebacker)—gliding from the stadium now on his coppertone ten-speed Paramount Road Racer. Here in Center more than thirty years ago he had played football in the crimson of Brest, caught a forward pass or two no doubt, tackled a boy or two no doubt, the facts were cloudy, his memory faint, and his heart never so much in the game as the hearts of his mates and his townsmen were. But he had been a tall boy, and the coach put him where tall boys were put who were also swift upon their feet and sure-handed. It had sometimes seemed to Westrum that the entire object of the game was only to keep from being reprimanded by the awful, vulgar, bullying, cutting, foul sarcasm of the coach. Westrum would have been pleased enough to settle for a tie.

At the south gate of the stadium the pickets met, surrounding Harriet Weinberg there, and the principal of Paree High, too, who had lately likewise taken up the cause, and fourteen teachers from here and there about the county at the risk of their jobs, and fifty students from Center High and elsewhere, and twenty parents from Center, among whom only Westrum wore a faded gray cotton jumper and sat upon a bicycle. He held high the sign he had carried before, FOOTBALL = FASCISM, although he knew his message was too complicated, a historical intuition too far-reaching to be written so large in a space so small without the benefit of notes and citations and other explanatory data.

All pickets but Westrum wore their school sweaters. Harriet wore a Center High sweater of midnight blue, the letter C upon her breast. In the midst of the shuffling and milling and strategic arrangement of their forces, to make themselves look more numerous than they were, Westrum would have quickly kissed her had he not, at the last instant, caught sight of Terence, who carried no sign, but camera only, and who was bound to become, thought Westrum, rather witness to any

199

scene than actor upon it, historian upon film, as his father was historian upon paper. Terence greeted his father only by an acknowledgment of eyes, too weary to lift his hand to wave, and too weary to unsling his camera.

Harriet's sign read WHO CARES WHO WINS? which she carried upside down, as the rules demanded (they were technically engaged, by order of the police, in a "vendor's display," not a march) until, assuming her position on the line of display, she raised her sign to greet the arrival of the New Hamburg bus. It was a bus striped green, accompanied by its own escort of three cars of police, and its windows had been ordered closed. Thus Westrum saw not the faces of the boys within, but the palms of their hands wiping their own moist breath from the windows. "My mother was born in New Hamburg," said Westrum to Harriet, when the door of the bus folded open, discharging the boys and their coach and the coach's assistants, and smaller, frailer, lesser boys who were proud to be managers, aides, record keepers and water bearers. True to their instruction, the boys of New Hamburg walked single file and wordlessly from their bus to their dressing room, reading the signs of the pickets without response or any visible emotion except perplexity—FOOTBALL = FASCISM, FOOTBALL IS WAR, TEACHERS NOT COACHES, BLOCK THAT BUDGET, WHO CARES WHO WINS?—who had never thought of football as war or fascism, good solid boys, Westrum thought, doing as their lives had taught them to do, obeying orders, who'd die obeying orders when playing fields were suddenly battlefields, who had never been picketed before, never been flung in the face with signs, for whom, indeed, football might be the one road in a thousand leading clear of the granaries.

"Your mother was," Harriet said.

"They're bigger than we were," Westrum said. He had been the tallest boy at Brest, but half these boys were as tall as he, and half of those as broad, and already their beards were black and harsh. They'll settle for no tie, he thought, they came to play, they came to win, they'd get past Philip Benstock if they

200

could. Always some single heralded figure obstructed the way, someone to personify the enemy, someone against whom they had prepared themselves all week, in whose name they had chosen one among themselves to imitate his style of play, dressed him in an enemy jersey numbered twelve whom they would either outwit or outrun or avoid or overpass, as the logic required, and against whom they had set their minds, establishing him in their imaginations as not alone their opponent upon Saturday but an enemy as well to everything dear and permanent in their ongoing lives, who in their minds had certainly become (for Westrum had been through it all) not only a formidable linebacker in the jersey of the other school but a Jew linebacker in the jersey of Center, where green grass not granaries grew, where men appeared to live at leisure, where men appeared to be favored not luckless, whose industry was smokeless, whose streets were swept.

On the whole, the crowd at the main gate was friendly. It had come for football, not for political debate, and it intended to enjoy itself, the more so if the right team won. It read the picket signs with the same passive interest it read the floating, dissolving mist of a skywriter—*Osco* (Ford cars, new and used, New Hamburg, everyone knew Osco Ford)—shuffling, trickling, tickets in hand, jugs, blankets, binoculars, pennants, cushions, sunshades, raingear, through the funnel of the gate to watch the boys play football, someone calling to the pickets now and then, "Creeps . . . yellow . . . queers . . ." This week, as in weeks past, one elderly gentleman, patriot, football fan, paused along the picket line to offer two dollars to any picketing boy who'd use it for a haircut. How could football be war when football was only football?

It occurred to Westrum that it was less the game than the crowd he feared. His father had always hated the crowd, hating especially the jugs the crowd carried, for he thought he knew what was in them. His father had gone to the games to spy on the drinkers, and in the hope of his son's heroism. The old man had preserved newspaper clippings and photographs

201

from those old days, intending to paste them in a scrapbook someday, but whether he had ever done so Westrum never knew, nor whether the clippings existed still: perhaps they lay hidden in the house somewhere yet, too precious to burn, too painful for the old man's eyes to see, record of a good boy gone bad, sold out, duped by socialism, communism, foreigners, Democrats, eastern bankers, Jews, and the liquor interests.

Westrum would have exchanged his picket sign for uniform and cleats. The moment gripped his stomach with excitement, a familiar tightening felt first long ago at games, afterward in public debate, and later at love. He would see the game, violate his own picketing, cross his own picket line. He'd not grease his bicycle, nor buy golf gloves for his calluses, nor nap, but he'd find Benstock and get a ticket and see the game, following with his eyes the last of the New Hamburg boys into their dressing room, drifting now with Harriet among the pickets.

More than one hundred pickets had participated, and she was pleased. She was persuaded that this picketing, week after week, had been in some way successful. "We're winning," she said.

"We'll picket forever," Westrum said. "We'll never give up," and thought to himself *perhaps one hundred, maybe a little less.* But Harriet heard only conviction in his voice, never doubt, he cheered her, encouraged her, gave her to feel that she was winning, although Westrum's voice sounded to himself empty of conviction, even as his face had been empty of conviction in Terence's film on the screen in Harriet's very house. But he'd not cross his own picket line. He'd take Harriet to lunch. Yes yes, she was eager for lunch, and he was sorry he had asked. "I'll go home and change," he said. He'd go home and nap, he thought, and tell her afterward he'd fallen asleep; everything would be solved by an afternoon nap, he'd lie down while history worked itself through. He'd nap and write his Journal and go off somewhere and telephone his mistress and

202

they'd talk dirty at twelve hundred miles, and he'd chide her, challenge her—any new little invented stories of gentlemen creeping up behind her at her post-office box?—preferring dirty talk at twelve hundred miles to lunch with Harriet or even to bed with Harriet until or unless he recovered conviction. Everything was spoiled by his knowing too much. He knew too many points of view. He could as easily have picketed for as against, depending upon what he wanted from whom. He might have been picketing now on the other side of the question had he taken a fancy to the wife of the coach, searching the crowd at the main gate for Benstock, who had extra tickets.

Benstock would be late. He was always late. Nor had Benstock spoken to Westrum in more than a week. Benstock had spent much of the week, Westrum gathered, trying to convene the Seating Committee, which seldom met, which was unaccustomed to meeting, and which declined to meet now, having learned that the purpose of the proposed meeting was to deny Westrum a Seat upon the grounds (said Harvey Weinberg, supported by Kenneth Silvers) that the Chairman had formed an insane prejudice against the candidate. "Have you seen Benstock?" Westrum asked.

"Don't mention his name to me," said Harriet.

The pickets dispersed with the thinning crowd, carrying their signs upside down once more to satisfy the police, and hearing then the unified cheer of the crowd, its first cohesion, whose meaning could only be that the boys of Center High had come racing upon the field. Indeed, yes, there they were, as Westrum saw, straddling his bicycle at the main gate, Center High in midnight blue, and he read their backs for the number twelve, for Philip Benstock, *all goys there but him,* he thought, a wide, sound, solid boy who could run a hundred yards backward in fifteen seconds, hard, thick, unresisting, dogged, stolid, loyal, mute—"Little Gibraltar," the newspapers called him, failing to account, Westrum thought, for the boy's foremost quality, which was instinctual, of the mind, who possessed not only heft and the speed to meet the play, but knew where it was going to begin with, no child of words, intelligent and devoted, sturdy, willing, perfect soldier.

The second cheer was smaller. It was the voice of travelers from New Hamburg. The sound was thirty years and older in Westrum's ears, for the cheers of home and away were distinct and different, nor had the green of New Hamburg altered a shade. The game lay within understanding, it was clear, like a war or like an election, somebody won and somebody lost, New Hamburg wore green and Center High wore midnight blue, they always had, Paree wore orange, Brest wore crimson, he could match color and town throughout the county even now, thirty years afterward, but he had missed Benstock in the crowd, he had no ticket, and no money in his jumper. If Westrum played end against Center today he'd help get number twelve, it's what they'd do, they'd make his life miserable, it was all in the game. The boy who was the keeper of the picket signs took Westrum's sign from his hand. But where was Harriet? When he turned from his speculation to look for her she was gone. He too had been a boy in these parts and played this game, they'd hit him high, they'd hit him low, they'd kill him, intending no harm, it was only a word, kill, whose mother's arm had been tattooed when she was a girl over the sea and Westrum a boy in Brest—whose own mother had forborne to watch, for she disapproved his being so often knocked down— and Tikvah unknown to Westrum, nor Tikvah's hair yet blown from his skull, though he went shortly to the battlefields with all these running boys, all but Westrum who remained at home solitary among his books, as he was solitary now upon his bicycle, turning and wheeling away.

But of course, he thought as he laid himself down, *but of course, but of course,* he thought, as his head touched the pillow, it was Miss Sanantone's gentleman friend who wanted him back alive, *bring him back alive,* the makework detective making his own personal work there in the good old United

States Post Office and scaring Westrum's poor dear mistress half to death. So she hadn't made it up at all, lovely thing. It was no fiction. She had invented neither the post office nor the telephone. Like every litttle puzzle of history he had ever solved, this one had been solved by his putting it from his mind. Leave it alone and it came home, all things came clear in time, the mind ground replies to all questions while the legs ran or the wheels spun or the arms and the legs churned the water, and the head in the act of dropping to the pillow spilled out secrets as their time came due.

Of course of course, he knew he was right. Bring Westrum back alive, bring him back alive. That would be how her gentleman friend would put it, though it wasn't *him* he wanted, but *her*. Sitting in bed now in his pajama trousers, his ankle taped fresh, he began to compose the event for his Journal.

But how could he write this for his Journal? Miss Sanantone had come alive (it must have been she who gave the man the number of the postal box), she lived, she breathed, she was therefore no longer a mere mechanical attachment to his typewriter nor any longer a neutral moral agent. She had become, instead, a reader of his pages and a character upon them, and he'd need a new girl now—perhaps a young man, he thought. But no.

He left his bed. Below, the football game played upon the radio, but when he was dressed and went below he found only the cat and the dog listening, and Terence sleeping the soundest sleep at last on the living-room rug beside a can of film, his white crash helmet, and the fireplace bellows.

On the radio of his automobile the band played. It was half-time. Passing the stadium, lowering his radio, he heard the band with his own ears, brass and thumping drum, and passed beyond its sound soon again, turning up the volume once more without being able to detect by the tone of the announcer which team was winning or what had significantly occurred, only a statistical ritual in the mindless rhythm of Coach Wilson reciting the budget—first downs rushing, first downs passing, first downs penalties (total first downs), number passes attempted, number passes completed, number passes had intercepted (net yards gained passing), total offensive net yards, yards interception returns, yards punts returned, yards kickoffs returned, average distance punts, fumbles lost—followed by a résumé of half-time scores and quarter-time scores of games played elsewhere among high schools Westrum had never heard of, so many new districts having been formed in thirty years. Therefore he knew nothing he hadn't known when, entering the underground garage of the Center, he lost the radio altogether. It crackled, and he parked his car, ascending quickly to his suite.

Her slippers of cotton fleece with mismatched pompons stood in the well of her desk, left pompon blue, right pompon red, her ball-point pens in strict formation beside her typewriter, and seven packages of cigarettes stacked in a pyramid. She was closed for the weekend, whose little life had been too little real to Westrum. He was ashamed of himself. He had brought her here beyond her power, separated her from her lover, as in an old time wicked men trafficking in slaves sundered families and lovers. Such a deed was the more ironic for its having been committed by the author of *A History of the Past World*, for whom history was accessible only by a study of persons, of individual men and women consumed by private goals and passions, seeking glory in their own time by the humiliation of particular enemies, not by a study of reigning theories of existence but by the study of lovers and mistresses, wives and fathers and children. And yet, all this known, all this in the very *History* he had been making when she came to him, he had dismissed her uniqueness. But she, of course, had not forgotten that she was real, even in the act of copying his shorthand from tablet to typescript, keeping the Index to his Text.

What had he been thinking? Had he thought that at the end of the working day she went dark like the light, silent like her typewriter, empty like her slippers? Yes, when she telephoned

206

to say that her father was dead Westrum had given a bit of a start to think that she had a father at all, he hadn't thought of her as having one, or of having anybody. He was absolutely certain now that it was Miss Sanantone's gentleman friend who had accosted his mistress at the post office, seeking the fellow's name now in the Index to the Text. *Bastard, what is your name? Bastard, I looked you up only recently.* It was the short name of a fierce or loathsome beast such as a wolverine, but not a wolverine, not *snake*—cobra, rattler—perhaps a bird such as eagle, but not *eagle*, either, nor *tiger* nor *civet*. Therefore Westrum chose another route to the name, plucking from his Index Miss Sanantone's own entry—*Miss Sanantone, her father's funeral, pp.* 44,372-6—beginning:

> On Monday, the sixteen-thousand-four-hundred-and-thirty-fifth day of my life Miss Sanantone telephoned by nine o'clock to say that her father died (Friday night) and to extend to me a "cordial invitation" to attend his funeral, whereupon I dressed as black as possible, partly in selfish mourning for the loss of half-a-day's work. I seldom thought of her as having a father at all. I knew he was a policeman, and that was all. But then, she never mentions anyone to me, we keep our distance between, our little lives apart, our souls segregated, separate but equal . . .

Westrum read forward in the single account of Miss Sanantone to appear at any length in his Journal—funeral parlor, limousine to the graveyard, rain, priest, coffin, wreath—shocked by the sudden, abrupt end of the entry. There had been more. He had stood with her gentleman friend at the gravesite, and the rain had poured down off the fellow's hat. It was vivid to Westrum's memory of both the event and of the page as well, the fellow's absence all the more startling in view of his having been unquestionably there, bad teeth and all, cards in his hat, indented face. It could have been no illusion. Men and names existed if Westrum's memory said so. Lately, for example, he had recovered the name of the historian of Flor-

207

entine art who had passed his hand across Tikvah's head and said—looked it up the other day, and there it was, let Tikvah deny the event as he might. True, that name was now lost again—no matter, Westrum could retrieve it simply by driving over to the Clover Leaf Motel and passing his hand across the Naugahyde surface of the bar-stool, locking his suite behind him and returning to his automobile and to the crackling radio which burst from crackling to the high excitement of the football crowd whose single clarifying voice was the voice of the announcer. Some great deed had been performed, perhaps a long run, Westrum supposed, completed now, all tension relieved, excitement subsiding, a new kickoff, "a brand-new ball game," the announcer said, "unbelievable, unbelievable, you've got to be here to believe it," whom Westrum easily resisted, crossing the bridge to New Hamburg, which the boys of New Hamburg would themselves cross in their striped green bus before nightfall in a mood or spirit yet to be determined, perhaps jubilant, perhaps downcast: they'd have either got past the Jew linebacker or they hadn't, they'd have either won or lost or tied, past his Uncle Nelson's head on the frieze of the New Hamburg County Courthouse, beyond the courthouse, beyond the post office, and beyond the square itself.

Before Miss Sanantone's house, across the breast of the stone maiden, an election sticker had been affixed, FLECK FOR CONGRESS, and from her fingers odd bits of string dangled. Westrum strode past her, and through the courtyard, and hastened upstairs to Miss Sanantone's apartment, at whose door he both rang the bell and rapped with the knuckles of his fist in a fury he suddenly forced to submission. He might, after all, be wrong. His mind might have tricked him. Sometimes in the past he had imagined writing something when he hadn't. Often Miss Sanantone's mental system was more accurate than his in such matters, who located for him someone so grossly misplaced that his logic failed where her guesswork succeeded. Now and then she found on a page for June someone he'd have sworn he'd encountered in December.

Her eye appeared in the peephole of her door, and Westrum could see, seeing only her eye, that his presence amazed her. Never before had he gone to her. The smoke of her cigarette drifted through the peephole. "Dr. Westrum," she said. "My goodness." For the moment she associated his coming with Philip Benstock, for Dr. Westrum had written in his Journal only two days ago that Philip would be hurt, and today he was. He had just left the game. Dr. Westrum was fantastically smart, he had a sixth sense, he predicted many things before they even happened. Speedily she unchained and unbolted her door to admit him, apologizing to him, as he entered, for her not being dressed, she never dressed until evening on Saturdays, she said, and sometimes not even then if there was nothing at the show. But not Philip Benstock, no: Philip's father. She had her plan in mind, and she would not swerve from it. She would deny everything, *your mistress,* she'd say, *Dr. Westrum, please, ask yourself if I would say a thing like that,* simply deny everything, be indignant, weep, threaten to resign her job. She wore a pink robe with deep pockets, her feet were bare, and she hurried to her slippers, holding her robe at the throat. *Why would I have told him I'm your mistress when although I like you very well, Dr. Westrum, such a thought never crossed my mind?* On her radio the football game played. On a small table beside her television instrument lay a copy of *A History of the Past World,* which acknowledged her "patient silent assistance" in its preparation. But she had never read in it, and therefore never discovered her name.

"Where do you get those unusual slippers?" Westrum asked. The left pompon was red and the right pompon blue.

"In the drugstore," she said.

"So oddly matched," he said.

"I buy two pairs and mix them," she said.

He had never thought of that. Ah, she had a little life of her own, this one, and he said, "I'm sorry to come like this. Maybe I'm mistaken. Please don't lie to me."

"Dr. Westrum," she said, "please, did I ever lie to you?"

He was white, and therefore angry. Dr. Westrum held himself back when he was angry, hiding his eyes to hide his feelings, and she knew by his whitening that he was angry. Hawkes, for example, grew red when he was angry, and raged and swore and threw the furniture about, and destroyed things and tore things up and threatened to kill himself after first killing everybody else, especially her, but Dr. Westrum whitened and became extremely calm and kept a low, quiet voice, always establishing facts before proceeding to accusations, and he said now, "When I went to your father's funeral I met a man there."

"Oh," she said. It wasn't the question she expected, and to prepare her mind she took time to bring from her kitchen a backless stool with stair-steps. She sat erect on the stool, holding closed her robe, slightly higher than Westrum, who sat upon the couch and who experienced a certain difficulty in accusing upward.

"Now," she said.

"He was a detective," Westrum said.

"Who was a detective?" she asked.

"The man I met at your father's funeral," Westrum said.

"Yes," she said.

"I don't remember his name," said Westrum.

"No," she said.

"What was his name?" Westrum asked.

"Whose name?" she asked.

"If you lie to me," said Westrum, "I really must discharge you," but that, he sadly knew, was itself a kind of falsehood, for if she told the truth he would discharge her, too.

"I don't know what man you met," she said. "Dr. Westrum, won't you have a cup of coffee?"

"Will you turn the radio down?" he asked.

"Yes," she said. "Down or off?"

"I may be on the wrong track," he said. "If I am, I'm sorry. Do you know what I'm getting at?"

"Yes," she said, for now she did.

"You *do?*" he asked.

"If I lie you'll fire me," she said.

"If it's true I'll fire you too," he said.

"It's not even fair," she said.

"He was a friend of yours," said Westrum.

"The boss never fires himself," she said.

"Who was he?" Westrum asked.

"I was never fired from a job," she said. "I won't be fired."

"You took him out of the Journal," Westrum said.

"I don't know what man you mean," she said.

"He was a detective," Westrum said.

"My father's friends were detectives," she said. "He didn't have any other friends. He wasn't rich."

"He wasn't your father's friend," said Westrum, "he was yours. He had a short name. He wore a hat."

"A short name and wore a hat," she said.

"I'm sending you home," he said.

"I'm not lying," she said.

"You're not telling me the truth, either," he said. A thought occurred to him. "How stupid of me," he said, "it'll be in the carbon."

"The carbon in the bank?" she asked. "There's no carbon," by which she meant to say there was no bank, for the carbon was kept, as she perfectly knew, in the vault in the apartment where Dr. Westrum met with his mistress. "I know where the carbon is. You won't fire me," she said. Nevertheless, her hope had been engaged by the magic word *home—sending you home* he'd said—and wasn't that what she and Hawkes had wanted from the beginning? But she hadn't meant to be fired. "We all make mistakes," she said. Hawkes knew how to get things done, and now she'd be going home as planned and plotted, and he'd be ready for her again. After all, he'd just come off a case and he was flush, and he was entitled to run around a bit to rest up between cases. Nobody stepped on Hawkes. He never really failed her when she needed him.

"It's not mistakes I'm firing you for," he said, arising from the sofa.

"I might be able to think of his name," she said.

"I don't need his name," said Westrum.

"You'll pay my fare," she said.

"Oh God yes, I'll pay your fare," said Westrum, "and more than that. You can go home to whoever it is that wants you so much. He's a detective with a short name, a bird or a beast, he sneaks up behind people in the post office. I wish you'd gone at it another way."

"If not mistakes," she said, "then you're firing me for lying."

"Not for lying," he said. "For altering my Journal."

"Women lie," she said. "You and her exist by lying."

"Lie all you care to," he said. "The man was in the Journal, because I talked to him at your father's funeral. I remember him from there and I put him in the Journal, and you took him out."

"In the shorthand or in the typescript?" she asked.

"In the typescript," he said, although now that she raised the question he could not be absolutely certain. Often, reading shorthand, he visualized typescript. "I could be mistaken," he said.

"I always said to save the shorthand," she said, and she eagerly added, "I'll save it from now on."

"No," he said, "I'm not mistaken."

"Did you ever think," she asked, "that nobody went sneaking up behind anybody else in the post office, only she went sneaking up behind herself? She invented it."

"For a while I thought so," he said.

"She wants you," said Miss Sanantone, "nobody wants me."

He heard on the radio New Hamburg throwing forward passes—good sense, thought Westrum, to pass over what you couldn't go through. He listened a moment for Philip Benstock's name, but he did not hear it. "Your detective friend wants you," he said.

"How is Mrs. Westrum today?" she asked.

"She's just fine," said Westrum at the door. He could not re-call that Miss Sanantone had ever asked for Beatrice. "Why do you ask?"

"I always ask," she said. "If you don't want me to ask I'll never ask again."

She had chained and bolted the door behind him, and he fumbled with difficulty at the mechanism. She made no motion to assist him. "You'll go back Monday," he said.

"Then I'm fired for something I never did," she said. "She lies, and I'm fired. It pays to be rich. Poor people bleed. The boss never fires himself," she called, leaping from the stool and running toward Westrum at the door and slamming it behind him with a rattling of the chain, and calling through, "Her whole life is lies, she's a dirty Jewish bitch," and more, she said, which Westrum heard upon the stairway, not her words but her rhythm telling him he was right enough: of large injus-tice she was the victim, yes—so were they all—but not of the lesser charge, hearing the rhythm of her confession with the clatter and rhythm of his own feet upon the stairway of the old house, and past the stone maiden whose back and buttocks, too, he now noticed, sought Fleck for Congress, and into his car, and through the square, and over the bridge.

In the underground garage of the Center he lost the radio. The score was still unknown to him. Perhaps it had been men-tioned, but he had been listening poorly, returning to his suite and replacing among fifty thousand pages (for he'd need to be now, until he found someone else, his own Miss Sanantone) the five pages devoted to the funeral of Officer Sanantone, humble policeman passed down to history by the accident of association with Westrum; to whom several additional pages were devoted in the annals of the police of New York—it ran in the family, Westrum thought—in connection with Officer Sanantone's having in turn altered or corrupted several pages, a crime afterward duplicated, and in the name of friendship, too, by his daughter, for which daughter like father suffered penalties upon the job, and yet a kind of admirable crime, he thought, a crime of fraternal principle placing love above law.

He lay upon the daybed of his suite in the hope of a short sleep uninterrupted by brilliant illuminations. Perhaps he was wrong. Had he fired her in justice? Had he been just to her? Perhaps it was only one more instance of the persecution of the innocent: was he not perhaps retaliating upon Miss Sanantone for the difficulties he was having with Benstock? She was a scapegoat and he was Hitler—Hitler is alive and well and taking a nap, he thought. At the gateway to his nap he heard the drumroll of the Mortuary Unit of the Police Department Marching Band, unless it were a drumroll from the football stadium on somebody's radio down the corridor. Perhaps he would never awaken from this nap. God would punish him for avenging himself upon Miss Sanantone. The world might end at any moment. Someone at a switch, irked by the chairman of whatever seating committee defined his life, might blow up the world for the relief of his own irritation. Drifting to sleep, he felt the world go cold, and he sat up and brought the blanket from the foot of the bed to his shoulders, and slept well then while the world continued—the game ended, the stadium emptied, the boys of New Hamburg crossed the bridge in their striped green bus, the day darkened, and the telephone rang in Westrum's sleep. Apparently it had been ringing for some time, for as he reached it his caller rang off, and he showered, and he taped his ankle fresh, and he began to compose for his Journal his account of his firing of Miss Sanantone.

It was a certainty in Beatrice's face at the door that something alarming had occurred. She hoped he knew of it already, to save her the heavy task of telling. *Terence*, he thought. *Joel*. Tragedy would be his sons. *Nelson*, he thought, and next he thought *Miss Sanantone has killed herself*, and he saw her swinging from the ceiling by the pink sash of her pink robe, her mismatched slippers clinging to her feet. "You haven't heard," Beatrice said, and quickly, to end her husband's suspense, "Philip Benstock was hurt."

214

"In the game," he said.

"Then you heard," she said.

"I told Benstock so," he said.

"His face was all torn up," she said.

"His face," said Westrum. He had imagined ribs, knees, shin-bones, he'd not have gone for the face himself, it's not how they'd have done it in the old days out of Brest. No, the face was malice, vengeance, thirty years ago they'd have gone for working parts only, to put a boy out of the game today, not out of life forever, they'd have gone for the joints of limbs merely functional and operational and soon healed, only to hobble and harass him, not to disfigure him.

"His teeth," she said.

"Where is he?" Westrum asked.

"They knocked out all his teeth," she said.

"All?" he said. Beatrice often exaggerated medical things, especially when children were involved, but the vision of Philip toothless weakened Westrum, and he sat in his leather chair beside the picture window, where the bird sang in the tree, taking a writing tablet in his hand but not writing. "I fired Miss Sanantone," he said.

"I thawed the meat," she said, "but I haven't the heart to make dinner." It was her husband's way, in any crisis, to sit to his Journal. He always had. No event occurred until he had made words of it, she mustn't scold, she mustn't think him callous, she must move now with absolute clarity of mind, for the mood of the moment was the mood once again of that most terrible night of his violence. She refrained from asking why he had fired Miss Sanantone, weeping now with the sodden package of meat in her hands as if it were the meat she was weeping for.

Terence bare-chested passed through the room, inquiring about a "certain particular" white shirt, not just any white shirt but the certain particular white shirt he had intended for weeks to wear upon this night. It gave him confidence, he said. He had slept all afternoon, and that had given him confidence,

215

too, and bathed for an hour, and deodorized himself with manly scents, and attended his hair to the ultimate stray wisp to lend it the appearance of shaggy carelessness, and gargled with red Lavoris. He carried in one hand the fireplace bellows, and in the other a formal black tie. "I couldn't have ate anyhow," he said.

"We'll go to the Infirmary," said Westrum to Beatrice.

"What for?" asked Terence, first in confusion, then in fury.

"Not you," his father said, "your mother and I."

"What for?" asked Terence again.

"For the Benstocks," his father said.

"What *for?*" asked Terence.

"To be of help," his father said.

"You're not going to any damn Infirmary," Terence said.

"They need us," his mother said.

"*Need you shit,*" said Terence, not to his mother but to his father, his fury rising, his voice high in fear, and his eyes shining wth the beginning of tears. "If he needs you so much why is he firing you? That's how much he needs you," and he turned from his father in appeal to his mother. "That bastard," he cried to her, meaning perhaps his father, perhaps Benstock, perhaps somehow Philip. "What good are you going to do at the Infirmary? Are you going to hold their hand?" He hurled the bellows against the fireplace screen. "That bastard," he said. "He thinks Benstock will give it to him if he shows up at the Infirmary."

"No," said Westrum honestly, "I wasn't thinking that."

"I'll put money on it," Terence said.

"Do pick up the fireplace screen," his mother softly said.

"He brought it on himself," said Terence.

"Brought what?" his mother asked.

"Who brought what?" his father asked.

"Philip brought it on himself," said Terence, "because they wouldn't have been so rough on him if he wasn't a Jew."

"You sound like your grandfather," Westrum said.

"I sound like you," said Terence. "Everybody says so."

"Such as who?" his father asked.

"All the kids heard it across the river," Terence said. "He was asking for it. It's his attitude."

Think, thought Westrum, don't move. *Life is a bowl of pronouns,* he thought, and Terence was weary in spite of sleep, defenseless, all turbulence within, who had dreamed for days of massive failure, of his projector heating out, of unaccountable explosions, of film snapping and breaking, lights failing, sound track awry, all wires entangling, buried to his upper lip in dreams of film and tapes and wires and lights and sounds and power all in the same moment so far defying control that not a thousand geniuses resident at the Center could even explain it, much less assist.

"I'm thinking mainly of Sally," Beatrice said.

"When did they say it?" Westrum asked.

"They've been saying it for two weeks," said Terence.

"They say he asked to have his teeth knocked out?" Westrum asked.

"You know what I mean," Terence said.

"No I don't," said Westrum. "I want it explained."

"Tomorrow," Terence said.

"No," said his father, "now."

"Do it now," said Beatrice, "and be calm. Don't ruin the night. Let's not do something tonight we'll regret forever."

"It's his attitude," said Terence. "He thinks he's somebody. It's the way he walks and the way he talks."

"How does he walk?" his father asked.

"He gives you that big muscle walk," said Terence.

"Show me," his father said.

"I can't," said Terence. "He dared them, that's what he did. He's arrogant. It's the way he talks."

"Then show me how he talks," said Westrum.

"By his silence," Terence said. "He doesn't talk, he's silent. You can tell what he thinks by his silence. He thinks he's some-

217

body, he thinks he's superior than I am, he's a football player and I'm not, his father's the boss and you're not, he's got you in the palm of his hand. It's only revenge."

"For what?" said Westrum.

"Because you're superior to him," said Terence.

"Here's your shirt," said Beatrice, holding Terence's particular white shirt for his arms to enter.

"Don't talk about people being superior to other people," said Westrum.

"I'd as soon not talk about anything," said Terence. "I want to get out of here, and you better not go to no goddam Infirmary."

"Your grammar leaves something to be desired," his father said, but it was not Terence's grammar which appalled him— the grammar would repair itself in time—it was Terence's free use of ideas of superiority which appalled him, which had passed to Terence in spite of Westrum's every effort to destroy the cycle by a lifetime of inner cleansing. His rage was hot, and he saw that Beatrice saw that his rage was hot and that they were once again at that moment which was like that earlier moment when Westrum broke the boy's back, and he thought now *count to ten,* as he'd been told, and he thought *think,* and he thought, *How is this moment like that other moment?* "Your mother asked you to pick up the fireplace screen," he said.

Beatrice picked up the screen, and she picked up the bellows, too, and handed the bellows to Terence, who then dropped it where he stood, not accidentally, as he had once dropped the old blue Ancient Malacca Distinctive bowl, but with all deliberation now, to dare his father's rage or violence, to punish his father for having trapped him in lies about Philip Benstock.

"Pick up the bellows," his father said.

"First I'll button the shirt," said Terence.

"First you'll pick up the bellows," Westrum said. His voice was low, and he knew that no voice would move Terence, and he knew, too, now at last, the nature of the moment: that his rage had arisen then and now not because of a bowl or bellows upon the floor but because the moment was a moment of exile —exiled then by Lerman from Washington, exiled now by Benstock from the Center. It was all quite clear and simple. A man required only fifty thousand pages of Journal closely studied to explain himself to himself.

"It's all sooty," Terence said. "I don't want to button a white shirt with black hands." Slowly he buttoned his shirt, his eyes upon his father, and if Westrum flew for the boy now they would remember ever afterward in despair that the terror had erupted from a question no more urgent than whether Terence would pick up the bellows before or after buttoning a certain particular white shirt. Of such stuff was all war made, thought Westrum.

"All right," said Westrum, "button your shirt first."

"That's what I'm doing," Terence said.

"I don't want to hear any more talk about people being superior to other people," Westrum said.

"He thinks he's somebody," Terence said.

"Everybody is somebody," Westrum said. "He's a football player. A football player is somebody."

"I might have been a football player," Terence said, "if you hadn't broke my back," in a voice as low as his father's, speaking of that moment now for the first time, which he had never spoken of before but carried in his heart only, nor forgotten it, nor buried it, but saved it and preserved it to present to his father at such a moment as this, a threat of foreclosure, a debt undeniable. "You're not going to the Infirmary," Terence said, stepping over the fireplace bellows to the picture window and tying his formal black tie, using the window for mirror.

"Pick up the bellows," his father said.

"Right away," Terence said, but to the last moment it lay where he had dropped it, and even then it wasn't Terence who picked it up, but Reuben Weinberg, who dashed into the house with a checklist of items essential to their mission, and

219

checked his checklist against Terence's checklist, and dashed out again with Terence. They were dressed alike from the knot of their black ties to the gleam of their shoes, off into the night in white crash helmets on Reuben's Honda 300.

Westrum and Beatrice next saw the crash helmets by the beam of their headlights, turning into Harriet's space in the parking lot of the high school. The helmets rocked gently upside down, slung by their chinstraps from the handlebars. "It's a morbid sight," said Westrum.

"Turn off your lights and you won't see them," Beatrice said, and Westrum returned to the car and turned off the lights. "However good or bad Terence does," said Beatrice, "tell him how good it is. Congratulate him. Praise him," and she took her husband's arm and they entered the sound of the schoolhouse. It was the sound of joy, Westrum supposed. "Who won the game?" he asked Beatrice, but she did not know, and he asked the joyful girl who handed him a printed program, "Who won the game?"

"Who won the *game?*" she said, for she believed that he was joking, and he passed with Beatrice down the center aisle, and they sat in the same row, perhaps, give or take a row or two, or perhaps in the very row and even the very seats where he and Benstock sat nine days ago, and there was Terence's name in the printed program, and spelled quite right, too (the world had a tendency to double the *r*), and the hall filled, and he was cheered by its filling. He had once heard someone say somewhere, "Hell is a half-filled auditorium." He had always felt so himself. On lecture tours he specified his preference for small halls filled to large halls partly empty, he hated the sight of shining empty seats, and Terence would do better with a full house, too: for Terence was Westrum's son, not Beatrice's. Joel was Beatrice's, he'd vanish at the sight of six people, and Nelson hid his head at the sound of his own name, but Terence was his father's son with something to say to a listening crowd, the larger the better, and Beatrice said, "Harriet has a presence, hasn't she?" Harriet walked slowly to the center of the bare stage, turning to the audience and standing silent, hands clasped in patience at her waist. This morning, when Westrum last saw her, she had worn a sweater of midnight blue, whose breast had charmed him behind her letter *C*, and charmed him now in crocheted blouse, also of midnight blue, and her braid fell to her shoulder. Her eyes had found him now —what had happened to lunch today? she'd cleared the afternoon, she'd sent Harvey birding, she'd been ready, she'd been waiting—her turquoise clasp swung slowly at the end of her braid, and here she was again, and the hall grew quiet.

She was brief. She believed that students should direct their own enterprises whenever possible. Therefore she was happy to give over the occasion to last year's runner-up in the Father Contest, a little plump black girl, as it happened, one Linda Lee, whose father was Second Chief Maintenance Engineer of the Center—that was to say, in an older style, janitor. The girl was vigorously applauded. She was popular among her fellow-students. Indeed, she seemed to Westrum an honest child. She reviewed the rules of the contest, mentioned the wonderful prize awaiting the winner, and identified the three judges, inviting them to stand at their places. One was Weiss, a chemist, last year's winning father, whose son had sung his virtues in heroic couplets. He was scarcely five feet tall, and he stood at his place beside one Meister, who was the second judge. "Mr. Meister is a storekeeper," said Linda Lee, startled by the laughter which followed: the owner of Meister's Ordinary Super Market was more than an ordinary storekeeper. Her surprise was so true, her innocence so real, that Westrum saw she had meant no joke. She smiled until the laughter lowered, and her tongue was very pink.

She was immediately confused again, for when she named as third judge the Reverend Fullenweider he appeared not from the auditorium before her, but from the wing, to her surprise, extremely tall and white beside her. "I'm sorry I was in the wrong place," he said, and he reached with his hand for hers, holding his arm awkwardly extended while she transferred her notes from her right hand to her left, and they shook hands at last, and the audience, relieved of the tension of the minister's outstretched arm, applauded.

He offered the invocation more cleverly than devoutly, West-rum thought; coy, this one, a bit squeamish about the name of God—"our general Father," he called Him. Too rational for faith, he was a smart young man and he knew where he was, he'd not have anyone think he was *too* religious. "We seek," he said, "divine or worldly guidance," take your pick, avoiding all offense with tricks of ambiguity, neatly and swiftly and briefly therefore invoking a God equally pleasing to scholars of the Center and established local shopkeepers, passing to his seat below, surrendering the stage to Linda Lee, who promptly sur-rendered it to Shirley Able, who was not much able, Westrum thought, poor pale girl, who had written a perfectly grammati-cal, perfectly correct, perfectly lifeless account of her father's existence, noting the dates of significant events of his life, be-ginning with his birth and concluding with his most recent triumph—his election to the presidency of the State Society for Immunological Studies—and walking from the stage to make way for a boy whose name had been omitted from the printed program, who played "A Hymn On Drums For My Father," no doubt excellent, Westrum thought, but noisy.

The third contestant might have been Shirley Able again, though she was less pale, and her voice carried better. West-rum's ankle troubled him, and he loosened his shoe, and he made the most earnest effort to learn, as he listened, why this girl valued her father, who had always been, she said, "a good provider." She named many of the items he had provided for his family, but she avoided all word of the spirit in which they were given. "Just giving things is not enough," she concluded. Apparently she had written more, but she chose at the final moment not to read it, and ended her contribution suspended in the middle of her sentence, followed upon the stage by a boy named Wellesley Hacker. "I'll show you some tricks my fa-

ther taught me," he said, whose mind, inherited from his father, could retain upon sight any series whatever, such as a col-
umn of names chosen from the telephone directory (by Linda
Lee) or the numbers upon dollar bills in anyone's pocket; he
could repeat the names of any twelve people shouted out one
by one from the audience, or any ten automobile license plates
announced in the same way, or name the order of any common
series such as the fifty states in alphabetical order (or their
capital cities), or the Presidents of the United States either al-
phabetically or chronologically, or swiftly name in alphabetical
order varieties of material objects such as fruits, vegetables, ani-
mals, flowers, trees, rivers, or lakes upon demand. For this astonishing feat—or series of feats—he was applauded with di-
minishing volume, for repetition reduced wonder.

His successor upon the stage was greeted with laughter. He
was Charles Evergood Hartlin. "My name is Charley Hartlin,"
he said, "always was." He wore a T-shirt with the name *Charley* stamped upon it, and he was a famous fool or clown or
comic. He had first distinguished himself among his school-
mates with skillful satiric imitations and impressions of television stars, political figures, and teachers at Center High, but he
had learned in time to turn from that outward scene to his own
diverting character. He invented himself as his art flourished,
creating imitations of qualities he hadn't had until he thought
to acquire them. He was more real to himself upon the stage
than off.

Westrum admired the boy's conception, a dialogue between
the boy and his father beginning upon the morning of the boy's
birth, when his father declared to him that he would be known
forever as Charles Evergood Hartlin. Yet it was easy to hear in
the crying of the baby the sound of *Charley, Charley* against
the voice of his father repeating *Charles Evergood Hartlin.*
Those were the lines and the limits of the debate between
baby and father, both parts taken by the boy here upon the
stage for the eyes and the ears of everyone he knew or had
ever known. He swung in imaginary swings, he rode upon

imaginary tricycles, he skated, he built a snowman, with every action crying, calling *Charley, Charley,* his father's voice repeating, echoing, *Charles Evergood Hartlin,* until at last, carrying his case to the people, the boy stood with arms upraised in political fashion, breathless, engrossed and persuaded by his own performance, calling, "What's my name? Tell me, tell me."

Scattered voices replied, "Charley . . . Charley . . . Charley," and he called again for answer, for a better, fuller, louder sound to end once and for all his father's defiant resistance to another man's right to name himself, "All together now, in the name of liberty, what's my name?" and the assembled people responded now with a full, total, compact, gathered voice—Beatrice, too, caught up with everyone else, all but Westrum, who held his silence—"Charley . . . Charley . . . Charley . . . Charley . . . Charley," as in a cheer, together, unified, and the boy with wisdom and timing to know to end it upon its own peaking, blowing kisses to the left and to the right as he skipped from the stage, having brought the auditorium at last to life, which had had no opportunity through two prepared essays, one hymn upon drums and one exhibition of a freak memory to applaud with feeling, nor any opportunity (since Linda Lee shook hands wih the Reverend Fullenweider) to laugh at anything, continuing to laugh and to applaud for several seconds after the boy had passed from sight into the wing.

Thus the auditorium appeared to be applauding the appearance of a motion-picture screen as it was swiftly wheeled upon the stage by Terence Westrum and Reuben Weinberg, whose suits of formal black after the T-shirt *Charley* suggested that the true and formal business of the evening was about to begin, that everything going before had been but preparation for this, which was, in any case (although only by the accident of alphabet), the final presentation of the evening, begun to the sound of Reuben's flute *allegro*, who had himself disappeared behind the screen and found his path through the separation of the curtain, not to his flute but to the switchbox, and darkened the auditorium, whose only light now was the beam of Harvey Weinberg's Bolex 18-5 Super borrowed by Terence for this crucial occasion, who had concluded after long inward debate that it was superior to his own. He feared only the danger of its heating out, but even against that emergency he had come prepared with fireplace bellows.

Flutist, Reuben Weinberg said the title upon the screen, slowly washed away by splashing water, and behind the title appeared Westrum's head twenty times the size of life in water, too, swimming clean hard strokes producing other titles soon splashed away by water, and behind the titles the pendulum of the clock upon the wall of the principal's office in the schoolhouse at Brest—*My Father Produced by Terence Westrum, Camera Crew Terence Westrum, Associate Producer Terence Westrum*, a pleasantry which appeared to amuse the swimming father who smiled as he hoisted himself from the pool beneath the sign upon the pumphouse briefly seen, nor overdone, the camera neither lingering nor dwelling WE DON'T SWIM IN YOUR TOILET, PLEASE DON'T PEE IN OUR POOL. Westrum, where he sat, shrank from the sight of his own wet head twenty times the size of life, and yet he was bathed by pleasure, too, at the rolling laughter through the auditorium, for Terence's sake, who crouched in the darkness beside his machine, his face tense and illumined, listening only partly to the laughter because mainly for any sound of trouble within the machine, confident of the art of his film, doubtful of the machine only.

Now Westrum upon the screen kissed his black-and-white dog and his black-and-white-cat—*My Father Is a Kissing Man* and—kissed his mother in the house at Brest as if beneath (such was the trickery of film) the Lutheran steeple in Brest (*My Father Loves His Old Home Town*), and kissed Beatrice too in the low light of the tavern of the Clover Leaf Motel beneath the frank curious gaze of the bartender with his white towel upon his arm, and Westrum shook hands with his father who danced a sidestep jig to the piping of Reuben Weinberg's flute in the high octave, and sat, and received his leaping cat upon his lap, whose name was Nigger (a point not made by the film-maker), and whose ferocious Doberman was made to appear, by the silent art of Terence's film, winsome and meek, barking for love, and once more Grandmother Westrum (once more the Lutheran steeple, too)—grandmother to the film-maker, mother to the hero—swinging the gate of the fence shut upon the loving dog—*My Father's Father's Dog*—Old Road, old schoolhouse, old pendulum marking time, grave-stones and cornstalks flying by, policeman at Brest lifting his hand in a kind of salute to their very respectable existence, and the depot as dead as the graveyard, yet brought to life by Terence's sweeping camera as if at any moment trains would come grinding from two directions.

And here came Westrum with Beatrice now beneath the flag hanging drenched and limp upon the staff, his head implicated and associated with the flag as with the Lutheran steeple—too clever, Westrum thought, like the clever young minister, Terence hinting to any churchgoing judge that his father was churchly, too, if you wish, although no title said so, or not churchly either, if you wished him not to be. Here God was indicated only, for Terence, too, was a smart young man and he knew where he was, shooting his father as churchman, patriot, health addict, hard worker, dog-lover, cat-lover, wife-kisser, small-town, big-town, here shaking hands one by one at the door with Benstock, with Harvey, with Kenneth Silvers, standing tall above them.

"He's too clever for his own good," said Westrum to Beatrice.

"He needs to win," she said. Her head was bowed, her eyes were closed and resting.

"It's a fake," he said, "it's doctored," and yet he knew too that whatever was fake was also fakable, needing the hint of truth to go by, and that it was he himself he saw there, however partial or cropped or spliced or cut or doctored, for he had made the moments happen to put the film to, and the sweet flute. It was only his own critic wit seeing himself behind his own portrait on film, even as Tikvah, were Tikvah to see this film, would see Westrum true behind the boy's clever arrangement; or as Benstock would see him, whose intuitions of blood long ago taught them skepticism of anybody's film of anything: who mistrusted him not because he was hidden (all men were hidden) but because, by denying that anything at all was hidden, he supplied their imaginations with unlimited possibilities. Where nothing at all could be confessed, all the worst might be suspected. A little candor only would have set their minds at rest.

But there had never been candor at all, not the least, only the one pure role, himself cast as perfect man unrelieved by even occasional confessions of frailty—not a good film, they'd say, walking out of the movie house into the night air, too romantic, too good a hero. *Ah, what a handsome man up there*, thought Westrum, attracted to the sight, his mind returning to the film. It was easy to see the hero's attraction for women, how trim, how slim, how lithe he was, how open his smile, how even his teeth, twisting through the air in slow motion now, but reversing himself when his fingers reached the water, diving upward backward from the water to the high board—*My Father Defies Gravity*—and the laughter a single solid wave bouncing upon the walls of the auditorium. Beatrice raised her eyes to see what she had missed, but too late, and saw instead Philip Benstock taking upon himself a multitude of enemies at the line of scrimmage, cheered for his valor by this assembly now (lying in the Infirmary with broken face), most of whom had cheered him upon the actual occasion, too, and Gretchen's white gloves upon Westrum's lap, and Reuben Weinberg playing his flute upon the silent screen, so astonishing the real, sounding flute that both flutes appeared to halt together in confusion, and all was sudden silence, all still and frozen for a moment in order that the moment might flow to the next, and there he was—there Westrum was—upon the picket line, whose own face, when seen in that place before, had been vacant of conviction, but to whose face Terence appeared even to have added conviction, erased vacancy, unless it had all been

illusion to begin with, or unless, lacking conviction then, Westrum was unable to see it then, and having it now saw it now,
and there was Harriet beside him, principal of the school,
mother to the flutist, mistress potential to the changeable hero,
joined there by Harvey, father to the flutist, husband to the
mistress potential, vigorous friend to the hero, whose face was
the face of Turtleman, first of the succession extending thirty
years from Brest to the east and back again—Turtleman,
Tikvah, Lerman, Benstock, those squat, broad, unbudging
Jews bearing upon the whole significant resemblance one to
another, the first of whom his father had exiled from Brest, another of whom had become his brother-in-law, the last of
whom was Benstock. And Lerman . . . well, Lerman . . . and
had Westrum made a game of them, experiments upon human
beings, like any Nazi?

There swung the pendulum. There piped the flute. There
Westrum upon his bicycle raced against the piping of the flute,
riding into the camera, it seemed, with an effort not only physical but also moral, striving to burst from the screen, and always failing, and Beatrice said beside him, "Pray. It's a race
against time," for there was Terence in agonies of desperation
fanning the projector with the fireplace bellows. *Film Donated
by the President of the United States.* Oh yes, thought Westrum, on whose behalf, shortly afterward, Justice Lerman
called to say that Westrum would be no longer needed: what
the President really wanted, it appeared, was somebody
swifter than a historian, somebody who'd get today's history
into print right away, tomorrow morning if possible, quick,
fast, immediate, never mind this fussing around for posterity.
Or had it been (the thought came to Westrum now) Lerman,
really, making the decision on his own, exiling Westrum from
Washington not because the President wished it but because
Lerman himself wished it, even as Benstock took it upon himself, or Tikvah took it upon himself, to decide on behalf of the
Center or the University that Westrum wouldn't be needed,

couldn't be trusted, something fishy, and cast him into an exile from which he was powerless to return, into a fate over which he had no control. The day that Lerman telephoned him to tell him in a hundred affirmative tactful phrases, a hundred times Yes whose sum was No, he'd gone home and struck Terence down as he'd almost done again tonight, again in the moment and mood of exile, as before, his rage overflowing his body which, on the whole, he subdued by running, as he was running now, before his own eyes, upon the screen, behind the Oldsmobile Custom Vista-Cruiser with the key to his suite taped to his sweatband, chronometer upon his wrist, Terence shooting him from the window of the wagon, when Beatrice waved and he'd not acknowledged them with his mind but only with his body which suddenly, senselessly spurted and sprinted as if to overtake them and embrace them, and upon his face he saw now an expression as involuntary as his sprinting, of utmost devotion and affection, the runner torn and divided between the duties of health and the desire to love *My Father Is a Healthy Man* (he read), and he saw the heatwaves rising from the projector, and he received the faint odor of the machine heating out, or about to heat out, or having already heated out. Terence pumped the bellows, lying upon his back upon the floor. His face was grave but confident, for if the machine was almost at the end of its own hot endurance, so was the film almost at its own end, film and flute fading curtly together, snapping themselves off clean, decisively, without lingering. *Bravo*, thought Westrum, and upon the short, brief last note of Reuben's flute the flutist himself, hidden all this while at the switchbox, so promptly snapped up the lights that Terence moaned with chagrin to be discovered still upon his back beneath the projector, the fireplace bellows still filled with air.

Terence gained his feet. He expelled the air from the bellows, wiped his face with his handkerchief, and with all possible modesty (yet not so humbly that he should appear arrogant) he bowed to his fellow-students and their mothers and

229

their fathers applauding him for having said so much so amusingly, so uniquely, so entertainingly, so originally, for having blown away with his bellows the boredom of the evening, for having introduced humor and laughter by artful labor—for having wedded act to theme, devotion calling forth devotion, whose work, indeed, not only celebrated his father but paid his father the praise of imitation of his father's own industry, his father's own passion to unify, to organize, winning for his devotion to those old virtues, by swift unanimous vote of three judges, a free trip to a North American city of his choice. With his bellows he pointed to the stage where Reuben Weinberg stood, so that the flutist might also be applauded.

He had in mind no destination. He had never given it any thought. He had expected to win, but he had not thought beyond the work to the prize. Daringly, he thought he might reject the prize. He'd give the money to charity, he thought, surrounded by friends, rewinding his film. "It couldn't have went another minute," he said, "it was heating out awful."

"It was beautiful," his mother said, and kissed him. "It was beautifully beautifully done."

"The track didn't synch," he said, "the music kept running away."

"Some things only the artist notices," his father said.

"Your father thought it was beautiful too," Beatrice said.

"It was very fine," said Westrum, seeking more to say, succeeding at last in going so far as to seize Terence by the shoulder when Harvey Weinberg burst between them and swept away Westrum's hand and embraced Terence, and embraced Westrum for being the father of Terence, and embraced Beatrice.

"Let's pack it up," said Terence to Reuben Weinberg. Would that his own father were a Jew. Jews wept, Jews wailed, Jews embraced, and the two boys packed the projector and wheeled away the screen and went off with the boys and girls of their circle to the Victory Screamer, and Westrum and Beatrice, too, into the night, to the Infirmary, where Philip Benstock lay.

"Your American games," said Sally Benstock bitterly to Beatrice, but it was Westrum who replied, for he understood that her bitterness was for him.

"Not mine," he said. "Not really mine."

"She knows," said Benstock. "She's not herself." She lay upon a cot in the physicians' consulting room, light-headed and becalmed by a soothing drug whose effects she fought, refusing whatever sleep of peace it might have given her. She had always fought sleep. One night in her childhood, between waking and sleeping, she had been carried away to captivity in a stone church, nor ever restored to that bed or that house of green tiles or those parents from whom she had been taken, and she did not sleep well even yet.

"His American games," she said again to Beatrice, taking Beatrice's hand, and Beatrice sat beside her. Sally dissociated Beatrice from Westrum, the wife from the husband, the dark Jew from the fair Gentile, speaking of them sometimes as if they were not even acquainted. It was a fabulous trick of her mind which her husband had become aware of only now, in these hours of waiting. Benstock corrected her impression, or tried to, perhaps with no effect upon her, yet with the most definite effect upon himself—Westrum had been upon the right side of the argument, so to speak upon the good side, Westrum had *opposed* the games, not favored them, but it was a correction she was incapable of receiving, and she repeatedly asked her husband, "Then why did you quarrel?"

"Because I was wrong," Benstock said, "I'm to blame, he knew what he was talking about, he warned me," and Benstock said to Westrum in grief with admiration, "You knew the territory."

"It was because he was a Jew," said Sally.

"In a way, yes," her husband replied.

"Wasn't it?" she asked Beatrice, intending the question for Westrum. She had not yet, in the weeks of their acquaintance, met Westrum's eye except in the first moment of their meeting, and she could not meet his eye now. His face was vague to her,

like the face of Coach Wilson, whose eye she had never met,
either, or the face of the tall, blond Gentile neighbor, her cap-
tor and her savior whose hand was iron gripping hers when
they walked in darkness to the well. "We cannot find
Gretchen," she said to Beatrice.

On the rack in the corner of the room Harriet Weinberg's
coat hung below Harvey's hat, and on the floor lay Philip
Benstock's cleated shoes and shredded jersey of midnight blue
stained with the green of the grass and the brown of the earth
and the lime of the lines of the gridiron. The jersey had been
twice torn from his body, first by the boys of New Hamburg
and then by the shears of the ambulance nurse in whose eyes
he saw revulsion for his smashed face soon to be more or less
repaired, more or less restored, the flesh of the upper lip disengaged from the teeth of his lower jaw, his jaw returned to its
former place, and his flesh sewn. He would be altered forever
—"He'll want to grow a moustache," the surgeon said—almost
again as he had been before, but not quite, rather a fan of
football than a player, and he'd wear a moustache, as his
mother wore a number.

"Everything's great," said Harvey, returning with Harriet to
the consulting room.

"He's coming down," Harriet said.

"She's asleep," said Benstock, leaving his wife's side to wait
in the doorway for word more precise than Harvey's. His son
was under the knife, his wife beneath sedation, and he was
unable to locate Gretchen, whom he had left at the football
game when Philip was carried off. "My mouth is on fire," he
said, whose only solace was cigarettes, and he lit another. "I'm
scattered all over," he said. "Half my family's unconscious. As
soon as it's over I'll be back here myself."

"Did Beatrice come?" Harriet asked.

"She's finding Gretchen," Westrum said.

"We hope," said Benstock.

"She will," said Harvey.

In a soft voice, with her back to her husband, Harriet said to Westrum, "I waited for you for lunch."

"I fell asleep," he said.

"I'd have kept you awake," she said.

"I'm counting on nothing," Benstock said from the doorway.

"What a day," said Harvey.

"I should have been picketing with you," said Benstock to Harriet. "You were right and I was wrong. Forgive me for all my bad thoughts about the picketing."

"I fired my girl," Westrum said.

"Wonderful," said Harvey, "I never liked her looks anyhow."

"How can you fire your girl?" Benstock asked. Did a man fire a mistress? Was that how such things were done in circles above his own? But no, she was no mistress of Westrum after all who had had no mistress ever, for he said so himself. The man who knew the territory told no lies on any score, and Benstock's mind revoked every doubt he had ever had. The proof of all things was Philip. Westrum had stood in a public place and warned against the game, and stood upon the picket line against it, yet Benstock had mistrusted him, denied him, misunderstood him, opposed him, withheld his faith from him.

"She did a bad thing to me," said Westrum.

"What did she do?" Harvey asked.

"Never mind what she did," said Benstock. "We'll get you a new girl."

"She didn't have an honest face," Harvey said.

"We'll get you two girls," said Benstock, "or three."

"At last the committee is unanimous," said Harvey.

"We need you," Harriet said.

"I might find the right girl in New York," said Westrum. "We're taking a little trip."

"Bring her back," said Benstock.

"Now you want me," Westrum said, in excitement, in exultation, a whole new life before him here and a dark new mistress before him now in midnight blue with swinging braid. "Yes, certainly," he said to Benstock, and the warmth flowed within himself, and he felt again, for the second time this night, a tremendous affection for himself, as he had felt upon seeing himself in Terence's movie, lunging, sprinting, breaking his pace in the name of love. He'd give himself now to Benstock in a moment of that man's need.

"Not want you," Benstock said, "need you."

"We need you," Harriet said again, and Beatrice returned, having found upon the telephone where Gretchen was, and Philip came unconscious upon a rolling cart. He was bandaged to the eyes, and his father kissed him upon his bandages, and the boy was wheeled away, and the surgeon came.

The surgeon himself was only a boy, or so he seemed to Westrum. He was dressed in green, *pajamas*, Westrum thought, *track suit*, fixing the surgeon in his mind for his Journal, *cap, mask, sweat running, bloody wrists*, passing his gaze from face to face seeking the father of the boy. He knew that Benstock or Harvey Weinberg was the father of the boy, but not Westrum, for the boy was a Jew, and everyone the surgeon knew (the surgeon was a Jew) was rather proud that such a stalwart linebacker was a Jew, and Westrum thought *all Jews here but me*, and the surgeon said to him, "I saw you somewhere. I saw you at the game."

"I wasn't at the game," Westrum said.

"Maybe you saw him picketing the game," Harriet said.

"Yes," the young surgeon said, "picketing the game."

"I was picketing myself," said Westrum.

7

In the gray dawn he wheeled his bicycle out of the garage and spun away. He was prepared to favor his ankle, but he soon discovered that it was well, not simply firmer and stronger than it had been yesterday, but absolutely well, perfect, wholly healed, and he was therefore perfect, too, and everything was excellent. He had never felt better nor more hopeful. Perhaps today would be the best day of his life.

His rhythm was trustworthy again, and he pedaled with leisure and confidence to Old Road, where his course began: it was four miles down Old Road to the cemetery, and four miles back, and a long day ahead by whose end, he hoped, he'd have settled many a matter, cutting the corner sharp, full pace ahead even before he'd quite turned into Old Road itself, down between the cornfields where birds sang from the bush, whom Harvey Weinberg knew by their songs and calls, whom Harriet would send off now and again in search of the songs and calls of birds in the bush in faraway places, whom Westrum would love when her husband was gone, or love beneath her husband's nose when he wasn't, and the gray dawn lifted, and the day began to glisten now. *I'll untape my ankle,* he thought, and his legs were deep into their rhythm, and the rubber whined on the road beneath him, and the air of the dawn was motionless except for the breeze he himself produced by the speed of his own motion, propelling himself into this great day, his own breeze drying his own glistening upon his own sweating shining body, for on a morning so happy as this he was the first and final cause of all events, when his spirits were up and his theology was down. Soon he would be free of Miss

235

Sanantone. Soon he would be free of Tikvah. Soon he would be free of his mistress, with much regret.

Up ahead, beyond the cemetery, the young policeman walked beside his car, skimming stones to keep awake. He straightened as Westrum approached, to appear vigilant, to show himself on duty and alert, pulling his necktie to his collar and greeting Westrum with a hand uplifted exactly as he had saluted the eye of Terence's camera, and it was as if the policeman now were imitating saluting as he'd seen it done in films. The film was more real to Westrum than the policeman, and the policeman said, "Good morning, sir," which were the first words Westrum heard this day, Monday, eighteen-thousand-three-hundred-and-ninety-fourth day of his life. He turned in the road.

His chronometer showed that he had come four miles with little effort in eight minutes and fifty-five seconds. He was himself again, he was well, his ankle was well, he'd spare two words for this policeman, and he said, "Great day," and saw before him, with the faintest dismay in spite of his exuberance the long road he had come which he was now required to return, and he thought how wise he had always been to set himself every task without too far considering its complications, to get himself halfway out with no sure means of getting back, to strand himself, maroon himself, flirt with impossibility, as he had stranded himself somewhere far out in those trackless wastes afterward entitled *A History of the Past World* with no instrument but his own intuition, stating his unprecedented case and waiting for the verification. Had he known in advance the difficulties of doing the things he had done he'd not have undertaken them, not left, not married, not raised sons, not taken mistresses, not written the *History*, and certainly not undertaken to maintain a Journal of a life so difficult as his own— had he but known it! No, he'd have lived like a vegetable, it was better that way, drawn a line on the ground with the side of his shoe and said, as boys said in the schoolyard at Brest, "This is my territory, I'll keep my side and you keep yours," re-

236

treated like his father to rooms behind a fence, who would lie here in the cemetery—to Westrum's left now, as he went cycling by—to which Westrum intended to return, or so he said. Yes, he had told Harvey Weinberg how he intended to lie there, though it had been no part of his plan, really, until he'd said it. He had said it only for the sake of winning Harvey, and winning Harvey he'd won Seat and new mistress, too, and chosen a gravesite besides, arguing the case his whimsy preferred and ending by believing the case he argued. Football was fascism. If it was the way to Harriet's bed it was nonetheless the truth he knew in his bones. He had only to examine his own bones. *Am I the world?* Was his knowledge of himself a knowledge of the world?

Then the world was a violent place and he didn't like it—*the world must exercise the heart harder*, he thought, *alone on a bicycle, unarmed*, speeding past the cemetery where he would lie when the world had ended, at least until the road was widened, by which time, he was certain, he'd have risen to Heaven like a good boy anyway, beyond the blades of the bulldozers, and Terence would come motoring past with his car full of wife and children and say, "Shall we stop and see my father's grave?" and someone's reply, "On the way back," and then forget altogether, simply forgetting to stop and look at the dead. *You can't stop a car once it's moving*, he thought. *I'll be buried here because I told Harvey so*, he thought, *to prove in death I wasn't lying in life*, prisoner of his own lies, challenged to make them true, shackled to these long tasks he set for himself, like the long straight road before him now which he must conquer upon his bicycle at a certain speed, having set the task for himself as he had set all others whether useful or pointless, juggling as many balls as possible for the sake of the juggling, doing to be doing, playing games of possibility for stakes he no longer required, rolling up the score for the score's sake, as Justice Lerman gathered money for money's sake, pedaling steadily now, his time well-made. And yet—*you see*, he thought, *that's what I mean*—he sprinted the last quarter-mile to improve his time, veering from Old Road, stopping his chronometer, licking the sweat of his upper lip, swinging his right leg over the seat and standing, cooling, gliding upon the left pedal, and dropping off then and running with his copper-tone bicycle up the driveway, into the garage, and showered and shaved for his mistress and his wife and the events of the day or the night in whatever the order of their coming.

He counted his cash, and he studied well his tangle-free Winding Reel, keys to car and bicycle, house here, apartment there, suite here, office there, keys to his footlockers, one key to his briefcase and one to his gypsum vault in the apartment he and his mistress kept (for which he also had a key), and the keys to several suitcases, and he gently and lovingly awakened Beatrice, saying, "Wake up, wake up, it's a glorious day."

On second thought, he'd tape his ankle one more day, to be on the safe side. He taped it fresh and tight and firm. Tomorrow he'd run in Central Park. *I like the feel of elastic*, he wrote upon a tablet, *dawn gray, then clearing, cycled Old Road eight miles in 17:40 don't know why I needed ten seconds. Greed. Don't do that any more*, and he wrote Miss San-antone's final paycheck, adding to it four hundred dollars (two weeks' salary) in severance pay, and he sealed it in a plain white envelope, and he began then a search of the house to find the bedroom Terence was in who moved from room to room from night to night. He found, instead, a note taped to the newel post, "Don't wake me. Leave quiet. Have a good time. Write if you get work. Don't worry about me. I'll have a ball."

"It's too early to be glorious," Beatrice said.

"I did eight miles in seventeen-forty," Westrum said.

"That's lovely, darling," she said.

"I had my best night's sleep in two weeks," he said.

"I dreamed that I was dreaming," she said.

"It's so restful to have made decisions," he said.

"I'm practically up," she said, and Westrum carried their

suitcases below, one of which was empty for Beatrice to fill in New York with lovely things, and he carried below his brief-case, too, containing four hundred pages of carbon copy of Journal composed since his arrival here, presented to him (the briefcase was) by Justice Lerman on behalf of the President and engraved with instructions for its return in the event of loss—"Just in case," said the President, "you forget it in the wrong place." So, anyhow, Justice Lerman said the President said. Beatrice said in the car, "It is glorious, you're right, dar-ling, you brought me a truthful report."

"Only twelve hundred miles to bottles and bed," said Wes-trum, and beside him now this woman, this dark girl he hadn't thought he could possibly have, for they were alien. She'd not have come to his course in history at all, except on her broth-er's hunch. "Try it," said Tikvah, "I'm told that he's unusual," and she went to Westrum in spite of his alien name. He had never imagined himself marrying farther away than New Hamburg, passing over the bridge into New Hamburg now, and the Center fell away behind him, and the girders of the bridge sank in his rear-view mirror, passing his Uncle Nelson's head on the frieze of the New Hamburg County Courthouse, beyond the courthouse, beyond the post office, beyond the Square itself, and down the sidestreet to the stone maiden, where Miss Sanantone waited with her typewriter.

"I hope we didn't keep you waiting," Westrum said, but she did not reply. She wore her green plaid coat and black pumps, and she coughed her morning cough. Westrum climbed the stairs to her apartment for her old straw trunk and smart suit-case.

She drank from a bottle of Dramamine in anticipation of the airplane, and she flipped her cigarette into the gutter, and lit another. She had said at first that she'd go home by train, but something had changed her mind. He offered her the white en-velope with her check inside, but she would not raise her hand to receive it, nor raise her eyes to his with any kind of explana-tion, nor reply even to Beatrice's greeting, but sat behind them in silence and smoke to the airport, and sat across the aisle from them on the airplane, still in silence, rigidly, burning and fuming with anger, and deprived now even of her tobacco, awaiting her distress, holding her Sickness Bag before her, her head exploding and her stomach spinning although the airplane itself stood as still and as motionless as a mountain, its motors not yet even ignited. In preparation for this cruel moment she had not eaten in twenty-four hours, so that her retching and her vomiting, beginning with the first vibrations of the motors, produced for the bag she held to her mouth nothing but her gasping; from this she gained a small relief by holding to her nose not the spirits the stewardess offered but a fresh, unlighted cigarette whose fragrance reassured her that all was never lost, that the world remained before her yet, that life would begin again after this ordeal, this necessity, this flight from a place she deplored to her gentleman friend, Hawkes, whom she doubted and sometimes despised. He wasn't the man Dr. Westrum was. She thought of the advantages of death.

Westrum showed Beatrice in *The New York Times* the death of Paul Zutzky at forty-nine, of an illness of "several months," the obituary said. "Did I know him?" she asked. "You met him once," her husband said, recalling it clearly, "in a Chinese restaurant in Chicago." "I don't remember," Beatrice said, and Westrum replied, "Yes you do, you must," somehow annoyed that she didn't remember: he'd gone with her and Tikvah and Zutzky and two or three others from a meeting somewhere in Chicago to a Chinese restaurant on the South Side, and they had sat, he recalled, in a booth, an alcove with a curtain drawn for privacy, and Zutzky told of a battle he'd been reading up on against some private papers recently come to light, from which he could now incontrovertibly show that a certain great battle had been lost and thousands of men annihilated because the general had formed his plans and calculations from an obsolete map. "So if they'd had the right map," Beatrice said, "the other army would have died."

240

First, she thought, she'd open all the windows. She'd air the apartment. She'd be sure the bed-linen was fresh. She'd have lunch with Winnie Tikvah, dinner at eight at the Lermans', and she'd go home with Wes then to bottles and bed. *Champagne*, she thought, crossing the aisle to see if she might assist poor Miss Sanantone. She gave Miss Sanantone the white envelope containing her check, and Miss Sanantone tore it into two pieces, and Beatrice said, "Well, when you change your mind he'll send you another."

"He can't do it to me," said Miss Sanantone, and Beatrice sat beside her and held her hand for a moment and said, "Don't be unhappy, be proud of yourself, you lasted a very long time with him, he's not an easy man," and they smoked a cigarette together, and Beatrice returned to her own seat beside her husband and read Paul Zutzky's obituary.

Undoubtedly they had met, if Wes said so, she'd met a lot of people she couldn't remember, sat at many meetings she couldn't remember, and dined in many restaurants Chinese and otherwise. She disliked reading of men dying at forty-nine —Wes was fifty—but it was only natural that he remembered everything, having written everything down every day of his life for thirty years, who was even now recording upon his tablet five miles in the air at six hundred miles an hour God knew what. Miss Sanantone across the aisle dropped the white envelope torn in two into her black patent-leather handbag as if, upon further thought, she might yet paste the check together and cash it. Miss Sanantone was breathing deep upon the advice of the stewardess, her breasts were fine and full, whose breasts her gentleman friend would no doubt this night lay hands upon. It was somehow the gentleman friend who'd caused the trouble. Beatrice didn't know the details, and she didn't care. The less she knew the better, and Wes himself would lay hands upon her, too, this night in their own good bed when this long day was done. How good he'd be. He always was. New York set him up, he ran all day about his business, to the bank and wherever, and then he was always superb at day's end—it paid to exercise and stay in health—he'd go on and on and on and on forever for her, and please her in every possible way, who might have been the captain of this airplane approaching up the aisle now if he hadn't become instead not a goyim captain of airplanes but husband to the Jews. She said to the gray-haired captain, "Who's minding the store?" He smiled at her and touched her upon the shoulder, but his eyes were upon Westrum, and he guessed that Westrum was her husband, and he gave his attention instead to Miss Sanantone, who stared him quickly down with angry eyes, nor any invitation to pause and listen to her woe. "Nobody," he said to Beatrice, "I thought I'd just trust to luck today."

Beatrice imagined today, as she often did upon such occasions, that everyone else, too, was flying to a lovers' rendezvous. All men and all women became for her, in her own anticipation, travelers upon journeys purely romantic, sealing again, dedicating again, enforcing once more whatever marriages or compacts perpetuated under whatever luck. Now he concluded his business with his tablet and unlocked the briefcase at his feet and dropped the tablet in, and Zutzky's obituary, too, and locked the briefcase again and held it clamped between his ankles to prevent its being stolen by thieves the size of mice, no doubt, lurking beneath airplane seats, and reading a letter from her brother handwritten upon the stationery of the Office of the Dean which she had never known he had received and about whose contents she remained incurious, as she had trained herself to be incurious about anything Wes ever wrote or received. Sometimes, at his invitation, she read a letter from someone, but always indifferently, hoping to forget everything. *Dear Wes* she saw, and even that much in spite of herself, she'd never read a letter unbidden, nor a page of his tablets lying about, nor any part of his Journal except once when she came upon two pages fluttering loose from a cardboard carton on the shoulder of a truckman moving them into the house at Leipzig (or was it out?) wherein Wes was prowling around in a big house somewhere all full of Jews but him, trying to decide if his politics was only sexual. He suffered all his life the most awful case of chronic conscience. He was worried now if he was firing Miss Sanantone justly or unjustly, and here came the goyim captain again, he'd been to the lavatory, dear fellow, he'd never been circumcized. Her sons had been circumcized. The insurance company always declined to pay for the boys' circumcisions on the grounds of their having been done not by a physician but by a rabbi: therefore it was not medical but optional, and Wes said each time, "Jesus, it costs me money to be a Jew." He liked to say things like that. He liked to pretend he was a Jew, he had never really recovered from the shock of his own daring, his own defiance, his revolution against moral neutrality, and there went the goyim captain closing his door behind him, into the cockpit, he'd fly for anyone, that one, for airplane pilots on the whole were moral neuters like stewardesses and stenographers and football coaches and supergoy rocketing to the moon.

Beatrice was wholly certain of her husband, and he dwelled in the palm of her hand. As far as she knew, only she so fully trusted him. His face invited doubt, and his speech had never lost the accent of the inner country: on the telephone he sounded like a cowboy who had moved to town. Nobody else really and truly understood that Westrum's mistrust of himself was greater than anyone else's mistrust of him, and with less reason; that he tormented himself beyond necessity; that he suffered a moral concern too exquisite; that he pushed himself beyond limits, like businessmen pushing for profits beyond profits. His face and his voice were so deceptive they fooled even him. He feared himself. He feared that he carried within himself that seed of moral indifference which had permitted his father and his father's fathers down the line to take pleasure in war, hatred, and the violent advance of their own interests, all in the name of American duty and service.

If he had done her ill at all it was by giving her so good an opinion of the country. He was not the country. But he was filled with a silly hope for the country, which he imagined was day by day opening its mind to itself, even as he, by the daily act of composing his own confession and testament of himself there between his ankles, his own scrupulous relentless history all-inclusive, as when in the moment of violence against Terence he had struck the boy and cried, "You little Jew."

O perhaps he had. Sometimes she thought she had heard it, or sometimes she thought she only thought she heard it in retrospect, because he asked her so often what he'd said, if anything. She never really knew and she never really cared and she never really thought it had much meaning anyhow—Jew, goy, spik, nigger, mick, bitch, bastard—they sprang to the lips on the playing fields of the north Bronx, it was the coin of fury, and he'd worried so much and so long about it that she'd gone at last to her brother and told him the whole stupid thing from the breaking of the bowl to the blow of the hand aimed too well to the oath Wes thought he might have uttered, but Tikvah only shrugged and smiled and said, "What else is new?" whose letter Wes was reading now beside her, and she touched his arm and said, "Please pass me the newspaper."

> Dear Brother Wes,
> I have here your letter from the airport, watching airplanes come and go. My apologies for the delay.
> I also have here a very cordial and discreet letter—*two* very cordial and discreet letters I should say—from one Benstock, apparently your host and admirer there at the Center. In the first letter (which is the second letter— the first by date was the second by arrival) he asks me whether your papers (Journal) are available for removal from "the University bank" here to his repository there, whether any legal obstacles stand in the way of their removal, or whether the University would make a fight of the matter.
> Some misunderstanding exists. What can he mean by such a peculiar reference as "the University bank"? Since the University has never been fortunate enough to own

or in any way control your Journal it is obviously not our right to relinquish anything. We cannot retain what we were never given. I understood your Journal to be in a bank vault ten thousand feet below the ground, guarded by Justice Lerman himself, who owns the bank and the street it stands on. At any rate, I am thinking that you and I must clarify this matter before I answer.

In Benstock's second letter he tells me that you have recommended me for a Seat at the Center. It is as if Benstock as writer of the second letter, I as recipient, and you as intermediary, are by no means the same persons who played those parts in the first letter. I admire his ethical sense, his arduous way of keeping separate on paper matters which cannot be kept entirely separate in the mind. I gain the feeling of a man in constant struggle. But I have not done a stitch of work on *Potentialities for Fascism in America* in many years (I must even look at his letter to get the title right) and I probably will never write another line of it. I thank you for your endorsement. But you know (for you have frankly said so) that I am lazy, paralyzed. If I could save the world I'd probably forget.

All I can do against the potentialities is to do this Dean thing now as well as I can. We are thoroughly rebuilding the whole ancient mess here, looking forward to several retirements (mentioning no names) which will give us opportunities to build anew in vacant places. It is for that reason that you must make up your mind no later than Christmas whether you intend to return. If you do not return you *must* vacate your place.

It has lately been suggested to me that I am "forcing you out" (such a strong word as "exile" was used) because of some resentment I feel toward your success. Lerman is pressing me very hard to make me give you everything you ask, he asks, or anything you or he might think of asking in the future. I don't know why he keeps pressing

245

me for something he knows I can't give you. Won't give you. Can't because I won't. Won't because I don't think it's right. You have enough, other people have too little, I'm spreading it around as well as I can. He tells me I "resist" you, my submerged and latent prejudices are unknown to me, and for all I know it's true. He tells me I should be "grateful" to you. What for? What have you done except to be human to me? That's not a favor, that's a duty, the obligation of a civilized man. (Even if I am supposed to go on the rest of my life paying off some debt to you I'm not sure it's legal to do it with University money.) Don't think that I don't admire your triumph over your own heritage, but I say to you that you better damn well triumph over your own heritage or we'll wipe ourselves off the face of the earth. I mean you. I mean myself.

I regret I don't remember the name of the Italian fellow who patted my head and referred to his wife's ass, etc., etc., when I replied so wittily, etc., etc. I don't doubt my wit, I've heard you allude several times to that occasion, and I am pleased to receive credit for a distinguished repartee. To tell you the truth I don't remember it at all. Never did. Look it up in your Journal. You remember more about my life than I remember myself, there's no doubt of that. Keep me posted.

I am buying a wig anyhow. Twenty-five years I was bald, now I grew hair from a store. What a store!! I went to the wigmaker's store to buy a head warmer for $3.75 to wear at night to defeat the common cold. The salesman said, "You spend one-third of your life in bed, it's true you should have a cheap little head warmer, but you also spend three-thirds of your life living, you should have a whole new head of hair, the way you look now you're extremely undistinguished, your effectiveness is zero, a bald man's a joke, nobody looking at you believes you're a Dean, put hair on your head and you'll look like what you are. Here's a moustache, too, for only twenty dollars, here's a goatee-moustache combination sixty-five, here's a semi-beard for ninety, full beard for only a hundred and ten, sideburns fifty dollars a pair. I bought hair for my head only. Instead of spending $3.75 I spent $375.00.

Don't be shocked to see me with my head full of hair. Pretend to recognize me. I will be as I was before you first knew me. The problem was color. We took several wigs to my mother so she could choose hair the color I used to have, but she was indecisive. Brown, yes, but was it light, dark, medium, how? Now, watch this for historical reconstruction!! "Take a piece of white bread from the box," she said. "Be sure to close the box behind you. Toast it in the oven." How high should the oven be, I ask her. "The oven has only one high. High, low, medium, it was all one high, the dial gave it class only, toast the bread as long as an egg." How long is an egg, if I may ask? She closed her eyes and imagined herself performing old routines in the kitchen, the things she did while boiling one egg for me and one for Beatrice any morning before school forty years ago. "Now," she said, "now the egg is done, now take the bread from the oven, the bread is toast, close the oven door behind you, the bread is the color your hair was."

The war is over at last, my head is full of hair again. You were right, I now believe, wars end when men refuse to fight. I went and had my hair blown off (lucky it wasn't my whole head I always say), and now I refuse to fight with you. The Thirty Years War is over. You may return. You may not return. It is up to you. I must stop searching my submerged conscience to find out if I am wronging you because I am jealous of your moral superiority. I grant you your moral superiority. Congratulations, you win. Myself, I have succumbed to all sorts of temptations, I am indolent, I pick up strange women on the subway, I smoke myself to death, I tell lies, and with all these sins to accomplish I cannot compete with your industry, your good health, your iron monogamy. I will write out a certificate attesting to your virtue. Deans have certificates for all occasions.

Even so, you know I never really believed it. Little truths leaked out from time to time. Over thirty years that was inevitable. You are on the whole a most unusual and excellent man, but so am I, in my way. You felt my pain, but I was not incapable of feeling yours. I learned many things from you, and I am grateful, you introduced me to a part of life I might not have known, but now we are square, we are even, all accounts are settled except the money I owe the wigmaker.

I dread the dinner party at the Lermans'. I'll be wearing my new hair. I'll come drunk. I'll stay drunk. He has been on top of me all year to buy your papers (Journal) for the University before he outbids me and buys them himself. "Start bidding," I say. He says he can't start bidding unless I bid first—how can he win a race against nobody? To him, too, I am prepared to surrender. He has more money than the University has, you have more moral superiority than I have, I wish I had his money and your superiority, meanwhile I settled for a new head of hair, head of new hair, I am what I am, as Popeye used to sing on the radio.

> I'm Popeye the sailor man,
> I'm Popeye the sailor man,
> I yam what I yam 'cause I yam what I yam,
> I'm Popeye the sailor man, beep-beep.

At last, thought Beatrice, Wes at last finished reading her brother's letter, and now he must twist himself around in his seat again to dig down in his pocket for his keys upon his Winding Reel and unlock his briefcase once again and put the letter in and lock it up again to keep it from the eyes of mice

248

beneath the seats. Men were warriors. Six wars were going on at once in today's *New York Times.* Men were boys, and her husband's face beside her now appeared to her for a moment nothing more than the distinguished mask of a boy up to mischief, she'd borne and raised three boys and she knew the look. His rare good spirits glowed upon his face today. "You're a boy," she said.

"How can I be a boy?" he asked, squirming to work his Winding Reel back into his pocket. "If I were a boy I'd be going to Albert Lea, Minnesota." Terence had chosen, as the North American city of his choice, Albert Lea, Minnesota, not New York or New Orleans or San Francisco. He'd hang around a few days in Albert Lea and come home. "He has a flair for eccentricity," Westrum said. "Who'd think of Albert Lea?"

"Who'd think of the Center when he could have New York?" asked Beatrice.

"Nobody," he said, carrying her hand to his lips.

"You're way up," she said. "You keep smiling to yourself."

"It's the altitude," he said.

"You were smiling on the ground," she said.

"I'm free of her," he said—of Miss Sanantone, Beatrice understood. "I'll start over right with a new girl."

"We'll start everything over right," she said. New place, new home, new friends, they'd begin a new life in a new place. Soon, when Terence was gone, they'd be alone at last as they hadn't been in twenty-five years.

"I'll be free of Tikvah, too," he said. "He wants me out by Christmas, tonight I'll give him a Christmas present early."

"You're always better brothers at a distance," she said.

"We're starting down," he said.

"Tell him nicely," she said. "Be extremely kind to him."

"Of course I will," he said.

"As a favor to me," she said, "don't make him think it's some sort of failure of *his.* He's failed enough. He knows it."

"Right," he said. She was right. He must be civilized and graceful. In parting he must show Tikvah not triumph but

249

love. "I understand everything now," he said, "not that I'm free of them but free of myself"—that he had gone from Brest into the great cosmopolitan world, and met the test of it, and succeeded by every standard he respected: therefore he could go back home to the place where he had begun, and live and do his work there, and be above the local meanness, and far beyond his father. "Tell her she's supposed to stop smoking," he said, "in the bloom of my life I don't care to be blown up by her cigarette."

But the stewardess had seen for herself that Miss Sanantone continued to smoke. "Ladies and gentlemen," the stewardess announced, "the captain has *again* requested that you extinguish your cigarettes," but it was not until the captain himself spoke, male voice firm, no nonsense, that Miss Sanantone extinguished her cigarette and buried her face in her Sickness Bag, and they came down from sunshine through the undercast, and Westrum whistled Popeye's song, and he said to Beatrice, "I trust your friend the captain remembered to let his wheels down." When the wheels touched, color rose swiftly like a shadow along Miss Sanantone's jawbone and up into her cheeks, her ears, and the blood of excitement raced in Westrum, too.

To this city he had come, once upon a time, upright overnight twelve hundred miles in a railroad coach, his pockets filled with dollar bills and nickels, but the telephones were dimes now, and he and Beatrice and Miss Sanantone telephoned from three pay-stations back to back while awaiting their baggage, Miss Sanantone her gentleman friend, Beatrice to Winnie Tikvah, and Westrum his bank who had been sitting awaiting his ring for two hours. "Bank," he said, "I'm here."

"In town?" she asked.

"At the airport," he said.

"Thank God," she said.

"We will confer?" he asked.

"Of course," she said. "I'll be there." She always was, wasn't she? She never failed, whatever the hour or whatever the season, no disloyalty was ever more loyal than hers, but she'd be a bit delayed, she said, she had tracks to cover and a little dinner party to do a little shopping for. "I'll cancel my appointment with my ear man," she said, she was going deaf, she believed. "First . . ."

"First," he said, "hang up the phone."

"It's the most spectacular day," she said. The morning was gray. It was their kind of day, they loved gray or fog or night or rain, God couldn't see them, she said, though apart from Him she didn't care who saw them just so long as it was nobody they knew. She took a particular perverse pleasure, in the presence of strangers, in appearing certainly not as Westrum's wife but clearly mistress, illicit to the toes, good girl gone bad at last after much striving, clinging, kissing, talking dirty in crowded elevators, marching naked all over the Orient to the more or less delight of bellboys, bathboys, masseurs, and innkeepers. Safe with Westrum, she cared to be seen, she was upon exhibition, she thought the very finest day of her life must have been at the nudist beach near St. Tropez, and the best hours of her life with Westrum anywhere East or West in the shrouded light of the sun or the glare of lamps: beneath a roof she never left a bulb dark.

Wheels, he thought, entering the taxicab with Beatrice and Miss Sanantone, bicycle wheels at dawn, the wheels of his wagon, the wheels of the airplane. Here was the city where he had made his name. Here he had begun, and he felt that he owned it now. It was all his. It was all for him. Here he had come from Brest friendless and doubtful and made his way here among the Jews who took him in in spite of his appearance and who hadn't even, as he discovered, read the books he thought they had, nor thought the thoughts he had, and hadn't even that very ambition he was obsessed with, although lore and myth ascribed it to *them,* and they conceded to him, as he became known to them, virtues superior to their own, engaged him, advanced him, printed him, quoted him, respected him, celebrated him, befriended him, lay with him, and married

251

him, and it was all one perpetual excitement to him, city of old stone and high glass and every finery, city of the mingling of skins and tongues. But he was undeceived. He knew he was able to celebrate the city only because it had been so good and kind to him. When he'd first come his brain had been one mass of lumped and undifferentiated matter made of books he'd read in his father's attic, here reduced, clarified, synthesized, organized into sense by himself for himself, called a *History* for want of a better name, multiplied by machine and carried to the world, for which he received as his reward his most comfortable place in this fine city, one fine home, one fine University, and anything else within reach of the doorman's whistle— Hermie's whistle. Hermie assisted Beatrice from the cab, and carried her bags to the vestibule, and returned to the cab, signaling Westrum to roll down the window if he would, and thrusting his head into the cab.

"Dr. Westrum," said Hermie, "I'm wondering if you remember I took care of several matters."

"I gave you five dollars, you bastard," said Miss Sanantone.

"Dearie, you never did," said Hermie.

"I gave my friend five dollars to give you," she said.

"He never did," said Hermie.

"All right, then here," said Westrum, "we mustn't spoil our homecoming with disputing," and he gave Hermie five dollars. "And we thank you," he said.

"Now where?" the driver asked.

"Say where," said Westrum to Miss Sanantone, but she would not speak.

"She won't speak to me," said Westrum to the driver.

"I can't go if you don't speak," said the driver to Miss Sanantone.

"Let's get going," Westrum said, "I've got an appointment at the bank."

"Dr. Westrum," said Miss Sanantone, in her old familiar tone, as if nothing had happened, "I know very well that there's no bank."

"All right then," said Westrum, "let's say that I'm off to a rendezvous, it's all the more reason to be going. I'm awfully sorry it's been so unpleasant between us right here at the end. It shouldn't have happened this way."

"It's not the end," she said.

"I'll tell you what," said Westrum to the driver, "let me settle with you," and he paid the driver, and he wished Miss Sanantone all good fortune, urging her again to call upon him for any assistance he could give, and off she went, gone forever, and he stood upon the sidewalk with his briefcase between his ankles while Hermie whistled him another cab.

In the new cab he sang Popeye's song inside his head, permitting himself to be carried—not far—to his fine and private bank. Many a deposit he'd made here, and many a withdrawal. He walked past the doorman before the iron gate.

The doorman was a heavy, florid fellow, not so tall as Westrum, but broader, wearing a greatcoat of green and gold, upon guard to keep the wrong people out, like the college boy on the road to Brest. He looked upon Westrum now as someone he knew—someone he had seen, but not recently, a shadow of confusion crossing his face even as he permitted Westrum to pass. His colleague, however, who operated the elevator, was a new man, vast and robust, as the doorman was, wearing the doorman's colors, green trousers, green vest, golden shirt, and black bow tie, golden stripe dropping across his chest from his heart to his right hip and down his green trousers from hip to cuff, and he said, "Your floor, sir."

"Twenty," said Westrum.

"A moment, sir," said the elevator operator, hastening away to consult the doorman, and quickly returning, on the hop, apologizing for not having known Westrum, explaining that he was a new man—"I'm a new man," he said, "I mixed you up with somebody else. You've been away."

"To Greece," said Westrum.

"You're Greek," said the elevator man.

"I'm as Greek as the day is long," said Westrum.

253

MARK HARRIS

Here he was free. Nowhere was he so free. He turned his key in the door. Here he was not even Westrum but Mr. Bank of Greece who came and went by taxicab between here and Greece whistling Popeye's music. In the bedroom he drew apart the window-drapes, and there was the river just as he had left it, and the bridge last seen in his rear-view mirror driving west. He raised the windows. She would shut them tight again, for the air, she believed, was poisoned by nuclear fallout discharged by goyim rocketry. Oh, how he loved her! How she amused him! He rested a moment upon his palms at the windowsill, looking down upon a taxicab discharging someone—not she—and he withdrew, passing from the bedroom to an inner room bare of all furnishing except his gypsum vault which he unlocked and swung open with ceremony, singing in greeting *My life, I am back, I am here. There you are. Have you missed me?* singing Popeye's song as if it were an aria, and spying within not only his life but a memorandum of death, too, his last will and testament deeding to the world, at the discretion of his wife and sons, his Journal first to last. Perhaps they'd only lock it up again until such time as no one would care whose mistress had been whose or how the conversations went among the hundreds of people whose lives with Westrum's crossed, when all the wives and sons were dead and gossip had fermented to history, and Westrum would tell from his grave on the road to Brest his most inward secrets for the instruction of history, which might be eager, as Westrum in his own time had been eager, to possess accurate and detailed reports of the past composed, as Westrum's Journal was, by someone living with equal consciousness both in his own flesh and in the general history, and driven, besides, by the will, the power, the endurance, the pride, the arrogance, and the daily discipline to write it down in its passing.

From his briefcase he removed those four hundred pages of carbon copy of Journal composed at the Center, typed and made multiple by Miss Sanantone, and the Index to the Text compiled by her, and he placed the new pages in their proper

254

order upon the shelves of his vault, joining his recent past to his farther past, his life, his creation, his burden, his afterlife, and the fortune of his sons. Then swiftly he found in the Index *Miss Sanantone, her father's funeral, pp. 44,372–6,* reading swiftly forward for the man in the rain who had failed to appear, yet who had been there and would have been there yet had Miss Sanantone not destroyed the pages in the hope of destroying proof of the man, too, because he was here now, still rained upon, exactly as Westrum had left him.

So she *had* lied, he *had* been right, the man had been at the funeral and on the page, too. Then Westrum had fired her for cause, nor been unjust, nor persecuted her. He was wondrously relieved. But now he was where he had begun. Why had he gone to look this man up in the first place? Why was he looking him up now? Now that he had him, what did he want of him?

> At the cemetery one person stood slightly apart, one Hawkes, her gentleman friend, a detective of some sort, who told me something of her father. Poor fellow (Hawkes), his teeth were bad with big black holes. Calling cards stood in his hatband. He frequently begins sentences with the irrelevance, "I'm a poor man." He viewed me with suspicion. He declined to stand with me beneath my umbrella. The rain ran down his hat . . .

Yes, the rain, there they stood, the rain off the hatbrim like a waterfall, Hawkes bled by the rich, he said, face indented, nose down, chin up, cursed by birth. "I love her deeply," Hawkes had said.

Yet even now in that old rain renewed, hearing once more the tale of Miss Sanantone's father, his crime and his penalty . . . once more accused by Hawkes of dallying with Miss Sanantone . . . standing here unable to recall why he had sought Hawkes or the name of Hawkes at all. *Oh yes, because,* he thought—but he could not trick himself into it. He could not clearly think. Awaiting the arrival of his mistress he could

255

never concentrate upon anything but her coming, joining, being, touching, for whom each meeting was revival and renewal although they often declared to one another the private wish for longer and longer interims until one interim should so far prolong itself as to extend forever. Now and again, precisely in the midst of the most earnest discussion of their parting forever, they fell upon one another once again, giving and receiving every pleasure their imaginations could devise. He could not think why he'd wanted that man . . . already he had forgotten the name. She wanted him always to say her name when he was in her, and he surely would, anything for a lady, *her* name he'd never forget though she was never named mistress in his Journal—you could only catch her name if you caught them at their screwing—running water in their deep sunken pool. Here was a pool Terence never shot, nor his father swimming in it, nor his father's friend, for winning prizes in the high-school auditorium.

So he had fired her for cause, nor would he replace her easily, either. She was dishonest, a cheat, a thief, a racist, a liar, but a good typist and a good keeper of his Index to the Text from A to Zutzky—Zutzky, Paul, historian—to whom Westrum turned on the waiting page, discovering to his surprise that it had not been his wife but his mistress in whose company he had met Zutzky, not in a Chinese restaurant with curtains drawn in Chicago, but in the bar-café of the Commodore Hotel in New York.

> . . . Then occurred an adventure involving my mistress and me. After the morning session I went back to the Commodore for lunch with Tikvah, Zutzky, and Harold Finkelstein. Zutzky is filled with bloodcurdling anecdotes to illustrate historical accident. They drank. I ate. "You don't drink," said Zutzky. I had been drinking half the night with my mistress above. "He never does," Tikvah said. In most of Zutzky's anecdotes many people are killed

because of the forgetfulness, laziness, negligence, stupidity, or drunkenness of men of power and authority.

His current project is to track down something in the memoirs of Lloyd George. It led to a French lady, very old and free-speaking, whom Zutzky visited last summer to verify the following: that a certain British general, "pausing upon her doorway" one summer night, probably 1917, left behind, when he departed, a map of something known as the Passchendaele sector. Within this sector lay a salient. Unfortunately, without his map, and with no time to return to the lady's house to retrieve it, the general was required to produce the features of the salient from memory.

He was quite good at reproducing the map, but not *absolutely* good. Here and there he guessed an eighth of an inch off, with the result that "the chord across the base of the salient" (Zutzky) was several hundred yards too far north (south or east or west, as the case may be), thus forming a cul-de-sac where none should have been, and permitting a happy group of bloody Germans to stand upon the hillside shooting down Allied troops as fast as they could work their guns. Instantly my Terence leaped to my mind, and I am determined he shall not die at war. Thousands died for the general's pleasure, and other thousands die at war because other generals are suicidal or disappointed with themselves or out of love. Gibson of Massachusetts writes: "And when I remember what pains I took to hone this grievous and only jewel, my consciousness, I will not surrender it to any leader half in love with death, neither do I wear it in shame; nothing in his head is worth my life."

We were seated at table according to the following arrangement: I was beside Harold, facing Tikvah and Zutzky. It was the bar-café. Suddenly Tikvah's and Zutzky's eyes lit up at something coming along behind me who could only have been, by the light of their eyes, a beautiful woman. That she was not only beautiful but someone of importance became apparent when Tikvah made haste to rise in his place to greet her with proper deference.

This beautiful importance was my mistress, who walked past our table, but who, then, pretending the greatest surprise, caught Tikvah in the corner of her eye, stopped, and said, "Why, Professor Tikvah, I haven't seen you for some time."

We all stood, and Tikvah introduced us one by one, and she said, when she heard my name, "Not *the* Professor Westrum," and reached for my hand, as she had not reached for the others', ignoring them as if they were drainpipes and rainbarrels, and keeping my hand in hers, and gushing and fainting over me, and saying, "I can hardly believe I'm touching the famous Professor Westrum, I've been aching for *years* to meet you. Why have we never met before? My husband talks incessantly of you. He won't stop. He's determined to steal you for the Government."

To all this I was sufficiently circumspect not to reply. "Then, Madame, your memory lies at fault, for all last night we were in bed together directly north of here on the way to Heaven, and on the floor as well, and in the bath." This would have caused some curiosity among the company no doubt.

She wore carved jade earrings with little Buddhas hanging down. Tikvah invited her to join us. She declined. He followed her with his eyes as she passed between the tables and beyond our view, describing her to us as "the wife of one of the halfway decent Trustees."

My mind teemed with ironic thoughts. For a few moments I lost the direction of the conversation. Suppose Tikvah were to learn that the woman to whom he had just introduced me—in the belief that she and I had never met!—was in fact my most excellent, loyal, devoted, and established mistress. Would such a revelation not instantly smash our long years of friendship? Would it not instantly convert in his retrospective mind every past doubt to a bad present certainty, every possible lie to a certain lie? My having once persuaded him of my absolutely monogamous fidelity held him always in the throe of a spell. But now the truth would cast doubt upon everything I had formerly claimed as true, causing him to review our entire relationship and seeing all things (even the true things) in an opposite light, for whose particular benefit, in this drama of our lives, I have always played the part of perfect purity, industry, sobriety, and smokelessness.

Westrum's error bewildered him. There was nothing Chinese about the Commodore, New York and Chicago were different ladies, his wife and his mistress were different places, he was amused, and he said, "You're a bit buggy and so's your old man," singing Popeye's song *I am what I am 'cause I am what I am* and slipping Miss Sanantone's little white cards into their proper places in the Index to the Text, the roster of his recent acquaintance, all those little folk almost nameless to his mind, passed accurately to history—three Punjabi met upon the road at breakfast, the Seating Committee and Benstock's Rosalie, the man and the wife in dust alleviation, a red-haired young man with a wire-cutter, Bill and Betty Brown, old Weiner in chemical equilibria, the policeman at Brest, the bartender at the Clover Leaf Motel, Able, Hacker, Hartlin, Weiss, Meister, Fullenweider, Linda Lee black and pink, the surgeon in green pajamas—until he was once again diverted.

It was his mistress at the door. She rang a dainty bell. When he opened the door she was poised with her key still searching for the lock, her arms at full length before her, too short, even so, for her farsightedness. She converted imagined afflictions to comic postures and gestures, whether by design he never knew. When she wore her eyeglasses they slid down her nose and fell off, swinging by a length of ribbon until she remembered to replace them. Then they fell off again. She believed that her eyeballs were hardening, although the world's first authority on glaucoma reassured her twice a year that this was not so. She was convinced that her hair fell from her head daily by the handful, though to Westrum's eye it remained as abundant as it had been fifteen years ago, from time to time changing color, but never quantity.

Today it was black, to match her costume of "amnesty black" signifying her support for the rebelling University students—ragged black button-down woolen sweater, black stockings, black chiffon, translucent scarf. Only Westrum knew how well she really was, who said to her, "Madame, you may come in," for she had stood a moment in the posture of old hesitation, old mistrust, old disbelief, child of her mother's instruction who told her never to enter the rooms of strange gentlemen, and never, above all, the rooms of a gentleman so senseless, so debased, so depraved as not to have been born a Jew: dishonor at best was dishonor, of course, but Jewish men were one thing, Gentiles another—there was that saving degree, after all—hesitating even now upon the threshold of that Gentile whose mistress she had been through all the years in ten cities on three continents, entering, and flying to his arms, whose hands still held a fan of index cards and who complained, kissing her, that she had interrupted him at his work, walked right in on him in the middle of his indexing, which now, he said, crucial as it was, must wait, and the cards fell from his hands and scattered, and Westrum and his mistress fell upon one another, as it had always been, beyond control irresistibly, in the first moments of reunion all beast, clawing, springing from their bodies, unlocking themselves to let themselves out so that they might again become slow, patient, truly loving man and loving lady, and afterward at rest she said to him, "You forgot to mention my name."

"I'm no good at names," he said.

"You could have made one up," she said.

"I could have called you Harriet," he said.

"Is she your vile, diseased principal?" she asked.

"Yes," he said, "I have bad news."

"Poor little fellow," she said, to delay the bad news, for they'd been on the brink of bad news before, "his ankle has a bandage. Are you running around the world every day?" She closed every window and drew every blind and turned on every light. "Airplanes are bursting our eardrums," she said. "They cause fissures in the earth. That's why we have earthquakes."

"I cycled eight miles in seventeen minutes and forty seconds this morning," he said.

"Don't tell me bad news," she said. "Hold it and maybe it will go away," and they floated in their warm sunken pool. Slowly they drank. When they lay again upon the bed she blew smoke into his mouth, she poked out his eyes with her fingers, she picked his teeth with the sharp, pointed corner of a matchbook, she choked him to death, she pulled out his hair until tears of pleasure shone in his eyes, she froze his left ear with an ice cube, she bit off his nose, she flew through the air six hundred miles an hour and bombed him, she pounded his chest with her fists. They wrestled. She pinned him to the mat, but he was like Popeye, he ate his spinach, he came back from almost certain defeat, he extricated himself from her clever wrestling holds, overthrew her, and smothered her to death with a pillow upon her face (she liked that). Once she had quite frightened him by playing dead. If by chance she died upon the spot he'd have a devil of a time clearing away the evidence. He'd wipe the rooms clean of fingerprints, and somehow he'd cart away his gypsum vault. "They'd be searching for you all over Greece," she said.

"Unpin my bandage if you will," he said.

"Tell me your bad news," she said. "Stop looking down my mouth, it embarrasses me."

"I've got to go back to the Center," he said.

"For a long time?" she asked.

"Forever," he said. "It's right for me now."

261

"Then is everything over?" she asked, when the doorbell rang, and they lay still, soundless, motionless. Westrum put his finger to his lips. "It'll go away," he said.

Nobody had ever rung their bell before, and whoever had rung it now rang again, long and steady, knowing that he had been heard, and after he tired of ringing he knocked. "It may be a janitor," she said, "or a salesman."

"No salesmen get in," Westrum said.

"Mr. Bank, we know you're there."

"It doesn't sound like a janitor," said Westrum, and he dressed swiftly in trousers, shirt, and shoes without socks. In his shoe his bandage seeped. "Keep cool," he said.

"Keep our wits," she said. She was cool, she was fine. She lived in constant imagined fear, but in actual emergency she was always equal to the moment: she soothed startled policemen at the scenes of accidents, she directed confused firemen to burning houses.

Westrum locked his gypsum vault, and he went to the door and stood beside it and asked quietly in a voice only slightly uplifted, "Who's there?"

"Mr. Bank," said the voice.

"What do you want?" asked Westrum.

"Just a few words," said the voice.

"What are they?" Westrum asked.

"You better open," said the voice.

"I'll call the police," said Westrum.

"O.K., I'll wait here," said the voice.

His pulse raged wild. What knock was this? In his mind he saw Terence, and Terence held him prisoner now. Were it not for Terence he would scarcely care who stood behind the door, for only Terence, of all people dear to Westrum, still lived near innocence, and he saw his mistress then, standing in the doorway to the bedroom, and she was the author of this entrapment. But that was foolish, and he smiled at her to erase the hatred from his face, and even in this moment she amused him, as always: she was dressed, and she held before her face her chiffon scarf like a veil, as if she believed, as a child believes, that by hiding her eyes she hid herself.

"I want to see," she said.

"We'll see," he said.

"There's nothing to be afraid of," said the voice.

"Good," said Westrum, opening the door to Hawkes, whose face he immediately knew, but whose name, though he had read it an hour before, he could not recall, the man with the indented face, chin up and nose down on collision course yearning to meet in space, calling cards erect decorating his hatband, gentleman friend of Miss Sanantone, who would not tell his name when Westrum asked, saying only, "My name don't matter, my business does"—his brief explanation of himself, often given.

"I can't let you in without a name," Westrum said.

"I don't care if I come in," said Hawkes. He saw, beyond Westrum, Westrum's mistress, whose face was hidden in her scarf. "I know who she is," Hawkes said.

"So do I," said Westrum.

"He's the post office man," she said.

"How many women do you need?" Hawkes asked.

"He's old Bring Him Back Alive," said Westrum's mistress.

"I'm not armed," said Hawkes.

"Neither am I," said Westrum. "If you care to come in, you may."

"Say, you're in a low key," said Hawkes, stepping in. "Holy Christ, why all the electric bill?"

"Sit down," said Westrum. "Will you have a drink?"

"I'm armed," said Hawkes, "I'll stand, and you just stand, too, and no harm will come to nobody if nobody does anything. Not only bring her back alive but give her her job back, too." He held high for Westrum to see the white envelope containing Miss Sanantone's last check, torn in two, and he dropped the pieces where he stood. "Give her back her job or I'll spill everything," he said, "and here in town, not in the cornfields."

263

"She didn't do the work," Westrum said.

"She did the work," Hawkes said.

"She deceived me," Westrum said. "She altered pages."

"Not much," Hawkes said. "Only where you made a joke of my teeth and my face. I'm a poor man, I wasn't born with a silver spoon."

"Spill it to whom?" asked Westrum's mistress.

"I might be a poor man," Hawkes said, "but I never busted a kid's back, Doc." Eyes upon Westrum, he replied to Westrum's mistress, "There's always somebody listening. There's no sense hiding your face." Walking slowly backward, feeling his way along the wall, he opened the glass door to the sunken pool, and he gazed upon the pool. "Wow," he said. His hands remained in the pockets of his coat. He crouched beside the pool, and freeing one hand he felt the water. "Nice and warm," he said, "pools and women, coming and going, lots of paper for writing, and no work, it's how you live when you're rich. How many women does a man need?"

"He's Miss Sanantone's friend," said Westrum to his mistress.

"Her lover," said Westrum's mistress.

"I'm no such a thing," said Hawkes.

"Then if it's only money you want," she said, "we can settle for money." But she knew now it wasn't money Hawkes wanted, it was his girl he wanted, and here, not away in the cornfields, even as she wanted Westrum here, not away in the cornfields. Ugly fellow, yet he was the answer to her prayer.

"Nothing like that," said Hawkes. The idea had never crossed his mind. Yet it was a suggestion, too, and he turned it over in his head. But with one middle finger he pushed up his hat one inch to let it out, and he said again, "No, nothing like that," after fair consideration.

"Or did you know all along who he was?" Westrum asked his mistress.

"She said different," Hawkes said.

"We met at her father's funeral," Westrum said. How was Hawkes armed? He was at the front door again, leaning as if casually, but in fact in fear, and Westrum thought to seize him with a leap. The man was slight, slender, soft and pale, but he was angry, too, and his anger would strengthen him, for the matter was personal, no routine extortion of a makework detective, revenge of an old insult, poor man eye to eye at last with his rich tormentor.

"Here in town," Hawkes said, "and keep your hands off her."

"My hands never touched her," Westrum said.

"She said different," Hawkes said.

"Then she's a liar," Westrum said.

"You already knew that," said Hawkes. "Employ her accordingly. Knowing the worst is better than dreaming the best."

"And will that be the end of it?" Westrum asked.

"Unless you take off for the cornfields again," said Hawkes.

"Why don't you take off your hat," said Westrum—something of humor in him returning—"in the presence of a lady?" It was the name of a bird or an animal, a brief name, not long or entirely short, of the class of fierce devouring beasts, wolf, tiger, eagle, six letters or seven, he'd look it right up. Poor chap, his teeth were hideous.

"I'll keep it on," said Hawkes, "because I'm going."

Westrum's mistress lowered her scarf. Her motion attracted Hawkes's attention, and he turned his head to her. Perhaps she cared to be known to him without doubt, and so secure his case in his mind beyond all weakening. "Yes," he said, "that's who you are."

"I hope we won't see you any more," she said.

"I'll let myself out," said Hawkes, "don't move," his hand upon the knob. "There's no percentage in action or motion," he said, closing the door behind him.

"Save me," she said to Westrum, and she sank to the floor, but with care to keep her dignity, for her fear was feigned, as Westrum seemed to observe.

"I met him," Westrum said, ignoring her. "His name escapes me. I was looking at his name just before you came," but he had taken only a few steps toward his gypsum vault when the name came to him. "Hawkes," he said, and he sat upon the bed. Sensations returned to him. His bandage was damp in his shoe. His pulse nicely fell at a right rate, but in the slowing of his body the smell of his own chagrin arose, and when his mistress came toward him to embrace him and to comfort him he turned from her. His secret was out, he was a moral Samson shorn, reduced of his weight in the world. If he did not obey, all leverage would be gone, he'd be only one more goy dashing about like any other, unmasked, ridiculous, no doubt a private drunk, too, they'd say, Tikvah would smile, Benstock would smile, Justice Lerman . . . all the rest, everyone. His anger ranged from person to person, seeking someone to blame. Prisoner of Hawkes, prisoner of Miss Sanantone, exiled from Brest by Hawkes, it was unthinkable, it hadn't even the dignity of exile from Washington when Lerman called to say he'd be no longer needed there, for then at least it required a Judge and a President to exile him, no makework detective. When Justice Lerman called to say it was over—*fini*, said Lerman, as amiably as he could, *caput, terminante*, master of two or three words in thirty languages—the event had dignity and reason, and Westrum had gone home that night in exile, too, in this same stink of chagrin, though his body was cool and his pulse was down, and he had sat with Beatrice and Terence and talked the matter out in the most objective terms; it was politics, they knew, it was the name of the game, it was how things were, they'd known the rules when they came down for the job, and that was that, when Terence dropped the Ancient Malacca Distinctive bowl, and his father went seemingly mad, and broke the boy's back with a blow of his hand.

He removed his shoes. "I'm going to take a shower," he said, which was to say *alone*, and she said she didn't mind, although she did. "Isn't it selfish?" she said. "Nobody showers alone." He unwound the elastic bandage from his ankle and snapped it before him like a whip.

"Did you ever?" she asked.

"Ever what?" he asked.

"Ever fuck his girl?" she asked. "It's awfully unjust to be paying for something you never even had the pleasure of. On the other hand, darling, if you can't go back and be king of the cornfields there's nothing so terribly awful about being the king of New York," and she caught the end of the bandage whipping through the air.

"Let go," he said.

"Don't be sharp," she said.

"Turn it loose," he said, whose voice so moderated suggested hardly more than the disappointment of a morning gone bad, but whose eyes, his mistress saw, were distant with rage, but saw too late, arms wide, dancing on her toes toward him, her motion beyond recall. It was not she he struck, but someone else in another moment in another place, with studious deliberation, as if he were both assailant and witness, and his mind listened to himself and heard himself cry, "Turn it loose I said," not *Jew* or *little Jew* but only *Turn it loose I said*, and she fell. "You see," he said, "you see, I never called him that," and he knelt beside her.

"I see," she said (she'd see with only one eye for a while), and he lifted her to the bed, and she lay hiding her swiftly swelling face behind her chiffon scarf and moaning low, "Oh dear, oh dear, you've ruined my poor little dinner party."

Tikvah, impromptu, inspired, prankish, gay, loose, laughing, having drunk all afternoon to meet the crisis of this night, arriving by subway and foot with Winifred in the moment of Westrum's own arrival, raced to beat the doorman to the cab, twisting open the taxicab door as if he were the doorman himself.

The point of the lark was lost for the moment upon Westrum and Beatrice who expected, in any case, certain doors to open of themselves. For a moment they failed to observe that the doorman wore no uniform, and in the next moment they saw that he was Tikvah, with Winnie nearby, whom Westrum hailed not *Winnie* but *Sally*, as if she were not Winnie Tikvah

267

but Sally Benstock. He pondered the slip of his tongue, which nobody heard but himself, kissing Winnie, embracing Tikvah, and paying the cabman. The cabman, to so much laughter, thought to add his own idea—"You're going to have a fun time tonight," he sang.

"We always have a good time," said Westrum, not to the cabman but to Tikvah as they walked beneath the canopy, out of the floating, drifting rain likely to turn before morning to the season's first tentative snow. In Tikvah's presence he felt himself instantly adopting that good cheer he had always assumed upon every occasion of their thirty years. He was buoyant, he bounced upon his toes, he exuded energy, hope, optimism, to counterbalance Tikvah on their everlasting seesaw. Perhaps, for all Westrum knew, Tikvah too played the game of opposites. Perhaps Tikvah's gloom was false. Perhaps Tikvah was not always the downcast Jew he always was in Westrum's presence. Perhaps it was Tikvah's way with Westrum of recruiting Westrum's old American faith and optimism as brother in mood to Tikvah's old solemn Hebrew doom, each to nourish and fructify and leaven and modify the other. *I called her Sally,* he thought, *how foolish, how right,* rising in the elevator, fixing it firmly for his Journal.

"When did you get in?" Tikvah asked.

"This morning," Westrum said, "it's been a long day up and down on a lot of vehicles." *Wheels,* he thought, *wheels and vehicles,* those were the key to this day's Journal, bicycle wheels to Brest, wheels to New Hamburg, airplane, taxicab, elevator to the twentieth floor, and he was a long way from Brest now, piloted upward in this carpeted, mirrored elevator with soft, hidden lights and soft, hidden music by the Spanish operator pushing a button they could have pushed themselves except that here in this house nothing was left for anyone to do unless he were a servant. *All Jews here but me,* thought Westrum, *and the Spaniard,* who at last himself became a Jew today, he felt, exiled forever from Brest to the place of his true belonging,

268

city of the Jews. The elevator operator accompanied them down the hallway, although Tikvah assured him he knew the way.

But orders were orders, the servant served not the guests but his boss, leading them to Justice Lerman's door held open from behind by a starched Spanish maid hidden from sight so that someone so humble as she might not vulgarly irritate the eyes of guests so important as these. She had been informed by the Justice that the man who was coming (not the short man but the tall man) was extremely *importante—importante hombre*, said Justice Lerman as well as he could, especially so, *especial*, *diferente de lo general, un hombre que tiene grande autoridad*, more so than any man they had ever seen or heard of or dared to imagine, to be served first (so his wife ordered), even before the ladies, and the ladies second, after the tall man so *importante*, and the short man last, after which two servants were to station themselves beside Westrum to treat of his every desire at dinner for six, of whom Westrum was to be first and Tikvah sixth and last. A maid took Westrum's coat, and the women's coats, and Tikvah's coat finally.

But Tikvah declined even to remove his hat from his head, much less surrender it, saying to Westrum, "Now pretend to recognize me," and who, removing his hat, revealed that he was no longer bald Tikvah but Tikvah with hair now. Beatrice uttered a cry and fell upon her brother, kissing the boy's face better known to her than the man's. "My little small brother," she said, and Westrum surveyed the new scene—the transformation, so to speak—and said, "You look younger, smarter, happier, healthier, and more Jewish," embracing the new Tikvah once more, and embracing Lerman, too, whom he had not seen since Washington days, and Lerman introduced Westrum to his champion and shy admirer, his wife, dressed in a gown of amnesty black and with a black eye, too, acquired only this morning in an amnesty skirmish, she explained—in the most incredible, unbelievable manner, she'd tell them how: "I was struck in the face, my dear Dr. Westrum—and you too

269

my dear Dean Tikvah—by a ferocious young man demonstrating at *your* University."

"I have a scar on my scalp from a brick," said Tikvah, "but you can't see my scalp any more."

"She shouldn't have been hanging around there," said Justice Lerman, though indeed he was proud of her. "She's my radical front," he said. She did his daring for him. She had marched in every major march from Selma, Alabama, to the Pentagon.

"I want to watch the revolution in," she said.

"Where should I put my hat?" Tikvah asked.

"But I understand," said Mrs. Lerman to Westrum, ignoring Tikvah, "that it's not really your University any more"—permitting herself to be interrupted by the servant's recitation of available spirits, Westrum smiling *no*, the servant continuing nevertheless, for he was uninterruptible, unable to accept Westrum's reply until the recitation was done, and unable to believe when it was that the tall gentleman of so much magnificent importance required only a tall glass of iced water. "I'd forgotten," Mrs. Lerman said. "I'd *heard* that you don't drink."

"I'll have a bottle of champagne to go," said Beatrice. She had forgotten to buy champagne.

"Shall we chill it for you?" Justice Lerman asked.

"Just slip it in a paper bag," said Beatrice.

"Some people say it's why the President didn't want you any more," said Mrs. Lerman. "You didn't drink."

"No," said her husband, "the President wanted headlines, not history."

"I can hardly believe I'm sitting in the same room with the famous Professor Westrum," Mrs. Lerman said.

"I find it routine," said Beatrice, since neither Tikvah nor Winnie could say it. "Altogether unexciting."

"You and I did meet *once*," said Westrum.

"Impossible," said Mrs. Lerman, "I'd have remembered if we had."

"In the bar-café at the Commodore," said Westrum. "Tikvah was there."

"I don't recall it," Tikvah said.

"You and I," said Westrum, "and Harold Finkelstein and Paul Zutzky."

"Zutzky just died," said Tikvah.

"Yes," said Westrum, "that's what made me look it up. We had lunch, and Mrs. Lerman came by."

"So it wasn't me," said Beatrice. "I knew it wasn't."

"Looked it up where?" asked Justice Lerman.

"In my Journal," Westrum said, "at the bank."

"It must be so if he says so," said Tikvah. "He remembers me better than I remember myself."

"I'm immortal at last," said Mrs. Lerman.

"God help us all," said Beatrice.

"At what bank?" asked Justice Lerman.

"But I've decided to take it away from my bank," said Westrum, "and give it to Tikvah."

"To me?" said Tikvah. "My apartment is too small for all that paper."

"Technically," said Westrum, "to the University."

"On what terms?" Tikvah suspiciously asked.

"On your terms," said Westrum. "I capitulate. I'm coming back."

"You see how powerful I am with hair," said Tikvah.

"With some help from the Trustees," said Justice Lerman, for he was persuaded that the Trustees had produced this good effect, himself in the lead, his wife behind the scenes, bringing pressure to bear all along on Dean Tikvah's conscience, forcing Dean Tikvah to examine his buried prejudices. "A prophet is not without honor in his own land," the Justice said.

"Maybe my hair makes *you* magic," Tikvah said, who cared nothing for the details. It was accomplished. That was enough. The secrets of men of power were beyond his understanding, they wheeled and dealed, they struck important bargains,

271

those were things they could do and he could not, he hadn't
the attitude for it, lies were impossible for him. Then, too, of
course, they had the size and weight to do it with. He himself
was a small man. He was blissfully drunk. He was beginning to
feel confidence in his hairpiece tonight, it was clinging well to
his skull. Let these men have weight. He himself was weight-
less, the crisis of the night having beautifully resolved itself,
floating to the dinner table now, and seating himself, at Mrs.
Lerman's command, opposite her, between his wife and his
sister, so that Dr. Westrum might have—"our fantastically distinguished guest, after all," said Mrs. Lerman—the view from
the window of the pure falling snow, and Tikvah the view of
her blackened eye.